Everybody's talking about

RACHEL, THE RABBI'S WIFE,

the intimate portrait of a gifted woman struggling to maintain her own identity within the stifling confines of her husband's world. It is a totally absorbing story, so real that all women will recognize Rachel Sonnshein—and see in her something of themselves. "A DELIGHT TO READ . . . An intriguing eye-opener to Jewish and non-Jewish readers alike . . . A strong, moving, often eloquent story."—*San Francisco Examiner & Chronicle* "A good-humored, high-spirited, *haimische* novel involving some immensely likable people, types and odd-balls one might spot in any denomination." —*Kirkus Reviews*

CHOSEN BY THE DOUBLEDAY BOOK CLUB AND THE LITERARY GUILD

Rachel, The Rabbi's Wife

Silvia Tennenbaum

BANTAM BOOKS
TORONTO · NEW YORK · LONDON

*This low-priced Bantam Book
has been completely reset in a type face
designed for easy reading, and was printed
from new plates. It contains the complete
text of the original hard-cover edition.*
NOT ONE WORD HAS BEEN OMITTED.

RACHEL, THE RABBI'S WIFE
*A Bantam Book / published by arrangement with
William Morrow and Company, Inc.*

William Morrow edition published January 1978
2nd printing .... February 1978   4th printing .... March 1978
3rd printing .... February 1978   5th printing .... April 1978
Literary Guild edition March 1978
Bantam edition / January 1979

ISBN 0-553-12042-5

Published simultaneously in the United States and Canada

For Lloyd,
who first understood
my language

1

The troubles began in January, in the cold, dark part of the year. Rachel Sonnshein later remembered the very day. It was a Monday, and she awoke, as she usually did, thick-tongued and confused by the lingering presence of her dreams. The light, edging around the sides of the window shades, was wan—poured from a sky gray as lead. Rachel turned away from the light and the day, toward Seymour, asleep in the other bed. His sheets were in a tangle and his dark curly Jewish hair crept across the pillow. He looked vulnerable, as people do when they are asleep. Looking vulnerable, he seemed young as well, though he was forty-two and they had been married almost twenty years. Seymour slept in a T-shirt that said PENN STATE on it.

Rachel pulled the quilt over her face. The room was full of matinal disorders and her nose was cold. She looked down between her breasts to see if her stomach was still flat—a straight valley between the ridges of her hipbones. She stroked her smooth skin. Not bad for going to be forty soon. She touched the nipples of her breasts; they puckered under her fingers. Her breasts had always been small. When she was thirteen she had wished they would go away. She played softball with the boys after school and knew that they had noticed the titties pushing the shirt away from her body. Soon they would tell her she couldn't play with them. Rachel's left hand traced circles around

1

her breast and poked gently into the flesh. (She watched for signs of cancer, always. Everywhere.) She remembered the summer afternoons and the yellow dust of the playground. She felt the hollows under her feet where a generation of batters had worn away the earth beside home plate. Bobby Rosenbloom watched her from his catcher's crouch. "She goes for them low and outside!" he crowed to his pitcher, who couldn't seem to keep the big softball out of the dirt. They all pretended it was hardball they played and went through elaborate motions.

Rachel Sonnshein heard the ratchety sound of the toilet flushing and, a minute later, Aaron's footsteps on the stairs. She had long ago stopped getting up with her son, and only her mother still mentioned it. Aaron himself preferred to leave for school unobserved so as to avoid conversations about sweaters and raincoats and rubbers. Rachel turned from side to side, trying to fit herself into a pocket of warmth. The pale gray light of a January morning contrasted sharply with the bright yellow ball field of Rachel's memory. A ray of terror entered her morning confusion. Rachel was tempted to cry out but forced her mind back to the image of herself at the plate, in full control, under a hot summer sun. She had swung from the heels, the way Pete Reiser did; she had practiced throwing the ball like a boy for long hours in front of a mirror. She hit the ball and pulled it, over the shortstop's head, into left field. She rounded first, thinking she could stretch the hit into a double, but Jack Carroll, the red-headed second baseman, tagged her out. His worn soft glove touched her breast. Rachel remembered it exactly, even to the way the pleasure of that touch had plummeted to her crotch.

Seymour spoke her name. It was no more than a sigh, yet Rachel recognized it. The sounds of Aaron's departure snaked through the house. Rachel's terror was for her very life. "Good-bye, Mom." Aaron's voice floated up the staircase. Good-bye, Aaron. Good-bye. Rachel heard the front door slam and in its wake came the barking of the neighbors' dog. She climbed out of

2

her bed and into Seymour's. He turned away, loath to give up his own dream, but Rachel curved her body against his back and reached around him to take hold of his circumcised Jewish prick. It grew hard in a minute and Seymour awoke enough to turn over and embrace Rachel. He cupped one hand over her breast and the other around her buttock.

They made love in the cold morning of a January Monday. Their passions were muted by sleep, and when they had come they rolled apart and lay still in the still house. Rachel felt the sticky semen between her legs. She again burrowed into Seymour, who lay on his back breathing as though he were asleep. Perhaps he was.

The telephone rang, and Rachel fell away from its sound and landed on the floor before climbing back into her own bed, now cold. She never answered the telephone if she could help it. There was too much trouble at the other end, especially early in the morning or late at night. Seymour reached out, patting the air and the night table like a blind man until his hand touched the receiver. In the seconds it took him to put it to his ear he came awake and tuned his voice up to professional pitch.

"Rabbi Sonnshein speaking. No no no, I was awake."

Rachel knew the call was neither about sickness nor death—there was no tenderness in Seymour's voice.

"The *minyan?* Now? Oh yes, the *minyan.*" It was a sore subject, the *minyan.* "I don't know," said Seymour Sonnshein. "This is one of my busy days and my car's been giving me trouble lately on cold mornings. I might be late." Briefly he was silent. "Ok ok ok," he said at last—not very meekly, thought Rachel. "I'll try to make it." He hung up. *"Shit!* They want me for the *minyan.* Federbush has *Yahrzeit.*"

Seymour sat on the edge of the bed and picked at his sticky prick with one hand while he rummaged through the hair on his head with the other.

Rachel looked at him from under her quilt. He was thin and his torso was long. A Jewish prince. She had

3

never liked fat men. In high school, back home in Buffalo, New York, Seymour had been on the track team until they found the murmur in his heart. That murmur, once discovered, had seemed to give him a softer look—he held out the promise of suffering. His princehood became more poetic and Rachel began to pay attention to him, drawn by his now fragile beauty. They danced together at the junior prom. Rachel needed a vessel for her romantic fantasies. Seymour, son of a diaper-service magnate and grandson of a butcher, found her self-confidence and arrogance of style reassuring. The murmur separated him permanently from the jocks and his life soon became intertwined with Rachel's in the conventional way. They kissed one another good-night under a fragrant lilac bush and made love on the back seat of a 1947 Chrysler. Save for a cutting edge of sorrow and hysteria (attributed to Rachel's "artistic bent" and Seymour's "weakness"), which managed to sometimes turn their experiences into bizarre happenings, they might have been like everybody else. They might have lived the clichés fastidiously and without regrets.

"Will breakfast be ready when I get back?" Seymour asked.

"Maybe," said Rachel, who did not want to leave her bed just yet, to find the terror constricting to an ache somewhere, an undetected growth, a furrow of old age.

"Please make that maybe a yes," said Seymour, and wound his anger up. "The least you could do when I have to go out in the fucking cold for Federbush and his *minyan* is to have some hot coffee for me when I get home."

Rachel closed her eyes and burrowed into the covers like a cat. Seymour's smell was all over her, familiar as her own. The bed was warm once again. Seymour got up to put on his underpants.

"Are you all right?" he asked, buttoning his shirt over the Penn State letters. His rhetoric had dissipated the anger, and Rachel's resistance had melted as well. She usually did his bidding. "You're so quiet," he said.

4

"I don't like winter mornings."

Seymour patted the hump on the bed that was her ass. "I love you truly."

Rachel wore a trailing Arab robe down to breakfast. She liked being alone in the kitchen, attending to the chores. There was comfort in familiar tasks. She made juice from fresh oranges and coffee from beans she ground in a small French grinder that made a loud whirring noise. The orange squeezer whined, the kettle whistled shrilly and, in the basement, the furnace went on with a roar. Through it all Rachel could hear the hum of the fluorescent light. The sounds of day were taking over the muddled dawn of waking. Rachel's terror began to ebb. She knew that if she accomplished her tasks she would not lose the day.

The kitchen of the old Victorian house looked down toward the harbor of Gateshead, Long Island. In winter the water was visible beyond the trees at the bottom of the lawn. In summer the leaves formed a green scrim through which the wind moved. Rachel liked the view in every season and in the evenings when the trees turned black against the setting sun and fading sky. A picket fence described the property line on the right side of the lawn, a chain link fence on the left. A family named Grog lived on the other side of the chain link fence. They cut their grass with a power mower every Saturday morning from May to November, and in the seasons between they cleared away leaves and snow with the aid of other noxious machines. Their racket daily rent the air and made Rachel's small appliances sound like gently purring cats. For the Christmas just past, Santa Claus had brought the Grog children a mini-bike to go with their go-cart. Rachel and Seymour had never been invited to visit the Grogs. A fierce dog guarded their house. A sign that read:

Eddy
Betty
Willy &
Bitsy

5

stood on the front lawn. Below these names and next to the picture of a poodle, it said:

Ollie

Ollie was a Doberman pinscher.

Rachel poured the orange juice into wineglasses and put slices of Friday's *challeh* into the toaster. There was sweet whipped butter and Mexican honey and a bouquet of dried flowers on the round white kitchen table. Aaron had put his breakfast dishes into the sink, and Rachel saw that he had had toast and orange juice and a bowl of Cheerios and had made himself a peanut butter and jelly sandwich for lunch. Her eyes took in all things as though she had to make first judgments about them. The curtains that hung at the long, old-fashioned windows billowed slightly in the draft of an invisible wind. A few snowflakes drifted down from the coagulated sky and the dead leaves on the apple tree shuddered on their spindly branches.

The apple tree bore bitter green fruit in season and then dropped most of them into the Prawns' garden, on the other side of the picket fence. Sydelle Prawn, a writer of children's books, was resigned to the fallen apples because she loved the tree's springtime bloom. Her sister Clarabelle added the apples to the compost heap that fed their lovely English flower garden. The two sisters wore identical straw hats in summer and felt cloches in the winter. They did not otherwise dress alike, though their clothes appeared to have been designed in the twenties. When Rachel and Seymour moved into the house they had been invited to the Prawns' for tea. Rachel returned the invitation one Sunday afternoon when Seymour was at a religious school convocation. "Did the good rabbi absent himself on account of our age, our religion or our station in life?" Sydelle asked. She bore a host of grudges. Clarabelle, on the other hand, wished everyone well and ate too many pastries. The sisters, one gaunt, one portly, went abroad once a year.

Rachel saw that her own yard looked ill-kempt and desolate. She tended it sporadically, most often only

6

when inspired by a colorful seed packet display or a sale on fading mums. Seymour ignored the garden completely, having grown up in a world where gardeners cut the grass and trimmed the shrubs and no flower was allowed to rear its lovely head because the diaperservice magnate felt that flowers attracted flying insects. Seymour did not notice, as Rachel did, that the Grogs added their leaves to hers every fall, on days when they thought no one was looking. Rachel's complaints (written on lined notebook paper and left in the mailbox under cover of darkness) elicited no response, but now and then a beer can landed in among her rotting leaves. Eddy Grog smiled sheepishly whenever he saw Rachel; his wife and children were more suited to dirty tricks than he. Betty and Willy and Bitsy looked straight through Rachel and fixed their disapproving glance upon the very landscape in which she moved.

The telephone rang. Rachel, sipping her second cup of coffee, broke off her contemplation of the harshly etched winter garden.

"Mrs. Sonnshein? Cy Glatt speaking. Tell me, is the rabbi there?"

Rachel looked at the clock. It was exactly nine o'clock.

Cy Glatt was president of the congregation. He spoke fast and usually hung up before Rachel could say good-bye.

"The rabbi is at the *minyan,*" said Rachel, not without a touch of pious righteousness. Seymour deserved the credit, but had she gotten the tone right? Rachel had been told that Glatt found her cold and distant. ("Like a *shikse,*" he was alleged to have said.)

"Remind the rabbi there's a Building and House Committee meeting at the *shul* tonight. I'd like him to attend."

Glatt made it sound like a command. He ruled with a few chosen words and many phone calls. He had a warm Jewish heart, it was said. Rachel picked up a pencil, intending to write the message down, but the pencil had no point on it. Cy Glatt's voice had been replaced by the dial tone. Rachel drank the last of her coffee.

7

Seymour came back at nine-thirty with *The New York Times*.

"Any calls?"

Rachel shook her head. She had already forgotten about Cy Glatt.

The phone rang again and Seymour went to answer it. Rachel grabbed the newspaper. She never listened to his conversations. They struck her like soundings from another planet.

"That was Truscott Boothby," said Seymour, returning to the breakfast table. He snatched the newspaper from Rachel's hands. "He wanted to know about Brotherhood Week. He's the only person in town who still remembers it."

"What's he planning for this year?"

"He asked about a Freedom Seder."

"For February?"

"That's what I said, but it didn't seem to faze him. He thinks Jewish holidays can be moved around at will. He's trying to get some black militants to attend."

"I didn't know there were any left. And in Gateshead yet!"

"If there's one militant around, Boothby will find him."

"Is he going to have him ask the Four Questions or tick off the plagues?"

"I think he said they'd just 'rap.' "

"Truscott's terrific," said Rachel. "I love him."

"You do? I think he's neurotic as hell."

"Isn't it nice to have one neurotic friend who's a *goy*?"

Truscott Boothby was Gateshead's Episcopal minister. A large and handsome man, a favorite of the ladies. Clarabelle Prawn had said, "He can put his shoes under my bed any time." As a youth, the reverend had played football at a small Midwestern college and been most happy there. When he drank (which he did frequently) he talked about those days with joy. His best friend and fellow lineman had been a black man. Truscott Boothby had loved him. Simply and purely. He had married a young woman crippled by

8

polio, but it was not the same—so he had decided to dedicate his life to brotherhood. The celebrations he arranged each February were splendid. They resounded with soul music and cabbalistic imprecations. Truscott Boothby, his congregants said, devoted more time and energy to Brotherhood Week than he did to Christmas or Easter.

Rachel suddenly remembered Glatt.

"Glatt called."

"What did he want?"

"Something about a meeting tonight."

"What kind of a meeting?"

"I can't remember."

"Why didn't you write it down?"

"The pencil's broken."

Conversations with congregants dropped through Rachel's mind like stones through a clear pond. She stood leaning against the kitchen counter, her arms folded. She was aware of her own pose, the morning scene, the pale northern light, the bread on the table. She thought of the Chardin at the Frick.

Seymour finished his coffee and went to call Glatt from his study. It took him a while to get past Fern, the president's wife, who ran the office of Glatt's Creations, a family firm. It created (in its creator's words) *"shmattes* for the *shvartses."* The office was staffed by cousins and in-laws; the shop employed chirping Puerto Ricans who were bussed in from South Gateshead, the nearest non-union slum. Glatt gave generously to the U.J.A. and waxed sentimental under the influence of Chivas Regal.

Rachel read the sports pages while Seymour was on the phone with his president. She looked, in vain as it turned out, for news of spring training.

"A Building and House Committee meeting," said Seymour, when he returned to the kitchen. "I wonder why they want me there."

"I bet they're planning to sell our house."

"It's *their* house in any case, but I hope you're wrong."

"I love this house. They wouldn't really do that, would they?"

9

"They'll do anything, you know that. I mentioned Boothby's brotherhood scheme, but Glatt refused even to discuss it. He said that brotherhood meant one of two things to him—'Jesus on the cross or niggers in the neighborhood.' He didn't want any part of either."

"He didn't say 'shvartses'?" asked Rachel.

"He said 'niggers.' "

Rachel made a face.

"That's how he feels," said Seymour, "and you're not going to change him."

"I don't want to change him."

"You just want to kick his ass, I know, but you'll get nowhere with your righteous anger. He thinks you're nothing but a snob with radical pretensions and he's probably right. He can't believe that anyone in his right mind would think better of grungy welfare mothers than of *shul* presidents. Glatt is a man of substance and he made it on his own—as he'll be the first to tell you—so why should he apologize to you? And he considers that I am in his employ, so he can say to me what he pleases. It's only in the pulpit that I can answer him, but if I lose my job that's a hollow victory indeed. He's got the power. We're nothing to him."

"I am a person of refinement and culture," said Rachel, bowing from the waist.

"Glatt doesn't give a shit about culture."

Rachel had lined the stairwell of her house with revolutionary posters. Like Truscott Boothby, she did not give up easily. Lenin and Che and Malcolm X continued to look down on the just and the unjust alike, years after such defiance was fashionable. Somber cleaning ladies and nervous Sisterhood matrons were equally offended by all those threatening glances.

Rachel rinsed the breakfast dishes before putting them into the dishwasher. Once the kitchen was in order she went upstairs to dress. The bedroom was cold, drained of lovemaking and empty of sunlight. It was a wasteland of unmade beds and scattered clothes. Rachel put on the first things that came to hand—blue jeans and a T-shirt, a cashmere sweater pocked with

10

moth holes, socks and tennis sneakers. She combed her straight brown hair and washed her face in cold water. For the first time that morning she looked at herself, half afraid that her face had turned into a cabbage. It had not, though it was full and round. Rachel had clear skin, her eyes were Hazel, her nose straight. She had a handsome face and a good profile, but (having grown up on Katharine Hepburn) she would have given all that for a hollow face and a long stem of a neck.

Leaving the beds unmade and Aaron's room un-aired (that room which always held the putrescence of a sixteen-year-old boy—the mingled smells of sweat socks and semen), Rachel climbed the stairs to her attic studio. There, close to the single window, under four tubes of fluorescent light, she had cleared a space for herself. From the window Rachel could see the harbor beyond the trees. She gazed at it until the view displaced all competing images. She studied the shapes, played one against the other, and made collages out of the patterns. She used fragments of words and dark photographs culled from slick magazines and pressed against the pale blue skies of torn wallpapers. She painted small pictures as well—still lifes and land-scapes.

Seymour called up to her from the landing.

"What are you doing?" he asked.

"Looking out the window," she answered.

"I thought you were working." His head appeared above the attic floorboards. "Do you need the car to-day?"

"I'm working—I don't think I'll need it, not until the afternoon anyway."

"Let me see what you're doing." Seymour had climbed up the rest of the stairs. His dark hair brushed the rafters.

"I haven't done anything yet," said Rachel.

"You're lying," said Seymour. "Why don't you want me to see your work?"

He sat down in the old armchair which Rachel had drawn up before the foggy oval mirror in such a way that she could sketch herself. The mirror's image was flattering. Seymour eyed himself and stretched his legs

11

out before him. He had always been a performer. Miss Burrows had cast him as Liliom once. Had he not been Jewish she might have let him play Brutus too.

"There's nothing to see, as yet," said Rachel.

"You don't love me anymore," he said. He was his mother's only son.

"Yes I do."

"Why can't I see your work then?"

Rachel said nothing. Silence kept intrusions to a minimum. Her hands lay loose and open in her lap.

"I can't figure out why they want me at that House Committee meeting," said Seymour.

Rachel looked out the window once again. The sky had darkened to a slate gray. It was heavy with snow. The wind fluffed the water in the harbor and bent the creaking trees. For a long time, during her college years, Rachel had refused to take seriously Seymour's resolve to become a rabbi. She kept assuming that he would turn back, but he never did. He had become a good rabbi. He was compassionate. He gave freely of his time whenever he felt the cause was good, the need genuine. He truly loved Judaism. He was an excellent preacher and had always managed to keep his weaknesses hidden. A melodramatic force animated his life and his flair for public utterance served him well. When he was at the top of his form—when boredom and a certain species of unseriousness did not assail him—he could even turn disaster to his advantage. True, he was married to a reluctant rebbetzin, but the very nature of Rachel's stubborn and sometimes eccentric defiance gave him cause for pride. She fitted Seymour's tragic pose.

The telephone rang again and Seymour sprang from his chair and clattered down the narrow stairs. Rachel's respite was brief. Seymour's voice sounded loud and clear.

"It's Golda Garfinkle. She wants to talk to *you*."

"Oh, Christ," thought Rachel, "what did I do now?"

Golda Garfinkle was descended (on her mother's side) from a Galician dynasty of rabbis. She judged Rachel by traditionally severe standards and always found her wanting. She would have had nothing but

12

contempt for her, had she not been Rachel's classmate at Barnard. That bond sweetened her judgments and made her an ambivalent friend rather than a sworn enemy. Golda had wanted to marry a rabbi (at Barnard she regularly took her meals at the Seminary on 122nd Street), but had settled for an Orthodox dentist with clumsy hands and flat feet. Her father had given them a most magnificent wedding. Golda Garfinkle became the prompter of Rachel's Jewish conscience.

"Did you forget about the Sisterhood meeting this afternoon?"

Rachel had, indeed, forgotten about the Sisterhood meeting.

"No, no, I didn't forget," she said, trying to rearrange the day to set two hours of it aside for the Sisterhood.

"If you didn't forget, I also hope you remembered you promised to say the *D'var Torah*."

Rachel sighed. "Just tell me when I'm supposed to be there."

"You *did* forget! It's a luncheon meeting. Be there at twelve-thirty. Hadassah Kleinholz is talking on Jewish Renewal."

"Hadassah Kleinholz?"

"The rebbetzin from Roslyn. Surely you know her."

"Of course," said Rachel, though she didn't have the foggiest idea who Hadassah Kleinholz was.

Rachel hung up. The day was shot to hell. She would have to write the *D'var Torah*, get dressed up, go out in the cold, smile a lot and listen to a rebbetzin from Roslyn. She went down to see Seymour.

"What did she want, your nemesis, the dentist's wife?"

"To remind me about the Sisterhood meeting. I forgot it, of course, and I'm supposed to give the *D'var Torah*. There isn't much time. What can I say?"

"Read them a passage from the Bible."

"You mean I should take them literally? That would be the easy way out. Somebody named Hadassah Kleinholz is coming to talk about Jewish Renewal. I'll be competing. I'll be judged."

"The rebbetzin from Roslyn. Shlomo's wife."

13

"Do I know her?"

"You're blocking her out. Of course you know her. She once told you, at a convention, that behind every great rabbi stood an equally great rebbetzin, and that if I didn't have a 750-member congregation and an apartment in Israel in five years you weren't doing your job."

"Is the time up?"

"Just about."

"I wish I could remember."

"She jingles and wears her hair in an orange puff."

Rachel began to see her in bits and pieces. "I remember her now. White plastic boots. Makeup like Theda Bara. She can't close her eyes, the lashes are too thick."

"Shlomo once told me they only talk Hebrew when they fuck. Why don't you speak about sexual practices among the Jews and the uses of modern Hebrew?"

Rachel went into the living room and gazed at the bookshelves. A hodgepodge of their tastes confronted her. Literary criticism stood up against Matisse, and little green Shakespeares squeezed between Joyce, Proust and Eliot. A section had been kept for Malamud, Roth, Bellow. Uris and Wouk leaned against an old *siddur;* Shulberg had fallen sideways. Rachel took down a volume of Kafka and sat on the floor with it. Seymour had referred to some tales of the Chassidic masters in a recent sermon and Rachel had thought of Kafka. The stories, from Buber, appeared bland and pointless but left a residue of mystery, an aftertaste of slightly puzzling exaltation. Rachel decided she would read a short piece by Kafka and join it to a Chassidic tale. She would attempt no explanation. The *D'var Torah* was, after all, no more than an overture, an appetizer meant to arouse pious thoughts and give a hint of spiritual substance before lunch was served. Rachel was asked to prepare about one *D'var Torah* a year and to say a minimum of five blessings, though these had been drastically reduced since the day she got up in front of six hundred people and said the blessing over the Sabbath candles instead of the one over bread. At the annual spring luncheon she was

14

expected to give the invocation or the benediction—not much could go wrong with those. It was quite enough to begin with the words "Our God and God of our fathers," or the phrase *"Baruch atah adonai,"* which also never got anyone in trouble, and then go directly into the request for guidance, divine blessing, and courage for the task ahead.

Amen.

But a *D'var Torah* had to be better than that.

Rachel chose a story by Kafka entitled "The Next Village," and a short Chassidic tale, "The Light Behind the Window." They would fit together nicely.

It had taken quite a while to make these decisions and to copy out the texts on a legal pad. The morning was far advanced, the telephone had rung at least three more times and Seymour could be heard to mutter behind the closed doors of his study. His voice contained no hint of passion; it buzzed evenly like the drum of waves on a distant shore. He comforted the bereaved, the crazed, the sick and the lonely. Many of these were women. That some of them fell in love with Seymour was inevitable. Rachel viewed these troubled souls with the sharp eye of one who does not admit to feeling pain. Like an old hospital nurse, she protected herself against the spectacle of decayed flesh and disintegrating spirit by smiling hard and keeping busy. Seymour's women gazed upon him with brimming eyes —how could he help but be flattered? He thought he had lived long enough and gained enough confidence not to take their love songs personally. But there were times when their pain seemed to crown them with a halo of sensitivity, and then Rachel's certainty seemed like cold steel to him and he wished she might hurt just a little so that he could console her.

Rachel knocked on the door of the study.

"I'm on the telephone!" cried Seymour. "Wait a minute."

Rachel opened the door anyway.

"I'm getting dressed—remember, you have to take me to the synagogue at twelve-thirty."

In the bedroom, a cold wind rattled the western windows. Rachel looked through the clothes in her

15

closet. The congregation thought that she dressed carelessly. In fact, she spent far too much time choosing what she should wear. It was simply that in this, as in other matters, she was guided by a spirit of contrariness. She liked floppy hats, long skirts, silver jewelry and flowery prints. Rachel dropped her jeans on the floor and took a loose gray jumper from the closet, putting it on right over her moth-eaten cashmere sweater. The holes wouldn't show. She tied a silk scarf around her neck and wound a string of beads on top of it. She pulled on a pair of purple tights and her boots over them. Between jumper and boots, it would hardly be possible to see the purple tights. The other women would probably be wearing pants suits. One or two of them would have on dark belted mink coats. Rachel ran a comb through her hair and was startled to see Seymour's face appear beside her own in the mirror.

"Are you trying to put Hadassah Kleinholz in the shade?"

"Just holding my own," Rachel answered, and put on a purple hat and a black cape.

They drove down to the synagogue in silence. It was bitter cold and the radio predicted snow.

Gateshead had once been a seaport. Sailing ships and, later, steamers had plied the Sound, carrying cargo to and from Connecticut and New England, or to the Port of New York. Whalers had sailed from here. Now there were only pleasure craft in the harbor in summertime. On weekends, fishermen crowded the railing along the docks, and the benches in the small park beside the harbor overflowed with young people in colorful clothes.

The synagogue (founded by ten Orthodox Jews in 1922 and named Shaare Tefilah) was located on Church Street, a block south of Main, between a rooming house and a Chevrolet agency. It had once been a Baptist church and was soon to become a branch office of the Long Island Lighting Company. The congregation had sold it for a good price and was building a brand new synagogue in a field surrounded by tract houses in New Gateshead, five miles inland.

16

Most of the four hundred current members of Shaare Tefilah lived in New Gateshead, a town without a center. Its name was on every map of Long Island, but anyone looking for it had a hard time finding it. There were schools in New Gateshead, ball fields, a library, but there was no candy store, no luncheonette, no sidewalk, no bench, no movie theater. The streets curved round and round, school buses came and went and, in summer, ice cream trucks, but there was no place where two streets crossed and made the beginnings of what might—one day—become a village. Teenagers too young to drive to Gateshead or to the Big Mall Shopping Center squatted in the streets on warm summer evenings or sat on the curb near the sump, where the lights from the split-level houses could not reach them. There were rich parts of New Gateshead and parts that were not so rich (nobody in New Gateshead said "rich," they said "affluent"), but there were no poor parts. The very rich (called "wealthy") lived in estates high above the Sound along the northern shore of Gateshead harbor. There were few Jews among them, to be sure, and none of them were members of Shaare Tefilah.

A few of the original member families, going back to 1922, still lived in the Village of Gateshead: above their shops, in the Deacon Hill garden apartments, or in row houses along Church Street. But they counted for very little and were rarely visited, even by their children. The real estate boom of the fifties had failed to sweep them to greener pastures. They were among the losers.

The ride to the synagogue took Seymour and Rachel less than five minutes. The distance was roughly eight blocks and was meant to be walked—on the Sabbath at any rate. The membership of Shaare Tefilah, though Conservative by now, expected its rabbi (and his rebbetzin) to observe certain of the practices set forth in the Shulchan Aruch, that awesome compendium of Orthodox Jewish laws and rituals. It was thought proper for Rachel and Seymour to refrain from eating treif, food that was not kosher, and to observe the prohibition against mixing meat and milk.

17

It was expected that they not desecrate the Sabbath by riding in a car, lighting a match, writing a letter, or handling money. It was not believed necessary for the rabbi to wear earlocks and to keep his head covered at *all* times (at the Republican Club cocktail party, for instance), though it made the congregation feel nice and warm in their hearts to see him pluck a *yarmulke* out of his pocket now and then and plop it on his head. The rebbetzin was not expected to shave her head and cover her bald pate with a wig. Trips to the *mikvah,* the ritual bath, would have seemed excessive, even bizarre. Modernity exacts a certain price, they agreed—we do not care for fanatics. This is America, after all.

The large Victorian house that Rachel loved so well had been sold to the congregation by Sam Farber, its first president. In the early years it had served as a meeting place and parsonage both. The men held their *minyan* in the front parlor and the rabbi lived upstairs with his wife and children. He rarely stayed for more than two years. Photographs of past rabbis and their Hebrew school students hung in a neat row in the hall. The rabbis' faces resembled each other—pale swatches of cheek and forehead between the black hats and black beards. The pictures had been taken in the backyard, against the clapboard siding of the house, and the second row of pupils stood on orange crates.

After the war the congregation bought the old Baptist church building and the rabbi and his family had the house to themselves. Another generation of spiritual leaders came and went. They wore black robes in the Hebrew school pictures and high square *yarmulkes* far down on their foreheads, and they still didn't stay more than three years. There were few other congregations in the vicinity; the rabbis of Gateshead and their wives grew lonely. They were always poorer than their congregants and stricter in their observances. It was assumed that their lives were bleak, expected that they stretch the joy of Simchat Torah across the entire year. Why else did they become rabbis? In the memories of the Jews of Gateshead, rabbis carried the lint of the ghetto in their pockets and reeked of damp gabardine

18

and dusty books. No one remembered a happy rabbi in a sunlit world, and the weight of such somber memories bore down upon the rabbis, their wives and children.

When Seymour Sonnshein accepted the call to Gateshead in 1965, the congregation was joyfully expanding on the wings of the postwar baby boom and a resurgence of interest in Judaism among suburbia's first generation of young professionals. The rooms of the old house became flooded with light—Rachel had painted the walls and put white curtains at every window.

Rachel and Seymour arrived at the synagogue on the dot of twelve-thirty. Seymour parked by the meter directly in front of the building and propped the blue and white sign that said CLERGY against the windshield. The meter maid, a red-faced woman who wore earmuffs in winter and a white sailor hat in summer, was his friend. She never gave the rabbi's car a ticket.

Rachel felt the familiar winds of panic flutter up within her. She was ill at ease at public or social gatherings, except when she was in disguise or unknown, able to play the role of sharp-eyed observer. At synagogue meetings she was bound to stand out. She was the rebbetzin, *and* she had exotic taste. People said, "Will you look at the rebbetzin, she's got up like a hippie!" Had she worn dowdy dresses and dark felt hats, like the rebbetzins who preceded her, they would have sniffed and said she was mousy. She was caught between the wish to be invisible and the need to assert her individuality.

Had Rachel thought that she was liked by most of the people in the congregation she might have basked in the light of their approbation and become nicer and friendlier than she by nature was. But she knew (Golda Garfinkle had pointed it out) that there were many voices raised in criticism against her. She was accused of being incomprehensible, difficult, cold and snobbish. She was cited for being lax in her ritual observances, a Jewish illiterate. Because she knew that there was some truth to all the charges, she took them to heart, suffered, became more incomprehensible

19

still. She wondered about all those who disliked her, but could not bring herself to think about them for very long. Some of her enemies were cool, others fawned on her, but try as she might she could not imagine how they spoke to each other about her or what it was they actually said. Her imagination would not extend in that direction; when she was away from them their voices ceased to exist.

Seymour headed straight for his study, a dank room just off the auditorium that served as a sanctuary. Rachel followed close behind. The building was poorly kept. Everyone was anxious to make the move to the new one. The Sisterhood met in a high-ceilinged room at the rear of the old church building. A small kitchen was used to prepare dairy meals; there were no facilities to serve meat. It would be different in the new building. The smell of cold cigars was everywhere—it was the odor of absent men. Although they no longer appeared except for morning and evening prayers, their presence had soaked into the very walls of the building. Between the morning and the evening, the days in suburban Gateshead were governed by women. The rabbi, the janitor, and the principal of the Hebrew school spent their working hours awash in a sea of females. Each had adjusted in his own way. The janitor cackled his black laugh and made them forget their white fears for the moment, the principal whined and cajoled in an imitation of them so perfect it verged on parody, and Seymour, the rabbi—Seymour cocked his handsome head to one side and looked pensive. He rarely smiled his princely smile, and resembled—thought Rachel—the Man of Sorrows.

Rachel sat down on the overstuffed couch in Seymour's office. It had, like so much else, been donated by someone in arrears with his dues. Books and letters and boxes of outdated synagogue bulletins were piled in the corners. Rachel sat primly in the middle of it all.

"How long are you staying?" Seymour asked.

"As long as possible," said Rachel and began studying her pages of yellow paper. The words she had

20

copied down seemed to make less sense than they had in the book.

Millie Fertig, one of the secretaries, came into the room without knocking. "Hello, Rabbi!" she said. Millie had to walk clear across the auditorium to reach the rabbi's study, but she did not mind the trek. She liked rabbis. She liked Seymour particularly. Her sister-in-law Fay, who worked in the synagogue office part-time, had no special feeling about rabbis but didn't particularly like Seymour. She made the trip only rarely.

Millie Fertig's voice was husky and deep. "What are *you* doing here?" she asked Rachel, sounding surprised rather than hostile. Millie, widowed longer now than she had been married, lived alone and was condemned to silence much of the time.

"*There* you are," said Golda Garfinkle, entering Seymour's study freshly rinsed and coiffed. "We're waiting for you. Have you got the *D'var Torah*?"

Rachel smoothed the folded papers.

"My God, it's *long*!" said Golda. She ignored Seymour completely.

Rachel got up from the couch and followed Golda meekly into the crowded meeting room. Here and there a smile cut loose from a briefly glimpsed, familiar face and floated toward Rachel. Six tables were set for lunch, each one crowned by a centerpiece depicting a Jewish holiday. The walls were bright with Israeli travel posters. Golda led Rachel to the head table and left her at her place card, in a spot between Hadassah Kleinholz and old Mrs. Kantrowitz. Hadassah Kleinholz was, as yet, absent. Mrs. Kantrowitz had been an honored guest at Sisterhood luncheons since her seventy-fifth birthday. She was now eighty-six.

"And who are *you*?" she asked Rachel.

"You know me. I'm Rachel Sonnshein, the rebbetzin."

Just then, Hadassah Kleinholz sat down in her chair, breathless and full of bubbling friendly chatter.

"So good to see you," she said to Rachel. "It's been a long time. You people never seem to come to any

21

of the regional meetings. It's a shame, you don't know what you're missing."

Rachel started to answer, but Hadassah's questions were flying thick and fast.

"Are you still writing?"

"I paint," said Rachel.

"Oh, right. Did you make these lovely centerpieces?"

"No, I think the Sisterhood art chairman did."

"You should serve in that capacity, with all your talent."

"It's not exactly what I do," said Rachel, and was truly sorry, at that moment, that it was not what she did.

"It doesn't matter," said Hadassah. "As rebbetzin you must be active. You should set an example."

It had grown quiet in the room. Rachel thought her unspoken thoughts had reached the far corners of the room. Everyone was looking at her. She heard her name.

"Rachel Sonnshein, our rebbetzin, will give the *D'var Torah*."

Rachel got up. She walked with the legal pad in her hand to where the microphone stood, and it suddenly seemed quite mad to be reading Kafka to the Sisterhood.

My grandfather used to say: "Life is astoundingly short. To me, looking back over it, life seems so foreshortened that I scarcely understand, for instance, how a young man can decide to ride over to the next village without being afraid that— not to mention accidents—even the span of a normal happy life may fall far short of the time needed for such a journey."

Rachel paused for a brief moment, preparing to launch into the next short tale, the one about the Chassidic rabbi. Before she could begin, she heard Golda Garfinkle say Amen in a loud clear voice. That was the end of Rachel's *D'var Torah*. She returned to her seat and sat down.

"What was *that*?" Hadassah Kleinholz asked.

22

"Rabbi Yisakhar Baer of Radoshitz," Rachel lied.

"A wonderful tale," Hadassah told her.

Golda Garfinkle asked the Sisterhood president to make the blessing over bread. Rachel felt herself slipping out of the limelight. She said Amen and broke off a piece of roll.

Tuna fish and egg salad were served in rounded scoops. Mrs. Kantrowitz had a good lunch. White-green hard leaves of iceberg lettuce, radishes and pale tomatoes. Hadassah Kleinholz wiped her mouth. It was time for her talk. She did not wait for the ladies to quiet down. She knew from experience that her voice would triumph.

Hadassah Kleinholz said she was glad to be in Gateshead. "You have a very talented rebbetzin in your community, I've known her for a long time. She is a little shy but I have urged her to share her talents with you. I know she will."

There were smiles on many of the outstretched faces.

"Is she talking about you?" Mrs. Kantrowitz asked Rachel.

Hadassah Kleinholz spoke in tongues. Rachel tried hard to pay attention to what she said but it reached her mind as garbled, mutilated language. Hadassah Kleinholz had become transformed before the microphone. She snapped her fingers, pirouetted, strove for the high notes. Her private self had apparently been squeezed into a wad of gum and left under her seat. "Jewish is beautiful," she warbled. "Be proud you are Jewish," she crooned. "Be *shtolz!*" she sang. "Sisters!" she cried, "renew your commitment to Judaism, renew yourselves! Drink at the fountain of Torah. Don't be ashamed. Be yourselves. Be Jewish." She seemed on the verge of taking off her clothes.

Rachel looked out over the audience. The women were very still. They paid attention. Only Mrs. Kantrowitz had fallen asleep. Rachel's mind wandered, drifted from the sunken figure of Mrs. Kantrowitz to the windows, left the whole gathering behind, hovered (like one of Chagall's figures) above the roofs of the village.

"Your children are like tender shoots," Hadassah

23

Kleinholz was saying, ". . . like the first fruits of *Shevuoth*. Let them walk in the light of Torah."

Hadassah Kleinholz raised her voice to drum upon the ceiling of the old First Baptist Church. Rachel forced her wandering mind back to the luncheon table.

"Renew yourselves!" Hadassah Kleinholz cried. "Return to the spirit of your fathers. You can do it! The Holy One—Blessed be He—chose you to do it."

"But how?" a voice cried out from the audience.

"How?" Hadassah Kleinholz echoed the word. "How? The light of your history, the beacon of Jewish martyrdom, shines forth from each and every one of you. I can feel it and so can you. I can see it in your eyes." She paused to take a drink of water. "You must make your home a Jewish home, a safe harbor in the *goyishe* night. Light the Sabbath candles so they may bring inspiration from Sinai, signal rest to your tired soul. Make the Sabbath a festival, a gift from heaven dropped in your lap by the Almighty. . . ."

"When our husbands come home they're tired, and our kids want to go out . . ."

"Stop right there!" Hadassah Kleinholz commanded. "Your grandfathers were tired too. Your husbands didn't invent it. But your grandfathers let *Shabbos* renew them. *Shabbos* made them happy. Sing to your spouses a new song. Offer them chicken and chopped liver and *kneidlach* and *kugel*. For one night every week be an old-fashioned Jewish wife. Offer yourselves. Give yourselves to your men. It is commanded in the Torah for the Sabbath."

"Sex!" a woman in the front row said. "After dinner—after such a dinner!—they fall asleep. If I sang a song to my husband he'd take me and my song to Kings Park State Hospital."

A few voices hissed out to quiet the lady in the front row. She sat back calmly, satisfied that she made her point.

"When was the last time you talked to your rabbi?" Hadassah Kleinholz asked. "When did you last go up to him and look him in the eye, wearing a smile on your lips? Communication is a two-way street. Ask him to

24

lead you on a retreat. What rabbi wouldn't be glad for the chance to spend a weekend in meditation and prayer at the Concord surrounded by his congregation? Pray to the Holy One, Blessed be He, dance to the music of the cymbal and the harp. Think Jewish! Bring the message of Judaism home to your children. Let *Yiddishkeit* be your guide. I say to you: embroider Jewish, crewel Jewish and needlepoint Jewish. Your talented rebbetzin will be glad to direct you. She told me so. I remember her from our student days. Always sketching . . . she was a regular Rembrandt . . . I only hope she remembered to stop on *Shabbos*. . . ."

Laughter among the Sisterhood ladies.

". . . her cartoons of the faculty amused us all."

Applause snowed lightly upon Rachel. She smiled automatically, frozen in a snapshot of someone else. She had not known Hadassah in the time of Seymour's Seminary studies; she never did cartoons, nor had she attended classes given by the Seminary faculty. It was all a lie.

When Hadassah Kleinholz finally sat down she turned a beaming face on Rachel.

"How about that little plug?" she asked. Her black-bristled eyes shone with elation, and a blanket of sweat glistened below her precise hairline.

"Thanks a lot," said Rachel. Hadassah was above sarcasm.

"I had to fib a little bit, but I do it for effect. I took drama lessons from a famous coach. Did you like my little spiel?"

"It's very dramatic," Rachel said.

Hadassah Kleinholz accepted the ladies' many congratulations graciously. Rachel slipped away unseen. She looked into Seymour's office but he was no longer there.

"Did my husband say he'd be back?" she asked Millie. (She could never quite manage to refer to him as "the rabbi.")

"He was tired," said Millie. "He told me to tell you he'd see you at home."

It was three o'clock. Snow was falling upon the streets and roofs of Gateshead. Rachel left the syna-

25

gogue by the back door. She did not say good-bye to anyone. The cold air, wet with swirling flakes, closed about her like a wave. In an instant Rachel was cut off from any lingering connection with the hot meeting room and its heavy perfumed air. "I don't love the Jews enough," thought Rachel and said it aloud, testing and tasting her guilt. *"I don't love the Jews enough,"* she said. The fence behind the synagogue parking lot was covered with the squiggles of suburban graffiti. It lacked the splendid baroque quality found in the work of the city's subway Masters. It lacked assurance. Among the hearts and genitalia was a message that read "Turn TO the LOrD JESus and BE SAved YOU jews."

"We Jews ought to paint a mural over that," thought Rachel.

Rachel walked down a narrow alley to Main Street. It was growing dark but the snowflakes were touched and transformed into sparkling starlets by the light of the street lamps. The gray day was sinking without a trace. Snow danced across the storefronts of Gateshead. Here and there some god-forsaken Christmas decorations trailed through a dusty window. On summer evenings Main Street had the timeless quality of the small town about it, American myths seemed to have stroked its façades, words from O'Neill and Dreiser, Wilder and Inge fluttered across the hot sidewalk. But on winter evenings it all shrank to nothing. Words were lost. The sidewalks were frozen to silence.

The chill of the wintry afternoon weighed on Rachel. Once again she had lost precious time, had achieved nothing. The meeting had made her feel like a mute, stubborn child. She had not even done her smiling best to reflect well on Seymour. She thought she thought too much about herself. She stood far outside the harmless innocuous efforts the ladies made to do good. They meant well, they wanted their lives to be enriched, like a loaf of bread. They organized to dispense charity and to support worthy institutions, they met to be uplifted and to raise some new word or idea upon their horizons each week. And Rachel fled from them,

26

put them down, ridiculed them. Once again she had left precipitously, had gritted her teeth in full view of everyone and insisted upon displaying her proud and alienated heart. It did no good and the day was still lost to her. It gave her small comfort and did not restore a single minute of work time to her.

Rachel arrived home with cold cheeks and a red nose. Aaron sat at the kitchen table, eating a bowl of cereal and drinking a Coke. He too had curly Jewish hair, but it was rougher and bouncier than his father's and he had his mother's round face. He was an awkward and beautiful sixteen. Rachel loved him. She rubbed his head with her hand.

"Cut it out, Mom."

It was expected that he reject his mother's advances, even when she tried to cloak them in gruff locker room movements. Rachel had not wanted daughters. She hoped Aaron would do well at baseball. He played third base and was a switch hitter. The dream had brought them close.

"Why are you eating cornflakes at four P.M.?"

"Because I'm hungry."

"And drinking a Coke?"

"Because I'm thirsty."

"Your stomach will rot. It's less than two hours to dinner. You'll get pimples and bad breath."

"I already have all those things and worse. Anyway, we learned in Health that they're a natural part of adolescence."

"I *never* had pimples."

"You're a woman and a rabbi's wife and don't *need* them."

Rachel tried to kiss him on the forehead but he moved away and she got a lock of hair in her mouth.

"What happened in school today?"

"We had a fire drill."

"That's exciting."

"The fire marshal came to speak."

"What about?"

"He told us how to start fires."

"Really?"

27

"Do you believe everything I tell you?"

"I rule nothing out. I wait and see. You always start to laugh when you're putting me on."

Aaron let loose a sixteen-year-old's belch. He was not, Rachel thought, his father turned child again, yet he resembled him. A gesture here, a glance, the shape of his hands. But it was all mitigated by Rachel's softer, rounder shape, which seemed to mock the echo of Seymour's angular features.

"Where's your father?"

"Upstairs. He told me he had to rest up for the meeting tonight." Aaron wiped his mouth on the back of his hand and went to do his homework.

Rachel put the dishes into the sink and looked at the clock. It was four-thirty. Seymour came downstairs just then.

"How was your meeting?"

"Like all meetings," said Rachel.

"How was Hadassah Kleinholz?"

"Terrific. A *real* rebbetzin. You should have married her."

"What did she say?"

"Who listens? Isn't it enough I was there?"

Seymour sidestepped Rachel's sulkiness.

"Would you like a drink?" he asked.

"I haven't shopped for dinner yet," said Rachel, prepared to sigh.

"What are we having?"

"Fish."

Rachel had not given any thought to dinner. At such moments she always answered "Fish." There was a fish store down at the corner. It carried great quantities of fish and marvelous but forbidden shellfish.

"I don't feel like eating fish," said Seymour. He never did feel like eating fish.

"How about McDonald's then?"

"We'll meet twenty congregants."

Rachel felt the bite of familiar anger. "I'm tired of hushing up my passion for *treif* junk food. I'm like everyone else in that respect. I want to have a Big Mac with cheese and a pepperoni pizza."

28

Seymour made a pitcher of martinis. There were several small green olives in Rachel's glass, onions in Seymour's. He divided the pitcher of martinis equally and they sat across the table from each other (the way they did at breakfast) and drank. They drank judiciously, cautiously even, and ate pretzels while the snow swirled outside and Aaron listened to Mozart in his room.

Rachel suddenly felt better. Sharp and full of daring.

"Do you love the Jews?" she asked Seymour.

"Of course I love the Jews."

"Because you're a rabbi?"

"I became a rabbi because I loved the Jews. However terrible they become they're never as awful as the *goyim*."

"A dreadful attitude. Do you call that love?"

"It may be perverse, but it's love."

"Would you say that you loved *these* Jews? The Jews of Gateshead?"

"Why are you asking all these questions?"

"I felt this afternoon that I was derelict in my devotion, that I may well love the *idea* of Jews but don't love the Jews. At least not the suburban Jews of Gateshead who come to hear Hadassah Kleinholz and find her 'inspiring.' "

"Hadassah Kleinholz made you jealous?"

"Of course she did, for a moment, but that's not the point. And you must answer my question."

"Of course I don't especially love the Jews of Gateshead, but then I don't care for most of the people of Gateshead. Anyway, all this talk about 'love' is Christian and kind of sappy and makes me think of flower children running through a meadow and Albert Schweitzer sparing the lives of flies and ants. I'm sure Moses didn't love *his* Jews either."

"Do you think you're Moses?"

"I think, more often, that I'm Isaiah, but there comes a time in every rabbi's life when he thinks he's Moses. When you've lost that sense of identification you'd better go looking for something else to do."

"They love to hear you thunder at them. They

29

love being flagellated. But when I read them Kafka they're offended."

"They pay me to thunder at them. It's part of my job. But you're supposed to be the good cop. You're supposed to embody all the virtues of a 'woman of valor.' The *last* thing you're supposed to do is to question their values. You are supposed to be what they can identify as 'Jewish.' And you don't fit the picture when you read Kafka. He may be profoundly Jewish, but not in the way they understand it. You make them feel dumb and simpleminded when they're supposed to think *you're* dumb and simpleminded. Kafka! For God's sake, Rachel! You're hopeless, my dear."

The telephone rang. Seymour answered it, said "Just a minute please," and got up, drink in hand, to take the call in his study. When Rachel heard Seymour's voice booming in the distance she dropped the receiver in its cradle.

She felt pleasantly at peace in her kitchen, bright now and warm against the dark coldness leaning on the house like a black shield. The moment was a reprise of the morning; the only thing that had changed was the nature of the light. Morning light came from without, the light of night from within. One promised the world, the other promised peace.

The drink's first high had buzzed itself out in Rachel's head. It was too late, thank God, to go to the store. Shopping was one of the things that solved itself if it was ignored. Rachel prepared an omelette with chicken livers. She made home-fried potatoes and a tossed salad. When dinner was ready she called Seymour and Aaron. Aaron came down first.

"I love chicken livers," he said, "but we learned in Health that all the shit the chickens ingest, the pesticides and the chemicals they put into the feed, goes directly into the liver. It does not pass GO, it zooms right through the chicken and *bang!* into the liver."

"You're not going to eat it?"

"I'll eat it this time. I'm starved. But it isn't healthy for growing children."

Seymour came in. "Sorry I'm late," he said. "One of my congregants had a problem."

30

"Male or female?" Aaron asked him.

"None of your business."

"Female," said Aaron.

"What else?" said Rachel.

Seymour put too much salt on his omelette.

"Eggs are full of cholesterol," Aaron said.

"What happened in school today?" Seymour asked him.

"We had a fire drill where we learned how to make a fire."

"That's the third day in a row," Rachel said.

"Mom believes all my outrageous statements. I don't know what's the matter with her."

"Your mother is as innocent as a cucumber."

Aaron went to the refrigerator to look for dessert. He came to the table with half a gallon of Breyer's ice cream—butter pecan.

"Use a *milchig* plate, please," said Rachel. "You shouldn't be having ice cream at all."

"What's wrong with ice cream?" asked Aaron, full of mock surprise.

"You're *fleishig,* son," said Seymour. It was an old refrain.

"I always am," said Aaron. "I'm made of meat."

"Just keep the plates straight," said Rachel. "Don't make a mockery of the dietary laws or your father will be fired."

"That's a hypocritical reason for keeping them," said Aaron.

"I know," said Rachel.

Seymour went to read the paper.

Rachel kept track of two separate sets of dishes but her system was chaotic and worked only in her conscience. When she and Seymour had been newly married and full of enthusiasm for the details of their life together—flatware and linens had all been initialed —they sincerely believed in maintaining *kashruth;* it was a bond between them. Both sets of in-laws suffered outrage over what they considered the practice of a barbaric ritual. Now the bond was in their trespassing. Over the years, Rachel's convictions had worn a little thin, and the parents sighed with relief. It was only

31

their derisory attitude that kept Rachel from abandoning *kashruth* completely. When her mother visited, Rachel was careful to instruct her in the separation of the plates.

"I have to go," said Seymour.

"It's only seven," said Rachel.

"I might as well stop by the hospital and see who's sick before the meeting starts."

Aaron went to his room, and Seymour put on a scarf and gloves and his heavy coat and went out into the snow. Rachel was left alone. Once more she put the dishes into the dishwasher, scrubbed the pots and pans, did the wiping and sweeping and let her mind float free of it all. The house was still, except for Aaron's radio, which was tuned to WQXR. Rachel went up to the attic. She was tired, but under the humming fluorescent tubes her spirits lifted. She worked a while, drawing corners of the attic and pieces of abandoned things. Soon her hand felt swift and she went to work on a clean piece of Bristol board. She began a collage, and lost herself in what she was doing. The joy was so great it hummed in her ribcage.

Out of nowhere Aaron appeared. She had not heard him. He stood still at the top of the stairs.

"There's a lady on the telephone who wants to know if you're busy."

"Tell her 'yes.' "

He was back in a minute.

"She says it's Mrs. Garfinkle and she'll only be a minute."

Rachel went downstairs. She decided not to think, even as she was talking to Golda.

"You left so abruptly this afternoon," Golda said, "none of us had a chance to say good-bye. Hadassah seemed a bit offended."

"I like to be home when Aaron gets back from school."

"We all love our children, Rachel. But that's not what I called about. I wanted to ask you something, it won't take a minute. I know you're busy. Will you do a program for the Sisterhood?"

"What kind of program?"

32

"Oh—anything. It can be a demonstration. A talk about art. Hadassah said such nice things about you. Everyone was enthused. We thought, after that stimulating meeting today, you might be able to give us some pointers on how to decorate our homes Jewishly."

"She got it all wrong. I'm no good at any of that."

"Rachel, dear, don't be coy. You're a bright girl, you can come up with something. I remember you graduated magna cum laude. Don't play dumb."

"You remember I graduated magna cum laude because you graduated summa cum laude."

Rachel sometimes wondered how it had come about that bright girls like Golda had turned into boring silly women. The brightness had probably been sealed off. Contained in a bell jar. It had had an existence separate from feelings or appetites.

"I'm not good at public speaking," she ventured.

"You're the rebbetzin," said Golda. "You can do it. We haven't taken sufficient advantage of your talents. You might do a slide talk on Jewish art."

"When?"

"In the spring. April or May. I'll let you know."

Rachel went upstairs when the conversation finished and worked a while longer. She forgot Golda almost immediately. At ten-thirty she went to see if Aaron had gone to bed. He was reading, propped up against two pillows.

"You look sad, Mom."

"Sad?"

She kissed Aaron and he was sleepy enough not to object.

"I'm just serious, and tired."

"I think you look sad."

At twelve-fifteen Rachel heard the front door slam. Seymour came right up the stairs two at a time and into her studio. He was covered with snow and brought the clean smell of winter with him.

"They're selling our house! Stealing our home from under us, sending us to some crummy development, so I can walk to *shul* on *Shabbos*. That gang of hypocrites! Cy Glatt wants us to look at a couple of houses,

33

to help them decide. They never even asked me if we minded! Oh, Rachel ..."

"What can we do?"

"Not a damn thing."

2

Three weeks later, Sol and Cookie Wasserman stopped their white Lincoln Continental in front of the Sonnshein house and honked loudly. The weather had grown bitter cold and the sidewalks were icy. Many of the older congregants were in Florida. Sol Wasserman was chairman of the Building and House Committee and he had come to take Rachel and Seymour out to the housing development behind the new synagogue to show them three houses.

"We want you to be happy," said Sol.

"Then don't sell the house," Rachel muttered.

Seymour dug his elbow into her side, but Rachel was too angry to care. The Lincoln Continental was white inside too, and from its stereo speakers issued the music from *Fiddler on the Roof*. Conversation was difficult among the multiple speakers and Rachel was rather glad about that. She didn't like riding in white Lincoln Continentals with people she hardly knew. In order not to let conversation flag she would begin telling boring stories. She never knew where they led, her listeners became mesmerized and Seymour grew fidgety. If only she could remember the names of children or the colleges they attended! The Wassermans had a married daughter (was her husband a *goy* or a Moroccan Jew?) and a son on a commune. Rachel remembered that the son had an odd name. Or was it the commune that had the odd name?

"Bobo sends his regards, Rabbi," said Cookie Was-

35

serman, without turning around. "He's into TM and says he'd love to discuss it with you one day."

"I'm always available," said Seymour.

"What's TM?" said Rachel, and Seymour nudged her again.

"Transcendental Meditation," said Sol Wasserman. "After all the money his bar mitzvah cost me." Sol Wasserman owned a Ford agency and the county police department bought most of its cars from him.

"TM isn't against Judaism, is it, Rabbi?" Cookie asked.

"I wouldn't say it was part of the tradition," said Seymour, mildly. Rachel was always amazed how calmly he took these encounters.

"I saw one of those kids with the shaved heads in the subway recently," said Rachel, and couldn't decide where she intended to take the story. "It's funny how they look with ordinary shoes and socks and heavy sweaters over those orange robes. He looked Jewish. Does Bobo wear robes?"

"He's not one of *those*," said Cookie, "and besides, it helped him to give up drugs."

The new synagogue was surrounded by a sea of frozen mud. Its exterior was almost finished; the contractor had promised that the interior would be complete in time for the High Holy Days.

"Let's see if they're working." Sol Wasserman drove across the frozen mud right up to the front door.

Sol Wasserman was, as they said, "into" real estate and had been in charge of the new building from the beginning. He interviewed a dozen architects, wanted to meet Marcel Breuer, and was disappointed to hear that Louis Kahn had recently died. In the end, his committee decided that it wasn't worth the extra money it would cost to hire a famous architect, and the contract was given to a local firm. The design had not pleased everyone, and a few members of the congregation left to join the Reform temple in Gateshead West. Rachel, who thought the building an abomination, had no such options. She had offered her opinions to the Building and House Committee chairman at a cocktail party one time and he had ignored them.

36

"Let the rebbetzin mind the rabbi," he later said. "Just because she got a degree in art don't mean she knows shit about building a *shul*."

The firm of Snyder, Breitkopf and Fannelli specialized in false fronts. Basically, they had a single structural plan: a shoebox, done in cement block, veiled by a decorative sheath which alluded to one of three styles—the vaguely Oriental, the vaguely Gothic and the vaguely early-American. Shaare Tefilah's identity was established through a giant pair of Tablets of the Law, the sort it has been popular for centuries to assume were carried down from Sinai by Moses. The tablets rose up two stories on either side of the front entrance to the building. They were made of stucco and ten Hebrew letters were incised upon them and lit from within by blue lights.

The people across the street had been against permitting the construction of a synagogue in their neighborhood and were suspected of being anti-Semites. Their house was up for sale.

"*That* house isn't bad," said Rachel, pointing to the large colonial with its two symmetrically placed chimneys and the gracefully proportioned front door.

"It's priced way out of our range," Sol Wasserman said, opening the car door. "With what they want for it we could build a second *shul*. Excuse me, girls, I want to show the rabbi where they're going to install the Ark."

Rachel watched them walk gingerly across the construction rubble. Sol was short and dapper. Seymour was graceful and towered above the Building and House Committee chairman. But you could tell Sol Wasserman miles away. He wore a toupee.

"I never get to talk with you," said Cookie Wasserman. "We'd love to have you to dinner some evening." Cookie had turned around and was looking at Rachel. "But you know, we don't keep kosher."

"It's all right with me," said Rachel.

"You don't mind?"

"I'm not a fanatic."

"As an artist, Rachel, how do you like the new building?"

37

"It looks like a shoebox."

"I think it's the best we could get for the money."

The men were standing in front of the building. Sol Wasserman gesticulated authoritatively. Seymour nodded his head.

"Do you love your husband?" Cookie asked.

"Of course I do. Why do you ask?"

"It must be hard to be married to a rabbi. But then, you're probably not like other people. And you won't tell me the truth."

"I'm telling the truth. I probably wouldn't lie about it if it weren't so; it would be too obvious."

"Nothing's obvious. People lie all the time. Especially about sex. I bet you don't like to talk about sex."

Rachel did not, in fact, like to talk about sex. She wondered for a moment how they had gotten onto the topic so swiftly. She had been wondering what there was to talk about. Evidently, Cookie wanted to talk about sex. Just then, the men came back. Rachel was relieved.

"Damn workmen are goofing off," said Sol Wasserman. "The place will never be finished by September."

Sol drove through the development's identical winding streets.

"How do you ever find your own house?" asked Rachel.

"You learn," said Cookie Wasserman.

A few of the houses still had colored Christmas lights strung along the edges of the roofs. The cold kept children and mothers inside. The streets were empty. Here and there a car was parked along the curb or in a driveway.

"It's not more than five minutes' walk to the *shul* from any place in the development," said Sol Wasserman. "There are several houses for sale. One is a split-level with a two-car garage and another is a splanch."

"A what?" said Rachel.

"A splanch," Sol repeated. "That's a cross between a split-level and a ranch."

"Already I can't stand it," Rachel said, and got

38

another nudge from Seymour. "It's an awful combination," she insisted.

"Why don't you look at it first?" said Cookie.

They parked in front of a house that needed painting.

"We'll fix it up for you," said Sol. "Don't worry about how it looks now. Just notice the spacious rooms and the convenient arrangement."

The Sonnsheins and the Wassermans stood at the front door for a very long time before anyone answered their ring. The woman who finally opened the door was dressed in a bathrobe, the kind with cotton tufts. Rachel could not think of the word for it.

"Excuse the way I look," the woman said.

The house was dark. The curtains were drawn in every room, and Rachel had difficulty seeing the shape of the rooms.

"Could you open the curtains a little bit?" said Cookie.

"The sunlight fades my upholstery," the woman said, but then she drew the curtains back. A ray of winter sunlight fell upon the coffee table. It was covered with dust and seashells. The kitchen was filthy; the bathroom smelled.

"We can get it for a good price," Sol Wasserman whispered. "All it needs is a good cleaning."

"My husband lost his job last month," the woman said to Seymour. Secrets always floated his way, confidences found his ears. "I don't know how I'll ever leave this place."

"Is there a basement?" asked Rachel.

"Yes, but I wasn't planning to show it. My sister lives there."

"Thank you for letting us see the house," said Cookie Wasserman. They bumped into each other, all four of them, in trying to get out the front door.

Rachel remembered that the bathrobe material was chenille.

"How some people live!" said Cookie, when they got back into the car.

The next house was the split-level with the two-car

39

garage. There was a flagpole on its front lawn. Rocks the size of bowling balls had been heaped against the base of the pole and painted red, white and blue. A cartwheel was cemented into place next to the driveway, and the mailbox was mounted on its rim. A wooden eagle, painted gold, with a wingspread of about four feet, hung above the front door. The woman who answered the door wore a jogging outfit. She had curlers in her hair. The early-American motif had spread throughout the house. A spinning wheel stood in the entrance hall, red-white-and-blue bunting hung about a portrait of George Washington, and milk cans with eagle decals on them stood about like spittoons.

Rachel felt dizzy for a moment. The world seemed to be exploding with gimcracks. She felt as though the space she occupied was mutilated by the presence of too many objects. For relief, she gazed out of the large picture window. Unfortunately, it looked straight down on the back side of the new Shaare Tefilah. The backyard was narrow and contained a rusty swing set and the remains of a plastic pool. A hedge of forsythia was all that separated the yard from the detritus-strewn field on which the cement block shoebox of a building stood. The curved tops of the Tablets of the Law were barely visible above the flat roof. The rear wall presented a dull gray surface, unbroken save for three small windows in a stairwell and the large metal door that led to the kitchen. A sight, thought Rachel, to bring sadness to any heart.

Mrs. Jefferson, the owner of the house, said, "It's perfect, I should think, for a rabbi." She seemed to be addressing Seymour. Her smile was dazzling.

"How about the basement?" asked Rachel.

"Of course we have one."

"Can I see it?"

"It's a mess."

"That's o.k., I just want to know its potential."

Mrs. Jefferson took Rachel down a flight of stairs and turned on a very dim light. Everything in the basement was put up on cement blocks.

"Is there water down here?" asked Rachel.

"Not if you keep the outside stairwell covered,"

40

said Mrs. Jefferson. "We licked that problem." A plastic sheet hung over the door, a large hole gaped around the pipe that led out to the cesspool. "The excess runs off down there."

The last house they looked at was at the top of a small hill that rose behind the development. This house had been part of the original parcel of land (comprising several hundred acres) which the Pembroke family of Gateshead had sold to a real-estate syndicate. Trees grew close to the old house, its porch was dark and groaned with the noise of pine branches sweeping along its windows. The rooms were papered in yellow stripes, the woodwork was heavy and brown.

"I like this place," said Rachel. It was unoccupied. She could see herself in it.

"It needs a lot of work," said Sol Wasserman.

"So did the first one we saw."

"But here the work is structural, it's an old house."

The four of them stood in the bare kitchen, uncomfortable with one another. Rachel felt herself pitted against Sol Wasserman and knew that it was an unequal match. She would lose. Seymour wisely kept himself aloof. The view didn't matter to him. He was a prince and would be made comfortable anywhere; Rachel would see to that.

"Does it have a basement?"

Sol opened a door that led to a space beneath the living room. It smelled of oil fumes and earth. An ancient furnace stood at its center and bricks were scattered here and there.

"You couldn't use that," said Sol, in a satisfied tone of voice.

Still Rachel held on. The house commanded a view across a field that ended in woods.

"That's due to be developed next," Sol Wasserman added.

"I like this place," said Rachel. She spoke to Seymour now, and her eyes begged him to agree with her, even as she saw—as he had seen long before—that it was hopeless. The Wassermans had already selected the American eagle. It needed no repairs, it was an average sort of place, no better than the houses where

41

most of the congregation lived, and certainly more modest than those of its officers.

As they walked—gingerly and separately—back to the white Lincoln Continental, Rachel noticed the yard for a last time: the furled green leaves of the rhododendron, the still black pines (odorless in the biting cold), the matted grass entangled in the last dead chrysanthemums, the wild roses—and high above them, like a spare eye, a window in the gable of the house. Why did she feel that sweet longing for places such as this? The ache verged on the sexual. Love made under these eaves would surely be sweeter than love made in a splanch.

The Wassermans dropped Rachel and Seymour off at the old parsonage. The ride back had been silent.

"I bet they buy the all-American one," said Rachel.

"You liked the last one, didn't you?"

"And you?"

"I didn't particularly like any of them, but I saw it didn't matter. Taking us was only a formality."

"That house in the trees was so familiar. It seemed to have a history. A *real* history."

"They don't see the past the way you do, Rachel. They're busy improving on it. A lot of them remember tenements in Brooklyn and row houses in Queens. They think 'new is nice.' Old things make them melancholy. They didn't have a share in the America of small towns. Neither did you, for that matter, but you romanticize it."

"I just like the way those places look. Don't they care what I like? Maybe I'll lecture on the 'Art of Architecture' for the Sisterhood."

"Don't be an ass, Rachel."

It was lunch time and they sat at the kitchen table and finished the meatloaf from the day before. Rachel kept on lamenting her coming loss.

"None of the kitchens were half as big as this one."

"We won't be there forever. Don't fret. Consider it a way station. Once Aaron graduates from high school, we'll have one less reason to stay. And if my contract isn't renewed this November the house won't matter anyway."

42

Rachel detected resignation in Seymour's words. He had, she thought, been accompanied by a certain silence lately, as though his thoughts spun on without ever finding their way into speech. He was not usually prone to withdrawal, unlike Rachel, who locked her emotions away and liked silence and the peace of being alone.

"What do you have in mind?" she asked.

"Nothing yet. I've been thinking about it, though, and I'll make some discreet inquiries at the Placement Bureau. Maybe it's time for us to go someplace else, or even for me to do something else. But for God's sake, don't tell anyone!"

"Who would there be to tell?"

"Your friend Sally, who has a big mouth."

"I like your confidence."

"It was only a warning."

Seymour left his dishes on the table, as he always did, and went into his study. Rachel tried to think about the future, but the only tangible thing in it was having to leave the beloved house—the rest was all dreams. She felt depressed and when she tried to see the landscape beyond her window, it was through a veil of tears.

Rachel went upstairs to her studio, where the sun lay warm and yellow across the floor and the corners glowed in its dusty path. But she could do no work. She found no arrangement of objects that made sense. She could not even see properly. The same anxiety she had felt spring at her heart earlier in the day (at the picture window in Mrs. Jefferson's living room) swept through her once again. Rachel looked in the mirror, she looked the same, there was nothing about her face that was any different. She found no terror in her eyes. Her heart beat loudly in her wrists and death whispered in her ears. Rachel went downstairs to bed and fell asleep. Sleep was her only defense.

"What's the matter with Mom?" Aaron asked his father.

"She's not feeling well."

"Her period?"

"No, nothing so physical. It's called anxiety."

43

"It grabs you in the chest."

"How do you know?"

"We learned about it in Health."

They were eating grilled cheese sandwiches at the Pleiades luncheonette on Main Street. Several times during dinner, people came in and greeted Seymour.

"It's amazing," said Aaron. "Everyone in this town knows you."

"The village is small and I'm the only rabbi in the Pleiades luncheonette."

They walked home together, past the movie theater and the bank and the laundromat.

Late that night a warm front moved across Long Island and the temperature rose into the forties. Rachel woke up to the change—it was as though angels had descended from heaven. Seymour was fast asleep. The house was quiet, but Aaron's snoring could be heard in the drafty hall. Rachel went to her studio once more. She felt that she had passed through a small crisis of the sort that afflicted romantics. She worked until dawn on a new collage and heard the drippings of melted snow go gurgling down the drainpipe. The day would become soggy with spring, one of those unaccountably warm ones that blow in even in the midst of winter and make the earth smell sweet and the trees glow pink and brown.

Rachel returned to bed and slept until ten o'clock. When she got up again she found the house empty. Aaron had long since left for school and Seymour was at his office. He had left a note on the kitchen table, next to Rachel's plate. She heated some milk and drank her coffee white.

The doorbell rang and startled Rachel. Immediately she felt guilty for being found so late in the morning, undressed still, rumpled and dank from her bed, unkempt as though she were what her mother might call a slut. (Her mother always washed and dressed before she appeared in the morning, but her mother had always had Donella, who arrived each morning punctually at seven-thirty to fix the children's breakfast.)

On the way to answer the front door Rachel passed the mirror in the hall. She saw that her hair was tan-

44

gled and she ran her hands over it to smooth it down. She saw the crud in the corners of her eyes and moistened her index finger to rub it out. Through the large panes of dark glass that flanked the front door Rachel always noticed who was outside before she was seen. This morning it was Truscott Boothby in a loden coat, without a hat.

"Hi, Rachel," he said, as soon as she opened the door. "I've come to see your husband, the good rabbi, but I can see he's not home."

Truscott Boothby was a large man, but in addition to being large he took up a lot of extra space. His movements were expansive; he seemed to need a field or a cathedral to contain him. In his physical dimensions he was supremely blessed with Christian-American presence. What was odd—and appealing—about him was the mind and soul that came with his great bearish body. The mind was sharp, the soul sensitive. Truscott Boothby had made it a matter of honor to be accepted by blacks and Jews as "brother," and he flung himself about in this brotherhood with consummate joy and pleasure. When he encountered troubles in his own congregation he remembered the love of Jews and Negroes and did not answer his critics back.

Truscott Boothby stumbled over a pile of boots and rubbers and almost knocked over the stand that held the Sonnsheins' assorted winter gear. He took the opportunity, righting himself, to embrace Rachel with his strong arms and to kiss her upon the mouth with his cool outdoors mouth. She was besotted by night and he was ruddy with sunlight and salt air.

"How's it going?" he asked.

"I'm waiting for spring training," said Rachel.

"If winter comes, can spring be far behind?" Truscott quoted Shelley without knowing Shelley. He always struck the right note.

"Would you like a cup of coffee?" said Rachel. "Seymour seems to be at his office. At least that was what his note said. I just got up. Forgive the way I look."

"I like you so much I'm able to forgive you any-

45

thing," said Truscott Boothby and threw his duffel coat over the bannister. He wore a turned collar and a Shetland sweater and corduroy pants. He might have come straight from Central Casting to play the Episcopal minister. Whenever Rachel and Truscott had a conversation, they turned reflexively to sports. Thus were they able to deflect all desire into another channel —Rachel recovered the tomboy and Truscott the jock.

"How do you think the Mets will do this year?" he asked, sitting down at the white kitchen table, rubbing his hands, overflowing the bentwood chair and finally shoving the dirty breakfast dishes away from his place.

"I haven't got much faith in them," she said. "You know I can't really love them the way I once loved the Dodgers. I haven't got the same intense devotion. Kingman and Seaver don't mean as much to me as Koufax and Robinson did."

It shocked, and sometimes delighted men to discover that slugging averages, RBIs, and sacrifice flies were beloved and familiar terms to her. She could recall Mickey Owen's dropped third strike, Don Larsen's perfect game, and Bobby Thomson's home run— Dodger tragedies all. She loved the game passionately, albeit in her own quixotic way, tied to summer and long childhood days under its sun. She had learned to know her body playing ball, to feel it acquire the only grace it possessed until she discovered the grace of copulation.

Rachel's mother had, time and time again, begged her to attend dancing school. "You'll be sorry, when you're grown, to have so little poise. Young men won't look at you unless you learn to wear a dress and to move like a lady."

Rachel made fresh coffee.

"It would be fun to go to a ballgame with you. I bet you'd see it with an artist's eye."

Rachel didn't commit herself. "The Mets need a terrific black player," she said, knowing the subject was close to Truscott's heart. "They haven't had one with real style and flair since Mays retired. You know, I was there that night. I cried and cried."

46

Truscott Boothby had always liked football better. But he remembered Willie Mays.

"Guess what I heard?"

He put three spoonfuls of sugar in his coffee and drank it black. He ate what was left over of the stale rolls and took a banana from the fruit bowl. Rachel was astounded at the delicacy with which he ate all these things. He did it offhandedly with small and depreciating gestures. "The Jewish War Veterans have invited the right-wing rabbi from Borough Park to speak at your temple. I hope Seymour will raise hell about it. They plan it for Lincoln's Birthday. What a sham! During Brotherhood Week."

"The Jewish War Veterans have never forgiven Seymour for his stand on Vietnam."

"Did Seymour tell you about my idea for Brotherhood Week?"

"Yes, he did, but I doubt it will work."

"What is the matter with you people? Are you becoming defeatists? Rachel, is he turning his back on the struggle too?"

He reached for Rachel's hand.

"Dear Rachel, I was in Selma, Alabama. Did I ever tell you about it? We all marched together. There was so much hope, such promise in the air. Where did it all go? What's happened?"

Rachel tried to move her hand, but Truscott's lay like a paw upon it. She relaxed and let it lie, but she could give him no answer to his question. He was unaware of anything beyond the small circle—defined by the white table—where they sat. Rachel was listening for Seymour.

"You overestimate the liberalism of the Jews," said Rachel. "Seymour is getting a lot of flak. You know his contract comes up for renewal this year. He'll have a lot . . ." (she wanted to say *tzuris*) ". . . of agony before it's settled."

"I myself am thinking of quitting the ministry. My congregation are not merely Republicans, they're Conservatives. They think Franklin Roosevelt was a Communist."

47

"I don't think Seymour is thinking of quitting—yet. He wouldn't give them the satisfaction. He still believes he can be effective from within. He thinks they need him."

"What do you think?"

"I think about my painting," said Rachel.

"You're a remarkable woman, Rachel. How I wish we had met under different circumstances. I knew someone very much like you, down in Selma. . . ."

At that moment the front door opened with its accustomed warning clatter. Rachel withdrew her hand from under Truscott's. "There's Seymour," she said. Truscott leaned back in his seat and held on to his coffee cup with both hands.

"Hello there my friend—Seymour!" he shouted, in his deep full pulpit voice. "Boothby here!"

Seymour came into the kitchen. "It's like spring outside," he said. "I see you got up," he told Rachel. She feared that Truscott would defend her, but he merely rose and embraced Seymour. They were nearly the same height, yet Boothby's bulk blotted Seymour out completely.

"I must talk to you about the Jewish War Veterans," said Boothby.

Seymour kept his eyes on Rachel. She could not tell whether it was concern or jealousy bearing down in his gaze.

"What's this all about, Truscott?"

"I understand they've invited that right-wing rabbi —what's his name?"

"Baruch Seltzer?"

"Yes . . . to speak at your temple."

"So it seems."

"Aren't you going to raise any objections?"

"Like what?"

"Refuse him the premises! He's a racist, for heaven's sake."

"Let me take off my coat, Truscott, and I'll talk to you. Did anyone call, Rachel?"

"Not recently."

"Are you o.k.?" he asked, interposing himself between Rachel and Truscott.

48

"Yes, I'm o.k."

Seymour carried his coat out to the rack in the hall. It was an old Chesterfield that gave him the grave air of a rabbi from Central Europe when he did not, as he did that day, wear it with a plaid flannel shirt.

"Is something the matter with you, Rachel?" Truscott Boothby tried to reopen the private conversation which Seymour had pointedly shut him out of by asking a private question.

"I'm fine," said Rachel. "A little anxious at times, but an early spring will resolve that."

Seymour returned. "Do you want to talk to me in my study?" he asked Truscott Boothby.

"Can't we talk here and include Rachel?"

"I must go up and put on some clothes." She addressed both men equally and went out of the kitchen. Seymour and Truscott Boothby stayed where they were.

Rachel felt the weight of a disturbed night in her limbs. She took a hot bath, and thought about Truscott Boothby. In the ten years they had been in Gateshead Rachel had felt removed from other men. It was as if her sexuality had been locked into a box to which only Seymour owned a key. No man in the congregation ever looked at her with desire. Rachel didn't mind and yet she minded. Hard as it was to imagine herself embracing the men of Shaare Tefilah, she nonetheless felt offended to think that not one harbored lecherous thoughts about her. In junior high school, where she had first awakened to the sexuality of her body—not as it moved on the ball field but in response to the touch of her boyfriend—Rachel had decided that there was a whole class of boys who simply would not do. At the time she had arrogantly thought the choice was hers alone. She never thought—one way or the other—about the boys' feelings. She had, in youthful pride, conceived a clear image for herself. She was an artist. The jocks, the hoods, the Don Juans, the apple-polishers, the dopes, the bores—all the insensitives, in fact—had been banished from her mind. She barely saw them.

She was as startled to discover that a jock lusted af-

49

ter her as she was to find out that she figured in a bore's dreams. She could break hearts! It did not matter that it was unintentional, their suffering was a reproach to her. It left her frightened and guilty. Was she a monster? Was being a monster the price you paid for being an artist?

Seymour, whom she loved, had been so gentle about her needs. He accepted her enormous ego. As long as she took care of him and continued to love him, he let her be what she wanted to be. He never tried to destroy that image she had of herself. As long as she was faithful, he did not try to change her. They married, as many do, to put the romantic agitation behind them, to regulate sexual desire. To have babies. Rachel thought, perhaps, that she had married also, to have the peace and steady life to grow into an artist at last.

Who knew it wouldn't be quite so simple?

Rachel lay still in the hot bath, letting her legs float to make islands of her knees and her breasts. The hair at the back of her head was damp. Her fingers were shriveled. "Get up and go to work," said Rachel to herself, but she listened for the voice of Truscott Boothby downstairs. It was flattering to have him pay court to her. Those men in the congregation with ill-fitting toupees and leisure suits—even the Gentiles of Gateshead, the Republicans with short haircuts and square chins, the commuters with fashionably styled hair and faded denim slacks—were all so unattractive. They never turned around to look at her. She detested them. Truscott Boothby *saw* her.

"Gone at last," said Seymour, when he came upstairs as Rachel was dressing. "He gets on my nerves more and more these days. What can I do about the Jewish War Veterans? I can't deny them the use of the *shul*. All I can do is not show up or show up and ask embarrassing questions."

"What will you do?"

"I don't know yet. Truscott wants to set up a picket line. I told him it was not his problem, it was a Jewish problem. I think he was offended."

"He wants to remain involved. That's his life."

50

"He likes you," said Seymour. "Did he try anything?"

"What on earth do you mean?"

" 'What on earth do you mean?' " Seymour mimicked Rachel. It was something she detested. "You know what I mean."

"Don't be silly."

"Be careful. I don't trust men married to cripples."

"You shouldn't abandon Truscott."

"What about my job?"

"You never used to talk like that."

"But what if I lose my job?"

"Why do you keep bringing that up?"

"It's a very real possibility."

"I believe we ought to cross our bridges when we come to them."

"That's *some* philosophy, Rebbetzin!"

"What in hell do you want from me? Am I supposed to worry and cry, cry and worry? It's enough if *you* do it. It doesn't help anybody, it's only depressing."

The ring of the telephone ended the conversation. Rachel left the room as soon as Seymour had said "Hello." She suddenly decided she could not bear the sound of the voice with which he greeted his callers.

In her studio once again she opened the windows to the warm wet air and to the smell of breathing earth. She sat at her drawing board, thinking but doing very little work. Had she been led astray by love, by the demands of men? In those years before she married, when she ought to have been looking out for herself, had she misspent her time? A German painter with whom she had studied in Provincetown, a humorless man with small and clever eyes, had told her that she was frivolous. Perhaps because her pleasures were so abundant. Was it because she was a woman?

Rachel sat in her studio all afternoon, letting her hands work mechanically while she thought about her life. One of her drawings showed promise. She was too old for promise.

At five o'clock (and Aaron not home as yet) Ra-

51

chel's friend Sally called and suggested they go into the city the next day.

Rachel decided that it would be a worthwhile distraction. "All right, but you have to promise me we'll look at paintings."

"I don't mind. As long as we go to New York, I'll look at anything."

"Even silk-screened portraits of Ethel Scull and heaps of coiled rope?"

"Even those."

"Can you pick me up so we can catch the nine-o-eight?"

"What a waste of time," said Seymour, when he heard of Rachel's plans. "You're always complaining you don't have time enough to work, and now you're going to spend a day bumming around the city with your girlfriend."

"I'll be looking at works of art."

"You'll be gossiping. Isn't that what you two do?"

"We have sober and informed discussions on any number of subjects."

"Do you tell each other the secrets of your marriage?"

"Not usually."

"But sometimes?"

"Rarely, as I recall."

"You must share *some* secrets!"

"Only those that don't matter."

"All secrets matter."

"Not those which belong to the past."

Seymour did not pursue the matter. He had never trusted the relationship. Rachel made few friends but made them with a rush of feeling. Seymour assumed women *had* to bare their souls—they always did when they came to talk to him.

Aaron came home on the late bus. He'd been playing intramural basketball and gotten a crack in the teeth; his lip was bloody.

The next morning it was cold and wintry again. Rachel wore her warmest wool sweater and a cap that came down around her ears.

52

Sally, a native of the Bronx, was bright and funny. She taught English in the adult-ed program at Adelphi, where many of her students were housewives and accountants who wanted to give voice to their heartrending stories, or vent their humor in picaresque novels. Sally and Rachel had met at a P.T.A. meeting when their children were still in grammar school. They found that they had much in common, and the realization that they might well have been friends back in high school hastened the growth of their adult friendship. They laughed together often and hard, as adolescents do.

Sally and Rachel parked at the far end of the parking lot. Every other spot was taken. They shivered in the biting wind as they jogged to catch their train.

"Imagine having to do this every day of the week," panted Rachel.

"Would you rather we'd driven in?"

"Hell no," said Rachel. "Who wants to look for a place to park in the city?"

Their hearts were beating fast when they reached the railroad station, only to find that there was signal trouble and the train was late. People stood about, anxiously looking at their watches.

"Lucky our husbands don't commute like the rest of Gateshead," said Sally.

Her husband, Leon, was a musician. He taught at Stony Brook and played in an ensemble that specialized in modern and baroque music. Seymour and he disagreed on many things (including their tastes in music), but particularly on the need for Jewish institutions. Leon had, in classic fashion, struggled against an Orthodox father, and thought Judaism a tattered, worn-out garment, which he did not want to pass on to his children. Rachel and Sally rarely talked about their husbands; it was an understanding they had, which they never quite put into words.

The train left the Gateshead Station twelve minutes late. It was, however, pleasantly warm and not too crowded. The bulk of commuters left between seven and eight in the morning, when (in these winter months) the sky was only beginning to brighten, and the cold wind sang through the naked trees.

A pale, brown winter field lay between the railroad tracks and the Expressway. A year and a half ago potatoes had still been planted there in dark green profusion. Now a circle of shingled houses advanced across the field, over the raw earth, like a wagon train.

"Will you look at that," said Rachel—"false shutters and fake porticoes. The glory that was Greece come to America."

"I don't want to hear about it," said Sally. Her tone was good-natured. "You'll depress us both if you go on. I thought we were escaping from suburbia for the day."

Rachel resolutely turned away from the window. "Where shall we go first?"

"You lead, you're the expert," said Sally. "I'm just a fat Jewish girl from the Bronx."

"And me?"

"You're a high-class Jewish girl from Buffalo. You went to Barnard and learned all about Greek temples."

"You went to Hunter."

"That's not nearly as classy. Besides, I only read books. In my family pictures didn't exist, nobody ever taught me to look at one. I had enough to do in college just trying to read all of English literature."

They reached Penn Station in an hour. When they stepped out onto Seventh Avenue they both felt the city's embrace. They crossed the street against the light.

"Let's walk over to the Morgan Library," said Rachel. "We'll go to SoHo later. Those galleries don't open this early."

Rachel and Sally looked at Master drawings for a while and then walked back into the great dark library to look at an exhibition of Jane Austen memorabilia. Sally did not hide her pleasure at this foray into her own field.

"I thought you'd like it," said Rachel, trying to make sense of the delicate, even handwriting. There were also delicate, even engravings of English country houses. "You have to have a taste for this."

54

"She was a marvelous writer," said Sally. "She understood her people perfectly."

"Somebody ought to take a scalpel and do for the inhabitants of suburbia what she did for the provincial English gentry."

"You're obsessed, Rachel. Can't you think of anything else?"

"I wish I could move back to the city."

"Maybe you will, one day."

"I don't know how."

"Take things into your own hands."

"That's easier said than done."

"Not if you're earning your own money. You should get a job, Rachel. It would change everything for you. You'd win your independence from Seymour. . . ."

"I have my independence."

"It's an illusory one. You'll never know how dependent you are until you earn your own money."

"I had to give up something in order to have the freedom to paint. It isn't possible to do three things at once."

"Then you have to stop complaining about Gateshead. There's nothing to be done about it."

"Do you like it there?"

"It's better than where I grew up. For me it's a step in the right direction and proves you can be upwardly mobile in America. I can get enough of the city one day a week. We go to concerts all the time, we eat out. I want no more than that. Most of our friends at the University live on the Island. I don't hunger, like you do, for some phantom community of dedicated artists. You think they're any less tuned in to success than the average Gateshead commuter?"

They were on a Fifth Avenue bus, heading downtown. Sally enjoyed the role of devil's advocate; Rachel liked to defend her ideological positions. They were caught in their roles like an old married couple.

SoHo was alive with chirping groups of women —most, but not all of them, came on buses from suburbia. Culture was rampant everywhere.

"They all look Jewish," said Rachel.

55

"Jews are the only people on Long Island or in Westchester who know where SoHo is. And they all harbor dreams of becoming collectors."

"Not only collectors, but collectors who bought wisely and cheap."

"It's an innocent enough dream."

"I wasn't being critical."

"With you, I never know, Rachel."

"When it comes right down to it, I like people in the flesh, it's only in the abstract I can't stand them. Most left-wingers I know are just the opposite: they adore the masses and can't bear real people."

Rachel and Sally walked contentedly up and down the streets of SoHo. Workers, pushing carts filled with baled rags, whistled at them and they smiled at each other, smiles that were intercepted by the men. "Hey hey hey!" the men said.

"It makes you feel young and gorgeous," said Rachel.

"Only if you suffered in high school from being unlovely."

They looked at many works of art. They talked about what they saw, and were drawn together both by their enthusiasms and their prejudices. They said "uggh" and "wow," and Sally deferred to Rachel's judgment, but slyly. They were not terribly serious. In a plain and whitewashed loft they blundered into a group of women being led in pursuit of culture by Hildegarde Kaye, a feminist painter. Hildegarde Kaye's work focused mainly upon the crotch. She had—once upon a time, before she became a feminist—painted abstractions garishly derived from the work of Franz Kline. Since she had begun to devote herself to crotches, her paintings had become meticulously realistic. Hildegarde Kaye had just finished a series entitled "The Private Parts of Great Women."

She was speaking earnestly, holding a piece of paper in her hand. The women stood about her in a semicircle, paying close attention. The walls of the gallery were covered with jagged-edged scraps of paper on which penises, of different sizes and shapes, drawn in

56

colored chalks, were pierced by arrows and other instruments of war.

"Women are experiencing necessary anger these days," said Hildegarde Kaye.

"Kein ein'ora," one of the ladies agreed.

"They are exploring inner space," Hildegarde Kaye continued. "Symbols accrue. Patterns of representation emerge, which hint at obsessional themes."

"I prefer Jane Austen's irony," Sally whispered to Rachel.

"Let's go," said Rachel. "I've had enough."

They ran down the stairs like thieves.

"Let's find a place where we can have a drink with our lunch," said Rachel.

They sat in a booth and ordered martinis. The drinks made them feel pleasantly high.

"You never talk about your private life," said Sally.

"What's there to say?"

"You tell me I'm your friend, but I don't know how you live at all."

"I get up in the morning, make breakfast . . ."

"That's not what I mean. I mean that your life is a mystery to me. I never see you, except alone. It's as though you couldn't stand me intruding, either in your private life or your public one. And I *know* you have a public one."

"Get active in the congregation and you'll hear all the gossip."

"Don't be facetious. You know how difficult it was even to convince Leon the kids should be bar mitzvahed. I think you feel that kind of rebelliousness too. Which is why it's hard for me to understand how you live."

"I believe in religion. At least I believe in Judaism."

"You're being loyal to Seymour."

"And what's wrong with that?"

"Nothing at all. Except it seems a lot of hard work. You haven't any friends in common, that I know of, in Gateshead. You're trapped in your Judaism, your congregation, it strikes me, as though very much against your will. It's a little sad."

57

"I'm not to be pitied. I can't bear that."

"I know. But I still think you're getting the short end of the stick."

If Rachel had not been giddy with the unaccustomed noonday drink, she might have found Sally's probing tedious. But now she weighed her friend's questions in a slightly tipsy manner. She found that she wanted to talk about the past—in these surroundings the need seemed especially clear. And they were—were they not?—enclosed in their friendship, oblivious of everything but the talk they made. At this moment she wanted nothing but to be perceived in a true light by her friend.

"We had good friends when we were first married and still living in the city. Seymour was at the Seminary and I was in graduate school. We were caught up in the New York Jewish intellectual world. We all talked a lot, we were involved and passionate. Sometimes the talk was too much for me, but I missed it when we moved away, when Seymour got his first pulpit in a small town in North Carolina. We realized that we barely existed anymore, as far as our friends were concerned. We only had each other."

"Out of sight, out of mind?"

"Exactly. I don't resent it. . . ."

"I think you do."

"Do you? Maybe you're right. I have my regrets, they're bound to turn into resentments sooner or later."

"I can't imagine what life is like in a small American town."

"It's not so different from Buffalo."

"I can't imagine Buffalo either."

"Once we got to understand the subtleties we got to like it, in its way. We were big fish in a little pond. We knew everyone, everyone knew us, even the *goyim*."

"I don't think I ever knew any Christians before we moved to Gateshead. Didn't you miss New York?"

"I missed it less than I do now. We weren't as busy, but we had more to do, if you know what I mean. Not only were we big fish in a little pond, but we were really needed. What we did was worthwhile and we

58

were respected for it. We knew our congregants' names and their histories: we shared in their griefs and joys."

"If it was so great, why did you come back?"

"Ambition, I suppose. A lot of our old friends were going places. We thought we might too. And then, when we came to Gateshead and tried to take up with them, we found we couldn't. It didn't work. If we had come back to New York instead of to Long Island, it might have been different. Nobody wants to drag out to visit you. They didn't have cars, and in those days the last train back left around ten-thirty. We would go into the city to see people, but we were like out-of-town relatives, we weren't part of their daily lives at all."

"Most of the people *I* knew moved to the suburbs too."

"Our friends were the sort that didn't. They traveled in a very small circle, and knew only certain, predictable places. Cambridge, San Francisco, New Haven maybe. Chicago. East Hampton. They made it a point of honor to stay in the city, even when it meant private schools, crime, dirt, high rents. They bitched, but they stayed. And they can't imagine, to this day, what I'm talking about when I tell them that Gateshead is middle America—conservative, bigoted and culturally deprived. I became so much more radical in the sixties than they did because I had a bourgeoisie to revolt against. It's like they say, it takes a kid who grew up in Scarsdale to become your true revolutionary."

"And you made no friends in Gateshead?"

"You're my friend."

"I mean you and Seymour."

"No, not really. When we first came to Gateshead we tried to live as though it were a small town, but it didn't work. We got to know some of the people our age who were active in the congregation, but congregational politics always get in the way of friendship, and in suburbia the rabbi's place is more ambiguous than it is in a small town. He can never overcome the oppressive sense that, to a lot of people, he's just an employee. But the worst thing is the turnover in the congregation.

59

Every year there are more and more new faces and fewer and fewer familiar ones. You stay in one place, but the congregation changes. Before you know it, it's no longer the congregation you came to serve originally."

"What about other rabbis?"

"Seymour is a loner among them. None of his close friends at the Seminary stayed in the rabbinate for long—some never went into a pulpit at all. So he's an anomaly of sorts. He's never been 'one of the boys.' Rabbis are like cops, they feel comfortable only with each other, but they long desperately to be accepted by the people they serve. That makes them uphold the values of their masters—the rich and the powerful and the complacent. It allows them to be *used*."

"But they're well paid."

"So are the cops. That's America."

"You're so cynical it makes me think you're unhappy."

"I'm not. I still think I can change the world."

"Because you feel it rejects you?"

"No such thing."

"But you feel the congregation doesn't approve of you?"

"How could they?"

"Maybe they don't think about you at all?"

"Of course they think about me. What else do they have to think about?"

"I think, Rachel, it's *your* problem."

"I think, Sally, it's *their* problem. They may not know it, but it is."

"You sure have a terrific ego."

"Then don't pity me."

They had finished their drinks and eaten their large and juicy hamburgers. The waiter left a check. It was time to go. Rachel felt contented, triumphant even. She had, she thought, successfully defeated Sally's efforts to cast her into the victim's role. She felt generous toward her friend, who did not judge her harshly. It sometimes *was* a lonely life. They split the bill and left a big tip (for having sat so long) and headed back to the galleries.

60

An hour or so later, coming down the last steep flight of stairs at 420 West Broadway, Rachel and Sally passed a thin man with a shock of brown hair. He was dressed in a blue work shirt and chino pants, heavy shoes and a wool Air Force overcoat. A cashmere scarf was wrapped around his throat. Rachel looked at him. She looked at everyone. But then she stood still and kept on looking until the man saw her looking (his head had been bent, watching the steps and the toes of his heavy work shoes on the rubber stair treads) and raised up his head to look back at her. They found each other's eyes.

"Hello, Rachel."

"Hello, Ben."

For a minute they were very still and just looked at one another.

Sally stepped out of the way of a group going up the stairs.

"What are you doing here?" Ben asked.

"You know I'm an incorrigible culture-vulture," answered Rachel, adjusting to past banter. "And you?"

"I don't paint anymore," said Ben, "but I like to see what those who do are up to."

Rachel noticed the familiar hollow at the base of his throat. Ben looked away from her, and Rachel was released into the present.

"This is my friend, Sally."

Ben nodded, they shook hands, and Sally became part of the meeting, though Rachel and Ben continued to grope for a bridge from the past to the present.

"I'm married," said Ben. He stood a few steps below Rachel and had to look up to her.

"Me too."

"I knew that."

"I mean I'm *still* married."

"I taught her all she knows about art," said Ben, addressing Sally this time. "I pointed out the *important* painters, the ones they ignore in college. Sassetta and Paolo Uccello, Piero."

"They don't ignore Piero," said Rachel.

"But they talk about him for all the wrong reasons. They don't understand his modernity. They don't see

61

what painters see. I went to Arezzo after you got married."

"I know. You sent me a postcard."

"Did I?"

"Yes. From Pisa too. And Siena."

"Would you like to have a cup of coffee? The two of you?"

"We have about half an hour," said Sally. "Or would you rather be alone?"

"Not really," said Ben. "You seem a nice enough person."

They walked downstairs together and around the corner to Prince Street. They did not speak as they walked.

"What do you do?" said Rachel, sitting across from Ben in the restaurant.

"I'm a painter."

"A *house* painter?"

"No. A real painter. Ingres, Raphael, Poussin."

"I thought you said you didn't paint anymore."

"That doesn't mean I'm not a painter. A poet needn't write a poem a day, he can still be a poet. Are you painting?"

"A little bit."

"What's it like?"

"I learned some of what you tried to teach me."

"Sometimes I do a little commercial art, sometimes I drive a cab." He saw Rachel looking at him in the light of the restaurant with her old critical eye. "And I do paint rooms sometimes. My wife works. She's a teacher."

"Where do you live?"

"Long Beach."

"Long Beach?"

"Don't you know—I always liked the sea? Even though I don't much care for the sun."

"I'd bake in it and you'd scurry for the shade . . ."

". . . into the tunnel of love or the penny arcade."

"You have all that in Long Beach?"

"And cheap rent too. The place is full of old people and losers. . . ."

62

Rachel thought he was going to add, "like me," but we swallowed and said, "Where do you live?"

"A place called Gateshead."

"On the ritzy North Shore."

"We have to go where the Jews are. Seymour's a rabbi."

"There are lots of Jews in Long Beach."

"They couldn't afford Seymour," murmured Sally.

"They wouldn't like his politics," amended Rachel.

"I take it he's a limousine liberal?" said Ben.

"He's a left-wing Conservative rabbi."

"Whatever that means."

"It means there are fewer and fewer places will have him."

Ben looked terrible, older than his forty-five years. Rachel had often thought about him since she had left him to return to Seymour. In her mind's eye he had kept his softly youthful face. But Ben's drawn features were those of a man who had too often woken up in unspeakable places.

"I wouldn't like it in Gateshead," said Ben, and caught Rachel's eye squarely. "I bet it closes up by ten every night. I would be very lonely."

"You were never one to stay by yourself."

It was, she recalled, one of the things they argued about. He wanted to stay up all night with his friends, talking at the San Remo, talking at Minetta's, talking at Julius's. Rachel wanted to take him to bed. To have him to herself—alone.

"I asked you to come to Europe with me."

"I couldn't."

"Your parents wouldn't let you. You were obedient. You listened to them."

"I wasn't ready to cope with Europe then, and with your friends. You traveled in a pack."

(He had come back from Paris and stood in the shadows opposite the house she lived in—with Seymour, by then—on Bank Street, waiting for her. "I can't come back to you," she said and he kissed her, but she said "I can't" again. She gave no other explanation. She loved him, but Seymour would never wake

63

up in unspeakable places. "Are you angry that I didn't write you much?" he had asked. "I was," she said, "but I'm not any longer." Ben had stood in the shadows a few more nights—it was autumn and the nights were gentle—and then he disappeared.)

"You were so romantic and earnest. You believed in inspiration and the kiss of the muse," said Ben.

"Was that how I was?"

"That's how I remember it."

"But didn't my muse have a sense of humor? And look like a blowsy Rubens nude? I bet she tripped over her draperies and knocked down vases of flowers."

"Your muse was full of art history."

"Maybe she was, but at least she stayed with me."

"I think we'd better head for Penn Station," said Sally—"that is, if you want to get home for dinner." She gathered her things together, having waited as long as she could before trying to hurry things along. "But stay, if you wish," she said. "I'll go alone."

"Another time," said Rachel. "I can't miss dinner."

"You *are* the same," said Ben. "Earnest and punctual. Going back to suburbia on time, the way you used to go back to the Barnard dorms before curfew."

"I didn't want to get into trouble. I still don't. At least not for frivolous things."

Rachel and Sally caught the 4:36. The encounter with Ben left Rachel out of sorts. She felt less inclined than ever to return to Gateshead with the commuters. Because her mind was in such turmoil she kept still and Sally tactfully joined in the silence. They had bought a fat *Newsday* and shared it, but Rachel thought only about Ben. Their meeting had honed the edge of her longing for New York to a sharp point. It pierced her heart as the train sped out to the Island, home to Gateshead. She felt as though she were being deported to a strange country, prisoner of her own timid conformity. She recalled Ben's taut, lean body, smooth and hairless, and the intoxicating smell of oil paint and turpentine that clung to him in those days. He had been her guide not only to the Masters, but through the city as well.

64

At home everything looked exactly as Rachel had left it that morning. Nothing unexpected had taken place. Rachel was surprised, as always. Aaron was doing his homework. Seymour was reading the paper. "What's for supper?" they both asked. The automatic timer had worked and the roast was ready. Seymour fixed martinis.

"What happened in the city?"

"Nothing much." She started to say, "I met Ben," but she didn't say it. Swallowed it.

"Yes?" asked Seymour.

"We went to SoHo."

"And what did you see?"

She wanted to say "I saw Ben," but said nothing. "None of the shows were any good."

"A waste of time, just as I said," he crowed.

"I guess so. Did anything happen in Gateshead while I was gone?"

"They're buying the All-American house on Astro Lane for us."

"The one directly behind the *shul?*"

"Yes."

"I told you so," said Rachel.

Now each one had a small triumph. The roast, however, was tough.

65

3

In the first bleak days of February, Cy Glatt called Rachel to announce that her house had been put on the market and she would be expected to show it to prospective buyers.

"You don't mind, do you?"

"Yes, I do mind, but what can I do?"

Cy Glatt laughed heartily. "That's what I like about you, Rachel," he said. "No bullshit."

"Ask them to call me before they come."

"The agents know that, doll."

Rachel lit a fire in the marble fireplace almost every night. It was a cold winter. Part of the harbor froze and the black figures of the children skating on the distant winter-white surface made Rachel think of Breughel.

The first agent brought a young woman who stepped inside the front door and said, quite loudly, "It's so dark, and too old." Rachel took umbrage, even though the house was not hers to defend. She hoped they might not be able to sell the house at all. The agent shrugged and handed Rachel her card. Those little cards piled up in the salad bowl.

A slip of a girl who came to look with a friend and a baby said, "I don't think the backyard is wide enough for a pool."

"You've got waterfront," said the agent.

"Who wants to go swimming in that shit?"

The agents were always bright and cheerful, the clients glum and dour.

"Nobody wants an old house," the agents said.

66

The snow fell in windy gusts upon the bone-hard ground. It was the day of the Jewish War Veterans' meeting, not long before Purim. Seymour had talked to the Commander, Heshy Siskind, trying to find out what Rabbi Baruch Seltzer was going to say. He was told to mind his beeswax. Truscott Boothby was full of righteous indignation. Rachel made up her mind to go to the meeting and ask bright, embarrassing questions.

"You won't have a chance," said Seymour. "Nobody will listen to you. The visiting rabbi prays every day to God, thanking Him for not making him a woman, and the Jewish War Veterans loved being soldiers better than anything else they ever did in their whole lives. You really think they'll let you challenge their idea of what's good for the Jews?"

The meeting room was blue with the smoke of cigarettes and everyone there seemed to be fat. The folding chairs overflowed with flesh. The crowd was noisy. Sweaters and sportshirts matched in mustard, goldenrod, and burgundy. Young men and boys in battle dress stood against the walls. They carried billy clubs. A chaplain of the Jewish faith shared the stage with the Commander and his fellow officers. All of them wore their blue-and-gold J.W.V. caps. The lettering on them said: Mickey Finkelberg, J.W.V.

"Who's Mickey Finkelberg?" Rachel asked Seymour.

The man in front of them turned around. "He was the first Jew from Long Island to die in Vietnam."

A small commotion at the door caused everyone to turn around. It was Truscott Boothby and Abigail, his wife. She was in her wheelchair, a withered creature with a gentle face, given to asking questions in a high, clear voice. Truscott sometimes brought her along as a diversionary tactic. He had purposely worn his turned collar and black dickey. One of the young men now barred his way.

"This meeting is for Jews only."

"The rabbi invited me."

"What rabbi?"

"Rabbi Sonnshein."

"It wasn't up to him," said the young tough. "He's got nothing to do with this."

67

"It's *his* synagogue."

"Are they going to throw us out?" Abigail Boothby asked, in her clear loud voice.

The young man could neither be embarrassed nor moved. Not by crazy *goyim*. "Security," he said. "We don't want trouble."

Seymour got up. "I'd better go and rescue our friend," he said to Rachel and extricated himself from the people and overcoats clogging the row of folding chairs.

"There's the nigger-loving rabbi," said Joe Kristal, the plumber.

Seymour shook hands with Truscott and Abigail.

"Where's your black escort?" he asked.

"Should I have brought one?" said Truscott, not having perceived Seymour's irony.

"What sort of Negro could you bring to this place?" bleated Abigail Boothby. "They're keeping *white* people out."

"Sorry, Rabbi," said the youth, "I was told to allow no outsiders." He did not give way.

"I'm the rabbi of this synagogue," said Seymour, his voice like steel, "and *I* decide who may or may not enter this house of worship."

"Well said!" boomed Truscott Boothby.

The boy stalked off.

"These people don't look like any members of your congregation *I've* ever met," said Truscott.

"Mostly they're not," Seymour told him. "My congregation doesn't reach many lower middle-class Jews. They're Seltzer's natural constituency."

"I know what you mean," said Truscott Boothby. "It's a problem in the suburbs. We've created economic ghettos. I've noticed it in my own congregation."

A number of local dignitaries (all of them Jewish) sat on the stage and introduced one another with brief speeches. They included the young rabbi from South Gateshead and the middle-aged one from the next town who had twice been fired for improperly handling his synagogue's funds. He was much beloved by his present congregation, as he had, indeed, been beloved by all his congregations. Seymour had refused to join

68

his colleagues on the stage. The guest of honor, Rabbi Seltzer, was late.

Cantor Blech led the assembled crowd in half a dozen Hebrew songs. He was young, unmarried, and cheerful. It was said that he was cheerful because unmarried, but Rachel thought she detected a hysterical edge to his cheer. *Everyone* wanted to fix him up with a nice Jewish girl.

It occurred to Rachel that she spent an inordinate amount of time in this room, listening to speeches. The thought depressed her. The moments of her life were drifting away, swirling from her like snow, and could never be recovered. Why did she have to pass, week after week, through this dreary room and be soiled by pretentious prattle? She sighed loudly. She should have stayed home tonight. Abigail Boothby rubbed her dry hands together in her lap. "Why did you bring me here, my dear?" she asked her husband plaintively.

Rabbi Seltzer arrived at ten minutes to ten. Almost everyone in the meeting room stood up. Rachel remained seated; so did Seymour and Truscott and, quite naturally, Abigail Boothby. The visiting rabbi was a small man, intense and quick on his feet. To Rachel's eyes he appeared like a gangster. He was followed by a phalanx of boys in army fatigues and scarlet berets. Empty holsters hung from their belts. Their faces bore the beginnings of beards, but only the beginnings. They were still softly boyish beneath the harsh brows. Baruch Seltzer shook hands with the people on stage before he went to the podium to speak. The youths leaned against the stairs that led to the stage. The rabbi raised his hand and the audience sat down. It grew still in the room.

"I'm glad to see so many people here tonight," said the visiting rabbi. "It shows you that even on the affluent North Shore of Long Island there are Jews who care about other Jews."

The audience broke into applause. Rachel noticed that Rabbi Seltzer wore a small black *yarmulke* on his small round head. His hair was neatly trimmed.

"I used to think that American Jews had all become

69

knee-jerk liberals, but I'm learning on my travels that it isn't so."

"Alas," muttered Truscott Boothby.

"Better not say anything," said Seymour. He had to lean across Rachel to talk to Truscott. Everyone in the room had seen that the disruptive *goy* was with the Sonnsheins.

"I don't think I need to tell you who I am," said Baruch Seltzer. There were chuckles of appreciation from the audience. Rachel felt utterly isolated. "My list of credentials is a mile long. I go wherever Jews need me, wherever Jews are suffering. I am the Defender of the Jews."

There was prolonged applause.

"I come here tonight not to tell you about suffering Jews but about proud Jews, Jews with guts, Jews with guns at their sides and blood on their hands— Arab blood, Russian blood, blood of Nazis . . ."

Fists were raised in the audience, shouts of "Never again!" filled the air. Truscott growled a little.

"I used to be told by the 'good' Jews, the gutless Jews, that I shouldn't talk like that," cried Baruch Seltzer, "but I did. I kept right on talking and now everybody in the world knows who I am, everybody in America has heard my name. They wrote about me on the first page of *The New York Times,* and when they do *that* even the farmers in Iowa know you. The dumbest *goy* in Georgia knows you."

"Surely *they* don't read *The New York Times,*" said Rachel.

"Shhhh," said the man in front of her.

"I was the first to tell you to be proud, to warn you of the enemies within the Jewish community, to tell you of the traitors you harbor in your organizations, your synagogues, your neighborhoods."

Rabbi Seltzer knew how to play his audience. He was used to adoring crowds; he was not usually asked to speak before hostile ones. He said that Jews in the twentieth century had failed miserably on behalf of themselves.

"*I'm* not here to fail!" he cried. "Elie Wiesel wrote

70

and wept for years and years about the Jews of Russia, and nothing happened. It wasn't until I made a little trouble, not until my organization gave a *schrei* that things began to move. *We*'re not afraid of giving offense. We don't care about being polite, being nice to the *goyim*. We don't shy away from violence, we are Jews who *fight,* Jews who are prepared to kill. When was the last time a rabbi got up to tell you that?"

"Seymour sure as hell doesn't," Rachel said to Truscott Boothby.

"I'll tell you more. I've got statistics for you if you want them. Statistics about Jews who don't pussyfoot around, don't bow and scrape, waiting for world opinion to come around. Oh no!" he cried. "I'll tell you about Jews who go and build settlements on the West Bank, who create Jewish homes even if they have to do it in defiance of their own lily-livered government. . . ."

"I was under the impression he had come here to attack the black community," said Truscott Boothby, puzzled and restive. He patted his wife's knee several times.

"Are you disappointed?" Rachel asked him, in a whisper. She studied his face. The handsome, craggy features contained no trace of Jewish *angst.* Even without his collar he would have appeared out of place. He looked innocent. He looked simple. Among the gross and vulgar Jews in that room he was an anachronism. Rachel was suddenly annoyed with him. How could he possibly understand what this was all about? What right had he to judge them?

The visiting rabbi pounded on the lectern. "The Jews of Germany also said 'be polite'; they said 'don't make trouble,' even as they marched to their deaths in the gas chambers."

Shouts and cheers swept up from the crowd and drowned the high-pitched voice. The visiting rabbi wiped his face with a handkerchief and lifted his *yarmulke* and set it back again with a single nervous gesture.

"I think we'd better go," said Truscott Boothby quietly to Rachel. "Give Seymour my apologies. Tell

71

him I hope I didn't get him in trouble. This isn't what I expected at all."

He pushed his wife's wheelchair up the aisle and out the door. No one paid any attention to him.

"Believe me!" Baruch shouted, "if *I* had been there with *my* organization, things would have been different. Six million would not have gone so quietly to their death."

Photos of the camps, photos of the Warsaw ghetto flashed through Rachel's mind. Seymour had made her look at them, she hadn't wanted to. He had told her terrible stories of the Holocaust, she hadn't wanted to listen. "We mustn't forget," he had said, again and again. But he had never dared to suggest that the victims might have saved themselves from the fury of their oppressors. The Nazis were the State. All power was theirs. The Jews had been stripped of everything, even as they were finally stripped of their clothes before being murdered. It was blasphemy to use them, to exploit their suffering for the sake of a man's vanity, to seize power in their name. Rachel's anger lay like a stone in her belly. The crowd roared.

"I'll tell you what you have to do, how you have to act," Baruch Seltzer cried out. "Do you want to hear me out?"

The crowd stomped on the floor.

"Root out the enemies in your ranks. Kill the vipers in your midst. Do it before it's too late. You know who they are, they counsel compromise, accommodation and appeasement. They tell you to sit down with the anti-Semites, the Arabs, the Cossacks, the niggers. Don't do it! You must learn to turn on your enemies, even if they are Jews. Inform on the appeasers, disrupt their meetings, boycott their stores, get them fired from their jobs. Watch out for those Jews who talk about Brotherhood and Peace—they are traitors to Israel!"

Baruch Seltzer grinned at the people, standing on their feet, on the chairs, clapping in unison, shouting, calling his name. He doffed his *yarmulke* again. The young toughs stood in a long row in front of the stage,

72

their clubs raised high. Rachel put on her coat. "I'm going up there to talk to him," she told Seymour. He took her by the hand and held her fast.

"You're crazy," he said. "What's there to say?"

"I'll tell him he's a fascist."

"He'll laugh in your face."

"How can anyone be taken in by him? He's a hood!"

"He plays on their frustrations. Gives them solutions, easy answers, a sense of power."

"He's a new kind of Jew, Rabbi," said Joe Kristal, the plumber, who passed by them just then.

"If you become like your oppressor," said Seymour, "you're no longer fit to be called a Jew."

Rachel and Seymour walked out into the cold February night, their eyes smarting from the heat and smoke of cigarettes. Inside, the rabbis and Jewish dignitaries were embracing the visiting rabbi. The lights were out all over Gateshead, the moon's reflection rippled across the black Sound.

"I don't love the Jews enough," said Rachel.

"I don't love them a whole lot myself tonight," said Seymour.

"The Reverend Boothby called," said Aaron, when they got home. He was sitting in front of the TV, watching a late movie.

"We just saw him," said Rachel.

"He said he was sorry he made a scene tonight and asked you to call him, either at home tonight or at the church in the morning."

Seymour waited until morning to return the call. It was easier to put up with Truscott Boothby's clarion voice and infernal good cheer in the morning. The sun was bright and Seymour planned to stay home from his office all day. "Let's do something," he said to Rachel, and they decided to have lunch together in Locust Valley. Seymour spoke to Boothby while Rachel folded the laundry, a chore she disliked.

"He asked me to give the sermon at his church on the last Sunday in February. I'm the first rabbi who's

73

ever been asked to preach at St. James the Apostle," said Seymour, pleased with Boothby's invitation. "Truscott must be planning to get fired."

"Why do you say that?" Rachel asked. She could not find the mates to three unmatched socks.

"It was only a joke," said Seymour.

"He's had blacks in his pulpit."

"Blacks are Christians. Whatever they've done, nobody's ever accused them of killing Christ. Besides, *they're* not moving to Gateshead in droves."

"I wish we lived where they understood us a little better. It would be nice not to be out of step all the time."

"One day, Rachel, I'll take you away from all of this," said Seymour, full of his old, his first love.

"You said that to me at the senior prom."

"And I did. I took you out of Buffalo."

"To bring me to Gateshead."

"You could have married Ben."

"I don't think so. I wanted to be safe."

There was no one else in the house. Seymour and Rachel went into the bedroom to make love. The sun shone in between the white curtains like a heavenly ladder. From the bed only sky was visible through the windows. "Vermeer," said Rachel. The light had transformed all the very ordinary objects into gold-crowned pieces. Their place in the room (however random) seemed special and full of meaning. Rachel assumed a pose next to the window. She saw herself in the mirror, her robe fell from her shoulders, she was naked and Seymour's penis stood erect. Dust rose from the small desk beside her bed like a shower of gold. Rachel looked at Seymour, as though across the years, and her desire was fierce. It had not come over her like that in a long time. She had almost forgotten how it was. Most of the time now there were other things crowding out the need that had once seemed the only one her body had. Now there were accretions of thought, unfinished business, small discomforts. Seymour barely touched her. They stood facing one another, very little space between them. Seymour's penis bridged the space, he kept his arms at his side, and

74

touched Rachel between her legs with his outstretched member. Touched her in that hairy apex, the very heart of her desire. The touch alone sent spasms like breaking waves, like deep cries through her. He touched her again so that she almost came, right there. He had only the time to encircle her with his arms once before they fell upon the bed and came together with a violence so great and sudden they felt themselves go under in darkness.

The telephone brought them groggily back to life. It was Hadassah president Michelle Shulman Halprin, whose deep voice always sounded like a classy answering service.

"I wanted to ask you to come to our study group this Thursday. You haven't been in *months,* but maybe this one will interest you. It's going to be in memory of Joseph Kranz, a dead poet. You know, don't you, that he came from Gateshead? His mother is going to join us. Are you free?"

Rachel agreed to come to the meeting. She heard her own voice escaping her like a sigh. "Sure," she said. "When is it and where?"

"Thursday morning at my house. Didn't you get an invitation?"

"I sometimes don't look too carefully at my mail."

"That's what I was afraid of. We're hoping for a nice turnout. I'll see you then, at ten o'clock."

Rachel trilled an unlikely "o.k." into the receiver, hoping to sound alive and interested. She smacked Seymour across the bare ass with the palm of her hand.

"Ever hear of a dead poet name of Joseph Kranz? I'm going to wear my new wool skirt and silk blouse and hand-knitted sweater."

"Why?"

"Because you're taking me to lunch."

Seymour and Rachel washed and dressed, still feeling some slight vibrations from their lovemaking. The telephone rang again, just as they were ready to leave. Seymour answered it in his study. He was gone a long time. When he came back he was shaking his head. "Cy Glatt's mother is dying," he said.

"It will cost me our lunch."

"I'm afraid it will."

"If she's only dying but not yet dead, why can't we have lunch?"

"Please, Rachel, there are complications. I can't begin to tell you."

"I won't say anything to anyone."

"What you don't know won't hurt you—or anyone else either."

Seymour kept a certain amount of the congregation's *tzuris* out of his house. He did it, he said, to shield Rachel and keep some part of his life untouched by all the misery gathered like crumbling piles of old prayerbooks. Rachel sometimes thought he did it as well to savor the stories alone, although he was not one of the rabbis who indulge themselves in misery, who become the repository of all their small world's grief. Nevertheless, the shield that protected her also kept her out.

Rachel walked into town after Seymour had gone to see Cy Glatt and had a tunafish sandwich at the Pleiades luncheonette. She did not wear her new wool skirt and silk blouse and hand-knitted sweater. The day had remained brilliant with sunshine, Gateshead had a blue heaven above its façades and roofs. The harbor's ice floes sparkled with the sun's fire.

The decor in the Pleiades luncheonette had not been changed in forty years. Rachel felt at home in it. The pale green walls and sunburst shapes of mirrors, the plastic-covered booths, high-backed and sweat-provoking, were of the thirties and like the ones she had sought out back home in Buffalo.

Rachel ordered a tunafish sandwich even though she would have preferred a BLT (on toast with mayo). She was not brave enough. In the next booth sat a trio of Sisterhood ladies, all of whom worked in shops on Main Street.

That evening Aaron went to bed early with a fever and other signs of the flu. Rachel sat in front of the fireplace as the wind howled outside and Seymour talked on the telephone. He left shortly after eight o'clock and did not come home until midnight.

"What's the matter now?" Rachel asked.

76

"More trouble."

"Is the old lady dead yet?"

"No."

Rachel fell asleep in an unmade bed and dreamt about Ben. He walked beside her in a summer landscape and would not come out of the shade. He stayed close to walls and beneath trees. The houses were old-fashioned. Rachel had been there before but did not know the place. Ben was ill and near death, but would not allow Rachel to minister to him.

On Thursday morning Rachel took a bath and left Aaron (who was still in bed with the flu, listening to the radio and reading James Thurber) supplied with orange juice and ginger ale. Cy Glatt's mother had, in the meantime, gone to meet her Jewish maker. The funeral was scheduled for two o'clock and Rachel was expected to attend. She wore her funeral clothes to the house of Michelle Shulman Halprin so that she would not have to dress up twice in one day. Golda Garfinkle picked Rachel up at five to ten.

The ride to Michelle Shulman Halprin's house, early on a cold and windy winter morning, took every ounce of good humor out of Rachel. Anxiety stole over her like gangrene. Golda Garfinkle wore fine leather gloves and smelled of clean linen and expensive perfume. Her dark brown mink coat glistened—it might still have been alive on the back of a sleek and healthy beast. Golda's pale blue Cadillac purred contentedly and ran smoothly through the streets of tract houses. Golda felt expansive and wanted to talk about college days.

"You heard what happened to Gayle Gross?" she said.

"Was it in the Alumnae Bulletin?" asked Rachel.

"Good heavens, no! She ran off with a systems analyst."

The name was vaguely familiar to Rachel, she would have to look the face up in the yearbook. If truth be told, she could never quite remember Golda either. Perhaps that was because the woman who sat beside her now had completely replaced the girl she had known twenty years before. Golda sent messages

77

about her intellectual life to the Alumnae Bulletin. "I adore films, especially foreign ones, but I'd sooner read a good book than watch T.V. I'm a 'volunteer' and proud of it. Jewish causes and culture are first on my list of 'musts.' "

Rachel read the class news religiously. The correspondents always sounded cheerful, as though reporting on how they'd spent their summer vacations. ("We keep busy trying to make a good life for our retarded child. Bob and I have matured together and found a new kind of peace, doing our best to cope with our very *special* little girl.") ("Having just been operated upon for the Big C, I would appreciate hearing from fellow alumnae interested in starting a newsletter dealing with this topic. If current statistics can be trusted there must be hundreds of Barnard girls out there who can tell us how they conquered cancer.")

"Did you see those Bertolucci movies at the Cinema Club?" Rachel asked, unable to dwell on Gayle Gross's systems analyst.

"I can't keep up with things the way you do," said Golda Garfinkle, lighting a cigarette from the lighter on the Cadillac's royal blue dashboard. "I'm content to be what I am: a good wife and mother as well as a good Jew."

"That's very commendable," said Rachel.

Golda opened her window a crack with the electric button, to let the cigarette smoke out. "I think it's important to keep traditional values alive. You, as rebbetzin, ought to appreciate that. You may be a good painter—I really can't tell—but it's just as important to keep a truly kosher home."

Rachel could not argue the point. She kept silent and wondered how happy Golda Garfinkle was with her life.

Michelle Shulman Halprin lived in a house with columns on an acre of land near the water. The acre had cost thirty thousand dollars without the house. Or so Rachel had heard. She was never clear about such things, and sometimes forgot a zero or added an extra digit. Despite the proximity to Long Island Sound of the development, called Belle Ville au Bord de la

Mer, almost every house had its swimming pool. Some had tennis courts as well. They were fitted into the space behind the houses with great ingenuity and the use of many yews.

Golda parked the pale blue Cadillac next to a mate and they hurried through the biting wind into the house. The hall closet was unable to hold another mink, so Golda and Rachel were asked by the maid to put their wraps upstairs upon the bed in the master bedroom. Rachel's pea jacket soon slid disconsolately to the floor, even its Bonwit Teller label powerless to prevent its descent. Rachel rubbed her cold hands and smiled at everyone. She poured herself coffee and took some cake, which she balanced on her lap on one of the linen napkins. She had found herself a chair next to the window so she could look out and see the flat steel-blue water across which small tugs pulled strings of sand barges. In the middle distance a narrow sandbar divided the water from the sky and looked—when the sun came out—like a brush stroke of ochre paint. There were mimeographed sheets with some of Joseph Kranz's poems on them laid out on a card table next to the J.N.F. *pushkes*. Rachel took several of the sheets and began to read the poems.

They were romantic and precise. Rachel found them startlingly beautiful. They were not at all what she had expected from a poet born and raised in Gateshead. Joseph Kranz spoke without rancor or sweet sentiment of his family, of young love and the memory of his birthplace. He recognized conflict, his portraits were sharply drawn. It was clear that he had read Whitman, but he knew Eliot as well. There was a chorus of good poets behind him.

"Sorry to interrupt your poetry reading," said Shirley Caplan, the Sisterhood's fund-raiser extraordinary, "but I wanted to ask you did you get my invite to the Art Show & Sale?"

"Your what?"

"I sent you an invite to participate in our Art Show & Sale next month. Did you receive it?"

"No, I didn't."

"I know I sent it. In any case, we're trying to raise

79

money to decorate the ladies' lounge and I suggested an Art Show & Sale. We're asking the artists to donate 30 percent of their proceeds, but it goes without saying that we'll gladly take 100 percent, if anyone feels like donating their work. Especially those connected with the *shul*. We've invited some very talented Long Island painters. Do you know Harold LeNu's work?"

"No."

"I'm surprised you don't. As an artist yourself I thought you would be conversant with the work of well-known local talents."

"I mostly go to the city to look at new painting."

"You'd be surprised at the quality out here. And the prices are better too. I've seen what they charge in New York. It's a rip-off."

Rachel made one of her noncommittal sounds and shrugged her shoulders as though she gave credence to Shirley Caplan's words. She shifted the conversation back to the safer ground of logistics.

"When exactly is the show?"

"The first Sunday in March. I'll send you all the information."

"I thought you said you already had."

"That was only the invitation."

Rachel would not in a million years be clever enough or get up early enough of a morning to catch Shirley Caplan napping.

"Here's Esther with her mother now," said Shirley Caplan and moved off quickly across the Chinese area rug.

An old lady had entered the room, trembling on the arm of a woman in her early fifties. The women in the room rose and applauded politely as the old lady was led to her seat, a comfortable armchair covered in tiger stripes. Her trembling stopped when she sat down. She held herself erect. Both feet were firmly planted on the floor. The women sat down on their folding chairs and Michelle Shulman Halprin called the meeting to order. She suggested that the reading of the minutes of the last meeting be dispensed with so that they might all get on with the treat at hand.

"We are fortunate to have with us today Mrs. Etta

80

Rosenkranz, mother of a poet, a Jewish poet, who was highly regarded by critics of all persuasions. Many of you knew him. Unfortunately he died before he had fulfilled the great early promise he showed."

Michelle read from a piece of lilac stationery. She was, as she herself said, a nervous person. Everyone was quiet. Mrs. Rosenkranz was obviously impressed, though not intimidated. She peered from behind her rimless glasses with appraising eyes.

"Let me interrupt here for a moment," said Michelle Shulman Halprin, "to say that Joseph Kranz's sister Esther is here too." Esther sat, alert and tense, on a folding chair. "Now I will tell you a few things about the life of Joseph Rosenkranz. He was born right here in Gateshead. He attended public school in this town and his teachers remember him fondly. He graduated from Gateshead High School when it was still in the old building on North Avenue in what is now Elwood P. Armstrong Junior High. He went to Harvard College on a full scholarship—in those days that was unusual for a Jewish boy—and graduated with honors. A Ph.D. followed in 1958 and he then traveled to England, which he had always wanted to do."

Etta Rosenkranz nodded assent to every fact.

"In 1960 he married Louise Ferguson, herself a poet. They had a daughter Faith and were separated shortly before his untimely death in 1965."

"She had a nervous breakdown. She was crazy," said Joseph Kranz's sister Esther.

"It's not necessary you should say that," Mrs. Rosenkranz admonished. She had a strong Polish accent.

"There you have a brief outline of the poet's life," said Michelle Shulman Halprin. "I'm sure Mrs. Rosenkranz can flesh it out for us a little later. First I will ask Dottie Fine to read us some of Joseph's beautiful poetry."

Dottie Fine thought she was far more cultivated than the Hadassah ladies. She lived *almost* in Gateshead Bluffs and dressed like the WASPs did. She dearly loved poetry and read it dramatically. Dottie had given readings at the library and the Y.M.C.A. and was waiting for an invitation from the Gateshead Bluffs

81

Garden Club. She wore riding dress to her reading at Michelle Shulman Halprin's house. Her boots were polished to a high sheen and a silver horseshoe pin held her ascot in place.

She read about a dozen poems in a strong, didactic voice unsuited for the subtle and delicate poetry. The poems did not yield up their mysteries, but the women listened as they might have listened to a difficult piece of music, reverently, without comprehension. They drifted off on their own trains of thought and shook themselves clear of daydreams at the start of each new poem. A few jotted down notes for the discussion that was to follow.

Dottie Fine ended her reading on a crescendo. A polite wave of applause broke out and she read one more poem for an encore. Mrs. Rosenkranz had closed her eyes to listen and leaned back in her chair. Her daughter frowned.

Michelle Shulman Halprin took charge again. "Thank you, Dottie, that was very beautiful. Now perhaps, Mrs. Rosenkranz, you can give us some insight into these poems. We certainly need it."

Etta Rosenkranz looked up, startled. "Well, I don't know," she said, and her *w*'s were *v*'s. "What is it you want to know, exactly?"

"You know your son better than anyone else did, perhaps you can add a deeper level of meaning to his work."

"To tell the truth," said Mrs. Rosenkranz, "I don't myself understand the poems."

"He suffered a lot," said Joseph Kranz's sister. "His wife was crazy."

"They didn't ask me that, Esther," said the old lady. "They want I should explain the poetry, but I only knew my son as a boy, may he rest in peace. He was a good boy. He wrote poems all the time, even as a baby. His father used to get angry. 'Don't you got anything better to do?' he asked him. Yossel used to take the typewriter—he was older then, it was after his bar mitzvah—up to the roof of our building and type his poems where nobody bothered him."

82

"He and Papa never got on well together," said Esther.

"They don't want to hear from that," said Mrs. Rosenkranz.

"A poet's life is spread out on the pages of his books," said the lady with the jewelry, a Mrs. Jabotinsky, who firmly believed in statements of principle and liked to introduce motions at meetings.

"Some of his lines seemed to me to express anti-Semitic feelings," said Golda Garfinkle. "Was Joseph Kranz a self-hating Jew?"

"He married a *shikse*," said Esther.

"I don't know what you mean," said Mrs. Rosenkranz. "Yossel was a little bit selfish. I think he loved himself, he didn't hate himself. It gave him trouble in life. I used to tell him that was wrong."

"You were the one who spoiled him," said Esther.

Golda Garfinkle was not put off. "He makes a reference somewhere to 'those birds in black, those chattering hands, those *kikes*.' Doesn't that seem to you to be anti-Semitic?"

"An anti-Semite my Yossi was not."

"His wife Louise didn't like Jews at all," said Esther.

"Perhaps the word 'kike' stands for the universally despised and rejected Jews," said Evelyn Isaacson. "He may have meant to be ironic." She was a doctor's wife.

"Didn't he express his Oedipal rage in his poetry?" asked Ida Blumenfeld, who was married to a psychologist and had taken a degree in social work at C.W. Post.

"I don't understand you," said Etta Rosenkranz.

"Your daughter said he didn't get along with his father. Was he able to write about that? Did he give vent to his hostility?"

"He didn't hardly talk to his father the last ten years of his life. My husband wasn't the easiest person to get along with either."

"Anything further on Joseph Kranz's poetry?" Michelle Shulman Halprin asked. There was no answer. "In that case I want to thank Mrs. Rosenkranz and

83

her daughter for joining us today and hope they'll come back another time."

The women clapped heartily. Mrs. Rosenkranz nodded and dabbed at her eye.

"Better I should be dead and Yossel alive," she said.

"He was always your favorite," said Esther and took her mother by the arm to lead her from the room. They put on their dark cloth coats and went out slowly, across the flagstone walk and the pebble patches to the taxi that had waited for them. Rachel watched them go and, for a moment, saw them enveloped in the light of Joseph Kranz's poems. She felt a sense of kinship: she knew these women well—the circumstances of their lives were absolutely clear. They had nourished the poet and would wear his memory always, like a halo. It didn't matter that they bickered, that others didn't understand—the poems were there, the poet who wrote them lived.

Rachel went upstairs to use the bathroom, which was decorated in gold and black. The toilet seat was soft. Rachel almost screamed as she sat down and felt herself sinking. But it turned out to be so comfortable that she would not have minded staying right there with a good book. She sat studying the splendidly decorated bathroom until she felt the clammy air from the toilet bowl rise up to envelop her naked ass. "Better join the ladies," she thought.

Downstairs more coffee and tea was being served, and a new round of goodies: cheesecake and brownies and home-baked cookies. Rachel ate several of everything and decided to go without lunch. She had to wait for Golda Garfinkle, who had many things to talk about with the Hadassah women.

Golda dropped Rachel off at home at twelve-thirty. Aaron was asleep and Seymour was eating tunafish out of the can.

"I hope there's something good for dinner."

"Fish," said Rachel.

Rachel attended the funeral of Cy Glatt's mother in the flesh but not in spirit. She had on her black hat and only wished it had a veil so that she could glide

84

like a specter among the guests. It was hardly necessary, however, to wish for a shroud of anonymity, for there were so many mourners that Rachel was lost among them. Because Cy Glatt was an old and honored member of the congregation, and its president to boot, the funeral service was held in the sanctuary of the synagogue. Rachel signed the guest book and sat in the very last pew. She paid no attention to Seymour's eulogy; it went in one ear and out the other. She thought about Joseph Kranz. The morning had impressed itself upon her with an uncommon radiance. Joseph Kranz, a poet in Gateshead—how she wished she might have known him! Surely they'd have recognized each other's talent, become friends even. Perhaps collaborated on a book. Rachel imagined the pages, graced by her drawings: seascapes from a suburban window.

After the funeral service she saw Seymour briefly. "You needn't come to the cemetery," he said.

Rachel went home and put on her shabbiest jeans and sweatshirt. Aaron said he was much better and what could he have for dinner. "Fish," said Rachel, and this time she actually walked to Koerner's Seafood Shoppe and bought two pounds of filet of sole. They had poached filet of sole that night, with hollandaise sauce. It was delicious, though neither Seymour nor Aaron acknowledged it. Rachel ate more than her share. Seymour and Aaron each had a single helping.

"You know, tomorrow night is Purim," said Seymour.

"Noisemakers!" said Aaron. "I'm too old for that."

"I didn't ask you," said Seymour. "Suburbia has seen to it that we leave Purim to the tender mercies of babies and old men."

The night of Purim was bitter and a light snow was falling. The name of Haman brought raucous sounds from the children's groggers. Sheldon Greif, the principal, directed the children at their noisemaking, but they did not always follow his commands. Seymour was surrounded by the elderly men whose minds still clung to ancient rituals. They had preserved the lipsounds and the movements, even in the alien heart of Gates-

85

head. They did not care where they were or what the *goyim* thought. No one had come to hear the *Megillah* who was not either a little child or an old man wrapped in memories.

At the conclusion of the services, the children were bundled up and taken home; Roosevelt Staub, the janitor, served hot tea and *hamantaschen* to the old people. Mrs. Kantrowitz commented adversely on their quality. "Store-bought," she said. Seymour waited until the last of the old people left. The snow had let up, stars emerged, thin drifts covered the rough places. Driving was treacherous.

"How are you getting home, Mr. Gingold?" Seymour asked a delicate old man in a fur-lined coat, who stood timidly in the middle of the parking lot.

"The janitor goes right past mine door, thank you for asking, Rabbi."

"I'll see you soon," said Seymour.

"We should meet at *simchas*," said Mr. Gingold.

Rachel wondered for days what she would wear to Sunday services at St. James the Apostle. She was under the impression that she did not have the courage to wear *exactly* what she wanted to wear because she did not wish to stick out like a sore thumb. In fact she did stick out like a sore thumb because whatever she wore was touched by her contrariness. Even if she had chosen to wear the perfect thing she would foul it up in some obvious way.

Seymour wore his black funeral suit.

"Isn't it weird to be getting ready for services on a Sunday morning?" Rachel asked him. He muttered assent. Rachel saw that he was nervous. He had showered endlessly. "Are you trying to wash off the stench of the ghetto?" Rachel called out to him through the closed bathroom door. She was waiting to take her bath. The Sunday papers lay thick and tempting inside the front door; Aaron was pleased to have them all to himself. He had declined Truscott Boothby's invitation to come along. He was pale and looked to have lost weight since his bout with the flu. Rachel chose an old wool dress she loved and had been unable to give

86

away for years and years. She kept hoping it would come back into style but it was growing tight on her and she suspected it would no longer fit by the time it was stylish again. There was a button missing. She went to sew it on and heard Seymour's cry of "Hurry, hurry!" so she put a small pin over the spot instead. She wore her grandmother's locket on a chain around her neck.

"A hat, you need a hat!" said Seymour.

Rachel ran back upstairs and chose the floppy purple one. It kept sliding down over her eyes. "I didn't know it was so big," she said in the car. "Can I get another one?"

"No!" cried Seymour. "We're late!"

In the 1780s, when St. James the Apostle was newly built, it had overlooked the sleepy whaling port and had been surrounded by hills thick with laurel and gentle fields that stretched to the harbor's westernmost reaches. It had served as the picturesque subject of innumerable engravings, paintings and (beginning in the 1860s) photographs. Over the centuries the Village of Gateshead had grown very nearly to the church doors, Main Street had been paved, and a parking lot had spread out beneath the ancient oaks.

The congregation was rich and staid. It contained some "new blood," but not very much. The Gentile *nouveaux riches* in Gateshead tended to be Irish or Italian Catholics or, if Protestant, to attend the Presbyterian church, which promised better business contacts.

Truscott Boothby greeted Seymour and Rachel at the door. He was resplendent and looked larger than life in his robes. Seymour looked very Jewish beside him. His dark curly hair was clean and soft in the pale morning air. There was the hint of sunlight behind the fast-moving clouds. Abigail Boothby sat in her wheelchair in the church foyer. An elderly spinster, a lady who saw it as her mission to offer kindness to the minister's wife, hovered beside her, giving off saintly vibrations.

"There are a lot of *goyim* here," whispered Rachel to Seymour, who smiled wanly and hissed a small "sh" before he was taken away by Truscott Boothby.

87

Rachel was all alone. She debated with herself whether she ought to go and speak to Abigail Boothby, but the spinster resolved the dilemma by greeting her first and introducing herself. Rachel did not catch the name and was afraid to ask that it be repeated. She allowed how it was a nice day and perhaps going to be a little warmer. The two women agreed. Rachel's mind went skipping through its storehouse of small talk but came up with no subject proper for the occasion. She was saved from further comments about the weather by the arrival of Jane Winthrop, who wore hiking boots and a camel's hair coat (as she did every other day of her life) and had never for a moment thought twice about how she looked to others or what they thought of her. Jane Winthrop spent most of her time doing good in the black community of Gateshead, even as the black community had let it be known that it did not wish to have good done to it, particularly by brashly efficient white ladies in hiking boots. Jane Winthrop promptly took Rachel in tow and Rachel was grateful to her. She suspected that there were any number of blacks in South Gateshead who were glad to see Jane Winthrop come stomping into a room, no matter how strongly they might decry it in public.

Jane never had to stop to think what to say. Holding Rachel by the hand she strode rudely past Abigail Boothby and her friend (she had no patience with white infirmities) and introduced her to a host of parishioners, all of whom stood politely in their rubbers and galoshes, talking Sunday morning gossip. Rachel made no effort to remember names but smiled nicely and, she hoped, ironically, all the time she pushed the sliding purple hat back from her eyes. The smile held her face in a steady vise and soon she felt as though she had lockjaw. Out of the corner of her eye, Rachel saw that several members of Shaare Tefilah had come down to St. James the Apostle, as well as Dottie Fine, who claimed that she was no longer Jewish. Dottie did not wear her riding clothes; she had on a stunning print dress and a hat larger than Rachel's. She stood out from the crowd as none of the other Jews did. Rachel nodded toward several of the familiar

88

faces. None of the congregation approached her. It was understood that Jews were not to hang around together.

Jane Winthrop carried her own Book of Common Prayer to a pew. She sat Rachel down next to her husband. The organ began its churchly sounds and the choir marched in behind the crossbearer. Truscott Boothby and Seymour walked at the rear of the procession. Truscott Boothby's robe billowed behind him, he walked with broad steps and thrusting shoulders. Once in the pulpit he allowed his voice to roll out, booming the words of the Psalmist into the rafters. Rachel was struck by the powerful sexuality that emanated from Truscott Boothby. She had always found Seymour attractive in the pulpit, but she thought this was so because it was Seymour up there—the man she loved. It had not occurred to her, until this moment, that everything that went out from the pulpit might be sexual. No wonder women lusted after clergymen! There they are, high above the crowd, raising their arms to heaven in praise and in prayer, giving priestly benedictions, and bellowing out glorious rhetoric in the language of Othello or Lear. In truth, they *are* actors. They play on the emotions and free their listeners' dreams. They woo us, damn them, thought Rachel. Because it was Lent, Truscott Boothby wore a purple stole. He brought a message from the heavens, and the psalms of David sounded good on his tongue, though they didn't sound Jewish. The choir sang familiar hymns and the congregation joined in with lusty voices. The sun shone weakly through the pale stained-glass windows and bathed the unadorned interior in blond, even light.

This plain white American church contained no mysteries, though it was surely full of secrets. The richest, most powerful men in America had worshipped here at the turn of the century; some of their descendants still did. In its humble beginnings, it had served whaling captains; now captains of industry knelt in its pews. When it came time for the collection, they threw crisp new single dollar bills into the silver platters. The endowment of this chaste church was so large that all of

89

its operating expenses came out of income. How like the WASPs to cling to the hard wooden benches, the plain brass cross, the unadorned steeple!

Truscott Boothby introduced Seymour as his friend. He said that they had fought the good fight together. He talked not about the present but about the recent past. He sounded weary, a nimbus of sorrow hung over his words of praise.

Seymour based his sermon on *Mishpatim*, the portion of the week according to the Jewish calendar. He read from the twenty-third chapter of Exodus.

"Thou shalt not take up a false report: put not thine hand with the wicked to be an unrighteous witness.

"Thou shalt not follow a multitude to do evil."

Seymour spoke about the Jewish respect for Law. He hinted most slyly that Christians had misinterpreted that respect to accuse Jews of being legalistic. He said that Jewish Law recognizes both the reality of the life of the people in which it is rooted, and the idealism of the vision it proclaims. His voice was resonant. Neither as powerful as Truscott's nor as thunderous, it rang clearly but did not boom. A faint flat upstate sound adhered to it. Rachel thought, "They will not think that he's a kike. They'll hear all America in his voice."

Seymour spoke about the sanctity of a man's oath, the penalty for bearing false witness. He said that the Torah articulated most clearly the idea that man must speak the truth and that the truth may not be perverted to suit either the will of the powerful or the vagaries of public opinion. Seymour spoke without notes. He was good at that. His sentences were organic, spoken, articulated in the normal flow of his voice. What fire there was was banked. Rachel was pleased and felt proud of him, the pride flowed once again toward her desires. She looked around to see if the congregation was listening. Some of the parishioners had closed their eyes but none seemed to be sleeping. Jane Winthrop leaned forward as though expecting an exhortation to leap into battle. Everyone was very still.

Seymour spoke about the grave warnings in Jewish Law not to be influenced by the weight of wealth, prestige or power in seeking to do justice. But to that, he said, must be added the injunction not to "countenance a poor man in his cause." He said that this was not a popular idea among liberals who tended to equate poverty with virtue. Rachel saw some small smiles on the faces of the faithful.

"Also thou shalt not oppress a stranger: for ye know the heart of a stranger, seeing ye were strangers in the land of Egypt." The sound of the biblical words stretched like a tent over the congregation; Jew as well as Gentile felt the bond. These queer archaic words coming out of the mouth of the preacher (faintly ringing of upstate New York) joined them, for the moment, in an imperfect world. Seymour, who had consciously created that bond, now struggled to free himself from it. He did not merely want to make this congregation feel virtuous, he wished to scold them, to bring them a touch of guilt. He wanted them to know he stood apart with *his* brothers.

"We Jews are a pain in the neck," he said, letting the vernacular grate against the ancient text. "We're forever harping on society's injustices. We know we are strangers in America as we were strangers in Egypt. If justice is denied us, it is denied, in some small way, to everyone. A society is only as free as its most oppressed and afflicted members."

Discomfort flickered briefly in the sparse white church. It tasted of old times. Rachel remembered, as Truscott Boothby did, the days of civil rights and Vietnam. Of being strangers in the land, standing in clear cold Washington on a November morning, singing "Give Peace a Chance." They had, before that, in 1963, clasped hands with the blacks and sung "Black and white together, we shall overcome." They were a land within a land; a country of the righteous within the country of the damned. It had been the first (and only) time some of the members of this church had stood with Jews, with war resisters, with blacks and with Catholics. Did they understand, Rachel won-

91

dered, that those times were over? She knew that Seymour wanted to tell them that, to suggest that the coalition of the righteous was irreparably broken. He wanted to cry out to them that those who still cared were isolated now, and the Jews were more isolated than the rest. But in the end, Seymour summoned the sounds of past struggles. He spoke of community. He drew back from the prickly presence of his Jewishness and ended on a note of conciliation. She heard the benediction, in mellifluous Hebrew first, then in everyone's English, and breathed her Amen upon it.

Seymour sat down and the congregation pulled itself back to the familiar order of things. Children squeaked, books were opened, here and there a throat was cleared. Harrison Winthrop sighed loudly. Truscott Boothby stood in his appointed place and said "Let us pray." All the Christians sank to their knees. Rachel sat way forward in her seat, her knees bent toward the floor, but she did not kneel. She lowered her head. The floppy hat slid forward over her eyes again. Jane Winthrop smiled at her, but Rachel felt alone and odd. They *were* kikes, even though they came from Buffalo. The congregation sang another hymn, this one unfamiliar. Jane Winthrop held the hymnal for Rachel, who joined in tentatively. Holy Communion followed, and Rachel sat alone. She wished Seymour were beside her. She wished she were just waking up in an apartment in the city, going to have fresh rolls, reading the Sunday papers, having the day free and clear. A concert maybe. The Museum of Modern Art. Drinks at a bar with friends talking into the late winter dusk.

The organ burst forth with the final hymn. "Stand up, stand up for Jesus!" sang the congregation. Rachel liked the tune and sang along lustily. She crowed "Jesus" with a special glee. It was like the yells at a high school football game. "Hit em again, hit em again, harder, harder . . ."

Seymour and Truscott stood in the receiving line by the time Rachel had left the pew behind the Winthrops.

"Come join us, Rachel," said Truscott Boothby, and Rachel stood between the men and shook lots of hands.

"Do you always have such a crowd?" Seymour asked the minister.

"Of course it's Lent, but I think your presence aroused a lot of interest and curiosity too."

They were standing together. Abigail Boothby had been the last through the line.

"More enjoyable than the night at your place," she said.

"I thought you'd sock it to them a little harder," said Truscott Boothby. "Not that it wasn't a terrific sermon, a good text. I don't know how you do it, friend, without notes."

"As your first Jewish guest I didn't particularly want to cause trouble," said Seymour. "Besides, what is there to be achieved these days? You might as well holler down a deep well."

"Oh, Rabbi," said Dottie Fine, "that was lovely. I learned so much."

"You could hear him every week if you came down to the Temple," said Murray Resnick, who had edged over from the cluster of Jews nibbling on *goyische* cookies and drinking coffee from thick mugs. The Jews beamed. They were proud. The rabbi had not disgraced them. Dottie Fine hoped her campaign to become a member of the Country Club had made some advancement.

"We've missed you at the Interracial Council," Jane Winthrop said to Seymour.

"Something keeps coming up," he said, "but I'll try to make it next time."

"We hope to get busy on the day-care center," said Jane.

"An issue!" cried Truscott Boothby. "We need an issue. Day care is perfect. It will galvanize public opinion."

"More likely it will polarize it," said Seymour. "Nobody but the three of us will support it."

"What a cynic your husband is," said Truscott Boothby to Rachel. His smile was full and happy.

93

"Was I o.k.?" asked Seymour, in the car.

"You were very good," said Rachel. "But why didn't you go on about the Jews?"

"I looked out at all those pleasant faces and they struck me like a sea of SMILE buttons. I thought, 'What the hell.' "

"As long as it wasn't a failure of nerve."

"It was a failure of nerve."

They drove in silence. Clouds raced across the sun and a warm wind blew from the southeast. At home they found Aaron drinking a beer, glum and beetle-browed among the many sections of the Sunday *Times*. He said he wasn't hungry.

"What's the matter?" Rachel asked him. "I think I'd better take you for a check-up, you look peaked."

"I've fallen in love," he said. "It's worse than any illness."

4

March was blustery and cold throughout. Rachel always forgot that three weeks of March were still legitimately winter, and that the spring equinox did not usher in that season overnight. Spring training, it was true, had been in full swing for some weeks now, but it had not yet replaced the endless array of fall and winter sports from the pages of *The New York Times*. Now and then there was a report from the grapefruit league, or a photograph of men gathered around a batting cage in Clearwater. Pitchers stood with hands on hips, gloves dangling from their wrists, while batters leaned on their Louisville Sluggers. Everyone squinted into the tropical sun. Rachel immersed herself in baseball literature. No sooner had she finished *The Summer Game* than she began *Baseball When the Grass Was Real*. She never got enough of the reminiscences of old ballplayers. They were the best storytellers, the truest of heroes: they were innocents. Rachel opened *The New Yorker* impatiently each week, to see if Roger Angell had gone to Florida yet to report on the gravely ritualized preparations for the new season. She dreamt about taking a trip down there herself one day (just when winter got too much to bear), and the dream merged with the old ones of her childhood. Then she had often gone to bed early and burrowed under her warm quilt (while the lights of passing cars meandered across the ceiling). In those fantasies (made over from the movies she went to see every Saturday afternoon), she played the gamin sidekick (Veronica

95

Lake to Joel McCrea in *Sullivan's Travels*), the tom-boy who kissed the fevered brow of a fastball pitcher crippled in the war, and swore to ride the dusty rails with him for as long as he needed her. And sometimes, before she fell asleep, she would press the wadded sheets between her legs and imagine that he made love to her, and he did, and she came—sometimes several times—in imaginary boxcars and sleazy rented rooms.

Aaron had not said another word about his skirmish with love, had refused to answer questions put to him. It seemed to Rachel that he regretted having blurted out his one confession. During the first windswept week of March, the three Sonnsheins moved in their separate paths. Seymour left the house often, muttering about trouble; Aaron kept to his room, when he was not hanging out at school, and stayed close to the tele-phone. Rachel prepared for the Art Show. She had for-gotten her pique over the tardiness of her invitation and decided to try to make the best of what the show promised. If nothing else came of it, at least she worked hard for several weeks and completed a re-spectable number of pictures. Rachel spent most of her days—and many of her nights—in her studio. She dis-covered that it was easy to put distractions aside when once you had established a rhythm of work. She no longer spent hours driving from market to market to get her shopping done. She refused all temptation: no dollar movies in Deer Park with Sally, no lunches at the Pleiades luncheonette, no trips to the city. She stopped worrying about whether her face looked like a pumpkin or a Brussels sprout, and did not think so much about quarrels, insults, and other problems of social intercourse. She even found that she was less frequently assailed by attacks of anxiety. She did not linger in bed in the morning, but jumped up, brushed her teeth, and set to work. She stopped to put the dishes into the dishwasher and she cooked dinner most days and flung piles of laundry into the machine when she happened to pass by, but she also went back to her studio after dinner and often did not go to bed until 1:00 A.M. She planned to have at least a dozen small collages ready for the show, and perhaps twenty drawings and pastel sketches. Rachel felt good about her work, indeed she found that her euphoria was such that she actually became optimistic about her chances of selling something on the day of the show. She told herself that it was plainly snobbish to think that only *schlock*-lovers came to these things; in all of Gateshead, she thought, there must be someone who will understand what I am doing and look with favor on my work. She decided to keep her prices low to encourage the browsing esthetes.

At the end of two weeks Rachel had enough work on hand to go out and spend more than half the week's grocery money on frames.

The Art Show & Sale opened at eleven on Sunday morning, while Hebrew school was still in progress. Sheldon Greif, the principal, had objected in the most strident tones. Seymour had told him to take it up with the President and the Board of Directors of Shaare Tefilah, but Sheldon Greif lost his nerve. He could only do his bitching to Seymour, which was one of the reasons the principal did not like the rabbi.

Rachel wore an Indian gown and put earrings on. She had washed her hair and brought the pictures to the synagogue the night before. The spot assigned to her was near the fire exit in the social hall. Her neighbor was a pale young man with a faint European accent, who spoke deprecatingly about his own work. Rachel found it good—though rather too painstakingly conceived—but her "Oh no, it's very nice!" seemed to ring hollow. Perhaps he was the sort of person (more often than not they are women, thought Rachel) who gains his acclaim by belittling himself. He said nothing at all about her work. She wondered if they would be uneasy stablemates.

"What is your name?" he asked.

"Rachel Sonnshein."

"Hello, Rachel Sonnshein. My name is Eli Marx."

They shook hands. His eyes were clear, the color of a washed-out spring sky. They did not look to one place long. Rachel thought he was probably obsessed but interesting, and so she did not try to escape from him.

97

The entire building, save for the classrooms and offices, was taken up by the show. The place looked like a bazaar. If you didn't look too closely, thought Rachel, it might seem splendid—cheerfully folksy and unpretentious. But if you looked closely you saw that it *was* pretentious and, what was worse, pretentious kitsch. Rachel felt the black twinges of despair creep through her bowels. Why had she gotten involved in this? She saw what Eli Marx had obviously known from the beginning—that they were in the wrong place. There was some work in the show—mostly sculpture—that verged on craft, though the committee had been explicit in trying to limit entries to the "fine arts." Asked what that meant, they said painting and sculpture. So was painting on velvet acceptable? Yes. How about on burlap? No, not on burlap. Sculpture made of junk was o.k., as long as it was small. Tree trunks carved to look like drunken sea captains were permitted, but the line was drawn at painted stones. Pots and jewelry were banned. The consensus among the committee was that work should not sell for less than twenty-five dollars.

Rachel had set up her work against the wall and placed the smaller pictures on a card table. She felt like a curbside vendor. Others were more practiced than she. They had built large portable racks to show their paintings, folding cases for their sculptures. They brought pillows for the metal chairs and thermos bottles filled with tea or coffee.

"If you want to look around, I'll watch your things," Eli Marx said.

"Do you think there's a chance they might be stolen?"

"No, but you don't want to miss a sale." This time his smile was ironic.

The artists were happy to chat with Rachel. They were free with advice.

"Don't let them bargain with you."

"Never admit that you can't do something they want done."

But Rachel was to have no opportunity to make such

98

an offer. Very few of the morning's onlookers stopped at her table; those who did passed quickly on, realizing in a sudden dreadful rush that they ought to venture an opinion or, at the very least, make an appropriate comment. Most of them knew who she was. Rachel could not make herself invisible, though she had brought a book which she tried to read, pretending to be no more than the keeper of the works of art. Eli Marx had little more success than she did, though he made the viewers feel guilty by smiling ingratiatingly, and pointing out the reviews his work had received in *Newsday* and the *Long Island Press*. He had mounted the articles on large sheets of paper and underlined the most flattering lines.

Seymour stopped by around noon. "Any luck?"

"What do you think?" said Rachel.

"Maybe you'll get a better crowd this afternoon or evening."

"I'm Eli Marx, Rabbi. So pleased to meet you."

The artist looked at him with naked eyes of envy.

Ida Blumenfeld and Evelyn Isaacson stopped by to show Rachel the purchases they had made.

"You have to know how to shop these shows," said Ida. "It's like anything else. You can't expect to find bargains at Bonwit Teller's; that's the beauty of Loehmann's."

"I've never been there," said Rachel. "I shop as rarely as I can."

"I don't see you going around naked," said Evelyn. She had bought a purple abstraction and two copies of a Chagall etching.

They glanced briefly at Rachel's collages and, finding it impossible to say something favorable, left smiling vaguely.

Eli Marx said, "It was a mistake to come here."

"Yeah," said Rachel.

"Those ladies are very unsure of themselves."

"Not about bargains they're not."

"That's why they talk about them. If you'll excuse my saying so," Eli Marx went on, "I think you do not do it right. They glanced at your work out of the

99

corner of their eyes. But you make them uncomfortable. It would be good if you came, how shall I say it, toward them."

"You mean 'lick ass'?"

"That is a crude way to put it. A rebbetzin should not be so angry. They would eat out of your hand if you were friendly."

"I thought I was a very friendly person. I smile a lot."

"The smile does not come graciously. It is pasted on your face."

Rachel looked directly at Eli Marx. She felt sorry for him. She did not think he was good at the flattery he claimed to have mastered. He saw her look and smiled the foreign smile.

"There is a very pretty woman coming this way and I think her eye is on us. Or perhaps it is only on *you*."

The pretty young woman was Natalie Gould, a newcomer to Gateshead and to the congregation. She was not only pretty but long-legged and graceful. It was thought she was a strange and mysterious person. Rachel did not know whether there was really a mystery about Natalie Gould or whether it was simply an aura created by the gossips and given luster through Natalie's silence. She was a favorite topic of conversation in Gateshead, and had probably replaced Rachel as the number one topic among the Jewish ladies.

It was said that Natalie Gould had an interesting past, that is to say her past was different enough from the past of her observers to seem interesting to them. It was said she was illegitimate, not even Jewish, but had been adopted by Jewish parents and raised in an Orthodox house. She most certainly did not *look* Jewish. Her husband, Charlie, was strong in body and very rich. He gave generously to the synagogue and to the U.J.A. He had, once upon a time, been a football star at Dartmouth, but he carried his fame (or the echoes of it) without insolence and never boasted of it. He was a stockbroker and all his hunches had been fruitful. His money multipled. Natalie and Charlie Gould had no children. (Even here there was room for speculation. It was said that they had had a son

100

who died tragically.) They owned a condominium in Israel and kept an apartment in New York. All of these things were just enough beyond the range of experience of most of the Jews of Gateshead (but within the range of their fantasies) to engender a rich flow of conversation. Rachel (who thought about them too) found the Goulds to be more truly rootless than any of the other "new arrivals" she had met in Gateshead. This rootlessness, combined with a casual disregard of some of the middle-class amenities, gave them a slightly bohemian air. The Goulds rarely talked about their past, and no one in Gateshead had known them in a previous incarnation. The few Dartmouth alumni who dwelt in the vicinity remembered Charlie Gould as the hero of the 1951 Yale game, but had never given much thought to Charlie Gould, student, householder or businessman. He had not used his school connections to get ahead; he had always been a loner. Perhaps he was just a little bit crooked.

Had anyone in Gateshead possessed imaginative gifts he might have invented a fine story for Charlie and Natalie Gould. As it was, their story remained un-revealed and unembroidered. People merely talked about what they had seen.

"Did you see her new coat?"

"Did you see what they did to their yard?"

Natalie Gould was not a total enigma to Rachel. She had known girls like her at Barnard, and they were not mysterious at all. They were bright, came from "good families," and had led sheltered child-hoods; they were innocent in matters of Art, Sex and Politics. At Barnard they occasionally felt dumb: for the first time in their lives they met girls who were world-weary, having had experiences in all three of those domains. They were sometimes Jewish, though mostly not, and came from the suburbs or from St. Louis. Now and then one was found to have come from East 74th Street.

Rachel might have been among them, except that she had spent the summer of her eighteenth year in Provincetown, studying painting. That was where she had first met Ben—he was, she thought, the doomed

101

hero (the failed pitcher) among a variety of scruffy bohemians. She had not noticed those painters who smelled of success. Her best friend was a young woman who had read Joyce at fourteen, Proust at sixteen, and quit the Communist Party at seventeen, long before Rachel had even begun her flirtation with Marx.

Natalie Gould always displayed a pleasant smile—the sort one is taught, like manners and the two-step, in dancing school. She wore it now as she came over to greet Rachel. She spent some minutes looking carefully at her work—the first person to do so all day. It was two o'clock in the afternoon and the March winds howled outside.

"I like your work," said Natalie Gould. "It's very strong and sure."

"Thank you," said Rachel, for what else was there to say?

"I'm Natalie Gould, I don't think we've been introduced." It was so like her to admit it.

"I'm Rachel Sonnshein."

"I know," said Natalie Gould.

Rachel wondered whether she also knew that she was the subject of many conversations. She was surely neither dumb nor stupid. She did not seem hostile. She was just perennially inexperienced in certain of life's crucial areas, though she knew many many things that Rachel had never been taught. She could say, "We have never been introduced."

Eli Marx listened closely while pretending to arrange his pictures. Natalie Gould did not seem to notice. She continued looking carefully at Rachel's collages. Rachel found herself hoping she would buy one. She thought of all the money she had spent on frames.

"Perhaps you'll let me see some more of your work one of these days," said Natalie Gould.

Rachel felt the disappointment clog her voice. "Sure," she said.

"How much is this one?" asked Natalie. She held the smallest of Rachel's collages in her hand.

Rachel was flustered. "Isn't it marked?" she asked, her mind working like a whirring motor, trying to come up with a reasonable figure. "Thirty-five dollars."

102

"I'll take it," said Natalie, and took out her checkbook. Rachel saw that she made the check out to Cash.

"We ought to get together," said Natalie Gould. "I've heard so much about you."

"Yes," said Rachel. "Thank you." She felt embarrassed, and a little resentment covered her pleasure at the sale.

"How is Seymour?" asked Natalie Gould. "Is he here?"

Rachel was startled to hear her say "Seymour." Most people, especially strangers, said "the rabbi." Natalie Gould must have seen the very slight expression of annoyance which flitted across Rachel's face.

"He called on us when we first came to town," she said, "and was absolutely charming. The other temples merely sent questionnaires and membership forms. We appreciated his personal interest, and that's why we joined."

Natalie's cashmere scarf hung to the top of her boots, which were made of red leather, soft and elegant. A gray flannel skirt swirled to below her knees; a sheepskin jacket opened to reveal a white silk blouse. Several long strands of pearls lay upon it. Rachel felt graceless. There was paint under her fingernails. Natalie picked up the picture she had bought.

"I'm sorry I don't have any wrapping paper," said Rachel.

Natalie still smiled. "So good to have met you. I hope to see more of your work soon."

Rachel did not know why it was, but she could not respond with enthusiasm to Natalie Gould's polite utterances. "Sure," she answered.

"You should have asked for more money," said Eli Marx, in a low voice, when Natalie Gould had gone. "She looked as though she could afford it."

Rachel was glad when it was seven o'clock and the end of her vigil was in sight. She had eaten a peanut butter sandwich and drunk one of the Cokes the Sisterhood was selling—the only thing she had had since breakfast—and now she was hungry. Seymour had gone home and was back now, chatting with one of the younger hostesses.

103

"Come have some champagne punch," said Michelle Shulman Halprin, and Rachel gladly left her table. Natalie Gould's check rustled in the pocket of her dress. She drank some of the sweet punch and sought out Seymour.

"How come you know Natalie Gould so well?" she asked.

"What do you mean?"

"She calls you by your first name."

"A lot of people do."

"Not people I've never met."

"You haven't met her?"

"No, I haven't met her."

"If you went to more places with me you might get to know more people. Natalie is one of them." He turned away.

"Is one of what?" Rachel asked.

Seymour ignored her.

"Wasn't it an exciting show?" asked Shirley Caplan, pretending to be giddy from the bubbly punch. "Did you sell anything, Rachel?"

"One collage."

"We made several thousand dollars, I hear. Don't forget to hand in your sales slip and leave us a check for our commission. Aren't you pleased with Sisterhood's success?"

"I have to make a phone call," said Seymour. "I'll be right back. Then we can leave."

Libby Donoghue, the art critic of Gateshead's weekly newspaper, stood nearby, writing on a steno pad. Michelle Shulman Halprin turned to her. "Have you met our rebbetzin?"

"What is your name, dear?" said the art critic, her pencil poised.

"Rachel Sonnshein."

"And what is it you do?"

"I'm a painter."

"That's not what Mrs. Halprin said. She called you a rabbits . . . I didn't quite catch it."

"I'm the rabbi's wife," said Rachel.

Michelle Shulman Halprin laughed gaily. "I'm sorry I confounded you with one of our funny Yiddish

104

words," she said. "I promise I won't do it again. And here's the rabbi himself."

Seymour was wearing his coat.

"Are you ready to go?" he asked.

"Any time you are," said Rachel.

They carried the pictures out to the car. "Don't work too hard, Rabbi!" a member called out jovially.

The sky had turned a deep blue, the color just before dark, when almost all the light has been drained from it and the first stars glitter like sparks from a wet fire. It was cold and there was no hint of spring in the air. Rachel saw the new moon hanging high above Gateshead.

* * *

The warm front moved in that night, and the next morning the air was balmy. It was Monday. Rachel liked Mondays; they were a release from the cluttered weekends. She was alone again, at last. Rachel found it harder and harder to deny the streak of solitariness within her. She did not feel like working that day and so she walked down to the harbor park and sat for a long time on a bench, alone save for the weekday loiterers. Rachel knew them by now, the idlers like her, who found it better to be here than elsewhere. The old men and women sought the touch of the warm sun, the patients newly released from Kings Park State Hospital tried to measure their steps without fences, and the salesmen between calls looked for a moment's calm to restore their strength, a chance to smooth out their faces for the next assault on bored and sullen customers.

Rachel tried to observe the details clearly, to pin them down with her painter's eye, but she found herself returning again and again to the Art Show & Sale. Then her inner eye would conjure up a tableau of Shaare Tefilah and she would lose sight of the scene before her. The tableau was depressing. Rachel wished she had not been a part of it. How could she have thought the Jews of Gateshead would run to buy her work? They didn't even understand it, just as they

105

didn't understand her. She made them uncomfortable, always searching for words to explain herself or to elucidate Profound and Serious Concepts, while their minds danced over ideas like stones skipping across a pond. Only Natalie Gould had tried to approach her, and she was probably showing her a kindness. She had the money to do it. Rachel hated to be pitied. And Seymour—why had he been so edgy of late? Evasive when asked about his plans and the events of his days?

"I only asked to show some interest," Rachel remembered herself saying.

"All of a sudden?" he had answered. "I don't bother you."

"You always know where I am," she had said. "I'm in full view."

Sometimes, as though happy with an unexpected gift, he talked a lot, made extravagant plans for the future and told Rachel he loved her. But his joy seemed to have nothing to do with her at all.

When the twelve o'clock whistle blew, Rachel walked back to the house to fix lunch. Seymour was not at home. The house looked as though it needed a thorough cleaning. Rachel did not want to look at it, and decided to take a sandwich and a beer back down to Harbor Park. She made two egg salad sandwiches, took a cold Bud and put it all in her army bag, along with the black sketchpad and an assortment of felt-tipped pens. Sketching would focus her eyes on the panorama without; perhaps it would thus shut down the theater within.

The telephone rang. Rachel said "Shit," but answered it. Golda Garfinkle was on the line. She said some nice things about Rachel's pictures, but Rachel did not listen because she knew Golda had called for something else. She could hear it in the tone of her voice.

"Too bad you only sold one picture," Golda said. "I hear they made over two thousand dollars. Have you started working on your Sisterhood talk yet?"

Rachel said "Mmmmhum" and bent down to lace her shoe. The receiver clattered to the floor. When she

106

put it back to her ear, Rachel heard Golda say, "What on earth are you doing?"

"Tying my shoe."

"Rachel!"

"Yes?"

"I'm sorry to interrupt you, but I'm at a Sisterhood board meeting and we're discussing the calendar. We thought it was time we did something on the women's movement. We couldn't find any other time for it except the meeting we had scheduled you for. . . ."

"You mean I don't have to do it?"

"You don't. No. I hope you aren't upset. We'll get to you in the fall."

"Of course I'm not upset. I hate to talk. I mean I hate to speak. I love to talk."

"I'm so relieved. Really, I felt badly to think of you getting bumped like this. But"—Golda lowered her voice—"I couldn't do very much. As you know, the woman issue is very 'in' these days and a lot of our younger members are pressing for a program on it."

Golda's obvious relief made Rachel realize that she ought to feel insulted. On the other hand, she realized that Golda was annoyed that she cared so little for the honor a speech before the Sisterhood would bestow on her. It was a duty, but an honor as well.

"Most other rebbetzins come down to see what goes on at Sisterhood meetings. They want to be involved, they want to play a leading role in their husband's work. . . ."

"The women are probably delighted I'm not there to cause trouble."

"We'll discuss it another time, Rachel. I must get back to the meeting. You're welcome to come over even now, if you wish. We'll have a bite in a few minutes. It's at my house."

"Thanks, Golda. I think not. But thanks anyway."

Rachel gathered up her things again, put the pea jacket on and went outside. She wore neither hat nor gloves, for the first time that year. When the front door had closed behind her and Rachel stood for a moment on the porch, squinting into the sun, the telephone

107

rang again. Rachel jumped down the three steps and went sprinting down Sweetwater Street, skipping across the muddy puddles. Ollie, the Grogs' vicious Doberman, barked furiously at her, but he was behind glass and could not harm her. Rachel saw him pawing the storm door of the enclosed porch and yapping with extended tongue through bright bared teeth. His sounds drowned out the ringing telephone for good.

Rachel reached the park breathless. She sat down on a bench next to the deserted bandshell and rested a minute before she began to eat her lunch. The conversation with Golda Garfinkle occupied her mind. It was still fresh and new, but second thoughts and reflections upon it were beginning to crop up like weeds between the remembered words. No matter how hard she tried she could not tear Golda's insinuation out of her head. She tried to list all the things she had done for the Sisterhood or was prepared to do, but, like all such rationalizations, these did not alter the substance of what Golda had said, they merely gave Rachel reason for her feelings of truculent belligerence. "Fuck the Sisterhood," said Rachel to herself, and felt a little better. She wanted to do the "right thing." Too bad that interpretations as to what the right thing was differed so greatly. If only she could drain all emotion from the performance of her duties, if only her grudging assent were less visible. Her heart's distaste seemed to flash insistently to the world. Rachel's stomach was knotted and tender. Was it anger or her approaching menstruation?

Rachel watched the harbor through the spaces between the evenly planted maple trees. In summer their crowns met and joined until they became a green proscenium arch. Rachel liked that view. This time of the year the bare branches of the trees barely meshed; each tree retained a separate identity. Rachel thought of other views squeezed between two planes. Her mind wandered away from the idea. Her stomach hurt. The subtleties of views and planes were lost. Menstruation had, of late, become a real pain. Rachel had never liked it, had felt crippled by it from earliest times. It was one of the things boys did not have to contend

108

with; it marked her off from them most clearly. They never had to feel the blood trickling out the hole on hot summer days on the ball field, didn't have to sit on the bench, gritting their teeth over dull stomach cramps, worrying about the bloody stain spreading out across the crotch of their jeans. And the goddamn sanitary napkins! Rachel had never been able to make do with Tampax, had laughed at the dumb ads in *Seventeen* —her first taste of advertising nonsense—where girls danced on tippy-toes across a sun-dappled beach. That wasn't how it was at all, at all. On really bad days even the Modess didn't stem the flow. Blood was everywhere. Big clots of it, swimming in the red blood, flowing as from a wound. Was it a wound? Sometimes Rachel sat on the toilet and watched it flow out of her. Dr. Fleischer had clucked his tongue over her "fibroids" for some years now, but Rachel had had these bloody days ever since she could remember. Ever since her period had begun, in the summer of forty-seven. At the age of fourteen she once walked around school all day with a stain the size of a salad plate on the back of her cotton dress. She kept it hidden by tying a sweatshirt around her waist so that it hung over her ass and covered the damned spot.

She had been as strong as the boys at eleven years, still, and then at twelve her period came and she somehow knew that her strength would wane. Truly it was a "curse," but her friends had named it "Willie" and she called it that all these years and marked down "Willie" on her calendar regularly, like the phases of the moon.

The sun was gentle on Rachel in Harbor Park, though the air was still stiff with the breath of winter, the ground gave up its frost slowly, and there would be fog in the night. Rachel put the leftover trash from her lunch into one of the dockside chained baskets and sat on a rock to draw the complicated structure of the bulkheads and the moored tugboat hugging them. Drew it in a line, never stopping, letting it do its own distorting, never going back (it was, in ink, impossible), only rushing forward. She drew the rocks, too, and the benches and figures along the shore, and then

109

turned around and drew the bandshell, now seen through the same line of maple trees which had, in the first view, framed the shore.

Rachel stayed in the park until the sun was covered by the advancing bank of clouds and spring was swept away—save for its faint fresh smell and the tips of crocuses beneath the trees. She bought a cup of coffee from a vendor. Her face felt flushed from the sun. The harbor was still. Only a few boats bobbed at anchor. Rachel felt good for having spent the afternoon exercising her hand. She had almost put Golda Garfinkle out of her mind.

By nightfall Rachel's period had begun. She took a hot-water bottle to bed and curled herself around it.

"I think it's time you went to see Dr. Fleischer again," said Seymour. It seemed to be the only response he knew how to make.

The following Saturday had been set aside by many of the members of Shaare Tefilah for the bar mitzvah of Spencer Gewirtz. "A classy bar mitzvah," Rachel had said when the invitation arrived two months before. It was handwritten on vellum in brown ink, in the same script used to draft the Declaration of Independence. Three hundred invitations had been dispatched. It took two stamps to post each one, plus the stamp for the self-addressed envelope, in which "the favor of a reply" was requested before the 28th of February. Rachel returned these little envelopes conscientiously, hoping each time that she would be alive and well on the date in question. Saturdays (except in July and August) were almost invariably devoted to the celebration of bar mitzvahs. Since Seymour and Rachel were invited as a matter of course, it meant that they averaged over three dozen a year.

Debra and Murray Gewirtz had three sons: Spencer, Byron, and Blake. "What happened to Milton?" Seymour had asked Debra once, in a rare moment of drunken abandon. Spencer Gewirtz was a short fat boy with horn-rimmed glasses. Rachel had difficulty differentiating him from all the other short fat boys with horn-rimmed glasses. Even Aaron (before he shot

110

up at the age of fifteen) had been a short fat boy with horn-rimmed glasses. There were times, when Rachel was waiting to pick him up on a dark winter evening from Hebrew school, that she had waved fanatically at the wrong child. Since it was easier to pick out bar mitzvah gifts by the dozen, Rachel always kept a single face in mind when she bought that season's supply. It was usually the face of Spencer Gewirtz and she bought either a book on crustaceans and reptiles or one on the Gold Rush in Alaska. "He'll be grateful when he has to do a report," she told Seymour.

Saturday morning was not Rachel's favorite time of the week. When she and Seymour had first dreamt their Jewish dreams, the Sabbath had been (as it was meant to be) very special. They lived together for an entire summer in New York, observing it, cherishing it, making it the crown and glory of their week. Rachel cooked a fine meal on Friday, which they often shared with friends. Afterwards they sat (the candles glowed and the windows were open to the Village street; the sounds of its life floated up to them like wayward butterflies) and they talked until late in the night. They sometimes went walking during the day, on the Sabbath, but mostly they read and slept and ate delectable things. When sundown arrived and Saturday night, the city seemed to glitter with a most unnatural brightness. Then it was time to go out on the town, to summer concerts, and to the movies.

Those days seemed to have nothing whatsoever to do with their Jewish experiences in suburban Gateshead. Seymour woke early on *Shabbos* (often with heartburn) and wandered through the house, plucking at books, nervous about his sermon, worried about his shirt, his tie. Rachel's response was to sink into lethargy, which made him more nervous still. He would sit in front of his breakfast and look at the fresh *challeh*, the honey and jam pots, and most often merely drink a cup of black coffee. Sometimes the phone rang (even on the seventh day, the day of rest, when he wasn't supposed to answer). Usually it was someone with a minor problem—a guest who couldn't find the synagogue, a florist who needed to be let in, a visitor

111

who wanted to know how late he could arrive and not miss *Kaddish*.

Seymour left the house at eight-thirty for the preliminary service, which followed the Orthodox ritual and was conducted entirely in Hebrew. Rachel (like most everyone else) came in at about ten-thirty. Sometimes she was later than that, but she never missed the sermon or the reading of the *Haftorah* by the bar mitzvah boy.

The morning of the Gewirtz bar mitzvah was blustery with winter once again. There was even a hint of snow in the air. Rachel waited until the last minute to get dressed, had a fight with Aaron over the smelly sneakers he had left in front of the TV, and had to run most of the way to the synagogue. (Seymour took the car except when she got up to drive him, in her nightgown under an army coat, galoshes on her feet.) She got there just as Spencer Gewirtz was called to the Torah. The sanctuary was filled to overflowing. Everyone was dressed brilliantly, in spring colors and the very latest style. Mothers and grandmothers had had their hair done, aunts and cousins too, the odor of hairspray hung in the air. People swiveled around in the pews to see who the new arrivals were, but not one of the relatives recognized Rachel, the rabbi's wife. They all came from the more distinguished suburbs of Nassau and Westchester counties, as well as from northern New Jersey and southern Connecticut. Rachel sat down in one of the last pews, looked out over the heads of the people and tried to figure out how this bar mitzvah was different from all other bar mitzvahs. Through the years they had begun to flow together into one continuous event, at which she sat growing older and older, while the kid remained forever thirteen and the parents and grandparents merely changed their clothes. Sometimes they were richer, sometimes poorer, noisier or quieter, more vulgar, less vulgar, sometimes the kid was fluent, sometimes he got stuck, it didn't matter a whole lot in the end, not even to the kid. It was really the party that mattered.

Spencer had a high loud voice and he had learned his portion well. He was one of the ones who stood up

112

on the pulpit, all cocky and self-possessed, and belted out the *Haftorah* like a child star. He winked at his father when he was done and shook hands with Seymour. (Spencer won prizes in junior high school and was elected to office by the student body.)

Seymour stood at his lectern for several minutes before Spencer stopped clowning and the relatives calmed down. He wore a black robe and a plain black *yarmulke*. He spoke about the Jewish reverence for life and said that Jews ought not to place property values above human values. Murray Gewirtz was a lawyer or, as he said, an attorney. Most of his clients were in real estate. Seymour had not planned to offend them; he always connected his sermon to the week's Torah portion and let, as he said, the chips fall where they may. The question to which Seymour addressed himself that morning was the need for a day-care center for babies—mostly black—whose mothers earned their daily bread by cleaning house for the middle-class residents of New Gateshead.

Rachel was sensitive to the quality of Seymour's sermons. She knew better than anyone, except Seymour himself, when he was in good form, when great and when mediocre. She never said anything until a day or so had passed; she knew how "sharper than a serpent's tooth" badly timed criticism was (had suffered under it herself), especially to a performer high on the fervor of his delivery. On the day of the bar mitzvah of Spencer Gewirtz, Seymour was not inspired. He was merely clever and brittle, he was faking it, he had come badly prepared. His intelligence always shone through, but this day it neither glowed nor quivered with conviction.

The sermon lasted exactly twenty minutes. No need to squirm. When Seymour had finished the congregation rose to sing the *Aleinu,* feeling virtuous. They had sat still for twenty minutes, listening to the rabbi take them to task for their human failings when they could have been home in bed or out shopping or playing golf. They felt that they deserved credit merely for *listening*. They had no intention of changing their ways but it was good, now and then, to be made to feel

113

guilty. Good thing the rabbi wasn't on the Town Board or, God forbid, a lawyer working for the N.A.A.C.P. Let him stay in his *shul* and talk. A few, feeling *too* much virtue for having gotten up early and given up a leisurely breakfast, took real offense and argued that the rabbi did not know the facts of life, was an idealist out of touch with the realities of American Life. "I worked hard to get out of Brooklyn, build a nice home. You think I want Brooklyn to come after me?"

Rachel did not stand in the receiving line. No need to prove she'd been there. She let herself drift along between the furs, trying to listen to what the people had to say about the rabbi, but not wanting to hear them if it was going to be nasty.

"Some sermon," said a voice behind Rachel.

"At least it was short."

"If he was my rabbi he wouldn't be my rabbi for long. I'd tell him a thing or two."

When Rachel reached Seymour, she shook his hand and said "Good Shabbos, Rabbi" and Seymour answered "Good Shabbos, Rebbetzin." Rachel shook hands with Murray and Debra Gewirtz and said *"Mazel tov"* both times. Murray bent down from his bearish height and kissed her; Debra was scanning the crowd to find her mother.

"Why isn't Ma in the receiving line?"

"Go get your grandmother," she said to Blake, who wore a leisure suit to match his brother Byron's. Spencer, last in line, had had to be outfitted differently, in the Husky Shop.

"Good Shabbos," said Rachel, shaking the adolescent hand.

Spencer smiled his glitzy smile. "So glad you could come, Mrs. Sonnshein."

Rachel wondered briefly it he was going to grow up to be gay.

The Gewirtz family had provided honey and sponge cake and sweet kosher wine for *Kiddush* after services. "Don't eat too much," Spencer's aunt warned the invited guests, "there'll be plenty at the reception."

114

The uninvited guests—mostly men come to say *Kaddish,* faithful members and a few old-timers who came for the delicacies—crowded around the buffet table.

Seymour and Rachel did not eat the honey cake nor did they drink the sweet kosher wine. They went home instead, so that Seymour could change his white shirt for a striped one and his sweaty underpants for dry ones. Rachel had also to change her bloody sanitary napkin. She was still bleeding profusely (on this, her sixth day).

"You'd better call the doctor on Monday," said Seymour. "How many days has it already been?"

"Six."

Rachel had put on two Modess pads (extra large) and stuffed two more into her black silk purse. She popped two vitamin-and-iron pills into her mouth.

"What's that for?" Seymour asked.

"So I don't become anemic."

"Go see the doctor," said Seymour. "Please?"

They drove through Gateshead, out along the north shore toward the Sheep Hollow Country Club. Baled and cushioned by their good clothes, the car's erratic heater, and static-bristling arias from the Metropolitan Opera broadcast, Seymour and Rachel passed through the world of Saturday's suburbia as though in a spaceship. Main Street was crowded with shoppers; the Lions and Knights of Columbus sold raffles at every corner; McDonald's did a brisk midday business; and boy scouts held an encampment on the City Hall steps. The distance separating the Sonnsheins from this cheerful bazaar was measured not only by their Jewishness (though they felt like inhabitants of another country— strange as Chassidim on a Mississippi street), but by the extent of their intellectual baggage. Spread out before them was the sweet simplicity of a life-style they could not share, had not shared since high school days. Saturday in suburbia was a great homecoming feast with floats and pom-poms and marching bands. But weren't they headed toward another kind of suburban celebration, even more conspicuous in its con-

115

sumption? The Sheep Hollow Country Club (now the weekly scene of Jewish revels) had once been as exclusive in its membership policies as the church of St. James the Apostle. "It shows you how times change," thought Rachel, "even if they change only for the rich." She felt her isolation twice: the party they were about to join was only another facet of suburban life, it was not an alternative.

Rachel looked out at the throng and saw a group of teenagers lounging in front of the stationery store. "There's Aaron," she said, before she had even finished taking in the scene. Seymour (waiting impatiently for a traffic light) did not hear her.

Aaron was standing with a pretty girl, holding her hand. It was a casual gesture, intimate because it was so natural to them. The two barely touched except where their fingers intertwined. They were laughing, part of a group of about eight adolescents, part of the Saturday afternoon scene, part of their own and different lives. Rachel, tempted to roll down her window and call out a raucous greeting, resisted the impulse once she saw their clasped hands. She had played her tomboy role opposite her son as well as her lovers; now, in a sudden moment of self-recognition, she knew she had better draw back and shut up.

"Did you say something?" Seymour asked, once they were moving again.

"No, nothing."

The country club had once been an estate. It was surrounded by an eighteen-hole golf course, and twelve tennis courts were hidden behind a copse of birches and beech trees. The parking lot (at the end of a long curving drive) was also artfully concealed. Young boys met the guests at the manor house porte cochère and whisked their cars away. A sign near the door read: "Your Host Has Provided the Gratuities." The manor house itself was built of brick and limestone; two wings spread from the mansard-roofed central section. Great trees surrounded the house on every side, but a large swatch had been cut through them so that members, dining on the terrace, could look across the golf course, down to the bay and over the water to the spit of land that separated the bay from the Sound.

Rachel left her cape with the hat check girl, who looked exactly as though she could have worked for the original owners of the manor house—been their parlor maid back in the Roaring Twenties. She was red-faced and lilting, Irish, with bright blue eyes. Rachel saw her put the cape up between the minks without batting an eye. "It's like our Plymouth among the Cadillacs," said Seymour.

"That's an unusual dress you're wearing," a woman Rachel did not know, had never seen before, said to her just as they turned from the cloak room to face the event. Rachel wore an African robe bought on Lexington Avenue, and was certain never to meet anyone else wearing the same thing. It hadn't cost very much, but that was not obvious—exotic dress covered a multitude of sins, uncertainties, and bare-faced lies. It wasn't necessary to wear stockings underneath, nor a girdle, and the bold pattern covered the stains of stuffed mushrooms as well as of blood.

The country club's bar was crowded with bar mitzvah guests. Many of them had not bothered to come to the synagogue, but had spent the morning at the beauty parlor instead. Others had shed their covers and appeared half-naked now, dancing savage dances, tapping their feet in rhythm to the music of the band, letting their laughter ring through the white and silver room. The oppressive Jewish past did not oppress them here. How many miles was it to the muddy ghetto streets? How many light years to hunger and a single patched pair of shoes? Chivas Regal flowed like water; the bartenders neither sweated nor smiled, and performed their jobs like oiled robots.

"Jesus, I need a drink," said Rachel, like everyone else.

Seymour went to get her a vodka martini. He took a double Scotch on the rocks and they stood alone, just outside the circle of friends and relations, dependent on each other, apart, aware. She gazed outside through the double French doors, upon the bare and cold ter-

117

race. Debra Gewirtz had wanted a late spring bar mitzvah, but nothing she could do changed the rabbi's mind or Spencer's birthday. Rachel imagined what it would be like come summertime and blooming roses, and wished for that time herself.

Everyone at the party noticed the rabbi and rebbetzin (sent down from heaven to spy upon them, to report back to the boss on Mount Sinai), saw them stand close to one another, cool and undismayed, sensed their unspoken ambivalence and did not approach them until they had gotten a little drunk. Rachel sipped her martini slowly, afraid to get high fast and sick later. Waitresses came by with tidbits of every description: little pizzas, potato pancakes with sour cream and caviar, egg rolls and little pink hot dogs around a bowl of mustard, cold shrimp on ice and a dip with curry, spare ribs and duck sauce and little knishes, stuffed mushrooms and deep-fried hunks of chicken. The food was good; it was a non-kosher Jewish country club. Not that it wasn't any longer open to Gentiles; the Gentiles just hadn't hung around once the Jews (their money had saved the club from bankruptcy) came in any numbers. The few still there were Italians, who were hardly considered Gentiles, and a handful of WASPs with Jewish wives.

A smiling man in an electric-blue tuxedo came over and shook hands with Seymour.

"Remember me?" he said. "Joan's brother Harry." He looked at Rachel quickly, expertly. "I don't believe I've met your wife."

Seymour, cold sober still, took the man's measure. He had never seen him before.

"I'm Rabbi Sonnshein," he said.

Harry laughed. "I'll be a son of a bitch," he said. "Excuse me, Rabbi. I thought you were Murray Gewirtz's partner."

They were caught in a moment's silence, the band had stopped.

"I can't get over the resemblance," said Harry, as he edged away.

Rachel felt the blood squirting out of her.

118

"There's Natalie Gould," said Seymour. "Someone we know. Let's go and talk to them."

"*I* don't know her," said Rachel.

"I thought you'd met at the art show?"

"Only briefly. I never met her husband at all."

"Come over then, I'll see that you get to know them. She's very nice and you'll like him."

"I've never met a financier I've liked yet."

"He's different. Intelligent, a little crazy."

"A crazy football player?"

"A crazy capitalist."

Rachel, slightly fuzzy-headed from the effects of the vodka martini, followed Seymour in docile fashion. They threaded their way through a crowd of swaying asses and Rachel did a tapping two-step behind Seymour's back, wishing—for a drunken moment—that she could lose herself like the others, shake her awkwardness and move like a slinky temptress, finger-snapping on the lively floor. Seymour resisted the rhythms; his grace was all in bed.

"Excuse me," he said.

"Excuse me, excuse me," Rachel echoed behind him, and sometimes had to shove a little.

Natalie Gould wore a black silk suit with a long skirt; there was a skimpy blouse under the jacket. She looked stunning. Her husband Charlie's hand was at her elbow; his face was impassive and proud. He wore a simple dark blue blazer. His shoulders were wide and his face was faintly yellow with the remains of a winter tan. For a second they seemed caught in the perennial society-page pose, a beautiful couple, white on black, with gleaming teeth made brighter yet by the flashbulb popping right before them.

Rachel found the fuzziness a perfect shield behind which to greet the Goulds, shake hands, and loll her tongue in small talk. Natalie's blond straight hair was gathered behind in a silver clip. She looked briefly at Seymour with smiling eyes and then turned to Rachel, who saw the smile drop from her eyes to her cheeks, extending the mouth. "So good to see you again, Rachel," she said, and turned quickly to Charlie, who

119

was composed and aware and would never be caught off guard. He'd mug the mugger first.

"This is Rachel Sonnshein. I bought one of her pictures at the art show, remember?"

Charlie Gould had bigger fish to fry, but shook Rachel's hand, determined to be friendly.

"Natalie says you're a fine artist," he said.

"And a terrific human being," muttered Rachel, out of the buzz of the martini.

"What?" said Natalie.

"My wife's always muttering," said Seymour swiftly, but Charlie had heard. "Shall we sit down?" Seymour asked, and they found a table.

Seymour leaned forward and Rachel watched his eyes draw across Natalie Gould's hair and skin and silken blouse, and jealousy crept into her heart for the first time. She tried to see Natalie clearly now, to see what Seymour saw, but that was impossible. "There is no such thing as objective reality," thought Rachel. Warm with drink, aching with blood, Rachel asked Charlie Gould whether he believed in objective reality.

"Money is objective reality," said he, and went to fetch another round of drinks.

"How was your trip to Israel?" asked Seymour, who seemed to know all sorts of details about the Goulds' lives.

Natalie Gould waxed enthusiastic about Israel. "I hope you'll soon have an opportunity to make the trip," she said to Rachel. "Don't congregations sometimes send their rabbis to spend a sabbatical in Israel?"

"Not unless they love their rabbi very much," said Seymour.

Charlie Gould had returned. "We'll have to see that they do," he said. He had brought Rachel a wickedly strong drink. She decided that he didn't like her. She could tell that he didn't like her, but was cautious about Seymour. The sort of man who doesn't like women. Rachel didn't like either of them. Natalie wanted to please and Charlie wanted to be honored for what he thought were his gifts. The women who liked Seymour, thought Rachel, always wanted to please her.

Guests were beginning to drift over to their table,

120

now that Seymour and Rachel sat with the Goulds. Charlie leaned back in his chair and talked joshing male talk with the men. He was a member of the Sheep Hollow Country Club and a crack tennis player. Murray Gewirtz stopped by and couldn't find the words to tell Seymour how beautiful the service had been.

"Sorry I missed it," said Charlie Gould. "I had a business appointment this morning. Have to keep my wife in diamonds."

Rachel thought "Horseshit" and took a sip from her second vodka martini. The alcohol rode through her head like a subway train. She was just before getting drunk. She knew she ought to stop, but there was nothing to do but drink; she felt excluded from all the fun. She had tried to say things, but they fell on deaf ears. Debra Gewirtz waltzed by, in the arms of a dashing Italian gangster.

"Hi, Rabbi!" she yelled. "Enjoy, enjoy! Pinch a *tush* or two. You have my permission."

And the band played on.

Rachel excused herself. "I have to go to the bathroom."

"Does the whole world have to know?" said Seymour, with a smile Rachel knew to be false.

"I thought you'd want to know where I was, in case I disappeared."

As she got up, Rachel felt another clot plopping down her vagina. She walked gingerly through the crowd. She went out into the hallway that flanked the terrace and was bright with daylight. She looked out the windows, across the golf course and down to the bay. The view was soothing to her eyes. The sound of the band was muted here. In the airy room at the end of the hallway there were bridge games, mah-jongg games and gin rummy games. A thin line of smoke curled above the players' heads. There was little talk. In the corner a coffee urn percolated, surrounded by porcelain cups. A maid in black uniform sat sleepily beside it, a copy of the day's *Daily News* on her lap. Every room had its attendant. It seemed to Rachel as though the entire staff had been kept on from the time of the original owner. An old gardener raked

121

leaves outside, next to the rose garden and the wisteria vines. No doubt country clubs would soon be the only green and gracious places left in all of suburbia. "Say hurray for the country clubs," said Rachel —drunkenly, she knew.

"Where is the ladies' room?" Rachel asked the maid.

"Upstairs," said the maid, rousing herself to scan the paper again.

Rachel retreated and started up the grand staircase. She began to run when she saw the broad flat steps leading gracefully to the second floor. Her long dress billowed behind her. At the top she was breathless and dizzy, the blood pumping out of her. A long corridor, carpeted in pearl gray, like the stairs, stretched right and left. It was a little spooky, like a hotel. Two discreet signs jutted out from the wall. GENTLEMEN, said one; the other said POWDER ROOM. A matron sat in the powder room as well, crocheting squares for an afghan. A few other guests from the bar mitzvah party were there, touching up the dark around their eyes, talking over the toilet stalls. Rachel found an empty one and sat down, letting the blood flow forth. She felt very dizzy and had to hold herself straight and upright by putting her hands against the metal partitions. She didn't want to go back to the party and have to look at lovely Natalie Gould, all gold and ivory and small delicate bones covered with young skin. No stench, no blood in her pants, no varicose veins.

"Does she really think I'm talented?" thought Rachel. "Wise, experienced, a woman of the world?"

There was a rattle on her door.

"Just a minute," she said and began to put herself back together again. She had to be careful not to let the long robe dip into the toilet bowl.

Rachel washed her hands and looked at her face in the mirror. She looked better than she felt. She was flushed and her lips appeared wet and languid. Neither her dizzy fight with nausea nor her inability to stay with a thought showed on her face. Nothing. It was simply her face in a country club mirror, a little shiny perhaps. Dumb, for the moment. Rachel searched through her purse for money to put in the matron's

122

dish, but she had left her wallet home. There was only a penny in the bottom of the bag and she couldn't leave that. The matron pretended not to notice.

Rachel turned to the right when she came out of the powder room and headed toward what seemed to be a sun porch at the end of the corridor. She needed a breath of fresh air, an open window. There were doors on both sides of the corridor, leading into offices and conference rooms. They were silent and unused on a Saturday in March. One of the doors was halfway open and Rachel peered around it. She had heard what sounded like the scratching of mice but turned out to be a couple locked in the struggle of an embrace. They both wore party clothes. The young man pressed the girl against a heavy mahogany table and she bent stiffly backwards. He covered her face with kisses which she did not resist, though she tried hard to push his hand —plucking at her dress to reach her body—away. But he held her tight, he was the stronger. She said, "No, don't," and he said, "Oh, please," and Rachel watched as though it were taking place on the silver screen.

"Let me go," she said, against his kisses.

"Not now, not now," said he. "I want to get in you, please let me." Furious to assuage his need, he pulled and tore at her dress.

Rachel watched them through the half-open door, uncertain what to do. Perhaps she ought to intervene. She remained in her place, frozen, still, until the couple slipped and slithered in their locked embrace into an armchair (large and cushioned in chintz) and the girl suddenly grew limp and pliant. The young man had lifted her dress—her hands still fluttered to put it down—and was ripping open his pants to let his stiff cock out when he looked up all at once and saw Rachel. "Shit!" he said, and Rachel saw his face too for the first time. It was Bobo Wasserman, son of the Building and House Committee chairman, an apparent fugitive from his TM commune, trying his best to screw Dede Blumenfeld, the tennis champion of Gateshead High. Bobo Wasserman got up, holding shut his pants, and slammed the door in Rachel's face. His

123

own face was full of fury. Rachel stood there, looking at the door, listening to the sounds of their conversation. She could make out no words. But there was the angry clenched sound of Bobo's voice, and Dede's higher-pitched weepy contralto, sounding like water flowing down a rocky bed. When they changed to the whisper of thieves, Rachel remembered where she was and groped her way back down the hall toward the sun room. There was wicker furniture throughout the airy room. With difficulty, she opened a window enough to let some air flow onto her face. She breathed it down in deep drafts, but instead of making her feel better it set her head to spinning more. Below her was a neat bare garden with crocuses and a stand of birches and pines. It was a setting from a Russian novel. The sky above the pointed crowns of the pines was dark with storm clouds and snow was falling in large thick whirling flakes.

Rachel could not focus on the scene, her eyes were full of tears. She lay down for a minute (only just a minute, she thought) on one of the half dozen wicker sofas, and then she heard the voices, close by. She thought that Bobo and Dede had come down to find a more comfortable place to make love, but the voices were stridently angry and used to fighting.

"You always put me down," said the woman's voice. "You put me down in public. I can't stand it anymore."

The voice was familiar. Rachel knew it but, without seeing the face, could not for the moment place it.

"You're a first-class bitch and a whore," said the man's voice, also familiar.

Rachel held her breath, as though she might disappear into a land of private encounters.

"You know all about whores, don't you?"

"I don't parade my sex in public, not at my own son's bar mitzvah."

It was Murray Gewirtz. Of course, thought Rachel, it was a proper script from life. Murray and Debra Gewirtz.

"I wouldn't sink so low as to accuse you in front of

124

a lot of people, put you down where everyone could hear."

"You're the one who makes the scenes, you're the one who starts to argue and scream like a fishwife. The whole world heard you call me a jackass."

"Oh, but you are a jackass. You're lucky I didn't call you worse."

"I'm good enough to have brought you here. It was me who paid for this party of yours. Thousands and thousands so you could show off. What are you showing off? My money, that's what you're showing off."

"Don't pull that shit on me. It's your party too. I see a lot of your crummy friends. You know what I think of those bastards. I told you I've had it with those dreary, vulgar idiots and their boring wives. It's on account of them we have no friends."

"They made all this possible. They made you a lady in a ninety-thousand-dollar house and gave you the pool and the tennis court and your sporty XKE."

"And they all know we're up here, fighting."

"Let them know."

"How can you do this to my kids?"

"*Your* kids?"

Their hysterical voices sounded almost alike. Debra and Murray Gewirtz had the same fight once or twice every week. Their shrill voices seemed to come out of one mouth, the wretched, stale words formed by a single screaming torrent. The words seldom varied; it was the pain and fury that came in new waves, in ever greater strength. The words were insufficient to dole out the mounting anger.

Rachel raised her head from the flowery pillow to see whether she could escape without being seen. A balloon of vertigo burst in her forehead. The Gewirtzes were in a small dark card room next to the sun porch. The main entrance—the door Rachel had entered—was clear. She knew the Gewirtzes wouldn't hear the rustle of her robe if she moved now, they had no ears for sounds beyond their own. But Rachel was not sure whether she could, in her drunken state, navigate the varied spaces between herself and escape. She would

125

have to lift her dress and tiptoe out between the wicker furniture and tables and magazine racks and lamps and ottomans without tripping, and get down the length of the entire hallway without being seen. Clearly, she could not manage it. She kept her eyes on the red poppies and blue cornflowers and white daisies on the cotton duck cushion.

And then quite abruptly, the voices stopped as though a needle had been lifted from a record.

"What is it?" Debra asked, in a voice near to normal.

"What are you doing here?" said Murray, in a hoarse low voice.

A child's voice, crying, said, "I've been looking all over for you. Byron hit me," he wailed.

"Can't stand that child," said Debra fiercely.

"Why did you leave Spencer's party?" cried the child.

"We had to have a private talk," said Murray.

"You came up here to yell at each other," said Blake.

Rachel heard them twitter and shush and bustle out of the card room, angry together now, mad at Byron. It was the last Rachel heard of them. A door fell shut and Rachel was alone again.

She walked slowly back in the direction of the party. As she stood at the top of the great gray-carpeted staircase she thought of Scarlett O'Hara falling down and losing her baby. Rhett's baby. Rachel held on to the bannister with one hand and walked carefully, holding her dress with the other. The noise and the crowd at the bar swallowed her up in dark pain. Bobo and the tennis champ weren't back yet, but the Gewirtzes were having their picture taken, smiling broadly.

"Where in hell have you been?" asked Seymour, alone at the cocktail table. "The Goulds have already gone in to lunch. I asked Natalie to save us two seats." He swallowed some angry words when he saw that Rachel was clearly feeling sick. "What's the matter?"

"I have a terrible headache and I'm nauseous and I'm going to throw up."

"You don't want to stay for lunch?"

126

"I can't."

"Shall I take you home?"

"You'd better, I think."

"You don't mind if I come back?"

"Once I'm safely home I don't care what you do."

Seymour drove Rachel home through the spring snow. It was falling softly now and sticking wetly to the trees. Rachel clenched her jaws and did not get sick in the car. Once home she took three aspirins, pulled the shades down, and slipped into bed. The room began to turn around and around in great arcs before her eyes. Open or shut, it didn't matter, the room was there, cranking around like a carousel. Rachel went to the bathroom and put her finger down her throat and threw up. She threw up once more before the room settled down and she could fall asleep.

Seymour came home just before dark and fixed a pot of strong coffee. When Aaron came in they sat together for a while and talked about everything in life but love.

5

Rachel's appointment with Doctor Fleischer was the day the baseball season opened. Driving her car to his office in New Gateshead, she listened to the radio. The crowd at Shea Stadium was small, and Lindsey Nelson, the announcer, said they looked frozen. It was a cold April day that even the bright sun could not warm.

Seymour had called for the appointment and was visibly nervous on the days preceding it.

"Do you want me to come with you?" he asked, several times.

"No, you'll only make me worry."

Rachel preferred setting out on journeys of discovery alone and without talking. At least without talking about the journey.

Bert Fleischer was a member of Shaare Tefilah, but let it be known that he preferred a more Reformed service. He had, he said, an aversion to the gobbledygook of Orthodoxy. Rachel was not interested in Bert Fleischer's ideas about religion but understood that he found it necessary to talk to her about them. He did it in part to justify the many letters he wrote to the Board of Directors, but also because he believed, sincerely and wholeheartedly, that Rachel was interested. That it was her life, her work, her passion. Bert Fleischer did not bill the rabbi for services rendered. He could never quite remember what it was that Rachel did that was not connected with her being a

128

rebbetzin. Was she a writer? A pianist? He should have written it down on the little cards which he always kept in front of him when Rachel came into his office to see him after the examination. But there was no place for "Occupation" on his patients' cards.

Rachel sat in the waiting room with four other women. The radio played something that was not quite music, perhaps it was Muzak, even though an announcer came on now and then and said something in a mellifluous voice. If every woman took twenty minutes and she was fifth in line, it would be an hour and a half before her turn came. Rachel hoped Doctor Fleischer's partner was in and that there were two of them working the crowd. Three of the women were obviously pregnant and might take less than twenty minutes.

Rachel leafed through the pages of *Vogue*. What a place to indulge your fashion fantasies! If you weren't pregnant, you were probably in mortal fear of your life. Rachel thought the skinny models undoubtedly suffered from anorexia, but she liked to imagine herself in their garments anyway. Many of the clothes she looked at were so outlandish that she vowed not to worry any more about what she wore. Ethnic take-offs were on every page: peasant blouses, dirndl skirts, shawls and caftans. And denim, denim everywhere. Rachel decided that she had been a trend-setter at seventeen when she had gone to Army-Navy stores in the seedier parts of Buffalo to buy Levis and thick gray sweatshirts and surplus Navy pea jackets. All the things you now got at Bloomingdale's. In those days, she and Jackie, her best friend, were the only girls who wore such clothes. It was rumored they were lesbians, but they were merely ahead of their time.

A pasty-faced model with green eyes stared out of the slick pages as though in an opium trance. She wore a robe of many colors from Bendel's. It cost $670. Rachel figured she could damn well continue to wear her African costumes.

The receptionist finally appeared at the door and said, "Mrs. Sonnshein?" Rachel followed her through the maze of halls and cubicles, took the paper cup

129

with her tag on it and went to the bathroom. She left the filled cup on the windowsill and then followed the nurse into the examining room. She got weighed. No surprises there.

"Take off everything but your shoes and socks, put on one of the paper robes and lie down on the examining table. The doctor will be with you in a minute."

Rachel did as she was told. The nurse had rolled a fresh piece of white paper toweling over the table. Above her Rachel saw the familiar fluorescent light. "How well I know those lights," she thought. The ceiling was somewhat discolored and gray. The building was not old, but it was the sort that ages fast— acoustic tile on the ceiling, imitation wood paneling on the walls. The vinyl tile on the floors was peeling up in the corners.

The doctor's gleaming tools were laid out on a white cloth. The water in the sterilizer burbled; the fluorescent light hummed. There was no music here. It would not be difficult to fall asleep if the doctor took his time coming. Rachel always fell asleep to avoid things. Aaron had that habit too. When he was little and got angry he always went straight to his room, slammed the door and got into bed.

"Hello, toots," said Doctor Fleischer. He knew Rachel's name perfectly well, and if he didn't it was right there on the card he held in his hand. "How's it going? How's the rabbi? Tell him I'm sorry I didn't get to hear him at the Gewirtz bar mitzvah. They say he was terrific as always. I had a difficult delivery that morning. I thought I'd see *you* at the party."

"I was bleeding, that's why I'm here today."

"We'll have a look-see soon enough, sweetie."

He drew on his single thin rubber glove. The nurse stood at attention and said nothing. She never said anything except, "Take off everything but your shoes and socks." Doctor Fleischer told Rachel to slide down to the edge of the table and put her feet in the stirrups. Rachel assumed that her sweaty feet were well-protected by shoes and socks and would not send their smell into the doctor's face. Looking bland and slightly

130

simpleminded (Bert Fleischer was considered handsome, but Rachel thought his profile dated and his chin mushy), Doctor Fleischer thrust his gloved and vaselined hand up Rachel's cunt and let it feel around a while. He made little clucking noises. Rachel, always stoic, said nothing. It didn't hurt nor was it particularly uncomfortable. Doctor Fleischer, rummaging around now, his free hand on top of Rachel's abdomen, looked pensive.

"That's quite a fibroid you have there."

"Big, hunh?" said Rachel. The "hunh" was involuntary.

"About the size of a grapefruit." He poked around some more and continued to look pensive. "When was the last time you were here?"

"Last year, I think." His presence in her womb was vaguely uncomfortable when she talked. "What are you going to do about it?" she groaned, not meaning to groan.

"Come into my office and we'll talk about it," said Doctor Fleischer.

He also took a smear for a Pap test and felt her breasts for lumps. Then he disappeared with a smile crooking his face, and the nurse followed him, after giving Rachel a tissue with which to wipe the gook from between her legs. Rachel dressed and went out of the examining room, past several other rooms (the partner's office, closets, more examining rooms, and God knew what kinds of mysterious chambers) and into Bert Fleischer's sunlit office. It was definitely a "masculine" office. Mrs. Fleischer must have chosen the furniture. The armchairs were of leather, the large desk of walnut. There were spiky plants in the window, large bookcases filled with leather-bound medical volumes, an oriental rug, and, of course, diplomas. On the desk were pictures of Mrs. Fleischer and the children, and a little tennis player made of nuts and bolts and screws. On the walls were more pictures of the wife and children. The wife was pretty, the children handsome; everyone was wreathed in smiles. The profusion with which the pictures grew on the office walls

131

seemed, to Rachel, to proclaim as nothing else possibly could that Albert Fleischer, M.D., believed in procreation.

"Your kids keep getting bigger," said Rachel, who couldn't think of anything else to say.

"I've got two in college," and he paused for a tiny moment. "One at Harvard and one at Wellesley."

"That's nice," said Rachel.

"I think my youngest daughter, Beth, is in your son's class at Gateshead High."

Rachel tried to remember if Aaron had ever mentioned her. Surely she was pretty. Rachel tried to figure out which one she was in the pictures on the wall. Probably the one holding the kitten. The one on the left in the tennis court photograph.

There was also a model sailboat on Bert Fleischer's desk. He was shuffling through his index cards.

"How old are you now?"

He asked the same question every year and Rachel always meant to answer "a year older than last time" but didn't. She told Bert Fleischer her age. He asked about her bowel movements. He wanted to know if she had headaches. How often did she get up to void at night? Rachel rather enjoyed his questions. She described her nocturnal pissing habits minutely. Doctor Fleischer wrote and wrote. Rachel noticed that his hairline was receding. She hoped he wouldn't get a hairpiece. It would make his face look even mushier.

"Well, toots, I'm afraid it's bad news about that fibroid of yours. Has your period been rough?"

Rachel described it in dramatic detail.

"How large are the clots? Size of a quarter? A half dollar?"

"Well," said Rachel, "they're not always round."

He was on Rachel's favorite territory. She told him all he wanted to know, and more. As she was talking she realized how much of her life had lately been arranged around her periods. It wouldn't do to plan something good, like a Sunday doubleheader, right in the middle of one of those bloodbaths.

"I think, honey, the time has come to do that

132

hysterectomy." He looked at her with his big brown eyes. "I hope it's not a shock to you, but we'll only do a partial. You can keep the ovaries. You'll be as good as new. No problems. What do you say?"

He couldn't have imagined that Rachel would greet the news with pleasure.

"Thank God. No more menstrual cramps, no more bloodshed. No more diaphragm."

"I wish all my patients had that attitude," said Doctor Fleischer.

"I'm not a *kvetch*," said Rachel. It was not entirely true, but it made her feel momentarily superior to all the *kvetches*. "I expect to live to a ripe old age. I'm going to become a famous painter—why should I worry about my uterus? Tell me when you want to take it out."

Doctor Fleischer looked through his calendar. "How about the end of the month sometime? I have to check with the hospital."

"As long as it doesn't conflict with Pesach," said Rachel. "We're supposed to go to Buffalo for the *sedorim*."

"The what?"

"The *sedorim*. That's the plural of *seder*. You do know what a *seder* is?"

"My Hebrew is virtually nonexistent, but yes, I know what a *seder* is. We went to the Reform temple in New Rochelle when I was growing up, and read our little thing at the bar mitzvah in English. I've explained it to Seymour several times. I get the creeps when I have to listen to all that crying and shaking they have at the synagogue here. It's barbaric. I've always said that if I wanted to pray the way my grandfather did, I'd go to Williamsburg. Seymour is a bright guy and liberal too, why doesn't he modernize the service a little?"

"It's not entirely up to him."

Rachel had been studying her pocket calendar. She didn't feel like talking about Bert Fleischer's upwardly-mobile religiosity, nor did she particularly want to explain Seymour's rabbinic convictions.

133

"Pesach ends three weeks from tomorrow," she said. "We'll do it the Monday after," said Bert Fleischer.

Rachel went out to the waiting room to get her coat. There were eight women now. "Next," said the receptionist, as Doctor Fleischer, smiling gaily, went back down the hall to the examining room. "Hi, toots!" Rachel heard him say, just before he closed the door.

Rachel turned the car radio on again. It was the seventh inning; the Mets were behind. Seaver had been taken out. Almost all the fans had left. In Gateshead the sun was shining brightly. The shadows were long only in the few hollows behind the bluffs that rose high over the bay. It was April, delicate, lovely April. Every day the colors in the landscape seemed to change from winter shades to the softer pinks, greens and browns of spring. The forsythia was in bloom; its brilliant yellow flowers erupted against the still muted tones of other plants. Here and there the greens had turned strong and vivid.

Rachel passed the little park next to the ball field on top of Gateshead's highest hill. It had been part of a large estate whose owner had willed it to the town in the early years of the century. Next to the harbor, it was her favorite spot. When she wandered there, Rachel could pretend that she was no longer in the suburbs but in some more civilized place. The day was so full of spring's light and gentle airs that Rachel decided to walk a while before returning home. She wondered whether she ought to be thinking about the hysterectomy. Was there something wrong with her that she saw it not as a deprivation but a liberation? It said in Ecclesiastes that there was a time for everything, there was a time to have children (did it say that?) and a time for not having them; taking out the womb was merely hastening the time of not having children. Rachel did not think of herself as unnatural. A little eccentric perhaps, but not unnatural. Why did she grate on the nerves of both the feminists and the suburban housewives? She might discuss that with Sally one day.

Rachel walked down the macadam path between the still dark pines and the gray trunks of the ancient red

134

beeches. The pond below her was alive with orange and speckled goldfish.

She would have to tell her mother about the operation, and the news would travel through her mother's circle in Buffalo. Imagine the wagging tongues if she had cancer. She hadn't thought about cancer in a long time. When her work was going well she rarely thought about it. A row of willow trees bent toward the flat surface of the pond. Two swans glided imperially beneath the delicately drooping branches.

In the field beyond the honeysuckle-covered fence a baseball game was in progress. Rachel could not resist. She ducked through an old hole in the fence and strolled over to the bleachers behind third base. It was a pick-up game. The boys were thirteen, maybe fourteen years old. They had not as yet solidified into men. They played with an old hardball, for the fun of it. For spring. Rachel sat down on one of the wooden boards as she so often did in summer, but it was still too cold to be sitting there, especially toward evening, with the sun sliding down the hills beyond the bay. It wasn't summer yet. Just wait, just wait.

Rachel climbed down. The ball—thrown from the outfield, past the pitcher and way to the left of the catcher—rolled at her feet. She bent casually (as though she were not a fortyish woman, carrying a pocketbook and wearing a well-cut flannel pants suit) and picked up the ball. It was scuffed and worn, the thread holding the seams together no longer red. Rachel cocked her arm back and threw the ball to the pitcher. "Thank you, lady," he said.

Didn't he see how good she was? Didn't he notice she didn't throw like a girl?

Rachel followed the left-field foul line out of the park. She looked back once or twice, saw the kids do their small nervous dances waiting for the ball, saw the batter tap the plate with his bat in one hand, choke up on it like Felix Millan, saw the runner leading off first, crouching low, the way he'd seen Lou Brock do it.

Rachel walked slowly back to the car and drove home. Soon it would be spring. Really spring.

135

"Where in hell were you?" said Seymour. "I've been worried about you. I even called the doctor's office, and they said you'd left over an hour ago. Bert told me he was going to operate. Are you all right? What have you been doing?"

"Watching a ball game."

"The Mets lost, Mom," said Aaron.

"I know, I was listening on the radio. Did Seaver get the loss?"

"Didn't you know I'd be worried about you?" asked Seymour.

"Whatever for?"

"Hearing about the operation. Not coming home."

"I'm fine. Delighted. I'd hoped for such news."

"Hysterectomies are the most often performed needless operations," said Aaron.

"Yeah, I know."

"Are you going to get another opinion, Mom?"

"Is that what I'm supposed to do?"

"Always."

"I hope you didn't discuss that in Health. If all the doctors' children in your class go home and tell their parents, the school board will have a riot on its hands. By the way, do you know Beth Fleischer?"

"She's a cunt."

"Not bad for the daughter of a gynecologist."

Seymour sighed and ran his fingers through his hair. "Be serious," he said.

"I am," said Rachel. "You need a haircut."

"When does he want to operate?" asked Seymour.

"They'll let me know. Sometime after we come back from Buffalo."

Seymour sighed again. "I'll fix a martini."

"You're taking it harder than Mom."

Aaron stood in the door to the kitchen, looking at his father, then down at the floor. He was holding his schoolbooks. There was mud on his shoes. He turned to his mother suddenly.

"You haven't got cancer? Have you?"

He had found the words difficult to enunciate. He was as frightened of saying them as he was of the idea

136

they expressed. Rachel saw him standing there, uncertain, scared, defiant. He was stepping out of childhood but he still stood between it and the larger world of manhood. He wanted reassurance, he did not want his terrible words to hold the truth.

"What a nonsensical question!" said Seymour. "Where did you get such an idea?"

Aaron wavered. "I don't know." He was afraid that he had merely been foolish. He was still a child. "I just asked."

"It's only fibroids," said Rachel. "The size of a grapefruit. I looked it up in the encyclopedia. They are almost never malignant."

"I'm glad," said Aaron, and kissed his mother on the head, unbidden.

Seymour smiled. "Your mother will be around for a while."

But Rachel felt a small chill of fear. The idea had been articulated. It took its place in her mind. You never knew.

They had decided to drive to Buffalo and left early on the morning of the first *seder*. It was not yet daylight. Gateshead slept in pale mist, beautiful in an innocence few ever saw. The house was in order and the real-estate agents had a set of keys; Sol Wasserman had seen to that. The suitcases were packed and included a new black-covered sketchbook. Just in case. They would be gone no more than five days, but Rachel wanted to feel that she was always prepared to work.

Seymour drove the convertible and Aaron slept in the back seat. Rachel was sleepy and glum because it was early morning and she didn't as yet feel entirely alive. She preferred to be left alone with her view of the misty landscape. Seymour switched on the radio and its sound set up the space for each to crawl into his own thoughts. Rachel's mind wandered, as it usually did, between the landscape and her dreams of immortality.

"Full moon," said Rachel.

137

"It's the fourteenth of Nissan—Passover."

"We're so far removed from the moon and the seasons."

"What do you want me to do about it?" asked Seymour.

"Nothing, I was just thinking."

"How do you feel?" he asked, but it seemed to Rachel to be a routine question.

"Fine," she said, giving a routine answer. She was due to menstruate again, soon. For the last time ever. Could it possibly be malignant? Rachel teased herself with fear.

They were on the approach to the Throgs Neck Bridge. Queens was silent, asleep. Here and there a garbage truck wheezed through the street, below the pale orbs of the streetlights. Rachel closed her eyes. She was tired—the single cup of black coffee had not been enough to wake her before dawn. But closing her eyes was like stepping into a prison cell—she felt a pang of desperation when she couldn't see what passed outside. Rachel opened her eyes and looked into the night. The moon had come from behind her veil, and the shattered Bronx emerged in its light. Exit to Yankee Stadium (how long since she'd been there?). Last Exit in the Bronx. The Harlem River. Yeshiva University. Washington Heights. Last Exit Before Bridge. Indeed, the mighty Hudson. It looked magical from the Bridge, glinting in the moonlight. The houses along its banks were invisible, shrouded in darkness to merge with the cliffs. It was now as it might have been long long ago, wild and majestic: a moonlit ribbon between wooded bluffs and palisades. The moon kept appearing in different places, as though it were jumping around in the sky. Now it was visible through the girders of the bridge, now through the windshield directly to the right, now through the gaps between the trees. The Palisades Parkway was lined with trees.

Rachel glimpsed the dark eastern bank of the Hudson sharp-edged with cities. Yonkers. Where Ben lived. No, he didn't live in Yonkers at all, what had made her think that? Long Beach. It was Long Beach. Near the

138

ocean. The visit to his grandmother's house in Yonkers. Rachel let her Ben memories flick through her mind and lost herself in them. The ride to Yonkers, the walk from the railroad station, the old lady's two-family house. Rachel had thought that the visit established a new bond between her and Ben, made a bridge between the Ben of the San Remo and the Ben who had a personal history, a family, a photo album, closets full of old skates, bubblegum cards, records. But then Ben resented her for having glimpsed it at all. Ben waiting for her at 116th Street and Broadway, Ben on the bed in his small room on Thompson Street, where it was always night. She saw herself knotted in the gray sheets, saw Ben sleeping, unshaven, his straight hair sticking out in every direction, like trampled grass (like Stan Laurel's). The morning's anxiety (no one knew where she was), the thoughts of home and parents, Seymour at his summer job. She had felt dry-mouthed and guilty, a little scared to be where she was. An abyss yawned from the dirty sheets, and she would have to carry Ben's anxieties as well. She turned to fit herself against him, her head beneath his arm. He turned away and mumbled a name she did not know.

When Rachel woke up the sky was paling in the east and they were on the New York State Thruway somewhere in the Catskills. Aaron was awake too, sitting on the back seat with his knees drawn up to his chest. Neither he nor Rachel wanted to talk. Seymour was mesmerized by the road. The radio had drifted to a local station playing polkas at dawn. The sky grew lighter and lighter. The sun burst upon the Hudson Valley with breathtaking suddenness. Over the local radio station came the sounds of cheerful announcers selling cars, giving weather reports.

"It's beginning to seem like upstate, like home. We've lost WQXR. It's a different country," said Rachel.

"Do you want to go back?" asked Seymour.

"What do you mean?"

"I hear there's a job opening up in Rochester."

139

"Rochester?"

"Yeah. The big conservative congregation there is looking for a rabbi."

"Rochester? Why would anyone want to go to Rochester? Buffalo is bad enough," Aaron piped up.

"If I don't have a job in Gateshead, kid, we'll have to go wherever I can find one."

Aaron kept silent.

"Are you really worried about the contract?" asked Rachel.

"I hear rumors. There's a whole clique around Sol Wasserman trying to get me fired."

"Why don't you give up the rabbi racket, Dad?"

"And what would I do, Aaron?"

"There must be something else you're good at."

"When you find out what it is, let me know."

The further they drove the more wintry it got. The sky was a milky white, the sun rose higher, the land grew flatter. They had passed Albany and were heading west. The radio slipped from one city to another. Utica. The beer signs kept changing too.

They arrived in Buffalo a little after 1:00 P.M.

"Where are we going first?" asked Aaron.

"To Grandma Betty's house. We're staying at your father's old homestead, so we have to go see *my* parents first so there'll be no complaints."

"It's not so bad once you get there," said Aaron, "but I always dread the arrival."

The day was brilliant—in an upstate sort of way. The clouds hung much higher in the sky here than they did on Long Island. There were still stashes of snow. The houses were broader, the streets straighter, and there were sidewalks alongside them. *This* was home, the place to which Rachel could never return all in one piece. She saw that the Engles' house at the corner had been painted. Behind it, where once had stood a venerable mansion, the land was cleared and a small office building was going up. When she was a child, the mystery of the mansion had always been in her mind. She would sneak into the bushes to observe the formal garden parties. Later, when that family had dwindled and the garden had grown slovenly, Rachel

140

would try to catch a look through the windows, just before dark. An old man lived there, with his housekeeper; he was a staid Buffalo burgher. But he owned —and they were the cause of Rachel's fascination—a series of very large paintings, all of them copies of well-known baroque masterpieces. Rachel saw them through the tall windows and wondered what it would be like to live in such grandeur. (She didn't discover that they were copies until she was in college and was shown the originals.) She recalled, even now, a wonderful Rubens hunting scene, and imagined that she could smell the phlox in the summer garden.

They drove into the driveway of her parents' house and Rachel heaved a theatrical sigh. Seymour looked at her and at Aaron and for a moment they were held in a common bond of interchanged glances and they all smiled at each other and said "Courage!" and Rachel said, "Let's be cheerful, we won't be here very long."

Betty Diamant had been watching for her daughter all morning. She worried about accidents, fires, drownings and mid-air collisions, though she didn't like to admit to it. She did not want to be known as that kind of mother. Consequently, she had sat at her desk since breakfast (it commanded a clear view of the street) writing letters and paying bills. When she saw the car pull up in her driveway, she did not hurry down to greet the children. They were safe now; she could afford to be casual.

Betty Diamant and Donella, her maid, had done most of the cooking the night before for the second *seder*. They had also made a nutcake for the first *seder,* which was to be held at the Sonnsheins'. "I can't come empty-handed," Betty had said to Sadie Sonnshein, Seymour's mother. Had Sadie decided to take up the cudgel she would have insisted on bringing something to the Diamant *seder* as well, but competitiveness in the kitchen was not her style. Donella sat at the kitchen table, reading a newspaper and keeping her ears open for the sound of the children's car. She had worked for the Diamants for thirty-seven years and there were things she and Betty Diamant had told one

141

another that they confided in no one else. The two women both came from the South (from Richmond, Virginia, and Winston-Salem, North Carolina), and Rachel's mother often said, "We understand each other." Rachel used to bristle when she heard that and accuse her mother of condescension. But she discovered it to be the truth. The two women *did* understand each other. They even fought like sisters and sometimes didn't speak for days.

Donella carried herself with a grace that is peculiar to heavy women. She had always been beautiful but never pretty, and no one had ever spoiled her, though she had been loved. Her blackness was as little of a burden to her as blackness can ever be. She understood the white world (the way Jews had once—before they thought they could *be* them—understood Gentiles) and kept her own family safe, out of range of the clucking sympathy that passed for comprehension among the white folks. She didn't expose her sons to the burning heat of white betterment. They didn't accept jobs cleaning the yard or washing windows in the Diamants' neighborhood. Donella never offered their services, and when a neighbor asked if she knew a boy who could help to rake leaves after school (they always said "help" as though they meant to lend a hand) she politely said no.

Betty Diamant and Donella met at the front door. Rachel saw the two faces—like the moon, like the sun —behind the storm door, and her love for them mingled with the old embarrassment, with the concern that something might have gone wrong since she last saw them, and with the edgy expectation of criticism. "You look tired," her mother said, often as not. "You putting on some weight?" Donella asked, sure to know that Rachel would say "I hope not" and think about it the whole time she was there.

Rachel was home. She knew that her assurance, her sense of being an adult, responsible and capable in every sense, would vanish as soon as she crossed the threshold. She gave herself over to being a child again as soon as she stepped out of the car and saw that she had been seen. She waved and the two women waved

142

back. Donella opened the storm door and Rachel felt the familiar catch in her throat, seeing the two sturdy pairs of legs, the two ample bosoms. Oh yes, she was home, and it was going to be good to be loved a little with the love of women. She missed it, now and then, she realized, and walked more quickly toward the house.

The two women embraced her, embraced Seymour, embraced Aaron. They held her a little tighter. She felt their cheeks softly on her own. They began to chatter. Rachel looked around to see if anything had changed since the summer before when they had been home last. It was the same as ever. Thank God.

"Let me look at you," said Betty Diamant. "I do believe you look a little tired."

"We've been traveling since four A.M.," said Rachel. "Of course I'm tired."

"Leave the child alone," said Donella.

The two women always jockeyed for first place in Rachel's heart. Rachel was the middle child, a girl between two brothers. The women brought her different offerings. They had always wanted to warn her of the limitations of womanhood, and had been appalled when she ran with the boys. Rachel was not the girl-child her mother had dreamt of having, and Donella despaired of her hard-headed ways. Betty wanted to make a lady out of her, but Donella taught her to be strong without being hard. (Donella had had the right idea.)

They had bacon-lettuce-and-tomato sandwiches for lunch. "I know you don't get these at home," said Betty Diamant. Donella had baked the pecan pie that Rachel loved. Rachel felt herself being pried away from Seymour and Aaron in a most subtle way. They were treated politely, from a little distance away. Betty Diamant thought that men and boys had much the biggest share of the world's treasures, and she was forever making it up to Rachel.

The families gathered early for the *seder* at the Sonnsheins'. The children wore their best clothes. They looked as though they came from a long line of distinguished ancestors. Buffalo was an old-fashioned

143

town and it was deemed appropriate to instill a conservative sense of dress and deportment in one's children. A conservative sense of noblesse oblige also attended the relationship between the races in these circles. The black women, Donella and Opal (the Sonnsheins' maid), supervised the kitchen and the two helpers they had brought with them. Opal was thin, like Seymour's mother, but they shared no other common bond. Mrs. Sonnshein despised housework and Opal's strength lay in being indispensable rather than comradely. The two never worked side by side. Sadie Sonnshein paid most handsomely; Opal had no complaints on that score.

The fathers stood above such matters. Both Milton Sonnshein and Saul Diamant were of the generation of Jews born in this country of immigrant parents. Both were self-made men who believed (though they might deny it) that a woman's place was in the home. Milton Sonnshein was the businessman, Saul Diamant the professor. They did not often come together, but when they did they were cordial and found subjects on which they could talk and agree. Milton Sonnshein had taken over the management of a small laundry in 1924 and created a vast linen service from it. He supplied diapers when diapers were still made of cloth and had to be washed. Now, his business provided bed linens to hospitals, motels, and college dormitories. Saul Diamant was a professor of chemistry at the state university. He was a portly man who had worn a crewcut most of his life. He liked to say that the winds of fashion did not blow through his hair. He was respected in his field, and due to retire from the university before long. Rachel wondered how he would settle into retirement; he loved teaching, and his students adored him. At home he kept his children rather at a distance. Rachel thought that she had inherited her mother's smile-covered determination and her father's solitary, self-righteous cast of mind. Only God knew where her talent, such as it was, came from.

Seymour, Rachel, and their siblings had grown up together in the bland fifties, in casual friendship. They met each other all the time—at the Temple, at the

144

Jewish country club, and in school. The parents and their generation were mostly native-born. They came from Buffalo or from the nearby smaller towns and formed a Jewish professional and business elite. Though not yet as snobbish as the German Jews, they aspired to a comparable style. They meant their lives to be filled with symphony concerts and good works, and, on the whole, they were.

Seymour and Rachel had been among the few in their crowd to leave the well-worn paths and seek their fortunes in other than conventional ways. It was usually only the misfits who moved away, or those with ambitions too large to be contained by their hometown. Since neither Rachel nor Seymour seemed to belong in those categories, people were hard put to explain why they had chosen to be different. In Seymour's case, some said it was the Holocaust. Others blamed his heart murmur or went so far as to say he hated his father. It was, in most cases, only the poor Jews—those who hadn't made it in America—who let their sons go off to become rabbis. And bragged about it, yet.

As for Rachel, it was said that she had always been solitary and "artistic"; it was a mystery what she might do. People called her "idealistic," too—whatever *that* was supposed to mean. (Rachel thought it probably meant that she wanted to give her money to the poor and wipe their children's snotty noses with her mother's linen handkerchiefs. Saul Diamant had always been careful not to give her too much spending money.) In any case, the good Jews of Buffalo shook their heads. They thought Seymour and Rachel an odd couple.

Seymour's sister Claire was married to a doctor. She was pretty and had the same dark curly hair as her brother. She never told the truth. Not that she was a liar, she merely invented stories, most often in order to explain why the things she set her mind and heart to never turned out quite right. She was full of schemes and projects that came to naught. She had three children and had aborted four times. She had wanted to be an actress, a dancer, a writer. She dreamed of success in each of these fields, but her small talent was not

145

nourished by single-mindedness or hard work. She imagined herself adored (she was) and applauded (she was not) and parlayed a summer with a local repertory group and an appearance at the Y.M.H.A. into the dream of a career. She spent an hour a day keeping a journal and took dance classes three times a week.

Bill Gardener, Claire's husband, was the son of a tailor named Goldberg, who owned a number of apartment houses in the Polish section of town. Bill had pursued Claire single-mindedly, the way he pursued his profession. He was a surgeon and most happy in the operating room. Though he felt comfortable in this house—his father-in-law recognized his talent and was grateful to him for keeping Claire in good clothes and reasonably good spirits—he was impatient with social obligations and despised all the hours not spent in cutting diseased flesh or in pursuit of some other equally clear, starkly defined goal. He recognized something resembling his own passion in Rachel, but he did not like her—never had.

Rachel's brothers, Michael and David, had always, it seemed to her, been inhabitants of a strange country. That it was *she* who was the foreigner had occurred to her only very recently. David, the older, was a lawyer; Michael had a small business. He had studied chemistry, like his father, but his bent was more practical than theoretical, and so he came to market his skills rather than teach them to others. Both boys had always been serious. Rachel found them dull; she could not forgive them their lack of humor. They appeared to be good husbands and fathers, but their wives were nervous and in frequent need of counseling. Rachel had little patience with her sisters-in-law. She would not have been surprised (had they been members of Seymour's congregation) to meet them in his office, looking sad. And yet, and yet—that upstate conservative sense of substance and style (not to be confused with political conservatism) which clung to these families kept its hold on Elaine and Peggy Diamant as well. They were hospital volunteers and active in a multitude of good causes, both civic and Jewish, and had

146

worked for McGovern in 1972. Their roots were in Buffalo. Rachel had known them all her life. When she thought about them (rather than when she was with them and impatient) she found them, at one and the same time, more generous and more tragic than the women of Shaare Tefilah, whom they superficially resembled.

Gert Sonnshein, Seymour's spinster aunt, had also been invited. She was always and eternally grateful for signs of human affection and brought handmade objects as gifts. Sadie, her sister-in-law, hid them from view the very next day or gave them to Opal, the maid. Gert knew this but voiced no complaints.

The children in the family all sat at one end of the immense table. They waited, patiently or impatiently, depending on their age, to find out why this night, different from all other nights, deserved their homage. Rachel saw Aaron in earnest conversation with one of David's twins and wondered what they had found to talk about. Aaron usually sighed that his cousins were behind the times and talked about strange sports and even stranger teams.

These then were the people assembled for the *seder*. Rachel felt that they had tried hard to put all their irritations aside. The air was crackling with good will. Great bunches of daffodils had been set on the tables, the full moon hung white and flat over the city and was visible to all the Jews of Buffalo who cared to look up that night when they opened the door for Elijah, the prophet.

There was a brief discussion as to who should lead the *seder*. "My son the rabbi, who is a pro," said Milton Sonnshein, but Seymour declined, saying, "It's *your* house, Dad, it's up to you." This small exchange took place every year. Seymour always offered the prize to his father with grace. Rachel was touched by this. She knew that Milton Sonnshein was vain about his resonant voice and fancied himself a born leader, an organizer.

Rachel saw them all as figures in a large painting. Of course it was the model for the Last Supper, but here it was at once more involved—compositionally

147

and psychologically—and simpler than that. The faces around the table were grave reflections of individual lives. They were not participants in a miracle but actors in an ancient play, dressed for modern times.

Milton Sonnshein sat, a large pillow stuffed behind him, a black velvet *yarmulke* on his head, and looked with affection at his relatives. He chanted the *Kiddush* first. Donella stood near the sideboard, beside the kitchen door. She took a quick drink of wine from a kitchen glass when *Kiddush* was said, and then brought the pitcher of water, the bowl and towel for the washing of hands. Milton Sonnshein poured the water over his hands and looked questioningly at his son. "The *karpas*," said Seymour, and green parsley was passed around and dipped in salt water. Milton Sonnshein broke the *afikomen* from the matzohs before him and placed it behind his pillow. Donella later went to hide it, choosing a moment when the children's attention was elsewhere. Milton Sonnshein read the Hebrew when he could, and switched to English when he had to. Rachel looked up from her *Haggadah* every once in a while to smile at Aaron, down among the children, the handsomest of them all.

The Four Questions were recited several times, to give all those who wanted to be heard (every one of the children attended Hebrew school) a chance at them. Parents and grandparents beamed. Donella stayed at her post beside the kitchen door and paid close attention to the chanting. She knew the Four Questions herself by now and mouthed the lilting Hebrew silently, prompter and dark angel both. Rachel saw her as a hierarchic figure in a mosaic. Opal sat in the kitchen, minding her own business, occupied with her Bible, which she carried always in her handbag.

Milton Sonnshein read the answers to the Four Questions with zeal, in English. He told about the wicked, the wise, the simple and the as-yet-inarticulate son. He did it all with a fine sense of drama.

Rachel noticed that her father did not wear a *yarmulke*. He was the only male who didn't, but nobody had made an issue of it. Saul Diamant followed his

148

own logic. He never drew attention to himself, but you always knew he was there. To Rachel he appeared like Joseph in paintings of the Nativity. Joseph, busy with his carpentry in the triptych at the Cloisters, by the Master of Flémalle, building his mousetrap.

Milton Sonnshein read the story of the Exodus from Egypt with evident relish. It was obviously his favorite part. Rachel remembered that he had stopped once, right in the middle of the telling, and explained that he always envisioned his father's flight from the Czar's Russia in just this way. "Except," he said, "the desert was a snow-covered plain and the Egyptians were Cossacks." Rachel saw her father-in-law as a king in Israel: Solomon greeting the Queen of Sheba in Piero's Arezzo frescoes.

"And the Egyptians' evil entreated us, and afflicted us, and laid on us hard servitude. And we cried unto the Lord, the God of our fathers and the Lord heard our voice and saw our affliction and our toil and our oppression. And the Lord brought us out of Egypt with a mighty hand and with an outstretched arm and with great terror and with signs and with wonders."

Donella breathed out a small "Amen."

Rachel saw Sadie Sonnshein wince at Donella's spontaneous rejoinder. She had never particularly liked her mother-in-law. At this moment she detested her. Sadie was self-indulgent and mean, a caricature by Goya, one of his idiot royal family, a simple woman filled with malice.

"These are the ten plagues which the Holy One (blessed be He) brought upon the Egyptians in Egypt, to wit: BLOOD, FROGS, LICE, BEASTS, MURRAIN, BOILS, HAIL, LOCUSTS, DARKNESS, THE SLAYING OF THE FIRST-BORN."

Milton Sonnshein took a drop of wine on his finger as he read each of the plagues, letting it drip onto his plate.

Seymour looked pleasantly removed from the evening's proceedings. It seemed to Rachel that he had made his peace with his father (if only his mother would let it stand) and was no more bothered by the *mishpoche* than by a swarm of summer moths batting

149

against a sturdy screen. It had not always been like that. The disdain with which his parents had greeted his choice of profession had filled him with bitterness and rage. For years he had played the martyr (St. Sebastian, full of arrows). He had changed only recently. It was as if he had severed all connections, decided at last that his life was his own. Rachel, who knew his moods better than anyone, saw him in a variety of ways. Sometimes he was like the figure on an Ottonian crucifix, tonight he was more like Rembrandt's young David, playing for Saul.

Time for the *Dayenu*. The members of the family came to attention, the children squealed with happiness. Grandpa Milt said, "Let's all join in and sing together. Seymour will be the leader."

And Seymour led the singing, without having to pay much mind to it, for he knew it by heart.

Rachel looked at her brothers and saw them yawn. Michael was surreptitious about it, David was not. Their faces were like those in a crowd: saints of small magnitude, spectators at an enthronement, a funeral. David and Seymour had once been friends, back in high school, but their friendship had come undone over the years. David distrusted Seymour, thinking him spiritual. He had told Rachel as much. But he admired *her;* she was tough. Michael, on the other hand, loved David, to whom things came easily. Rachel saw him defer to David; perhaps he figured some of the gold would rub off on him. Michael did nothing right. His business was not spectacular. He did not prosper.

They said a psalm of praise together. "Let us then sing before him a new song: Hallelujah!" The voices did not ring in unison. The reading was ragged. Seymour's voice was the strongest, his father's the loudest. Claire read with feeling, as though she were doing Blanche in *A Streetcar Named Desire*. Rachel found her beautiful but was frightened by a certain glitter, a laugh too shrill, the effect of too frequent changes in her style. She imagined her face ripped off a subway-station poster, to reveal another, and another . . .

"Praised art thou, Lord God, King of the Universe, Creator of the fruit of the vine." Milton Sonnshein

150

made the blessing both in English and in Hebrew. Donella had refilled the glasses with wine. They all drank the second cup and then Milton Sonnshein washed his hands again.

The *Hillel* sandwich was prepared, the bitter herbs eaten with the matzoh and with the sweet *charoset*. It was time for the meal to begin.

"It's so nice that we're all together," said Betty Diamant. She always dealt with the thing at hand. Rachel knew that she savored all she saw around her, noted all the details and spread her love and criticism equally among children and grandchildren. She gave a name to all things and saw unhappiness as a sign of weakness. She was lovely and stately, in the manner of Veronese.

Donella and her helpers brought in the fish and then the soup. Opal was an excellent cook and had long since mastered the secrets of Jewish cuisine. Sadie Sonnshein never went into the kitchen except to see that it was clean and to check that nothing was missing. It was after eight o'clock and everyone was hungry. Rachel looked around and the pictorial possibilities of the scene struck her full force. During the reading of the *Haggadah* she had studied everyone by the light of the candles and the crystal chandelier. She had noticed their gestures and observed how stylized they might become. Now she thought about doing a large painting. The idea excited her. It would be a group portrait, a combination of the Last Supper and a host of other meals. Why not? Rachel saw the faces around her stilled, monumental as in Piero, flattened against the bright patterns of their clothes and the shapes of the foods and the vessels before them.

"Did you bring a camera?" she asked Seymour.

"You want to take pictures?" her father-in-law, who heard everything, asked.

"I'd love to," said Rachel, eating a matzoh ball. It was soft and large and floated in the pale yellow soup, among green flakes of parsley. The painting would have to have food in it, cups of wine and hard-boiled eggs. The delineation of simple objects was all Breughel; as the meal progressed it would become entangled,

151

sloppy, would become all Jordaens. Leftover food on the plates, half-eaten potatoes.

"Never mind," said Seymour. "We'll take pictures later." He tried to catch Rachel's eye, but she knew it and would not look at him.

"I'd like to have one of everyone around the table," said Rachel.

"You're crazy," said Michael.

"You'll disturb the entire company," said Betty Diamant.

"Go up in our bedroom, Aaron," said Grandpa Milton, "and look for the Polaroid for your mother. It's in my closet, I think," he shouted after him.

Elaine and Peggy, the sisters-in-law, looked at each other. They both thought Rachel ought not always to have her way.

Aaron brought the Polaroid down.

"You're going to discommode everyone," said Rachel's mother.

"You don't have to do anything, pay no attention to me."

"That's the story of your life," said Michael.

Rachel did not begin to think of Michael's bitter crack until later. She stood on a chair in the corner.

"Be careful," said her mother-in-law, and Rachel obediently took off her shoes and stood on the cushion in her stockinged feet. She took one picture. Everyone was stiff. She had not been able to get them all in.

"Relax!" she cried, and took another. This one had Donella in it, clearing away the plates. Donella was the only one who didn't seem to mind the picture-taking.

"Are you finished?" asked Michael.

"Just go on with what you're doing," said Rachel. She persevered and got six pictures in all. They had to be passed around for everyone to see. Now that they had been taken and were actually visible, it was agreed that it had been an excellent idea.

"Don't forget they're mine," said Rachel.

"You won again," Michael told her.

Once Rachel was home and found her family reacting to her in their prickly ways she fell into the role of

152

slightly spoiled brat. Not that she actually saw herself in the role—she simply assumed it was expected of her and so she obliged.

Chicken in wine, with almonds, was served. Sliced carrots and green asparagus added their color to the table. Mounds of potato *kugel* steamed on the china platters. Milton Sonnshein talked about business. He let no scrap of conversation go by without attending to it.

"How's your congregation?" he asked his son.

"Fine," said Seymour. "How should it be?"

"I understand rabbis always have trouble," said his father-in-law.

"We have to move, is all," said Rachel. "They are selling the house."

"That charming place?" said her mother.

"It's what comes from being dependent on a bunch of jerks," said Milton Sonnshein. "I always warned you about that."

Seymour made a face at Rachel. His father hadn't noticed.

"You become a rabbi, you have to learn to beg," said Grandpa Milt.

"We're not begging," said Rachel. "It's just that I like the house."

"Buy it then."

There was a pause. Milton Sonnshein looked directly at Rachel, but it was his son he had challenged.

"I can't do anything until I know whether I'll stay there," said Seymour. He continued to look with hard annoyance at Rachel. Sweat had suddenly formed on his palms and the nape of his neck. Rachel pretended to be involved with a drumstick.

"Is there a chance you won't?" said Milton Sonnshein.

"There's *always* a chance I won't. How did we get on this subject anyway?"

Seymour's Aunt Gert, trying to be a help by changing the topic of conversation, directed a tentative, quavering question his way.

"Do they have urban renewal down your way?" she said.

153

"Not yet," said Seymour, grateful to the absurd old lady. "What's new is considered pretty, what's old is historical."

"You wouldn't believe what goes on in this town," said Gert. "It's become a jungle."

"There's no future in the cities," said Grandpa Milt, who had opinions on everything and felt he deserved the last word.

"Where you live is nice," said his sister. "Where I live is a desert."

"A jungle or a desert? Make up your mind," said Milton Sonnshein. "It's a fact that more people live in the suburbs today, or the southwest. People are moving to the Sunbelt. Soon we'll all be Texans."

"The suburbs are hotbeds of reaction," said Rachel. "Most of the people who live there don't give a shit about anything. They spend millions for snowblowers and don't want a cent to go toward welfare." She was glad to be able to preach a little social gospel.

"I don't think you need to use such language," said Betty Diamant. "You didn't used to."

"She's never been delicate as I recall," said Michael.

"You want to start telling people how they can spend their money?" asked Bill Gardener.

"A country that doesn't look out for its poor deserves a revolution."

"My daughter-in-law, the armchair Marxist," said Grandpa Milton.

"The congregation must love you," said David.

Rachel was enjoying the stir she had caused.

"I think Rachel deserves a lot of credit," said Gert. "She wasn't raised to be a rebbetzin." Gert thought it was her duty to prevent the spread of dissension.

"Why must you argue, Rachel?" said Betty Diamant. "You'd think we could all find something pleasant to talk about when we're together like this."

"How about the Epsteins' condominium?" said Rachel.

"Who told you the Epsteins bought a condominium?" asked David, somewhat sharply.

"It was just an educated guess. Aren't they always buying things?"

154

"The *seder* is traditionally the time for family arguments," said Seymour. "People have spent a whole year storing up resentments. A *seder* without an argument is like a rose without a scent."

"A lot of people commit suicide at Christmas time," said Peggy.

"Not Jews," said Rachel.

"I don't know, the statistics I read didn't break it down ethnically."

"Did you hear that the Herzog boy threw himself out the window of a hotel in Syracuse?" said Betty Diamant.

"He was a *faigele*," said Milton Sonnshein. "You knew that, didn't you?"

"Maybe he thought he could fly," said Michael.

"Don't joke," his mother told him.

"Homosexuality is on the rise," said Elaine Diamant, "even among Jews."

"Especially among Jews," said Seymour.

Dessert was being served. The sweet wine had clogged heads all around the table. The children were becoming cranky.

"Don't forget my nutcake," said Betty Diamant.

"Time for the *afikomen*," Grandpa Milt called out. The children ran about looking for it. David's oldest son found it behind the dictionary stand in the living room. He brought it back and Milton Sonnshein gave him a crisp new dollar bill. The younger children yelled "No fair!" but Grandpa Milt had shiny quarters for them all.

The third cup of wine was poured and Seymour suggested that they sing the grace after meals. His father thought it was superfluous.

"I love the melody," said Rachel.

"Enough is enough," said her father-in-law.

"If you do this after every meal, it's a wonder you get any painting done," said Claire.

"I can sing and paint at the same time," said Rachel.

"Let's get on with it," said Seymour. "I'll lead."

The third cup of wine was drunk.

"Time for Elijah," said Seymour, and the children —those who were still listening—ran to the door and

155

opened it. A draft of pleasantly cool and fragrant air entered the house. The full moon was visible, for a moment, high above the trees.

"What now?" said Seymour's father.

"Hallel," said Seymour.

"Let's skip it," said Milton Sonnshein.

"The kids are restless," said his wife.

"The grownups too," said Saul Diamant.

"I'd like to sing at least a song or two," said Aaron.

They drank the fourth glass of wine, as was prescribed, and Seymour said, "Next year in Jerusalem!"

"Amen," cried Donella, and "Amen," said Opal, in the kitchen, looking at the clock. It would be two hours' work cleaning up.

The family went into the living room. Soon the women had drifted together, while the men talked about stocks and taxes and negligence. Rachel sat on the arm of Seymour's chair. The kids were mostly in front of the TV, the smallest ones were falling asleep. There were wine stains on the Peter Pan-collared shirts and the starched pinafores were rumpled. Rachel felt the weight of the food holding her down like a sack of stones. Her mind lay on top, unmoving and dark. There was nothing to talk about. They had been home less than twelve hours, she thought, and there was nothing left to say.

The parents looked at their watches and yawned, said what a great dinner it was, and promised to see each other the following night. Saul and Betty Diamant got up to leave. They kissed Rachel and shook hands with Seymour.

Betty Diamant stopped by the kitchen to see how Donella was doing. She gave the other help each an extra five dollars and told Donella to come in late the next day. "Get some sleep, and take the rest of the nutcake home with you."

The others all gave her hard looks.

"That woman is something," said Opal's niece.

"Mind your own business," said Donella.

"They all something," said Opal.

"Take the rest of the nutcake," mimicked the pret-

156

ty dark girl, who was studying to be a dental technician.

"Shut your mouth," said Donella. In her heart her love warred with the outrage that always lay right beside it.

Rachel and Seymour lingered briefly in the living room.

"I think I'll go to sleep," said Aaron.

"I'll go up with you," said Rachel, and followed him to see that he had everything. To be alone with him for a minute. Aaron had the small guest room. It was like the room of a charming country inn.

Rachel kissed Aaron good-night.

"It's boring here."

"I know," said Rachel, "but it's only a few days more."

"Don't they ever talk about anything interesting?" asked Aaron. "Was it like this when you were little?"

"It must have been. I know that by the time I was your age I used to feel that they were the most provincial people on the face of this earth. But since I've lived in Gateshead I realize they're not so terrible. They have redeeming features."

"You sounded like a troublemaker tonight. But I bet you wouldn't like it if I made trouble."

"I play the role that's been assigned to me. You have to earn your part. Your uncle Michael once said that I had to let the whole world know when I walked into a room."

"He's jealous of you."

"With good reason, I'm sure."

"In Gateshead it's easier to escape—there's New York."

"*That*'s the best part about Gateshead."

"I bet you couldn't get lost in Buffalo. I mean you couldn't disappear, like a fugitive."

"Fugitives always come to New York City."

Rachel went back downstairs. She thought she ought to say good-night to her in-laws even if she didn't feel like it. On the stairs she heard weeping. She could see obliquely into the living room; only part of

157

the couch was visible, one armchair, and a large part of the rug. Sadie Sonnshein sat on the couch, a handkerchief balled up in her hand, tears streaming down her face. Seymour was not visible. His father sat in the armchair, his profile stony and still.

"Why didn't you say anything?" said Seymour.

Rachel heard the measured tone, imagined him serious, sitting on the ottoman, legs wide apart, or standing with his hands in his pockets, chewing on his lip.

"Your mother likes to make a drama," said Milton Sonnshein. "There are simple procedures to be followed. There's no need for this."

Rachel turned back and went upstairs. The tableau was complete without her. It had been a long day, she was exhausted. She barely heard Seymour come in. "I think my mother is very sick," he said, but Rachel was asleep.

The next morning they went over to the Diamants. They also visited everyone else. It was necessary not to leave anyone out, to admire the children and dogs and new purchases. Seymour's mother's health was discussed. It seemed suddenly that everyone knew that she did not feel well. Bill Gardener got her an appointment for a battery of hospital tests. The second *seder* was supposed to be a replay of the first, but Milton and Sadie begged to be excused. The rest of the family got together anyway and the *Haggadah* was read in very short order. Conversation ebbed and flowed; everything had become old and familiar all at once.

The next three days passed quickly. Soon they were all three in the car again, headed for the Thruway and home. Rachel had not mentioned the hysterectomy to her mother. There was enough excitement about Sadie Sonnshein; Rachel was glad not to add to it. And the less chance her mother had to lay plans, the better. "I'm a big girl now," thought Rachel. But that wasn't really it. She was scared of her mother's concern. She didn't want to contend with the awful apprehensions that lurked forever in Betty Diamant's mind.

"Are you worried about your mother?" Rachel asked Seymour.

158

"Oddly enough, I'm not. She's both tough and hysterical. Those kinds of people always live to a ripe old age."

"Are you worried about me?"

"A little."

"I'm tough, too."

"Not as tough as you think."

"There's not a thing wrong with me."

"I know that. But I'm responsible for you. I love you."

Rachel checked into the hospital on the last Sunday in April. It was a muggy day and the leaves—still frail and tender—had burst open on every tree. The lilacs were not yet in bloom but azaleas blazed red and purple all over Gateshead. Rachel called her mother just before the operation. She tried to sound casual but Betty Diamant thought she heard distant explosions of anxiety.

"Why didn't you tell me sooner?" she asked.

Rachel began a long explanation which, while true, was distorted enough to sound as though it had been invented.

"Besides," she hinted, "we were all thinking about Sadie. . . ."

"You mean you knew when you were in Buffalo?"

"I was waiting for confirmation."

"So I was right to think you looked peaked."

"How *is* my mother-in-law?"

"Home now. They didn't find a thing wrong with her, but that didn't convince her. She's lost a lot of weight. But I'm more concerned about you at the moment."

"I'll be all right."

"Shall I come down?"

Rachel had waited with trepidation to hear the offer made, but when her mother finally uttered it the sound of her voice betrayed her own reluctance.

"No, no," said Rachel, relieved.

Seymour accompanied Rachel to her hospital room and sat on the leatherette armchair while she put away her nightgowns and robe, set her toiletries up in the

159

bathroom and arranged her books on the night table. The second bed in her room was empty. Seymour chewed on a fingernail. It made Rachel nervous to see him so distracted. "Go home," she said, already feeling the embrace of the hospital and its intractable routine. It had begun the moment she checked in; the very forms that had—endlessly—to be filled out seemed calculated to divorce her from the world of the normal and the healthy. Seymour asked anxious questions of the nurses who came and went, performing their myriad duties. They answered him indulgently. They knew he was a rabbi; they had seen him on his weekly rounds.

"I want to stay with you," he said.

"You're driving me nuts," she told him. He was free to come and go while she had become a patient, a prisoner in the land of the sick.

The sun shone into the room, across a purple bank of low clouds, and left a large yellow rectangle on the floor. Then Seymour went home, at last, promising to call, promising to be back first thing in the morning. The sun set slowly, the rectangle disappeared from the floor and the pale sky gave off its dying light.

Nurses' aides came to shave Rachel when visiting hours were over. Looking at her bare pussy she wondered what Hildegarde Kaye would (or could) do with it in her crotch-paintings, now that it was as bald as Yul Brynner's head. There were other things to occupy Rachel's time. No sooner had she started on the Sunday papers which Seymour had left her, when a long line of residents appeared to ask innumerable questions. They marked her answers down on secret forms on their clipboards. Rachel liked being the center of so much attention and answered their questions carefully and at length. She wondered if they were merely in training to ask questions, or whether they were actually keeping a file on answers to questions like "Do you know what you're here for?" Sometimes a resident asked a question she had already answered for the previous resident. Were they checking up on her or on each other? She found it all immensely gratifying.

160

After the residents had left, a nurse appeared to announce that she would be given an enema later and that she was not to eat after 8:00 P.M. She was followed by an aide who brought supper on a tray. Rachel had trouble recognizing the various foods, save for a half a canned peach and a roll. She decided to eat only those things that seemed to be made of edible materials—there were not many. She felt prickly where she had been shaved.

Before long the anesthesiologist appeared, introduced himself and sat down to discuss the anesthesia. Rachel found him unimaginative. He meant to be forthright and make the patient feel that she was not being treated like an object, but he was not good at public relations and obviously hated this part of the job. Knocking people out was what he was good at.

All the attention had given Rachel so much confidence and filled her with such joy that she began to look forward to the operation with some pleasure. Suppose she didn't wake up from the anesthesia? That wasn't a bad way to go—she'd never know what happened.

The enema was big and soapy. It was dispensed by a voluble nurse who talked on and on while it flowed in and Rachel tried to concentrate on holding on to it and, when that was no longer possible, reaching the bathroom in time. Blessed relief! The voluble nurse talked even while Rachel sat on the toilet. She was straightening the bed, fluffing pillows, adjusting things. When Rachel finally crawled back to bed, cleaned out and empty, she saw that it was only ten-thirty. The hospital was still, only night sounds chirped from the darkened corridors. Rachel considered masturbating to pass the time and establish her own fantasies on this beachhead, but her shorn private parts were too prickly and slightly sore from the effects of the razor. Anyway, it was better to be awake at night than early in the morning. Rachel turned on her lamp and read almost the entire *Times* before she fell asleep around 1:00 A.M.

She was awakened by sunlight and hospital bustle before seven, though she tried hard to go back to sleep and stay in the dream, which was rapidly fleeing. It

161

had been about Barnard. Had she won a prize? Was she back there again? Because she had failed? Because she was studying for an advanced degree? She had sat in the library over manuscripts and picture books, going to devote herself to a life in art history. It was a pleasant thought, the dream was good, she had not failed after all. The bright day was spreading over the room. The morning nurses came and went; the noise of hospital activity was everywhere. She remembered she was going to have an operation.

They gave her a hospital gown and hooked her up to the infusion at half-past eight, but didn't come to take her away until nine, just after a deceptively delicate nurse had plunged a needle into her buttocks. Rachel got high as a kite. They rolled her onto a stretcher and wheeled her down the hall into an elevator and up to the operating room. Rachel felt like waving to everyone. Hi there, hello! She saw the world cockeyed, of course; it was largely ceilings, and bent-over faces of people in which chins were prominent. When she tried to raise her head to see something else they told her to lie down. The voices from on high. Conversations between orderlies ricocheted from wall to wall. She heard soft laughter. Giggles. The rustle of uniforms. She smelled clean starched cotton. She was flying skyward on her sensations. Strapped down, helpless, but free in her head. The operating room lights were bright. Doctor Fleischer was there, in green cotton, looking handsome and proud to be there. In charge. He was talking to the anesthesiologist, who was more at home here than he had been at her bedside. He joshed Bert Fleischer about his tennis game.

"Ready to go, toots?" Doctor Fleischer asked.

Then Doctor blank—why didn't he wear a name tag?—put a different bottle on the infusion and that was the end of Rachel for a time.

The next thing she knew she felt the pain in her belly.

"It hurts," she said, aloud, and opened her eyes, but they fell shut again before she could see out of them. A little later, on another trip back to the surface, she saw the infusion bottle and a clock. The clock

162

said twelve-thirty. A lot of disembodied voices hummed on the horizon. Mummified figures wandered in and out of her vision.

A woman's voice said, "You're all right. It's all over. You're all right."

"Have I lost it?"

The nurse said, "What, dear?"

"I can't remember," said Rachel, "but it hurts."

It really did hurt. Rachel hadn't thought it would hurt so much. She let herself go under again but the pain persisted. She tried to feel her stomach, which seemed to be wide open.

"Don't touch the dressing," said the nurse.

Later, back in her own room, Rachel saw Seymour's face above her.

"It hurts," she said.

"You're o.k."

"It hurts a lot."

"You're fine."

"Stop saying that!" said Rachel, disgruntled. She fell asleep again. The bed next to her was still empty.

When she came to again, Seymour was no longer there. The pain still was, and now Rachel felt nauseated too. A nurse buzzed around. "I'm going to vomit," said Rachel. The nurse put a cool steel dish next to her cheek. "Use that," she said, but Rachel clenched her teeth and dozed off again. The curved dish nestled in her damp hair. Some time later she heard voices cascading down a stream of words. The words were very clear but made no sense because Rachel couldn't follow the stream. By the time a word had reached her, the sentence had already been swept away. One of the voices was Seymour's.

"You're back," she said. The yellow light of evening floated into the room. "What day is it?" she asked.

"Monday," said Seymour.

Rachel noticed that there were bars on the sides of her bed. She put her hands on them and saw that her wedding ring was taped to her finger with adhesive tape. "Take it off," she said. He fussed with it a while before he got it peeled away. Rachel's lips were dry.

Lucky Seymour, she thought, can walk out anytime he wants, can run in the spring air, the April dew.

"What did you say?" he asked.

"Did I say something?"

"It sounded like it."

"Go home. I'll talk to you tomorrow."

"Visiting hours are over," said the nurse, white and brisk.

"I love you," said Seymour.

"I'll never bleed again," said Rachel. "Imagine that."

After Seymour left, Rachel tried to lift her head, but it was too heavy. She reached under the heavy white hospital gown to steal a touch of the dressing. Her stomach felt as though it was ripped open from hip to hip, but the dressing was small and covered only a narrow strip between her navel and her shaved pussy. "It's over and done with," she thought and fell asleep again, feeling at once heroic and smug. She continued to wake up at intervals throughout the night. She could not turn over to lie on her side; she was stiff and her belly ached fiercely. She had no dreams—her mind was buried deep inside her hurting body. The stainless steel dish still lay beside her head.

Rachel felt better the next morning. She was able, once again, to make connections between words, to see the room whole, to move without the winds of nausea. A nurse came and washed her. It was a lovely sensation. She put on a clean hospital gown. Rachel waited happily for Seymour. "I can talk to you today," she said, when he came.

Seymour sat down in the leatherette armchair and said, "Well, what shall we talk about?" Now that Rachel had successfully emerged from her operation, he was edgy with untold small concerns.

"I can tell you lots of stories," said Rachel.

"What'll I give Aaron for dinner?" Seymour asked her.

"Fish," said Rachel.

"Maybe I'll take him out for Chinese."

"He doesn't like Chinese," said Rachel.

164

Seymour left before Rachel could tell him about her operation. "I have other patients to see," he said.

That afternoon, the deceptively delicate nurse came to take Rachel for a walk. She was strong like an ox. "They'll give you solid food for dinner tonight," she said. Rachel's stomach hurt like hell but she walked bravely, albeit like an old lady, bent and cautious, all the way down the hall and back.

The solid food they brought for her dinner consisted of a gelatin dessert made entirely of chemicals. Rachel read the label and announced she wouldn't eat it. "Honey, I don't give a shit what you do with it," said the aide. She looked like a princess from the Sudan and wore a uniform that ended just below her crotch. Rachel found that she'd grown very aware of the sizes and shapes of bodies. She drank her milk and the chicken broth and left the gelatin dessert to quiver in its tinfoil cup. That night she went walking by herself and looked into all the rooms. Most of the patients were watching television or dozing under their covers. The nurses at their station were eating candy.

The following afternoon, Seymour brought Aaron with him. Rachel found it hard to make conversation. After three days it seemed that she already knew nothing but hospital stories. Her world had shrunk to four walls and a corridor—it even held her imagination in check. Rachel described her pain and talked about enemas. "They keep wanting to give them," she said, "even though I've eaten nothing."

"I tell people you feel terrible," said Seymour.

"I do."

"Maybe it'll discourage visitors for a few days."

"They keep calling," said Aaron, "and their voices sound positively funereal: 'How's your mother?' they ask, and call me 'dear' because they can't remember my name."

"Oh, Lord," said Rachel.

"The whole congregation must have called. I'm getting tired of answering the phone."

"The ones that can't stand me, do they call too?"

"They don't tell me whether or not they like you."

165

Aaron had brought a card and a bunch of flowers. Tears welled up in Rachel's eyes.

"You're being sentimental," said Aaron.

"I'm a sucker for sweet gestures. Grubby hands that hold a nosegay of wilted daisies—it makes me cry all the time."

"My hands are clean and the flowers aren't wilted," said Aaron, "but I know what you mean. Grandma said to tell you hello. She called too."

"I'll talk to her when I get home."

"The place is a mess."

"I don't want to think about it," said Rachel.

By the next day she felt almost like her old self. Doctor Fleischer came in, fresh from another operation.

"Hi, toots! Tomorrow we'll take the stitches out."

He sat on the leatherette armchair and lit his pipe. Rachel had no idea what they were going to talk about.

"Any questions?" asked Bert Fleischer.

"What are they made of?"

"What?"

"The stitches."

"Nylon."

"The food in this place is terrible," said Rachel. "The dieticians go to Cornell for four years and come up with plastic jello and white bread. It's incredible. Rats fed on white bread die after a week. Did you know that?"

"There are a lot of very sick people here and they all need special diets. Are you getting kosher food?"

"I would if I thought it would be an improvement."

"How's your bowel movement?"

"I've hardly eaten anything, how should it be?"

Bert Fleischer got up and peeked daintily under Rachel's gown. He lifted the dressing and clucked in admiration.

"It's a nice big scar," he said. "That fibroid of yours was a lulu. But don't worry. In a couple of years it will fade and you can wear a bikini again."

"I don't wear bikinis. My legs are too short."

166

Doctor Fleischer looked puzzled. "I'll see you tomorrow, sweetheart."

Sally came by that afternoon and brought Rachel a copy of *Humboldt's Gift*. She also carried a jar of tomato juice in her bag. "Bloody Marys," she whispered, even though there was no one in the room, and they drank them stealthily out of the hospital paper cups.

"Guess what?" said Sally.

"What?"

"The rumor going around town is that you have cancer."

"Maybe that's why I haven't had any visitors."

"Well, I scotched it as best I could, since you don't like people to feel sorry for you."

"I don't mind a little pity, as long as it's for something I haven't got. Let them treat me like a dying princess for a little while. They'll catch on soon enough that I'm not about to shuffle off to the cemetery. Besides, they might have second thoughts about firing Seymour if they think I'm mortally ill."

"You're terrible, Rachel!"

"I could have told you that long ago."

"A lot of people think you're sweet."

"It's because I smile a lot."

"You *want* to be liked, you know."

"What makes you say that?"

"You worry about it when somebody doesn't like you. You worry about the impression you make. You're funny that way; you don't want to conform, but then you sulk when your non-conformity meets with disapproval. And you're very, you should excuse the expression, elitist about your good taste and your intelligence and your talent. At the same time you want to be 'Everywoman,' simple, plain and honest, like the lady at the vegetable stand. That's a contradiction you can't resolve."

"The Bloody Mary is delicious," said Rachel.

After Sally left, Rachel walked down the hall to the pay phone and called Aaron.

"Let's go to a ball game when I get out."

"You've been drinking," said Aaron.

167

"Celebrating my recovery with Sally. Will you go to Abraham & Straus and buy a couple of good tickets?"

"Reserved seats?"

"Why not."

Rachel thought it seemed like summer, beyond the hospital walls. The men cutting the grass wore only T-shirts; the nurses strolled leisurely across the courtyard. She opened the window in her room and the fragrance of linden trees came in.

The measured walk up and down the hospital corridors had become part of Rachel's daily routine. She still walked slowly and held her belly, but she went further and further afield on her voyages of discovery, especially at night when all the visitors were gone and no reminders of the outside world obtruded upon the hospital's ritualized inner life. On her next-to-last night, she saw a death. The cardiac team had been called to her floor. Rachel heard it on the P.A. system. They rushed past Rachel, into a room already crowded with nurses and residents. The door had been left open and Rachel saw them beating on an old man's chest, pummeling him with their fists. He bounced up once or twice and then fell back. Just then, a nurse saw Rachel and shut the door in her face. By morning the room was empty and the bed all made up, clean and flat, waiting for a new patient.

Rachel had two visitors from the Sisterhood. They brought flowers and official greetings. The room was already filled with flowers; they were arranged along the windowsill and got in the way of Rachel's view.

"The rabbi says you feel terrible," one of the women said. "You *look* fine."

Rachel slid down in her bed and said "Ouch."

"Are you all right?"

"Just a twinge in my incision."

"Should we call a nurse?"

"No, no," said Rachel. "I'll be o.k."

She had pulled the sheet up to her chin. Her hair was stringy and dirty.

"Are you enjoying the Bellow?"

Rachel nodded vigorously. "All except the stuff about Rudolf Steiner," she said, "which I skip."

168

The visitors did not stay long.

Late that night, unable to sleep, she called Seymour. Aaron answered.

"Where's Dad?" asked Rachel.

"Gone out."

"Did he say where he was going?"

"No, he didn't, Mom. He just said 'out' and not to wait up, he might be very late."

Rachel called an hour later, and there was no answer; Aaron was asleep. Rachel tried until 2:00 A.M. She went to bed angry, but fell asleep anyway. The hospital had taken over her life completely—in a few short days. She might as well be dead. Did they think her dead on the outside? Where in hell was Seymour? At seven in the morning the thermometer person came in and woke her up. Rachel thought about calling home but didn't, she was not sure whether it was because she didn't want to be *that* sort of wife or because she didn't want to know whether or not Seymour had gotten back.

She was ready to go home before noon. Seymour came to fetch her.

"Where were you last night?"

"I had someone with lots of trouble, I can't tell you about it now."

"Not even who it was?"

"No."

"I think it was Natalie Gould."

"You can think what you want to."

Rachel had to walk carefully and lie down a lot. She watched baseball on the TV.

169

6

Rachel saw sunlight dancing on the water. She had taken a reclining chair out of the basement and into the yard and was lying on it. It was warm enough to stay in the sun, but not so hot as to produce sweat and the need to go into the water. Rachel still moved gingerly. Little red droplets of blood oozed from her incision. Alarmed, she had imagined a hole going deep into her belly like a mine shaft, but Doctor Fleischer had said no, it was not like that at all, it was merely some surface bleeding. Rachel wore shorts and a T-shirt. She had washed her hair, taking great care not to strain her stomach. The lilacs were in full bloom next to the house, and the massive bushes shielded the yard from the street as well as from the eyes of the Grogs. The fragrant clusters of purple flowers reached toward the sun and bobbed in a gentle wind. Rachel asked Aaron to climb the fence and cut her some of the blooms. Ollie barked furiously and tried to snap off his foot. Rachel shrieked loudly and her shrieks brought Willy and Bitsy Grog running. "Get your fucking dog away!" Rachel screamed. She sounded as vulgar and hateful as a fishwife. She sounded like Betty Grog.

The Prawn sisters were working in their garden. They waved at Rachel and pretended they hadn't heard her screeching. The apple tree was in bloom above the Prawns' stately tulips; its white blossoms filled the blue sky. Sydelle and Clarabelle had been to visit Rachel when she first came from the hospital. They

170

had brought her some fancy imported chocolates and discussed operations, doctors, and the high cost of hospital care. It was a pleasant visit. Seymour had not been at home.

"We hear your house is on the market," said Clarabelle Prawn.

"We'll miss you," Sydelle added. "I hope the new people will turn out to be as congenial as you, my dear." She had lately been bothered by a persistent and troublesome cough.

Rachel's back was turned to the Grogs' chain link fence—she looked the other way, toward the view she preferred. A sketchbook was in her lap, opened to a clean page, and she wore sunglasses to shield her eyes from its white glare and from the bright sparkle of the water. In the fullness of summer the Prawns' garden recalled the palette of the Impressionists, but in these less richly painted days of May, it was a more sharply etched scene she saw. It too reminded her of another time (fair landscapes always seem to reach into the past), but one that was not rooted in painting. Rachel thought about this and tried to evoke its model. She raked over her memory for movie moments and for that sudden clear image that tugs at the heartstrings. She imagined a Golden Age, a time (before the Fall) when only the life of the imagination mattered, and she could escape into fantasy. Rachel didn't particularly want to think of the present. She did not want to admit that she was troubled by Seymour's skittish behavior, his defensive refusal to discuss his nocturnal absences, his monumental silences and preoccupation. Rachel was not by nature suspicious—she spent too much time thinking about herself and making up a personal iconography for her work—but there was clearly something in the air between her and Seymour. No, not really between them, but rather off to the side. A shadow in a photograph. Seymour had begun to develop a secret life. Perhaps it was a small secret life but it was there just the same. The shadow—a small tumor, a minute malignancy. Rachel thought she would not stoop to spying (not yet, not now) or snooping. She

171

would never open a letter "by mistake" or listen in on an extension phone. But when she stumbled over something, a clue, it would lodge in her mind like a seed in her tooth. She could understand how it might become an obsession to find the "truth" and how bitter and masochistic a journey she would have to take.

The sun shone down on her and slowly it would turn her brown. She tanned well; she started off early and went by easy stages to polished burnt umber. Rachel tried to imagine Seymour in bed with someone else, but her resistance to the idea was so great she could not form the image. She would not look on Seymour making love to anyone else any more than she would look upon her parents copulating. She hated pornographic photographs, but paintings or drawings were another matter. Perhaps it was that they were more like what she saw in her mind's eye and less what she might see through the keyhole. Rachel wondered whether it was, as she had surmised, Natalie Gould who had entangled Seymour in the folds of her slinky silken skirts. Natalie had sent a charming nosegay of flowers to the hospital; it was by far the most tasteful bouquet she had received. Rachel wondered if anyone knew, wondered if Seymour had found a trysting place, some secret corner in a dark and expensive restaurant. She wondered if people were talking, if they had seen what she had not, if the gossips said "Poor Rachel!" The thought that anyone might say "Poor Rachel!" disturbed her most of all. That night she asked Seymour whether he was having an affair. "Don't be silly," he said, and would say no more. The subject was closed, she had no second question. Perhaps she was wrong. Perhaps he would come to his senses before she was proven right, before it was too late. Too late for whom?

Betty Diamant called regularly to check on her daughter's progress. She dispensed medical advice and asked searching questions intended to elicit all the details of Rachel's recovery. She even offered to pay a visit and see to Rachel's needs herself. The idea that her mother might, at this time, come blundering into her life gave Rachel some anxious moments. She did not

172

want to be scrutinized. She didn't want her mother sniffing at her tender spots, rooting at her weaknesses. Betty Diamant liked Seymour well enough, but she *loved* Rachel and could (with a mother's instinct) detect small signs of unhappiness or discontent. Rachel knew this all too well. She feared the comfort her mother would bring her. It would have to be paid for, most likely in confidences, admissions of failure, bonds of dependence. Rachel had, long ago, brought these gifts to her mother freely, but that was before she discovered that they could, with more reason, be brought to a lover. A lover—though he often gave little comfort—returned the gifts in many delectable ways and allowed for a most satisfying secret life as well. Mothers struggle all their lives to conquer their daughters' beaux, to become, once again, the sole confidante."

"Shall I send Donella then, to help you with the housework?" Betty Diamant asked.

"No, I don't think so. I can manage alone."

"Acting the martyr, are you?"

"No, no," said Rachel. "But as long as we're on the subject, how's my mother-in-law?"

"They still haven't found anything wrong with her. She's been to the very best doctors. If you ask me it's all just a bid for attention. Sadie Sonnshein was always neurotic."

"Maybe she knows something the doctors don't."

"Then she should tell them."

"I don't mean that. Maybe she's got an intuition about her death. For all we know she's really dying, only we've gotten so used to believing the doctors . . ."

"The rebbetzin is full of wisdom today," said Betty Diamant. Rachel thought she was being unduly nasty.

"Why are you harping on the rebbetzin bit?"

"Because you've always criticized your father and me for our bourgeois ways and yet you sit there, among a bunch of very ordinary Jews, and let yourself be tyrannized."

"What brought this on, all of a sudden?"

"I worry about you, Rachel," said Betty Diamant.

173

"Take care of yourself. Don't let anybody—not even Seymour—belittle your efforts or change your ways. You have so much talent. . . ."

"What's the connection between all this and the state of Sadie's health?"

"I don't know—you sounded odd before. I keep wondering if there's something wrong. You're still young, Rachel, you've got a long life ahead of you. Are you sure you don't want me or Donella to come?"

"I'm sure, Mother. And I promise to behave and look after my talent."

It was a relief to end the conversation. Rachel thought about it late into the night, and was curt with Seymour when he asked her what the trouble was.

On the afternoon that Rachel and Aaron had tickets for the ball game, Rachel picked him up at school just before lunch. She had given him a note that read, "Please excuse Aaron Sonnshein at noon today. He has an appointment to attend a cultural event." The school frowned on frivolous activities, and Rachel did not invoke doctors lightly, for reasons of superstition. They drove to Flushing, parked near the subway station, and took a train one stop to Shea Stadium. It was a ploy to keep out of the Shea Stadium traffic in the rush hour. Rachel's belly was still tender. Doctor Fleischer had cautioned her about driving, but she kept his admonitions to herself.

The day was mild, the sun hot, especially in those dusty corners shielded from the breeze. Rachel hugged Aaron in full view of the stadium, up on the elevated platform of the Flushing line of the IRT. Although his body was hard and lean, he felt softer now than he had before the tense edge of his awkward adolescent self had started to crumble. Rachel wondered about that too—had he slept with a girl? She added that thought to her other unspoken ones. The crowd streamed happily out of the subway, mother and son walked among them, swiftly, eager to get to their seats. It was a perfect day for a baseball game. On such a perfect day at the ball park, the need to work was not so great a burden (the guilt was put away with other

174

dark thoughts) and could be borne. Rachel had not touched her paints since the Art Show & Sale. There had been Passover first, and then the hospital. Three weeks out of her life. "Don't be so compulsive," Seymour had said, and she had tried to swallow the driving impulse which sometimes seemed to make her rigid with frustration. She hated that sharp and rigid self—a puppet on a string rattled by tensions. So she lay in the sun and read and fell into a torpor. She finished *Humboldt's Gift*, and then, because it seemed that everything else that came her way was short, she started to read *Anna Karenina*. She always carried her black sketchpad with her. Lately she had written many notes and observations in it, but made no drawings. It was difficult—after the enforced idleness of the hospital—to get back to painting. Rachel wanted a word of encouragement; she needed confidence to begin work on her group portrait at the *seder* table. One conversation with another serious artist might be enough, one trip through a great museum or a stunning exhibition. Was it really possible to be an artist in Gateshead? Could it ever happen as long as she remained adrift in that desolate landscape? Rachel wondered if she should run away.

"Are you paying for everything?" Aaron asked as they walked through the turnstiles.

"Yes, I am, my dear," she said (having taken twenty-five dollars out of her savings account).

"Then how about buying me a scorecard?"

Rachel bought two scorecards. They had seats in the mezzanine section, between first and home, immediately behind the boxes. Rachel gave Aaron five dollars and put dark thoughts about money out of her mind too. She tipped the usher handsomely. "Maybe we can sneak into the boxes later," she said to Aaron, and bought a beer. He bought two hot dogs and a Coke. They wrote down the batting order in their scorecards. Rachel looked up and out beyond center field, and saw Queens delicately drawn in the haze of the spring sunshine and abruptly cut off by the left-field bleachers. From this distance the seats looked flat, like an element in a collage.

175

"What are you thinking about, Mom?"

"The view. Why do you ask?"

"I don't want you to be melancholy."

"Who, me? Melancholy?"

"I just thought I'd check."

He turned his head away so that she saw only his profile. He was studying Dave Kingman taking batting practice. The seats beyond them were filling up, Aaron's profile stood out against yellow sweatshirts and orange T-shirts.

"You've lost your virginity, haven't you?" she suddenly asked him.

He turned his face full back to her.

"What makes you say that?"

He was tanned down to the neck of his striped shirt and his hair was reddish from the effects of the sun. He played baseball with his friends on the park diamond every afternoon until the six o'clock whistle.

"You seem so self-possessed," said Rachel.

Aaron's brown eyes were on her. She didn't know what he saw but they were amused, liquid, a lover's eyes. "Yes, I have lost my virginity."

"Are you in love with her?" his mother asked. She was certain it was the correct and only question.

"Don't you know? Can't you tell?"

"I thought I could tell, but sometimes my mind is on other things."

"I *am* in love with her."

"Do I know her?"

"I don't think so. Her name is Frannie."

"Were you holding hands with her on Main Street the day of the Gewirtz bar mitzvah?"

"I might have been. We do hold hands."

"Too?"

"Yes."

"I saw you as Dad and I were driving by."

"Did he see us?"

"I didn't point you out to him. I think I was a little shocked and wanted to get used to the idea. I don't mean 'shocked' really, but it was a new experience, something I have to get used to. You never told me anything."

176

"That's part of it. Not talking about it when it's all over your mind. But I'm not a kid anymore. What did you think of her?"

"I don't think I really saw her. Not the way you do when you know that you are meant to see a person. I saw *you*. She was merely an appendage. Something growing out of your hand."

"That's a terrible thing to say, Mom. I'll never introduce her to you."

"Well, I suppose I'll see everyone you bring home to me a little that way at first. Don't be hard on me. I'll let you go."

"I think you'd like her. She's very nice."

"Does it make a difference to you?"

"What?"

"That I like her."

"I think so. I'd like to believe it doesn't, but I'm afraid it does."

"Are you happy?"

"Yes!"

"There aren't too many complications?"

"Mom!"

"Am I intruding?"

"You're terrible. They told us in Health about people like you. But no, there aren't any complications now, though there may be in the future, but I don't want to think about that."

"She's not Jewish?"

"No, she's not Jewish."

The names of the starting pitchers had been announced, as well as the line-ups. Cheers and boos in the ball park. It was time for "The Star-Spangled Banner." Rachel and Aaron stood up. The organ quivered over the P.A. system. The players held their caps over their hearts as did some of the men in the stands. Rachel sang "The Star-Spangled Banner" in a piping bad voice. It was an impossible tune. The words blinked into place on the scoreboard: ". . . o'er the land of the free"—what a hopeless note!—"and the home of the brave." The crowd's chatter swelled into a roar on the last word. It was time to begin. The umpire shouted PLAY BALL! The Pirates were up at bat, the Mets had taken the field. They were playing the lead-off hitter straight away.

The elderly man in front of them was neatly dressed in pressed working clothes; he had filled in his scorecard with loving care. He was waiting to begin a conversation. He was all alone.

"I'm glad the Mets still use grass," said Rachel. "The ball field doesn't look like a recreation room that way, and there's dirt between the bases."

"Can't use Astroturf," said the man, "the water table is too high at Shea."

He had successfully made contact; he kept Rachel informed about his life and baseball memories for several innings. He was a retired mailman and lived in Kingston, New York. He came down for as many games as he could. Took the bus. Had always been a Giant fan, no damn Yankees for him. His wife was dead, God rest her soul.

The lead-off batter hit a low line drive to right field. Mike Vail ran in and caught it at his feet. There were shouts and claps of approval. Rachel scored it 0–8. She was torn between scoring and merely watching. Sometimes the rhythm was interrupted when she tried to get it down correctly on the paper. Sometimes she even missed a play. Who started that double play? she might have to ask, having watched the runner dancing off first as *crack!* the ball left the bat and the fielders moved swiftly to make the play. But if she merely watched, her mind would drift off to the theater in the stands, and she would not be able to say, in the seventh inning, as Millan came up for the third time, what he had done before.

The pitcher bent down, looked for the sign, reared back. The tension built, as it always did, at that moment. The batter swung, not well, and the ball bounced to shortstop. Harrelson fielded it cleanly. Rachel scored it 6–3.

"I do declare I love baseball," said Rachel.

"You love yourself loving it," said Aaron.

The third man up drew a walk. He flung his bat toward the dugout and loped to first. Willie Stargell, up

178

next, looked fierce. He twirled his bat like a mythic woodcutter about to fell a tree.

"Reminds me of Johnny Mize," said Rachel. "Used to scare the shit out of me. I saw him once at Ebbets Field."

A quick sharp question stung Rachel's mind just then. Where was Seymour at this very moment? She did not ask with love but in a panic stab of pain. And blanked it out again as Stargell hit a high fly ball deep to left field. A lot of people groaned, a few cheered. Rachel saw that it was not going out of the park. Kingman ran back and caught it on the warning track. The players loped back to the dugout and the Pirates took the field.

"I saw Mize in his prime," said the mailman, who had become a member of the family—"a great ballplayer, power like a bullsnake."

It was an odd turn of phrase, a weird description. Big Johnny Mize. The rush of baseball memories made the mailman voluble. He recounted the things he'd seen. The great catches and the shutouts. He had been to ball parks everywhere. He collected ball parks, and treasured the dead ones. Shibe Park. Comiskey Park, Ebbets Field, the Polo Grounds. Rachel remembered things differently; the activity in the bullpen of her mind was sporadic, always turning about her own self. It was not only that she had played the game, but that it had also become a metaphor in which the events of her life fitted and were recalled without threat. She remembered the playground games, and the dawn of her awareness of becoming a woman. All at once she was no longer asked to play with the boys. In high school she had been on the girls' softball team and played in the blue gym uniforms on the cruddy field next to the tennis courts. She disliked those blue uniforms, without lettering or names or emblems. They had pleated skirts over elastic-banded bloomers, a belt and collar. One team was given red pinnies to wear and that was how you told them apart. Rachel loved patches and labels, the drama of men's uniforms. A Polish boy who liked her let her wear his blue and

179

gold satin basketball jacket and she came proudly home with it. "You look like a hood," her mother said. "And don't accept gifts from boys. They'll want something in return."

The first player up for the Mets fouled off four pitches before he looked at a third strike. Millan hit a clean single over third base. He stood on the bag and talked to the first baseman; he talked to the first base coach too. Everyone moved easily, stood expectantly. The fans stirred, beginning their excited bird chatter.

Joe Torre hit a line drive between short and third which the Pirate third baseman went valiantly to his left for but didn't catch hold of. Millan held up at second. There were two men on now and only one out. The fans buzzed, only the experts in the crowd stayed cool. The mailman did not get excited, nor did Rachel and Aaron.

"They always leave men on base," said the mailman. "The Mets leave more men stranded than any other team in baseball."

Gulls circled over the stadium, the pennants fluttered in the breeze. The trees in the parking lot were a new green. The sun glinted and glittered over the tops of the cars. Rachel's arm rested against Aaron's, which was brown, the soft hairs on it sun-bleached. The runners edged off the bases. The pitcher threw a fastball down the middle. Another followed quickly, in the same place. Strike two. The base runners returned to the bags. The pitcher took his sign, threw another fastball. Crack! The sound traveled, everyone heard, moved, saw the ball skip across the green infield, saw the shortstop take a few steps forward, come up with the ball, toss it to second, saw the second baseman leap expertly to avoid the sliding runner as he threw the ball to first. Double play. Side retired. The fans let out a sigh, settled back, looked around for beer, for peanuts, for ice cream.

"Six to four to three," said Rachel. "A classic double play."

"At least only one guy got left on," said the mailman.

"Are you sorry you married Dad?" Aaron asked. The suddenness of the question startled Rachel.

"No, of course not," said Rachel, vehement with a rush of love and guilt, affection and loyalty billowing up in her. What was she doing, treading such a dangerous path? You didn't choose your parents, nor even your children; the only person you chose was your husband. "I only wonder, sometimes, about the way life snuck up on me. I suppose it's the human condition. It happens to everyone. But I had the idea I wanted to be an artist, and thought it meant living only for your art"—Rachel gave it a haughty sound—"for your pure experiences. But the years pass and while I *know* I'm a wife and mother, I still wonder can I call myself an artist. Nobody knows who I am."

"If you're *really* an artist, what does it matter?"

"It shouldn't matter, but it does. I think it matters to me because I'm full of doubts. And Gateshead only reinforces the doubts. The artist is invisible in suburbia. The rebbetzin is visible, the woman is visible, the mother is visible, but nobody sees the artist."

The Pirates were up once again. Koosman, who was pitching, walked the lead-off hitter on four pitches. Grote walked out to the mound, said a few words, patted him on the rear, went back, crouched down, and waited for the delivery. Rachel bought another beer. There was mustard on Aaron's chin.

"There's mustard on your chin," said Rachel.

"Can I have a beer?"

"If you're old enough to screw, I suppose you're old enough to drink," said Rachel, and bought him a beer too.

Koosman got the next batter out on a soft fly to right field.

"Did I ever tell you about the time I almost ran away from home?" said Rachel.

"No, you didn't. Is it an interesting story or a boring one?"

"I'll tell it and you'll see."

"Maybe you can lie a little."

"There he goes!" said the mailman. The Pirate runner had stolen second base. Some of the fans booed.

181

"I was a junior in high school—your age—and Seymour had taken Marcie Kubelik to a party, and then to a dance. She was a ballbreaker and had had her eye on him a long time. I was upset, and in my foul mood I went out with this Polish guy. He was a lot older—I mean, he was twenty-two or twenty-three—and a communist. A *goy* a communist! A Polack a communist! Imagine it. He was also one of those people who love the Jews with a kind of abject hysteria."

Koosman struck the next batter out. The umpire's call of a third strike was directed dramatically at the Pirate bench. Koosman stood a little way off the mound, relaxed, studying his infield. It was only a moment, though, before he stepped back, his toe on the rubber, his eye on Grote.

"Grandpa made a terrible scene when he found out. He threatened to confront the guy—even Grandma Betty thought that was too much. I remember hearing them whispering in closed rooms; it was like angry hissing snake sounds. Donella said I had no business giving my parents so much grief. Grandpa wasn't speaking to me and that *really* hurt. I was a pariah, and suddenly I started to hate Buffalo, it was the first time, I think, that I was in real conflict with everyone at home. And the Polack didn't help, he translated all my rebelliousness into social terms, talked about Marx and Revolution. I think they all thought he was taking me to bed but he was only trying to radicalize me."

"Who was the first person you slept with?"

Koosman pitched, the batter swung, the ball rose into the sky. Rachel watched the outfielders, saw Kingman run back, saw him slow down, stop. The ball landed in the visitors' bullpen. The crowd was very still. The Pirates were ahead, 2–0.

"That's neither here nor there, Aaron."

"I just wondered."

"It has nothing to do with the story."

Rachel drew a little diamond shape with four lines growing out of it on her scorecard and wrote a 1 in it. Then she finished the diamond of the man who had walked and put a 1 in it.

"I finally decided I was going to leave home. I had all sorts of romantic notions about what it would be like. Mostly they were based on movies I'd seen and books I'd read. The thing about artists, you see, is— they believe more strongly in the reality of art than in the reality of life. Even when they talk about copying nature or think their fidelity to it is what matters most."

"Did you run away?"

"No. Actually, my communist Polack prevented it. He knew enough not to mess with a sixteen-year-old who'd seen *The Grapes of Wrath* once too often."

"Were Grandma and Grandpa grateful to him?"

"They never knew."

"Why are you telling me all this?"

"I think there's a moral in it somewhere."

"I love you, Mom."

"Thank you, Aaron. I love you, too."

Koosman had taken stock after the home run, pitched carefully, and gotten the third out on a weak tap to the mound.

"What happened to the guy?"

"He left Buffalo and went to New England to organize. I never heard from him again. And I realized (though it didn't happen as easily as I'm telling it now) that it was probably my fate to sit in my room reading *Union Square* and *Jews Without Money* rather than to live in a New England mill town, preaching Marxism to the workers."

Rachel saw a swarthy man in the row in front of her, a little to the right, look up at her as she said *Jews Without Money*. He was listening to her conversation now.

"I never *heard* of those books," said Aaron.

"They probably weren't very good. I couldn't tell, I loved them so. But of course the Jews of suburbia don't read them. They think about other things and don't want to be reminded about the Jews without money."

Rachel saw the man stiffen; his head was half turned toward them.

"Isn't that all right?" Aaron asked. "I mean, if they didn't have it then and have it now? Isn't that progress?"

"Not if they no longer give a shit about the other guy. The Jews of suburbia are all fat and flatulent now."

"Watch out what you say about the Jews, lady!" said the swarthy man, now fully turned around. He wore a large golden *Chai* around his neck, on his white T-shirt, as did his two children.

"I can talk all I want about the Jews, sir," said Rachel. "I am a rebbetzin."

"Says who?"

"You want I should show you my credentials?"

"You should be careful how you talk," said the man. "I don't let racial slurs get by me. We Jews have to fight."

"Not with each other," said Rachel.

"Sometimes Jews are the worst anti-Semites."

"How right you are."

They made up. The mailman went out to get a beer. When he came back he sat down in one of the empty box seats. Aaron had looked away during the entire conversation. He was not quite pretending not to belong to Rachel, just getting a little distance between them.

"Where was I?" she asked.

"There are two strikes on the batter," said Aaron. "The Mets are up. They're behind two runs."

"Ah, yes," said Rachel, and scribbled on her scorecard.

"Watch the game," said Aaron.

The batter hit a high pop fly to the right side of the infield. The second baseman was under it, took two small steps while waiting, and caught it. The ball went quickly around the infield and back to the pitcher.

"Did you really plan to run away?"

"I plan to run away all the time."

"And you never do?"

"I haven't so far. Maybe that's because I discovered that, for me, the pleasure is all in the imagination."

The next batter hit weakly to the left side and the third baseman came up with it. Rachel bought another beer and poured half of it into Aaron's cup. The game moved smoothly on. Neither team threatened. Rachel

184

felt the sun hot on her shoulders and sweat in the small of her back. The concrete under her feet was sticky with ice cream and soda; peanut shells, popcorn, and paper cups swirled around her sandaled feet.

"Watching a ball game is one of the sweetest pleasures in the world."

"You romanticize it too much," said Aaron, not without affection.

"There is no objective reality," said Rachel, somewhat archly.

She leaned over to kiss him on his down-soft cheek. He did not shy away but instead put his arm around her shoulder and kissed her back. On the forehead, because he was the taller. He had learned how to kiss. His body knew how to move with love. Rachel was startled.

"In the middle of the ball park," she whispered. "What will people think?"

Aaron gently disengaged himself. On the field a third out had been made and the teams were changing places once again.

"What happened?" Rachel asked her new friend, the swarthy Jewish man.

"A pop fly down the right-field line, caught by Millan. Are you really a rebbetzin?"

"Cross my heart and hope to die."

"Where's your husband's pulpit?"

"In Gateshead."

"Are there a lot of Jews in Gateshead?"

"Enough for a congregation."

It was the sixth inning. The Mets had left a man on base in every inning, and were still behind, 2–0. In the bottom of the sixth Kingman hit a home run with two men on, and the fans let out a substantial, happy roar. Aaron and Rachel stood, along with the others, and clapped as he came around third. His teammates slapped his palm as he crossed home plate. The Pirate pitcher and catcher stood, hands on their hips, a little to the side, one near the mound, the other near the plate.

"Are you glad you had me?" asked Aaron, when they sat down again.

"Of course I am. What kind of dumb question is that?"

"If you had to do it over, would you still have me?"

Rachel wondered whether he was asking the question in place of another, or asking it for its own sake. Did he need reassurance? Had some shadow crossed her face, had she slipped from him, far away, in that moment since the kiss? Or was he trying to free himself at the same time?

"I've never for an instant been sorry I had you," she said, and he smiled.

"It's nice to be at the ball game with you," said Aaron.

They returned to watching the players on the field. In the seventh inning the Pirates suddenly had the bases filled. It seemed to happen without fanfare: a scratch hit, a walk, a shot deep to third on which a play was impossible—it was scored as a hit. There were no outs, and a conference took place on the mound. The manager was there and the catcher and shortstop. The runners stood unconcerned on the three white bags. A cart appeared on the warning track and chugged toward home plate. A silly contraption. They had done away with the walk from the bullpen, which lent a certain pathos and dignity to the drama of replacing the pitcher. Koosman walked slowly off the mound and into the dugout. Sporadic applause rained down on him. The sun had sunk below the rim of the stadium. It was growing cool; a shadow stole toward the mound. Bob Apodaca, the relief pitcher, threw a number of warm-up pitches. Rachel observed the familiar movements. Every stance and every gesture was timed-honored, like the steps of a ritual dance. It was absolutely necessary, in watching the game of baseball, to be on intimate terms with it. Only intimacy prevented moments such as these from being dull. And then, quickly and suddenly, the tension resumed. Apodaca faced the batter, who had stepped back into the box. The runners took their lead, the fielders assessed the situation. Apodaca threw the ball.

He got out of the inning safely, retiring one batter

186

on a strikeout, a second on a pop fly to the third baseman, and the third on a long line drive to Vail in right field. Going into the bottom of the seventh it was still 3–2 in favor of the Mets.

In the top of the eighth the Pirates put two runs across to go ahead again. They did it neatly, on two doubles and a single. The game was Apodaca's now, to lose or to win.

"Do you think Dad's got a girlfriend?" asked Aaron while the Pirates took the field.

He asked this monstrous question hesitatingly, but it seemed to Rachel to be no more than an extension of her own thoughts. She was not surprised.

"I think perhaps he does," she said. "Why do you ask?"

"He was gone a lot while you were in the hospital. He used to say, 'I'm going to visit your mother,' and stay away a long long time."

Rachel felt shaken (any confirmation, whether demanded or not, is unwelcome in such a case). She felt her heart drop at the same time as she found herself springing to Seymour's defense.

"Your father is always around women. A suburban congregation is full of women with nothing to do. They have the time and the energy to busy themselves doing good deeds and bad deeds. It's awfully hard for a rabbi —or a minister—to resist them."

Aaron kept silent. The Mets went down in order in the bottom of the eighth inning.

"You don't have to explain it to me," said Aaron. "I know all about it. I just wondered what you knew. Do you have any idea who it is?"

Rachel lied with a beating heart, but quickly and easily. "I have no idea. I haven't even tried to find out. I've stayed away from the whole thing."

Rachel did not realize until she spoke that what she thought was a full lie was only half a one. She had not really shown any concern or interest. It was as though it did not have anything to do with her.

"Maybe it doesn't have anything to do with me," she said.

187

"Are you that sure of yourself, Mom?"

"Not that sure of myself—I'm that sure of your father."

Having said it she believed it and saw that Aaron believed it too.

With the Pirates ahead a lot of people began leaving the stadium. Rachel and Aaron stayed. The swarthy Jewish man's children were bored, and he left with them.

In the bottom of the ninth the Mets began to stir. The first batter up drew a walk; the second hit a double to deep left. The tying run was on third. The crowd clapped and shouted and stamped in joy. With none out, the winning run was on second. The man danced off the bag, clapping his hands, moving in anticipation. Two pitchers were warming up in the bullpen, but the Pirate manager left his starter in. He struck the batter out and got two strikes on the next one. He was pitching well but without certainty, and the air was still alive with hometown hopes. Yogi Berra called on a pinch hitter. A black man came out of the dugout to bat for Apodaca. It was John Milner. He took two balls, looking, and then swung hard. It seemed clear, from the moment the bat hit the ball and the *whap* reached up and the ball flew out, that it would fall safely. Through the hole into right field. A single. Two runs scored. The game was over. The Mets had won it, 5–4.

Rachel looked at the bleachers one last time. Only a small corner was still sunny. A single man sat there and read a newspaper. The sky was still pale blue. The bleachers ended—still—in that sharp clear line. Summer was so close you could almost touch it. Rachel thought it would be nice if only she could grab hold of the day, just as it was, and carry it home with her to savor on a bitter cold morning in winter.

Rachel and Aaron took the subway back one stop and drove home along Northern Boulevard. They stopped at a Burger King, though Rachel would have preferred a bar. They tried one, but the bartender wouldn't serve Aaron. "I don't care if you're his mother," he said. "You could be the mother of God and I

188

wouldn't give him a beer, he's not eighteen." They got home at seven-thirty. It was barely light, and they sat a brief while in the backyard. There was a note from Seymour: "No need to plan dinner for me. Hope you had a good time." Rachel said nothing. The day had been full, but it was ended now.

When Seymour returned home he was cheerful and affectionate. He said he had been to a dinner meeting with new members. Rachel believed him. She wanted to believe that her life would go smoothly and evenly so that she could return to work. She had taken the pictures of the *seder* gathering to be enlarged, and she began to do a series of drawings from them. Slowly her lethargy left her. She stopped lying around reading fat books, and left *Anna Karenina* for the last hour of the day, for bed, for just before sleep. As she worked (every morning from eight until noon), she began to conceive of the large composition. The idea grew slowly, but it was beginning to encompass all her waking hours. Her drawings began to rely less on the photos and more on each other. She thought, all it needs is discipline. She was happy, safe again in her studio at last.

But not for long. When they had made their plans, weeks before, to attend the convention of Conservative rabbis, Rachel hadn't thought about the time it would take away from her work. She never thought about future events until they stared her in the face. When Seymour said, "I'd like to leave by nine o'clock in the morning," Rachel told him she had planned to use the morning to work.

"That's all you know these days," he answered. "You hardly come out of your studio anymore."

"I wasted time in Buffalo and in the hospital. Then I rested. Now I need to paint."

"And you complain about me."

"What do I complain about?"

"You don't like me to be out so much."

"It depends on what you're doing."

"Here I'm taking you away on a few days' vacation, and you're quibbling about a couple of hours, as though you didn't want to spend them alone with me.

189

Did you ever think I might need a respite too?"

They talked out of earshot of Aaron. They always closed the doors when they argued.

It was still wintry in the Catskills, even in May. The outdoor pool was empty. Its bottom was cracked, and cigarette butts and faded Coke cans clung to the rain puddles. Seymour and Rachel had not been to a convention in years. They found the hotel an anomaly. It was surrounded by parking lots and outbuildings which housed the help. Fair nature was kept at arm's length; the outbuildings looked like slums. A gas station immediately outside the guarded gates to the hotel backed up against an open dump. The view from the hundreds of rooms was largely of hundreds of other rooms. The slums were visible, the lake was not. A ski-lift towered above the trees. Dead tulips languished beside the walk that led from the gate to the main entrance. Having properly identified themselves to the guard, Rachel and Seymour drove up to this entrance in their Plymouth convertible. Bellhops met them with racks for their clothes and carts for their luggage. They had brought only a small handbag each.

Once they entered the great indoors, all traces of mountain air and mountain sunshine vanished. It smelled of chlorine and fried potatoes.

"You know," said Rachel, "it feels as though we're on an ocean liner, but we're not going anywhere."

She thought the simile particularly apt and repeated it several times during their stay, but no one thought the remark amusing.

"I think you were praised too much as a child," said Seymour. "You seem to be struck to an extraordinary degree by the cleverness of your observations."

"I don't insult easily, either. That provides a balance to my self-satisfaction."

A bellhop led them to their room. Because it was sixty degrees outside, Rachel and Seymour had a wrangle about the need to run the air conditioner. Seymour said it was stuffy without it. Rachel said she would catch cold if it was on. In any case, the room smelled

190

like the locker room adjacent to the indoor pool.

They dressed up for dinner. Rachel wore her colorful African gown and Seymour wore a navy blazer and light gray flannel slacks, a striped shirt open at the throat and an ascot. He looked debonair. Rachel looked exotic. Everyone remarked on it. Several of Seymour's colleagues thought he and Rachel were trying to draw attention to themselves. Rachel muttered "Rabbis rabbis rabbis" as they wandered among the clergymen and their wives. She approached these hundreds of Seymour's colleagues with a mixture of exasperation and compassion. They had come (on their congregations' "convention allowance") to escape their flocks for a brief time; they did a lot of complaining about their members, the *balabatim*. They uttered the words with the same strength of feeling an earlier generation had reserved for their "bosses." They were delighted to have escaped, even briefly, from their congregations, yet they were at a hotel in the Catskills which was a member's fantasy come true, a monument to their very tastes and aspirations. Seymour was greeted by rabbis right and left. Some of the rabbis said *"Vie gehts?"* which was as much Yiddish as some of them knew. It sounded folksy and proper for the time and the place. There wasn't much of the old country stuck to most of them, but they shared the common nostalgia.

The foyer of the hotel was filled with booths and salesmen. Many of the latter were Orthodox or Israeli or both; the bazaar-like atmosphere was as close as the convention came to resuscitating the past. Torah covers, torah crowns, torah pointers, breastplates and candelabra. They were all there. *Seder* plates, tablecloths for all occasions, *challeh* knives and covers, *Kiddush* cups. Pictures of elderly Jews—on velvet, in tile, and on wood; on copper and glass; "traditional" and "modern." *Mezuzahs* in all sizes, for doors and for around the neck. Silver and gold Stars of David. *Chai* and miniature law tablets. Prayer books and *Haggadahs*. Greeting cards and kits for the kiddies, packets for the Holy Days. Dreidels and groggers. Barton's candy, chocolate from Israel, *yarmulkes* and

191

taleisim. Booklets on marriage, on law, and on ceremonies. Pamphlets on child-rearing, community relations and fund-raising. "How to get the most media coverage for your money." Retirement plans. Rachel was given a plastic bag that said EMPIRE KOSHER POULTRY on it. She thought it would be a good bag in which to carry her paints and books through Gateshead.

A cocktail party preceded dinner. The rabbis ordered Manhattans and whiskey sours. The room was lit by blue and white lights.

"I wish something would happen," said Rachel. "It's too much like a bar mitzvah. Why did we come?"

"It was a free trip."

"Free is no good if you're miserable."

"Do you want to leave?"

"As soon as possible."

"We're signed up for two nights."

"To hell with that. Let's leave tomorrow and go to New York. I'd sooner fuck in the Big Apple than the Borsht Belt."

A rabbi had come up behind them. "What language you use, rebbetzin!"

"Hi yah, Harry," said Seymour. Harry had been in his class at the Seminary.

"Howya doing?"

They might both have been salesmen. Conventions seemed to do that—Seymour was always much too hearty.

"Did you hear about Chaim?" asked Harry.

"No. What about him?" said Seymour.

"He got fired."

"I thought they loved him."

"That's always the ones they fire."

"Did you hear Toledo is open?"

"So it seems."

"The place is going downhill."

"It used to be a good congregation."

"What about Rochester?"

"They have a lot of competition from the Reform congregation. There's a crackerjack rabbi who pulls them in at the other place."

192

"Joe Levine is leaving Milwaukee."

"I was told he was very happy there."

"I think he's going to teach full time."

"You still in Philly?"

"Yeah. And you, where was it? On Long Island?"

"Gateshead. My contract comes up this fall."

"I wish you luck. Nice to see you, Rachel."

They looked in vain for old friends, familiar faces. But the men Seymour had been close to in his student days didn't go to conventions. They had put all of that behind them. They taught or counseled or wrote.

The stampede toward the dining room had begun. Most of the men in the crowd wore *yarmulkes*. A few congregants were present. They wore them too. Surrounded by so many rabbis they acted very deferential. Those who had accompanied their own rabbis tried to show the others what good friends they were. In that case, the rabbi had to act deferential. Or jolly. It all depended, but in most cases it was a bore. Rabbis went to conventions to forget about their congregations, even if they found themselves talking about them all the time.

Seymour and Rachel managed to find a nearly empty table. They sat down with a morose young man and a middle-aged couple eager to smile. Seymour introduced himself and introduced Rachel.

"Where are you?" said the middle-aged rabbi.

"Gateshead, Long Island," said Seymour.

"Detroit, Michigan," said the rabbi.

There were baskets with rolls and rye bread and black bread on the table. Also dishes with celery and olives and a plate with pickles and pickled tomatoes. The seats around the table filled up slowly. There were a couple from Chicago and a classmate of Seymour's named Moshe who wore a diamond ring on his pinky and had a suntan.

"You still in Miami?" asked Seymour.

"I've got a life-time contract," said Moshe.

The last to join them was a stately elderly couple from Springfield, Massachusetts.

A rabbi on the dais was asked to make the *hamotzi*. Dinner was served. There were many choices, all of

193

them kosher. A container with a non-dairy "cream" sat on the table. It was kept in the container so that one and all could see that it was, in fact, not milk being— God forbid—served with meat. Everyone dug in as though starved. Eating a lot was the only way the paying guests could get back at the hotel (there was no way of getting even) for charging them a hundred dollars a day. There appeared to be an endless variety of food, beginning with the chicken soup and *kneidlach,* the consommé madrilene, the chopped liver and herring salad, the fruit cup and the melon. Some of the dishes had French names but proved to be ordinary Jewish brisket and *flanken* when they arrived. Boiled chicken, veal stew, roast beef, chicken paprika.

"Are you a graduate of the Teachers' Institute?" the stately rebbetzin from Springfield asked Rachel.

"No, I'm not," said Rachel, sounding apologetic.

"Do you participate much in congregational activities?" she was asked.

"Not if I can help it," Rachel answered, with a smile she hoped was guileless.

"Good for you," said the stately rebbetzin. "Don't let them think they can make a slave out of the rabbi's wife."

The rebbetzin from Chicago was interested in talking to the men. "What's the response to late Friday night services in your congregation?" she asked the rabbi from Springfield. "And do you allow bingo?"

The couple from Detroit answered yes to everything. "We are Jewishly alive in Detroit."

"I never get to see my husband except at conventions," said the rebbetzin from Chicago, "and then he talks shop all the time."

"Late Friday night services have become obsolete," said the rabbi from Springfield.

"They certainly don't work in suburbia," said Seymour.

"Is your husband very busy?" the rebbetzin from Chicago asked Rachel.

"He does a lot of private counseling," said Rachel, and received a sharp look from Seymour.

"We have bingo twice a week," said Moshe. "We

194

bus them in from all over town. Made so much money we redecorated the sanctuary last year. It's the most gorgeous in greater Miami. This year it's chandeliers for the whole damn building."

"Bussing poor people into your *shul* to gamble is disgusting," said Rachel. "I bet you wouldn't bus them into your neighborhood school."

The word "disgusting" had sent an unpleasant shock through the dinner guests.

"Are you socially-conscious, dear?" the rebbetzin from Detroit asked.

"They love it," said Moshe. "Better they lose their money to us than to the numbers people."

Rachel chewed angrily on her breast of veal. The others ignored her. Only the rebbetzin from Springfield looked upon her with friendly eyes.

Rachel turned toward Seymour. He always seemed more lovable at conventions. Rachel liked him a lot when she saw him among his peers. She always loved him, but sometimes he was hard to like. In company such as this, she thought, he shines like a beacon in the coal-black night.

The dais was chock-full of important rabbis, professors, lay people and their wives. The dining room blitzed with the lights of flashbulbs. Photographers were busy taking pictures of each and every guest at the head table. Several rabbis dashed from place to place, speaking words of welcome, delivering messages, arranging introductions. They kept a careful lookout for the photographers, so that they might raise their smiling faces to them. A revered old professor, the guest of honor, could not eat because rabbis kept coming up to shake his hand. Each time he was approached he would wipe the corners of his mouth with the napkin and raise his behind about an inch from the chair. His velvet *yarmulke* often nearly toppled from his mane of white hair but he always caught it in time with a practiced hand. He wore a long white beard and looked magnificent. He had always impressed the world—especially the Gentile world— with the magnificence of his looks. He had been unloved by generations of students. Most of them, rabbis

195

now, had forgotten how little they had loved him. The light of public opinion and institutional reverence (he had devoted his life to the Seminary) blinded them to his past meannesses.

"What a bastard he was," murmured Seymour.

The white hair stood like a saint's halo about the professor's pinched face.

"A true scholar, a man of God," said the morose young rabbi, who spoke and ate little.

The salad was bitter and made up mostly of endive and chicory. Also iceberg lettuce. The rolls had all been eaten.

"Do you have children?" the Detroit rebbetzin asked Rachel.

"A son."

"Didn't you bring him?"

"I believe in taking an occasional break from motherhood," said Rachel.

"Up here you don't have to see your children all day."

"Where are you?" Seymour asked the morose young man at long last.

"I'm looking for a job right now. I was an assistant to the rabbi in Short Hills."

Seymour groaned.

"What a ballbreaker you picked out," said Moshe.

"We got along well," said the morose young man.

"So why are you out of a job?"

"The congregation found me too traditionally oriented. I think they were threatened because I was bringing the message of Torah to their children. I turned them on to God."

"In Short Hills?" asked Rachel, incredulous.

"You'd be surprised how hungry they are for spiritual experience in that gilded ghetto."

Moshe brayed at him. He was the sort of man who answered criticism by belching and said "bullshit" when he encountered intellectual subtleties. A man of the people with a diamond pinky ring. "You really think that it's *spiritual* to observe six hundred and thirteen *mitzvahs*?" he said. "I tell you I have yet to

196

see a truly spiritual rabbi in this entire organization. I hope I don't offend you?" He hoped no such thing.

"Not at all, this is my first convention." He added, "I *also* noticed the absence of a spiritual dimension among the members of the Rabbinical Assembly."

"The traditional values are the true values," said the rabbi from Detroit.

"Let 'em come to me," growled Moshe. "I'll give 'em a spiritual dimension."

"Bingo you'll give them," said Rachel.

Conversation died down briefly while decisions were made about dessert. The group at the table had not established any great rapport. Rachel decided once again that she loved Seymour. She had come to understand this world in which he moved. They had been through it all together. Natalie Gould would never do. She too would say, "Go without me, I don't want to have anything to do with those boring people. I don't know how you stand them." But she had not been present at the beginning. The question was, of course, whether Seymour was ready to seek to forget the beginning.

"Do you have a good cantor?" the rabbi from Chicago asked the rabbi from Detroit.

"He wishes he could make a career in opera, but so far, thank God, he hasn't succeeded."

"My cantor wants to be a rock star," said Moshe. "I could do without that, but the people in my congregation, they love him."

"My cantor wants to be the rabbi," said the rabbi from Springfield. "He shows up everywhere. He pays hospital calls, *shiva* calls. He gives benedictions and invocations for the Lions and the Rotary. My only hope is he'll lose his voice."

Dessert was served. It grew quiet around the table again. The men were thinking about the troubles caused by cantors. Rachel ordered strawberries. "We're all out of strawberries," said the waiter. The public address system shushed the rabbis and rebbetzins to relative silence. It was announced that rabbi so-and-so from Denver would lead the grace after the meal.

197

Seymour fished the *yarmulke* from his pocket (the other men at the table wore theirs at all times) and joined in the *bentshing*. Here, Rachel was no longer the expert she had been in Buffalo. She had to fake a lot of the words, she did not know the whole thing by heart. Most of the rabbis and rebbetzins did. She joined in the very last section with special gusto; she remembered the words because they were part of the abbreviated form used at congregational dinners. Then the speeches began.

Many rabbis had vied for the honor of honoring the world-renowned professor. Being rabbis, they spoke at length. The world-renowned professor cackled to himself when a joke was made and bowed his head modestly when his great knowledge, unique scholarship, and becoming humility were mentioned. Two learned papers were read in his honor. They concerned the use of a particularly obscure word used in an ancient text regarding the spring festival. The rabbis held contrasting views on the matter and it was not resolved. When the world-renowned professor rose to speak it was nearly eleven o'clock. He did not resolve the question raised in the two papers though he hinted that he had a solution in the works and that it might involve a third view. He told anecdotes about his life and times at the Seminary. They were self-effacing, modest and amusing. They tended, always, to end triumphantly for the professor or for his point of view. He always came out ahead. He was never bested. His voice tinkled with mirth.

"I am nothing but a simple scholar," he said, again and again. "A simple scholar, a rabbi and teacher in Israel. And if you asked me, now, to choose between the profession I have pursued, among my books and my papers, and the profession I might have—like all of you—followed, in the pulpit leading a devoted flock, I will tell you that I would choose (if I had to do it again) the pleasures and rewards of the pulpit. For they are truly blessed, who serve as a preacher and teacher in Israel."

"Bullshit," said Moshe, but he stood up, along with

198

everyone else in the room, to clap and cheer for the world-renowned professor.

After dinner, many rabbis and their wives remained in the lobby, chatting with each other. Rachel and Seymour went to their room. It still smelled of chlorine. The windows could not be opened. Another argument over the air conditioning ensued. Rachel fell asleep quickly. But she dreamt that Natalie Gould stood alongside Route 17, hitchhiking. "Don't pick her up," she told Seymour, but he stopped the car and told her to get in. They all three sat in the front seat and Seymour drove very fast. "STOP!" said Rachel, but he drove on and on, past all her destinations. Rachel woke up. There was spittle on her pillow. She was angry with Seymour. She turned over in the large bed in the hotel room and muttered "Bastard!" Seymour had pulled all the covers on top of himself. The air conditioning hummed, but the room felt stuffy.

"Son of a bitch," said Rachel, a little louder.

"What?" Seymour groaned and burrowed into the covers.

"You're a bastard."

His face was rendered askew by deep sleep, his hair was matted. Rachel pulled the sheet from him and turned away. The curtains at the window were so thick it was impossible to know whether it was daylight. Seymour, coming awake, had an erection. He said, "Rachel, where are you?" and searched for her. She felt his hard penis up against her backside. Still angry because of her dream, she said, "Don't touch me," and recoiled from him.

"What's the matter?" he asked, almost awake now.

"You're an unfaithful son of a bitch," she said, and Seymour withdrew as though stung. He rolled to the furthest corner of the bed and Rachel knew he was hurt. It relieved her anger somewhat but also fanned her guilt. She ought not, she thought, be devious. But she could never ever win a confrontation. "I'm sorry," she said. "I had an unpleasant dream about you." They went back to sleep for a while, each keeping to the edge of the bed, far from the other. When they woke up again, they had almost buried the memory with the night.

Breakfast brought them together with two young couples. Introductions were made but conversation languished. Who could talk to strangers at the breakfast table? Rachel and Seymour ordered herring in sour cream and scrambled eggs. They had fresh onion rolls and sweet butter. They ate melon and blueberries in rich cream and drank coffee with half-and-half. They would surely have to skip lunch.

"Let's go home soon," said Rachel.

"I heard you," said Seymour. He was still skittish about their nocturnal encounter.

She went to a meeting of the rebbetzins. It was held in a sunny lounge of the hotel. Rebbetzins tended to go about in small, closely-knit groups at conventions. Many of them knew each other from the days when they had been students at the Teachers' Institute of the Seminary. They met regularly, when their husbands did, at Chanukah dances and regional gettogethers. At Sisterhood conferences they sought each other out, proud of their bonds and traditions. Back in Eastern Europe they had once been addressed as "Rebbetzin" as surely as their husbands were called "Rabbi." They did not consider their roles demeaning; they were proud to be defined by what their husbands did, and endeavored to fulfill the demands made upon them faithfully. Over the years, of course, the conviction had grown in many of their hearts that they were as learned as their men and could do what they did just as well—or better. So they sometimes competed with them. Congregants joked about this, as did certain rabbis. But only a small minority among the rebbetzins were feminists.

The meeting of the rabbis' wives was loosely structured. There was supposed to be a discussion about the problems they all faced, but not all of them saw the problems clearly. Or saw them at all. The feminists recited a long list of abuses, from the prayer men said each morning, thanking God because he had not made them women, to the prohibition against women serving

200

as witnesses. Others merely complained that their husbands' souls were sapped by the demands of the congregation. They bewailed their loneliness. The feminists were opposed by a number of vocal women who believed that matters were best left unchanged, sanctified as they were by centuries of habit and usage.

"I wouldn't even want to be called to the Torah," one rebbetzin said. "Those scrolls are heavy. Suppose I drop one? Do you ladies realize what Jewish Law requires of a person who drops a *sefer torah?* Forty days of fasting. Some penance! No thanks—I'd rather be kept in my place."

Rachel decided to go among the men to find Seymour. The room was crowded with rabbis. Feelings ran high. There was much discussion; many men had asked to speak. Rachel did not see Seymour in the swarming room. She sat down on one of the gold-colored chairs and listened to the discussion.

"Aren't you Seymour Sonnshein's wife?" the rabbi on her left asked.

"Yes, I am."

"He's going to speak shortly."

"On what?"

"I don't know, but I think he's against it."

"Against it?"

"They tell me he likes to make trouble. They say he doesn't believe in ritual."

"Seymour believes God put the Jews on earth to 'do justice and love mercy,' not to worry about whether the light in the refrigerator goes on when you open the door on *Shabbos.*"

"Rabbis have to make a living too. Show me *one* who can feed his family preaching social gospel and I'll show you a fraud."

Seymour spoke briefly and eloquently. He defended the right of rabbis to follow their conscience in the matter of ritual observance. Behind Rachel two men scuffed their feet and showed displeasure by making the kinds of sounds that children make when they have to listen to the substitute teacher explain the day's rules and regulations.

"I hear he eats *treif,*" said one voice.

201

Rachel did not turn around.

"My sister-in-law belongs to his congregation and she says he eats Chinese. What can you expect from someone married to a *shikse*?"

"His wife's not Jewish?"

"That's the rumor. I may be wrong. My sister-in-law says they are a couple of oddballs. He's one of those social-justice types. Against Vietnam, for the *shvartses*."

"Same old self-hate. No wonder he eats *chazzer*."

Rachel kept her eyes on Seymour, but she no longer heard him. She tried to think of a clever response to the detractors behind her, but she was tongue-tied. Quick wit was not her style. She moved slowly through the world of words; it was pictures she saw and remembered. Seymour had sat down to scattered applause. The men behind Rachel left. She had not turned to look at them, had caught no glimpse of their faces. The moderator of the discussion thanked the rabbis for their contribution to the day's enlightenment and for the wisdom they had contributed. Nothing had been decided, and, because it was almost time for lunch, few of the men were listening.

Rachel and Seymour met outside.

"Two guys behind me said you ate *treif* and I was a *shikse*," said Rachel.

"I hope you corrected them."

"You *do* eat *treif*."

"And sometimes I wish you *were* a *shikse*."

"They thought you were filled with self-hate."

"Let's get out of here."

Rachel and Seymour drove back to New York. The closer they got the more like summer it seemed. The trees along the Palisades Parkway were green, their leaves unfurled. The city was bathed in strong metallic light; everything was crisp and clear. They went to the Museum of Modern Art and sat in the garden. They told each other that they loved one another. They drank a beer and Rachel lectured Seymour on Matisse. He did not mind. They checked into an old hotel on Seventh Avenue and opened the window of their room

202

to the setting sun. It was a funky room; the carpet was stained, the furniture old. But it was not a ship going nowhere. They saw a movie downtown at the Waverly Theater and ate in SoHo and had another beer. They felt young and shouted out their joy in the streets.

Late that night they returned to the hotel and made love on the lumpy bed and fell asleep to the sound of street noises many floors below.

The next morning they drove back to Gateshead. The pad beside the telephone was full of messages. A funeral awaited Seymour. A Board meeting had been rescheduled. A buyer had been found for the house. Sydelle Prawn had been taken to the hospital in an ambulance.

7

June was usually the month of promise: the beginning of summer, the end of the school year. It was a time of hope and of lengthening days. Rachel loved summer. Its demands were few, its pleasures as profuse as the scented roses climbing the backyard fence.

Rachel worked hard on her *seder* painting during the month of June. She spent every possible minute in her studio and when her work went well she felt great pleasure and strength. When it went badly she became depressed, thinking she had no talent and was wasting her time in pursuit of a chimera. Was she, after all, a suburban lady with too much time on her hands, indulging herself? She talked with no one about it, not even Sally, with whom she went to the movies often. Some evenings, when her eyes would seem to be bursting with too much looking, she walked along the beach down to the town dock and watched evening fall, the sky paling as in Magritte, the water yellow, turning black swiftly. Once Seymour asked her if she had a lover and Rachel grew angry with him. She accused him of attacking her in order to defend himself.

"I'm not unfaithful," she said, though she knew that her fierce commitment to her work was a kind of unfaithfulness. Ambition kept her in bondage almost as a lover might.

Rachel tried to let these discussions drop before they could veer into arguments. She could not spare the emotion. She would not allow herself to speak the angry accusations that sometimes rose to her

204

tongue. Seymour was often away at night. There were many congregational meetings; they ran into the early hours of morning. Seymour said he was mending his fences, giving his detractors no further cause for discontent. He met with his supporters for lunch and coffee and for drinks. Rachel asked no questions. She refused to be embroiled in a fight; she welcomed the chancé to be alone with her work. But discontent simmered beneath the summer surfaces of their lives. Natalie Gould's shadow crossed their paths. Autumn would bring disruptive change: the move, contract negotiations, uncertainty and *tzuris*.

Rachel realized that the hysterectomy had affected her more than she might admit. It put her into menopause—how could she deny it?—and brought her that much closer to the end of her life. To death. She really *had* to work; soon there would be no more time. Half her life was gone, even if she lived to be eighty.

When Aaron was a baby Rachel used to sit in the kitchen of their house in North Carolina with a friend and talk over coffee while their children played on the floor or slept in the playpen. She had spent her days like most of the other women and worked at night, a few hours here and there. She shopped and cooked and baked and washed and cared for her baby. The hours she had spent talking with her friend were good but somewhat ephemeral in retrospect, though not as ephemeral as the eternity spent at Sisterhood meetings, Hadassah meetings, worship services, bar mitzvahs and U.J.A. dinners. Still, Rachel had gone to all those things without complaining. In North Carolina they had seemed proper and part of the shape of her life. Even in Gateshead, in the beginning, the pattern had not been too intrusive. Rachel still worked at night, a few hours here and there. She had accepted the idea that she must be furtive about her art. Art was *not* her life. She had become a wife, a rebbetzin and a mother. It was irrevocable. Who cared that she had talent? Lots of people do. It takes more than talent to be an artist. But then—and she could not pinpoint the moment when it happened—she had looked at her work and decided it deserved a better place in her life.

205

Perhaps the life she had made was *not* irrevocable. She did not want to look back (when she was eighty) and see only the ephemera of devoted service spread across her years.

No doubt the women's movement had helped to define her ambitions, had helped her think about sorting out the things she wanted put on her gravestone when she died. During the summer between her freshman and sophomore years at Barnard, Rachel had worked with a scenic designer at Tanglewood. "You're very good," the man told her. "Where shall I study then, when I finish school?" she asked. "Oh, don't bother your pretty head about it," he said. "You'll only get married and have babies." Of course, she had. There were other epiphanies. Six years ago, at a party at their house, held to raise money for Clergy Concerned About Vietnam, Rachel had met a museum director. He had looked around at the paintings hung on the living room walls and asked "Who did these?" Rachel told him that she had. He was clearly surprised. "You have a talent," he said, "but I don't want to encourage you. It's too late for you to begin a career now." The words still burned in her mind.

Seymour had been asked to officiate at a big wedding, early in June, right after Shevuoth. It was to be held at a catering "facility" near Gateshead, a place almost as grand as the palace at Versailles, but located in the midst of a parking lot rather than a park. Three other rabbis would be there; the family of the bride was very distinguished.

"We have to go to the reception, even if you don't want to."

Rachel had planned to go swimming that Sunday and work in the evening. Her plans were always infused by too much optimism.

"Oh, shit," said Rachel.

"It's important, they carry a lot of weight. My contract is coming up for renewal."

"What's their name?"

"Whose?"

"The bride's family. The ones giving the wedding."

206

"Glass," said Seymour.

"Who's she marrying?"

"A medical student."

"That's nice—what's his name?"

"Minsk. Will you remember it?"

"No. Will I have to?"

"Not past today if you've sent a present."

"Damn. I forgot."

"Then you'd better remember the name. And send something."

"Like what?"

"You're the expert in housewares."

"I'll send a book: *The History of Post-Impressionism.*"

"Don't be funny, Rachel. They barely read."

"They can look at the pictures then."

The entrance to the catering facility was a mixture of Newport and the old South. Boys in livery took the cars and spirited them to the far corners of the parking lot. Two giant black men stood on either side of the doors to open them. They too wore livery, knee-breeches, and powdered wigs. The large foyer inside the entrance had a fountain in the middle; a staircase wound around it to the second floor. On the opposite wall, about a hundred feet away, was a waterfall. Colored lights played on the waters of the fountain and the waters of the fall. The sound of Muzak wafted through the spaces. Plastic plants grew in every corner of the dim interior; mirrors reflected the lights of a thousand small, candle-shaped bulbs. Video screens listed the names of the participants in each "affair," and indicated the room. There was a Roman room, a Louis XIV room, an Aztec room, a Byzantine room, a Chinese room, a South Sea Islands room, an African room and an Imperial (Viennese) room. There was not, however, an American room. America was what created the whole thing, American taste and know-how; only the entrance reflected the native style. The place was owned by Charlie (King Kong) Martucci, and it was the best on the Island. A rabbi was on the premises at all times, to see that the kosher

207

food was kosher and that none of the Chinese pork, the Byzantine shrimp, or the Aztec kidneys got mixed in with it.

The Glass/Minsk wedding was in the Louis XIV room, the largest in the house. The *chuppah* was made up entirely of white flowers. Daisies, lilies, carnations and roses were wound in and out of the latticework. Four rabbis in all had been invited to participate, as well as two cantors. Seymour had brought his black robe. He left Rachel alone and went to look for Siggy Glass to discuss logistics. Champagne was served to the waiting guests, kosher champagne and salted nuts and red caviar. Rachel took a glass and held on to it. She didn't like champagne—especially the kosher variety, which tasted like ginger ale.

"Four rabbis and two cantors!" she heard it said.

"Imagine what it cost."

"Don't worry, Siggy's got it."

"They're going to Europe on their honeymoon."

"Four rabbis and two cantors; I still don't believe it."

"I wonder did Siggy invite the *shvartse*."

"You'll see soon enough. He'll stick out like a coal in a bag of marshmallows."

"He's not so dark."

"I know, but he couldn't pass either."

Rachel looked around but could find no black face in the dim light.

The crowd was dense but well-behaved. It was difficult to move among the bodies and the yards of long dresses. Rachel allowed herself to be carried along. Now and then she took a tiny sip of her champagne.

A man looked at her and said, "Pardon me, but aren't you the rabbi's wife?"

"*A* rabbi's wife," said Rachel.

He wore a ruffled shirt. "How are you?"

"Fine."

"I'm Beryl Krieger, co-owner of the Gittleson funeral home. Tell the rabbi to give us a call sometime."

"What for?"

208

"We can always use an extra man. We like to keep a large stable for availability. And he can give us business. We help him, he helps us."

"Will I get a cut-rate funeral?"

"We can discuss that when the rabbi comes in. You're a young lady yet, but it's always good to be prepared. At the moment of death everyone is too excited to tend to these things. Here's my card."

Rachel shoved it into her purse.

"What are you interested in?" he asked. He was at no loss for conversation.

"All sorts of things," said Rachel.

She did not want to have a conversation about serious matters with the funeral director. He had sideburns and a mustache that twirled up at the ends.

"You're happy just to be a rebbetzin then; that's highly unusual these days. Your husband is a lucky man."

"I collect swizzle sticks," said Rachel.

The man looked nonplussed. "How interesting."

"And I also have a lovely collection of dwarfs."

"Dwarfs?"

"Plaster dwarfs, you know."

"Oh, of course—the kind that sit in your yard?"

"Exactly. Not very Jewish, I admit. For my Jewish collection I save *yarmulkes*. You wouldn't believe how many I have. We go to a lot of bar mitzvahs, you understand, and weddings. . . ."

"We have plain black ones with our name on them," said the funeral co-director. "You'd be surprised how many people forget to bring their own to a funeral. And some don't own one."

"Mine are all colors," said Rachel. *"L'chayim!"*

"L'chayim!" he answered, smiling at someone else. "Excuse me," he said, and left, as good at extricating himself from a conversation as he was at initiating one.

"There's Rachel Sonnshein," said Golda Garfinkle to her husband, the dentist. "I have a bone to pick with her."

"Hello, Golda," said Rachel, and inclined her head

209

slightly in the direction of Morris, whom she could not bear. His face was large and his eyes small. He looked like a schemer.

"You never showed up at the U.J.A. luncheon," said Golda to Rachel.

"What U.J.A. luncheon?"

"We sent you an invitation. I know we did."

"Maybe I was at the convention."

"All the other rebbetzins were there."

"I mean when the invitation *came*. I'm sorry, Golda. I'm truly sorry." Rachel flushed with guilt. "It might help if you called to remind me of these things."

"I'm not your secretary, nor am I your conscience."

Rachel would have loved to create another such conversation as she'd had with the funeral co-director, but now she felt inhibited. She didn't want to be mean. Besides, Golda knew her too well.

"It was very embarrassing," said Golda, "and reflected badly on our *shul*, on Seymour, and on you."

"I'll try not to let it happen again. You know, by the way, that I was in the hospital?" (What wouldn't she do to save herself?)

"We *all* knew it. Didn't you get the flowers the Sisterhood sent you either?"

"Yes. Of course I did. I believe I wrote a thank-you note to the secretary, as soon as I got home."

"I hope you'll be at the next meeting. It's on the women's movement. I think we talked about it."

"I can hardly wait."

"Rachel, let me ask you a question," said Golda, looking into Rachel's eyes with her own, which were wide open in fright and defiance. "Why are you so hostile?"

"Me hostile? What in heaven's name do you mean?"

"Let's go," said Morris. "They are about to begin the wedding."

"It goes back to when we were at Barnard. I've always rather liked you. But you were cold then, now you're hostile. I don't understand it."

Morris steered Golda away by taking her by the elbow. He leaned down and whispered in her ear. Golda drew back from him. Rachel was unhappy about

210

their conversation but had little opportunity to think about it. Naomi Shapiro, a redheaded social worker, plucked at her sleeve. "Come with us," she said. "You look lonely." Rachel allowed herself to be led to a seat. The room was nearly full. The folding chairs were placed tightly together. A red runner had been laid down on the floor. It was strewn with white flowers. Rachel wondered idly whether they were real. She decided that she was becoming obsessive about such things, and didn't touch the flowers to find out. She sat down on a folding chair next to Naomi Shapiro, grateful that she had been asked. Now it would look as though she had friends.

A spotlight was on the bride as she walked down a long incline between pillars, into the Louis XIV room and the *chuppah*. She wore a slinky white satin gown (it most certainly did not go with the decor) with a huge train. Her arms were covered with long gloves, up to the capped sleeves of her circa 1935 gown. She was very beautiful. She walked gracefully and two flower girls went before her, scattering more petals.

Naomi Shapiro said, "She's a fool to get married. Just look at her! Gorgeous and free, giving it all up for that future doctor of America."

Rachel was not the only one who heard her.

The groom stood under the *chuppah*, surrounded by rabbis and cantors, waiting for his bride. Seymour stood taller than all the others, including the groom, whose frizzy hair stood several inches up from his head and was crowned by a royal blue *yarmulke*. It took young Ms. Glass a long time to reach the *chuppah* and its gaggle of waiting men. The wedding guests sent forth small exclamations of delight as she approached, the spotlights playing on her resplendently; the sound of a symphony orchestra cascaded through the hall. When the tape recorder stopped and the lights dimmed to a romantic dusk, the rabbis began their ceremonies. Each one had been given a specific task to perform. The cantors sang. There were blessings, psalms, more blessings, several little speeches. The bearded rabbi in the broad-brimmed hat said a few words about God the matchmaker and then yet another rabbi urged the

211

couple to establish a Jewish home. He said a Jewish home was the best bulwark against assimilation. "Beware of assimilation! It does not hit you all at once but sneaks up on you without warning." He illustrated his point with a parable about a lobster. A lobster thrown into a pot of boiling water, he said, thrashes about madly, fighting for life. But put him in a pot of cold water and turn the heat up slowly and he'll never know what killed him. "Not that I, God forbid, would boil a lobster, but I keep my eyes open, so I can learn from life and impart my knowledge to you, my children. Don't let assimilation sneak up on you."

"The lobster gets cooked either way," said Naomi Shapiro.

The cantors chanted the seven blessings in unison. The bride marched seven times around her groom. The fourth rabbi read the marriage contract in a flat, Midwestern voice. Seymour pronounced Minsk/Glass man and wife. The wineglass was put on the floor. The groom stepped on it but it didn't break. He stepped on it again and this time a loud crunch was heard in the hall. Mazel tov! said the four hundred guests, and the tape recorder was activated once again, this time to peal forth Mendelssohn. The wedding party marched out while the spotlights danced in time to the music.

The feast was sumptuous and took the better part of the night. The waitresses wore white gloves. Seymour and Rachel sat at a table with Naomi Shapiro and her husband, an elderly cousin from the bridegroom's side who was quite deaf, and a couple from Great Neck who wore (man and wife both) white muslin Mexican shirts.

"The Jewish wedding ceremony is barbaric," said the wife.

"Do you remember the rabbi who married us?" the husband asked. "He smelled of garlic and was filthy."

"Did they rehearse this bit?" Seymour asked Rachel in a low voice.

"Maybe they don't know who you are," she answered.

"Walking around the groom like that, seven times,

212

what male chauvinism!" said the lady from Great Neck.

"That's the tradition," said Seymour. "The bride agreed to it. You can't change the past, only the present. She seems not to want to change the present either—she's planning to lead a strictly Orthodox life."

"We used to be Jews," said the man from Great Neck, "but we're people now. Citizens of the world. Citoyens! *Our* daughter got married on the beach—we had an Indian mystic, a Jehovah's Witness, and a Muslim lead the prayers. We built a bonfire and went swimming in the nude after dark. The surf was high. We ate nuts and cheese and drank dandelion wine. It was so good and open and free. Why don't the Jews learn to be a little more radical? Everyone else has changed for the better in this century. They lost us the day that rabbi breathed garlic on me."

"Garlic is a natural food," said Rachel.

"Judaism has survived worse than weddings in the surf," said Seymour. "And do you call the murder of six million a change for the better?"

"I *knew* you'd bring that up sooner or later, Rabbi," said the man from Great Neck. "You people always do. The numbers are greatly exaggerated."

Rachel saw the black man before the others did. He was bearded and wore a conservative dark suit. There was a white woman in a pale fur with him, thin as a model. They walked toward the table where the Sonnsheins sat with the others and two empty chairs. The dancers parted to let them through.

"I guess that's Norma Glass's sister and brother-in-law," Seymour said, quietly, to Rachel.

"You know them?"

"I know about them. Don't you know I know everything?"

The men rose as the couple came to the table. The man from Great Neck shook hands with the black man. A smile wreathed his face.

"I'm E. B. Jackson," said the black man, "uncle of the bride. This is my wife Jean."

"Norma's sister?" cackled the deaf cousin.

"Yes," said Jean Jackson.

213

She looked older than her husband. Rachel thought she detected a wariness about the eyes, a tense stretch around the mouth. She was forever expecting insults, receiving rebuffs.

"Are you the writer?" Naomi Shapiro asked.

"I am," said E. B. Jackson. He was more at ease in a crowd than his wife.

The couple from Great Neck were thrilled. They beamed in unison; bright and literate questions formed in their minds. Excitement also gripped the others at the table, a kind of heightened awareness, now that they knew a celebrity sat amongst them.

Crêpes stuffed with a creamy chicken mixture were brought to the table by the white-gloved waitresses. The dancing stopped briefly; the band played on. There was a delicate chicken broth, not with matzoh balls but with little tiny noodles and bits of vegetables. Then a mixed salad sprinkled with sliced raw mushrooms and grated red cabbage, spinach leaves and light green romaine, thinly sliced tomatoes and purple onions.

"Quite a delicious meal to be so kosher," said the man from Great Neck. "Rabbi," he said, in a voice that stilled the rest of the guests at the table, "Rabbi —don't you find that Jews are becoming more racist?"

"Perhaps," said Seymour, "but so is everyone else. Jews," he said—wearily, having made the point so often before—"reflect the society in which they live. On the whole, I'd say, they are probably *less* racist than other whites, just as they are generally more liberal. Even if not as liberal as they once were."

The man from Great Neck was playing his role for the black writer, who looked bored, having been in too many places where conversations between others were slyly addressed to him.

"I beg to differ, Rabbi. You are propagating a myth." The silver jewelry on his chest shook with his passion. "I have Catholic friends who are more liberal than any Jews I know."

"Good for you," said Seymour. "Or should I say 'good for them'? I am talking about statistics. Numbers. A broad experience."

214

"Whose?"

"Mine for instance."

"Your experience does not count. You live in a ghetto, you have to do only with Jews. You dispense opium to the Jewish masses."

"That's better than dispensing cant or bullshit," said Seymour.

The black writer sat impassively, drinking his whiskey. His wife picked nervously at her food. Rachel had grown angry.

"Comes the revolution you'll be the first to hang," she muttered to the man from Great Neck.

"Now wait a minute, sweetheart. The rabbi and I were having a friendly discussion, but you're being nasty."

Naomi Shapiro had said something to her.

"What?" said Rachel, distracted from her pursuit of the ass from Great Neck. "I'm sorry I didn't hear you."

"I said, 'Have you read any of Mr. Jackson's books?'" Naomi was trying to keep the peace.

"Why yes," said Rachel. She looked at the writer. She knew she had read one or two of his books. She couldn't recall their titles but seemed to see the jackets clearly: brownstones on a Harlem street, sensitive young faces. E. B. Jackson wrote urban novels. He wrote with wit about the black middle class in white America.

"I wonder if he'll write about *us*," said Naomi. She addressed the writer, in her blunt, straight way. "Will you, Mr. Jackson?"

He smiled a cool, public smile. "I never know what I'll write about until I actually begin."

"It won't do me any good then, to tell you the story of my life?" Rachel asked playfully.

"And who are you?"

"The rebbetzin . . . rabbi's wife."

"Mrs. Sonnshein paints," said Naomi Shapiro.

"Isn't that unusual for a rebbetzin . . . rabbi's wife?" said E. B. Jackson.

"*Shall* I tell you the story of my life?" Rachel was feeling high.

"I can't promise how you'll turn up in one of my

215

books," said E. B. Jackson. "Writers are a nasty lot. I wouldn't trust one if I were you."

The mother of the bride came over to their table just then. "Are you having a good time—everybody? Hello, Jean," she said to her sister. "Why so late?"

"Traffic was incredible," said her brother-in-law.

"I didn't think we had to make a special effort to be on time," said Jean, "since we were barely invited."

Norma Glass ignored her. She wore peach chiffon. Her hair was losing the order and the sheen her hairdresser had teased into it.

"My husband wants to see you before you leave," Norma Glass said to Seymour.

"Aren't you going to greet us?" said the man from Great Neck. He got up from his chair and gave Norma a small kiss on the cheek.

"I'm surprised you're here," said Norma. "I didn't think you went to Jewish affairs."

"It's been very enlightening to talk to the rabbi. We haven't discussed Israel as yet," he said, casting a malicious glance at Rachel.

He seemed to have developed a curious affection for Seymour. The Viennese cart was coming around. Mrs. Glass had done her duty.

"What you were saying about the Jews," said the man from Great Neck, "do you apply that to Israel too?"

"The poor Arabs," said his wife, "exploited by the white man."

"I think I don't want to talk about Israel," said Seymour.

E. B. Jackson looked at his wife. They got up.

"We must fight that traffic once more," said the uncle of the bride.

The men all rose.

"If we ever meet again you must tell me the story of your life," said E. B. Jackson to Rachel. The smile on his face took the edge off his words.

The man from Great Neck turned to Seymour as soon as they were once again seated.

"I assume you support Israel?" he said.

"We Jews don't have much choice," said Seymour.

216

He touched Rachel's arm. "I'll go say good-bye to Sigmund Glass. I'll see you downstairs."

He disappeared without a word to the others at the table. Rachel was left to make the farewells.

"May we meet only on happy occasions," said the deaf old lady.

"Let's get together some time," said Naomi Shapiro.

"Peace!" said the man from Great Neck.

Rachel and Seymour met at the fountain.

"Look what I got," he said, and pulled a crisp new hundred-dollar bill from one of Sigmund Glass's business envelopes.

"Wow!" said Rachel. "It isn't often that I get to see one of those. Not bad for a half hour's work."

"I worked a hell of a lot longer than that," said Seymour, "if you count the time spent listening to that idiot from Great Neck. Besides, Siggy Glass spent twenty thousand dollars on this wedding, he can afford a hundred bucks for the rabbi."

"He could have given us free passes to all his movie theaters. Wouldn't that have been nice? Free movies forever?"

"Nothing is forever," said Seymour.

June was hot and humid that year. Most days Rachel worked in the mornings when the attic was still cool, and went down to the beach about one o'clock, with a hero sandwich and a can of cold beer. She carried her sketchpad and a book (*Anna Karenina* still, though she sometimes varied the fare and read Chekhov stories) and stretched out far from the mothers and the children, at the very end of the Town Beach where the sign said *STOP—Private Property.*

Sometimes she walked along the pebbly shore past all the warning signs; the only thing she feared were suburbia's dogs. She carried a stick against them. On many days she felt so deeply drawn into her work that she could not bear company. Only when she was alone did she feel content, open to all the visual impressions.

One afternoon, toward the middle of June, Rachel went down to the beach as usual, to sit near the

217

rocks at its easternmost end. She was almost the only one there. School had not yet let out; the only teenagers around were obviously playing hooky. A young couple was necking on a blanket. Their transistor's beat did not affect the rhythm of their lovemaking. For a short minute Rachel wondered whether Aaron too came here and laid his girl on a blanket in the sand. She sketched the rocks and the opposite shore, taking note how it had changed since the winter.

Rachel ate the sandwich she had brought and drank the beer. It had been a long morning since breakfast —she was hungry and thirsty both. After she finished eating she read a while, lying on her stomach to let her back and the back of her legs tan. This time she had Chekhov with her, but the beer soon made her sleepy and she put her head down on her arms and fell asleep. She slept for an hour or so, deeply, and didn't wake up until a sudden chill crossed her body. A large white cloud had come out of nowhere and blotted out the sun. She put on her sweatshirt and looked at her watch. It was after four o'clock. Rachel got into her car and drove the long way home. She liked the back streets of Gateshead. They seemed to echo long-forgotten scenes. Their secrets were unknown and could only be imagined.

There was an unfamiliar car in front of the house when Rachel returned. A cream-colored Mercedes. Rachel was annoyed because it blocked the driveway and she had to park in front of the Prawns', where a sign read "2-Hour Parking 7 A.M. to 7 P.M. No Parking on the Streets of this Village from Midnight to 6 A.M." This regulation was meant to discourage lovers and burglars. Lovers and burglars were not easily discouraged, but Rachel had gotten a ticket once when she left the car out front overnight.

She burst into the house with a little too much clatter, all because she was uncertain who was there and did not know how to appear. She saw Seymour first, stretched out in his armchair, long-legged and tousled, wearing an old plaid cotton flannel shirt and white house-painter's pants. Old blue sneakers were on his feet; no socks, and holes in the sneakers, too. Across

218

from him and his sneakers, on the couch, sitting up primly behind the coffee table, as though ready to leap up and leave, was Natalie Gould. Rachel was surprised but not confounded. As soon as she saw Natalie Gould she thought, "She is here to talk to Seymour about the congregation. She is interested in both, she wants to help him, she is going to be a strong supporter, he needs that, Natalie Gould will be here all the time from now on, making plans. I only hope she leaves me out of them." It took her a short while to get through *those* thoughts and to begin on the others, the unpleasant ones. She sat down first, wet ass and sandy feet and all, on the other chair, the Thonet chair which wouldn't stain from the saltwater or mind the sand. She took her sunglasses off and wiped her nose with her hand, in an exaggerated gesture again, because she was uncomfortable and half-naked and sticky-haired and Natalie was very chic and cool and clean. Only after she had sat down (legs apart as she used to sit on the bench during a baseball game) did the other thoughts come tumbling through her mind. "What are they doing here? Did they make love? How long has this state of affairs existed so blatantly right beneath my eyes?" Again, the thoughts did not have such clear shape; they tumbled around like laundry in a dryer. Rachel saw Seymour in his chair, all stretched out and languid, and Natalie on the couch, composed. She felt she ought to say something (as though it were she who was the intruder) and so she began telling about her afternoon on the beach.

"I fell asleep on the beach, after my beer and hero sandwich, trying to read Chekhov." (She had not planned those exact words and yet they came out as if rehearsed. Drinking beer and reading Chekhov. Rachel was drawing up the picture of who she was.)

"You look a little sunburned," said Seymour, "on your shoulders and your nose."

Rachel felt the heat on her skin as he mentioned it.

"The suntan suits you," said Natalie. She was more crisp and cool than ever. "I'm allergic to the sun and have to stay out of it as much as I can. I envy you your sun worship."

219

She, too, drew up her qualifications. She wore stockings. A hot day in June and Natalie Gould wore stockings! She wore Gucci loafers, too, and a white cotton suit. A small sand drift had gathered under Rachel's chair. She felt the bathing suit chafe between her legs and on her burned shoulders. Seymour seemed at peace, enjoying his place there between them, all stretched out. Rachel felt that she had intruded. That she was the outsider begging to come in and join them. But at what?

"Seymour and I were just discussing the congregation," said Natalie. "You may know that there is a small group of us working very hard to see that Seymour stays in Gateshead."

Rachel did not want to think about the congregation, let alone discuss it with Natalie Gould. She felt badly that she didn't want to, but it was none of Natalie's business. Whenever she thought about Seymour's situation she grew angry, but her anger did no one any good and only exhausted and distracted her. But that was none of Natalie's business either.

"What can I do?" said Rachel.

"We didn't mean to imply that you should do anything," said Natalie. "I was just telling you what we were talking about. Seymour needs friends and supporters. We have to work hard . . . if he wants to stay, that is."

Natalie wore large glasses, tinted about the edges. Her neck was long and smooth. Two strands of pearls encircled it.

"I think I'd better go get the sand off me," said Rachel. "I'll see you when I get dressed."

"I'll probably be gone."

Rachel noticed that she had had a drink. The glass sat in a small puddle on the coffee table. Seymour's was on the carpet beside his chair.

Rachel went upstairs. The door to Aaron's room was closed. He was listening to a ball game and doing homework. Rachel knocked and stepped in before he answered.

"How long has she been here?" she asked.

"I don't know. She was here when I came home."

220

"In the living room?"

"Where did you *think* she'd be, Mother?"

Aaron rarely said *mother*. Rachel shrugged. No need to entangle Aaron in her problems.

"I think I'll take a shower."

Rachel sat on the unmade bed after she came out of the steaming shower. She had washed her hair, too, and felt clean and healthy. Summer made her bloom, it uncovered what she thought of as her true self. Sitting cross-legged among the tangled sheets, she saw herself in the mirror that was attached to the closet door. She was pale where the bathing suit covered her body. The red nipples of her breasts were round and dark; her arms were deep brown against her white stomach, against the sheets, her hair damp and matted from where she had toweled it. "How come, Seymour, you need that bitch?" she said, aloud, watching her mouth move in the mirror. The knowledge that Natalie's presence in Seymour's life was real could no longer be denied. She was in the house, he had brought her home, he was trying to insinuate her into Rachel's life. "Oh, no you don't!" said Rachel to the mirror. She liked the way the narrow glass framed her from ceiling to floor and shut out the sides. The window behind her (shuttered against the afternoon sun) gave the picture depth. Rachel got up and inspected Seymour's bed for fresh semen. There wasn't any and the bed smelled only of him. Maybe she exaggerated, maybe it hadn't gone as far as she thought. She had been denying her suspicions, now they had come in an overwhelming rush, like the final awful acknowledgment of the disease that's been ignored, despite the lumps and muddled pains, the daily exhaustion.

Rachel pulled on a sweatshirt and a pair of ragged Levis and stepped into her thongs. She tied a kerchief around her wet hair and put some face cream (a pointed gift from her mother) on her cheeks and nose and went downstairs. Natalie Gould was saying goodbye. Rachel saw her standing on the porch, beyond Seymour, who was framed by the doorway. Rachel thought she saw Natalie withdraw her hand from his, but she might just have been brushing at a summer

221

moth. Seymour stood very still in the open door, holding the screen behind him. The late afternoon sunshine slanted through the maple trees and fluttered in the shadows of the porch. Rachel had the sense, again, of being apart, in the dark of the stairs. Hadn't she seen a hundred movies in which it happened just like this? Natalie walked gracefully down the porch steps and into her cream-colored Mercedes without looking back. Seymour let the screen door slam and stood in the hallway, facing Rachel.

"I didn't see you," he said, "sneaking down the stairs."

"She left," said Rachel.

"She had to go home. She said to tell you good-bye."

They were short with one another and uncomfortable. Rachel picked up the glasses in the living room and wiped the water puddle with the sleeve of her sweatshirt.

"Tell her not to park in front of the driveway next time."

Seymour said nothing. Rachel took the bottle of Jack Daniels that stood on the coffee table and carried it with her to the kitchen. The kitchen was golden with the light of the sun going down over the trees at the bottom of the yard. In summer they blotted out the hills across the bay. Rachel poured herself some of the bourbon and added ice and tap water.

"What's for dinner?" Seymour asked, trailing after her, his hands in the pockets of his white painter's pants. He had decided to pretend that life was normal.

"Did you sleep with her?" Rachel asked.

"What do you mean?"

"You don't understand English? Did you fuck her?"

"Today?"

"Today, one day, any day, did you?"

"Rachel?"

"Answer me."

"Rachel, you know I love you."

"So you *did* sleep with her."

"I love you, Rachel, better than anyone in the whole wide world."

"How long have you been carrying on?"

222

"I'm not 'carrying on.' "

"Whatever you call it then."

"She's a good friend. She's been a lot of help."

"Do you reward all your helpers by sleeping with them?"

"She means you no harm."

"That's a lie."

"It isn't a lie. She likes you."

"It costs her nothing."

"She wanted to tell you."

"What?"

"About us."

"And?"

"I said you'd be angry."

"What did she say?"

"She said that she could explain. She said that if you loved me you'd understand."

"I don't want to hear about it from her. That makes me an accomplice."

Rachel drank her bourbon. She looked out the kitchen window. How often had she looked that way and seen the view, in every color and every season? In white fog and under a moon, red with autumn, and pure gold like this, aflame in summer sunlight. But she didn't see it now. She looked and didn't see it. Her mind, boiling over with words, was too full. Words were always a curtain, a hedge against seeing. That was how you walked across the street and got hit by a truck. Seymour still stood while Rachel sat and refused to look at him as long as they were both silent. He was waiting to touch her, he wanted to be forgiven. The whole thing was ludicrous. Rachel probed her anger and hurt and felt the edge of play-acting all through it. She knew beyond a shadow of a doubt that Seymour loved her. She had known it way back then, in high school, when she had won out against the cheerleaders. And Natalie Gould, she told herself, Natalie was a cheerleader. She was one of those girls whose lives were a cheerful whole—football games and proms and dates on Saturday night. Natalie had it all organized, like her bedroom with the dolls and pennants, and she was queen of it. Then. Was she still queen of it now,

223

in Gateshead? Was Gateshead no more than high school grown up? Rachel thought, "Now I will have to fight the same battle all over again, but if I do, surely I'll win again." If she had a mind to.

Seymour came over to her, sweetly, like a little boy —Aaron had never been as sweet a little boy as Seymour could pretend to be—and kissed her on the head, on the kerchief that covered her wet hair.

"I love you very much."

And, despite her anger (or perhaps because of it, intertwined with it) Rachel felt desire stirring in its hairy place. "Don't come at me like that," she said. "Don't come sneaking in to me now and think all is well."

He cupped her breasts under the sweatshirt in his hands and kissed her, and Rachel felt her cunt open and close in answer to her damp lips, opening and closing, yearning and reaching. She pushed Seymour away, but with only half a heart. Then they heard Aaron on the stairs, clattering noisily toward them. They moved apart, but he saw them still near each other, almost touching, not having been able to break the spell completely.

"Shame on you," he said, "kissing in the kitchen, in full view of your son."

He broke the thread. Rachel was glad. She wanted to nurse her angry hurt a while longer.

They didn't talk about it again, for a while, but thought about talking about it, stealthily and cunningly, both of them, watching for signs and portents.

Rachel continued to work on her painting of the *seder* and a series of related pictures. Family tableaux based on old photographs. Still. Posed. Abstract. Full of secrets. She had found a photo album in her old room in Buffalo and brought it back with her. She was absorbed in her work.

Rachel went into the city, once a week. She spent most of her time there at the Metropolitan Museum or the Museum of Modern Art, looking. Checking out problems, searching, *seeing*. Sometimes she called up Sally to go with her, but more often she went by

224

herself. She saw more when she was all alone. She could step back and not find it necessary to comment and explain; consequently the view was full and clear and spoke directly to her. She only wished she had another painter at her side to see what she saw. She thought often about Ben. She carried her black sketchbook and wrote short comments next to the drawings she made.

Coming home on the train one afternoon, just before the rush hour, Rachel saw Truscott Boothby. The train was one of the old ones, with a diesel engine, headed out to Port Jefferson. The air-conditioning didn't work and Truscott stood with Rachel on the platform and watched the landscape thundering by. The train was filled with students from Stony Brook and patients and attendants from Kings Park. A motley crew. Truscott bought Rachel a drink and then he had a second one and stood very near her, smelling of whiskey.

"I like you a lot, Rachel."

Rachel was pleased that Boothby liked her and said, "You're o.k., too." She never quite knew what to do with a compliment.

"They don't know what a dandy rebbetzin they have, down there at your old man's synagogue."

His blue eyes looked straight into hers and Rachel thought that they were *goyishe* eyes indeed. Did he want to go to bed with her? The thought came to Rachel oddly, as though Seymour had conceived it. Truscott Boothby was not a figment of Seymour's imagination, but his relationship to her somehow hung on Seymour. As though he wanted something that Seymour had. Would he have picked her up on the train? If she had stood next to him in the bar car, nursing her cold can of Bud, would he have looked at her?

Truscott bent over and touched her hair, his outstretched arm propped against the doorframe of the train to steady him. He held his drink in the other hand. Rachel did not move. She read the signs of desire on his face and was pleased. His mouth was slightly open, he swayed with the movement of the train. He drew closer; it might have been the lurching car.

225

"Rachel, I have wanted to tell you for a long time that you are beautiful and warm and kind and compassionate. I am going to kiss you."

Rachel did not move. Truscott Boothby kissed her, the train crunched to a sudden stop and he fell against her so that she hit her head against the metal doorframe.

"Ouch," said Rachel.

Truscott Boothby apologized. He had spilled some of his drink. "I can't do anything right," he said, and grew glum. "Why don't I meet you in the city some time. At a location less public and bumpy than this?"

"I'll have to think about that."

"I mean you no harm."

"I know that, but I'm unused to planning dates with men other than Seymour."

"We could go to a movie, I know you like movies. And have a drink. Maybe go to a Chinese restaurant. We wouldn't be bound to a speeding train then, or the prying eyes of Gateshead."

Rachel was flattered by the idea of such a meeting more than she was concerned with its actual realization. It would be complicated to arrange. She had no time in her life for complications. And she always told Seymour where she had been, what she had done, whom she had seen. She never made anything up. (Most of the time her recitations bored him.) She was so literal about details that he barely listened. But he would surely sense it if ever she made the whole thing up. It was one of the things at which he excelled. It helped to make him a perceptive rabbi.

"I'll call you one day when Seymour is not lurking about, and we will make a date. You are wasted on Gateshead, Rachel. It is too mean and narrow a town for you."

"I'm there because of Seymour. I'm not wasted on him."

"On Seymour too," said Truscott. "Jewish men expect the world of their wives. I know they are said to make good husbands, but I think that they are often spoiled. They imprison their wives by their helpless-

226

ness. The wives become strong and competent, but are denied a life of their own."

Rachel was startled. He was always so direct. So simple.

The conductor came by to pull up the trapdoor that covered the steps. "Gateshead," he cried. A line of passengers stood ready to climb down from the train. Truscott Boothby helped Rachel to navigate the high stairs, though she wanted to show him how like a sprightly jackrabbit she was, hopping on her toes. They saw familiar Gateshead faces.

"Good afternoon, Reverend."

"Hello, Mrs. Sonnshein."

Truscott Boothby said good-bye to Rachel and smiled a happy smile.

She felt desired. She felt pretty. She was certain that if she passed a mirror just then, or even a shiny surface —a darkened window, a piece of gleaming steel—and saw herself, she would appear beautiful. She never truly saw her face, she knew; she only felt it and put it together from the light of affection in other people's eyes.

Rachel came home with a loud "Hello, everybody" and put her shopping bag of Zabar's goodies on the kitchen table. It was a guilt-offering for not planning to cook dinner that evening. Herring filets in cream sauce, shiny fresh bagels, succulent whitefish in its golden skin, and pickled lox.

Seymour fixed martinis and allowed Aaron to drink the dregs from the icy pitcher. Aaron's face and arms were tanned the color of an Indian. There was a soft bleached fuzz of hair on his arms and cheeks, and Rachel imagined his girl fitting herself against him, her breasts softly pressed into his flat chest, feeling his hard collarbone with her arms, trying to lick his ear-lobe. Because the picture was all in her mind it excited her. She looked back at Seymour, who was silent and preoccupied.

"What are you thinking about?" she asked him.

"I had a call from the placement bureau," he said. "They have recommended me for a job in Omaha."

227

"Omaha, Nebraska?"

"The big Conservative congregation there is looking for a rabbi. Their old rabbi is retiring after thirty-five years. It's a coup just to be asked to go for the interview. A lot of people would give their eyeteeth for the job."

"In Omaha?"

"It's one of the best-paying jobs around. It's prestigious. The rabbi there is the biggest frog in a pond that's not even so very small."

"Omaha doesn't even have a museum I ever heard of!"

"I'm not going to try out for a curator's job, Rachel."

"You've decided to go then?"

"I'm waiting to hear from the congregation. The Seminary said they would call to arrange for us to go out there."

"Us? You mean I have to go to Omaha with you?"

"You don't *have* to."

"Suppose I don't want to go to Omaha?"

"I said you don't have to."

"I mean altogether. If you try out for the job you might get it. If you get it we'll have to move out to Omaha. Aaron will have to change schools for his last year in high school. That's crazy."

"And suppose I get fired this winter?"

"You haven't gotten fired yet. In any case, it won't take effect until next summer. That's a long time away."

"I'll be graduated by then," said Aaron.

"It's not often such a recommendation comes my way," said Seymour. "It would be irresponsible not to go. I don't want to sit here, awaiting my fate. *That* would be crazy. If they know they don't have complete control, maybe they'll treat me a little better."

"I thought your friend Natalie was going to see to it that you stayed on here?"

Seymour started to react to the mention of Natalie Gould's name, looked at Aaron, and thought better of it.

"No one can guarantee such a thing."

"Don't I have anything to say about it at all?"

228

"You can say what you want to say, but unless you're ready to support this family, I'll have to make the decisions. You can paint in Omaha as well as in Gateshead. How come you're suddenly so attached to this place? I thought you hated it."

"But it's near New York, at least. It's not out in the middle of nowhere. I'm finally at the point where I think I'm beginning to get somewhere. I'm finally seeing myself as possibly, just possibly, having a career. I dare not even mention that word, but there it is. And then to go dragging off to Omaha—my God, it's like telling me I'm going blind!"

Seymour stiffened. Rachel felt him quite literally grow hard and tense with opposition. She had merely been throwing out words at him; she had said exactly what came into her head. She had not stopped for even a moment to think the problem through. Undoubtedly, her heart would soften once she had seen the other side, considered the alternatives. She stopped herself in her tracks and squeezed her voice back down into her throat, lowered it to speak softly.

"Never mind now," she said. "We'll talk about it another time."

"Omaha," said Aaron, in a kind of wonder—"I don't think they even have a baseball team."

"I thought we'd stopped talking about it," said Seymour.

The evening was mild. The kitchen windows were open and the air was fragrant with the wild growth outside. The west wind carried the smell of the sea. Rachel looked out and saw one of the Grog kids throw an empty soda can into her bushes. Rachel got up in sudden absolute fury and stormed outside. Emboldened by the martini she held in her hand she went straight down to where the can had landed and (without looking directly at the family next door) heaved it back. It landed with a clatter on the flagstones of the patio, and the dog began its furious howling. Betty Grog stood up (Rachel did not recognize her immediately, she had dyed her hair black) and began cursing at Rachel. Her voice was shrill and very clear. Rachel

229

tried not to hear her, but that was not possible. "You filthy Jews!" she screamed. "You dirty pigs! Keep your garbage in your own yard."

Rachel said nothing but walked quickly back toward the kitchen steps. The same soda can dropped about three feet from her. A little bit of the sweet sticky soda sprayed from its open hole. Rachel picked it up once more (it was a can of Tab). "It's your fucking can," she screamed, aiming it directly at the dog and letting it fly. "You sonofabitching Nazis!" She missed the dog and hit a pot of geraniums instead. Ollie raced toward the fence and barked like one possessed. Rachel went back into the house, blind with rage.

"Goddamn suburban shit," she said, and drained the last of the martini from her glass.

"You were magnificent," said Aaron.

"You think people don't fight with their neighbors in the city?" Seymour asked. "You think this same stupid crap doesn't go on in the whole wide world? I'm certain they threw stuff at each other back in the old country and cursed better than you'll ever curse. Calm down."

Rachel tried to forget the moment, but could not put it out of her mind for days. Her anger welled up again and again, like a blush, whenever she thought of the incident and remembered the spiteful hate-filled faces of the Grogs and her own shrill response.

The following Sunday, about noon, the president of the Omaha congregation called to invite Seymour to spend two days with them.

"And bring your wife," he said. "We'd love to meet the little lady."

"I'm not a little lady," said Rachel to Seymour. "Did you say I'd go?"

"I told them I would talk it over with you. Will you go?"

"I suppose so," said Rachel. "Anything to tear you from the arms of Natalie Gould."

The retiring rabbi had graciously invited them to stay at his house. "He can spy on us that way," said Seymour. "He probably has the guest room bugged." He was glad that Rachel was coming with him.

They flew to Omaha on a humid rainy weekday in the latter part of June. They flew over the checkerboard country, over mountains that looked like green moss and plains on which long straight roads converged in spaces that looked immense even from the air. It was clear in the Midwest; the sun surrounded the plane, set its wings aglow in silver light. There were cities spattered about way below. Some of them were pasted on rivers. You could not miss the Mississippi. Omaha was on the Missouri, of course. Aaron had looked it up. "There's no place near it," he said. "It's all alone out there." They arrived after noon. It was bright and hot in Omaha. They were met at the airport by the retiring rabbi, a dapper man with a small white goatee, wearing a gray straw hat. He did not wear it in the fashion of Orthodox Jews—he was not wearing a hat to keep his head covered, but because he was a man of seventy years and old-fashioned and liked to keep the bald place on his head shaded from the sun. He wore sunglasses and drove a very large and beautifully appointed Oldsmobile. He apparently noticed Rachel looking it over and said, "I could have had a Cadillac, but I thought it better not to have a Cadillac." He was a man who noticed everything. Rachel disliked him immediately. "I invited you to stay with me," he said, "so that you would be sure to have kosher meals and be in relaxed surroundings in order to tell me all about yourselves." He seemed to have taken an instant liking to Seymour and had several times already put his hand on Seymour's shoulder, but now he looked at Rachel and added, "Unless you don't care whether or not you eat *treif*." Quickly, before Rachel could utter a word, Seymour said, without hemming or hawing but in the voice of a compliant disciple, "I appreciate your thoughtfulness, but I must tell you that we *do* eat *treif,* though we keep a kosher home of course."

"The people here like their spiritual leader to be a traditionalist," said the rabbi, "not that I don't enjoy a good steak now and then. But it is, in many ways, a small town. I know most of my six hundred congregants by name. I ministered to their parents and even

231

their grandparents. It is not a place to keep secrets. Do you like to have secrets, Rebbetzin?"

"She's very open," said Seymour.

Rachel understood that it would be well if she said very little in Omaha. She kept her head turned toward the window and looked out at the flat landscape.

The rabbi lived in an elegant house not far from the synagogue. And he had an elegant wife, a dainty woman who looked younger than she was. Rachel was reminded of Buffalo as she studied the wide streets and large, squat houses, the elms, and the sky that arched over the plains. The rebbetzin too was familiar, in the way of upstate relatives. She presided over a perfectly appointed house which might have been considered too conservative by the Jewish citizens of Gateshead, even a bit drab. There were no picture groupings on the walls, no plaids clashing with coordinated florals, no color accents, no suits of armor or brass-plated Chinese chests. There *was* a painting by Marc Chagall over the couch in the living room. Discreetly as it was hung, it dominated the whole room and Rachel went directly to look at it.

"Oh," she said, "a Chagall."

"You recognized it quickly," said the rebbetzin.

"She's an artist herself," said the rabbi.

"Of course," said the rebbetzin. "I forgot. Do you like it?"

"Yes. It's charming," said Rachel, enchanted by the idea that there was a real painting by a real painter in this house—however late and decorative it was.

The rebbetzin was quick as a cat and moved as silently. There was a maid in the kitchen who served tea and, later, a delicious dinner. She wore a white uniform to serve the latter; at afternoon tea she had had a gray one on. A pair of heavy silver candlesticks stood on the dining room buffet. The absolute assurance and order in the house was amazing. Rachel and Seymour whispered about it in bed that night.

At dinner, the rabbi quizzed Seymour, without quite seeming to do so, and the rebbetzin asked mild questions of Rachel. They were as expert as C.I.A. agents, the small dandy with his white goatee (he wore a

232

yarmulke at dinner, so Seymour donned his as well) and his gray cat of a wife. No one would ever get the better of them; no wonder, thought Rachel, they had been here for thirty-five years. They were the sort of people who did not make mistakes more than once. They had no children.

Rachel had providentially worn her good linen summer suit, and she hoped her pantyhose would not rip. Though her legs were brown enough not to need stockings, she knew that she would be expected to wear them in Omaha. She had brought a pair of pants, but it was clear she would have no chance to put them on. Good thing she had brought a simple blue cotton dress with white pinstripes, too.

After-dinner coffee (fragrant and black) was served in the living room. The rebbetzin told Rachel small delicate stories about her life in Omaha.

"I believe in setting a good example," she said. "I have never quarreled with anyone."

("Do you believe it?" Rachel asked Seymour in bed that night. "No," said Seymour.)

"Some women are so anxious to assert themselves, these days," the rebbetzin said to Rachel. "I hope you're not one of them?"

"She asserts herself in her own quiet way," said Seymour, but his tone and smile were affectionate.

"I don't think any of us can help being affected by the women's movement," said Rachel.

"Of course you people in New York are a lot more neurotic and aggressive than we are out here," said the rebbetzin. She had found her own explanations for all things under the sun.

"Once, when we first came to Omaha," she said—not merely to Rachel—"we were invited to the home of a very rich man. He's dead now, may he rest in peace. He wanted to impress us with all his possessions and he wanted us to know how brilliant he was ..."

"My God!" thought Rachel, in the very midst of the rebbetzin's story, "I am going to miss the Sisterhood meeting and I didn't let Golda know."

Her heart fell. She knew she would have to listen to Golda's pained recriminations once more. And she

233

deserved them. Each and every one of her complaints. She should have remembered to call. It was inexcusable. In the meantime, the rebbetzin's story ended in a burst of Yiddish, which Rachel did not get. The rabbi laughed delightedly and Seymour chuckled. It must have been a story that was one of the rabbi's favorites—he was not in the habit of allowing his wife to dominate any but the women's conversations.

(In bed that night, Seymour whispered to Rachel, "You know that story she told? She stole it from the tales of the Chassidim, it's in Buber.")

The Men's Club social was crowded with prosperous-looking couples, most of them in their middle years. Seymour gave a talk which, for the sake of its announcement in the temple bulletin, had been entitled, "Isaiah and the Prophetic Tradition." It was a good talk. Rachel had heard it innumerable times. It was Seymour's favorite for out-of-town speaking engagements. He was graceful and witty. He wore his *yarmulke*. His mind was on what he was doing. Rachel tried to gauge the audience's response. They were polite, listened carefully, and did not whisper during the talk. They *were* more polite in Omaha. After he was finished there was considerable applause and much rustling, whispering, and moving about on the chairs. Rachel tried to listen, to catch some comments as they floated through the air, but she sat next to the rebbetzin and of course everyone knew she was the visiting rabbi's wife and kept their comments turned away from her. The rebbetzin was mildly enthusiastic. "Your husband is an intelligent man," she said. "I hope his heart is as large as his intelligence. A rabbi must have heart, above all else."

There were a few tentative questions, most of them asked by the men.

"Rabbi," they would all begin, respectfully. "Rabbi, tell us, do you believe in God?"

Rachel knew the questions. She knew the answers too.

"Not a personal God," Seymour would say, "not an old man with a beard, sitting in heaven on a throne." He went on to amplify and refine his idea of

234

God. After this the questions would veer away to other subjects.

"Rabbi, how do you feel about Israel?"

It was not difficult, if you had been in the rabbinate for a while, to judge the attitude of the questioner and to know the answer he expected. The trick was to answer in such a way as to satisfy the questioner, without compromising your own position. Seymour was usually mild and answered gently; he counted on his quick-wittedness to see him through. Only if he sensed great hostility or great stupidity (or both) did he become a touch nasty, a touch arrogant. Rachel always cringed when he waxed sarcastic. She was glad she did not have to run this gauntlet.

"Rabbi, do you believe women should be called to the Torah?"

Seymour answered him with a simple "Yes." The audience murmured excitedly. Rachel felt them drawing up in opposition. It looked as though there would be some discussion. Maybe they had rejected Seymour then and there. Rachel did not want Seymour rejected, even though she didn't want to go to Omaha. At a nod from the retiring rabbi the Men's Club president got up and stilled the audience.

"We will have a chance to ask Rabbi Sonnshein some further questions tomorrow," he said. "I want to thank him now for his stimulating talk. We will adjourn for cake and cookies. Those who wish to greet the rabbi and his wife personally may do so."

Pleasant chatter rose all about Rachel. People greeted one another and cast appraising glances at Rachel. She felt demure and awkward and tongue-tied. Nobody knew who she was. If they came to Omaha she would have to learn to distinguish each of these people. It would take months and months. She would be unable to work. She would have to learn to know the new landscape; she might lose years. How could she live so far from the sea? So far from escape? The sea promised the world of distant shores, it promised discovery.

The next morning the rabbi woke Seymour at an early hour and they went to the *minyan*. The rabbi

235

explained that he had been faithful in his attendance early in his career, but had—with the advancing years —become a little lazy. He expected his assistant to go.

"It is necessary that the people know one of us is there to pray with them. I show up often enough so that they remember that I am one of them. In the past I felt it necessary to be in attendance because I did not want anything in my congregation to be outside of my ken. That's important, my dear Seymour. Never let them create anything in which you have no part."

The Sisterhood meeting went smoothly. Seymour spoke about Shevuoth, so recently past. About Naomi and Ruth. Rachel did not listen. She was tired from her effort to be friendly and sociable. It was a strain to be a guest, a strain to be among people every minute of the day. Rachel felt herself afloat again, carried away on a sea of faces. She longed to be alone.

A dairy luncheon was served after the meeting. Small talk buzzed around Rachel. She answered the questions she was asked. Often she made her answers up as she went along, spinning them out so that they careened along on the edge of being lies. She often lost track and could not remember what had just been said. She forgot where she was headed. Seymour was tired too.

After lunch the rabbi suggested they take a ride with him. They drove around Omaha. Rachel liked seeing the sights. The rabbi loved his city and was completely at home in it. He showed off his love as much as the views. Everything he said proclaimed that they were strangers here, but he was not—the place was his. The rabbi drove easily, though he sat low in his big Oldsmobile. They came to a large hospital.

"I must go inside briefly," said the rabbi. "A member of mine is in there. An old friend and big contributor."

The rebbetzin stayed with them in the car. There was very little left to say. Everyone tried hard to fill the lengthening gaps. The cars in the parking lot, the heat, the size of the building, the doctors—all these

236

were scrutinized to provide a subject for their deteriorating conversation. The rabbi returned after fifteen minutes. He told the rebbetzin about the patient he had just seen. Like all old men he was at once scared to see the great wings of the angel of death, and glad that they beat about another's head.

Back at the house, the rabbi took Seymour into his study and they had a chat. The rebbetzin served Rachel a very small glass of sherry and left her alone in the living room with a six-months' supply of old *Commentary* magazines. It was still and summery. There were vases filled with red and white peonies in the living room, perfectly arranged with a collar of shiny green leaves to set them off against the crystal vase.

Rachel thought about the rebbetzin. She was like an evil stepmother, full of cunning and malice. It was good to be going away. Rachel had seen nothing in the time they had spent in Omaha that had changed her mind about living there. It would be impossible. She would go crazy or wither and die. The people had been nice and friendly enough, but they inhabited a different world. She hadn't the strength to get to know them or it. And the flat horizon was a mocking reminder that this was the heartland indeed, and there was no escape.

The rabbi and Seymour came out of the study. They were both smiling. The rebbetzin appeared, in a cool clean dress, and they ate supper. It was a pleasant, short meal; the coming departure buoyed everyone. The rabbi and rebbetzin basked in the light of their own hospitality. Their house would soon close up around them again, and breathe its peace. Seymour and Rachel could count the minutes to freedom. The rabbi drove them to the airport. The sun was still above the horizon (that flat endless Nebraska horizon, rippling with wheat), but its light had dimmed and its heat had gone out, though the pavement held it a while longer.

"I'll leave you here," said the rabbi. "I've got to pay a sick call. It's been a pleasure."

"Thank you, very much," said Seymour.

237

"Thanks," said Rachel.

The rabbi drove away and Rachel and Seymour were left alone at the Omaha airport.

"He as much as offered me the job," said Seymour. He sounded happy.

"Is it his to give?" asked Rachel.

"You didn't notice how he runs things in this town?"

"What did he *say?*"

"He said he was very impressed with me, with the way I handled myself, with my honesty, my erudition. He said he would do everything in his power to see that they offered me the job. He thought I'd be a worthy successor to him."

"You let yourself be flattered deaf, dumb, and blind by an old fart."

"They pay extremely well."

"I don't want to go to Omaha," said Rachel.

"You don't want to hear what they're paying?"

"I don't care about that. I don't care if they pay a hundred thousand dollars a year plus tips. I won't go to Omaha!"

"You'll go if I get the job. Of course you'll go!"

"You wouldn't last a year. Not with that bastard hanging around in his retirement, with nothing to do but poke into our lives. Not with that awful rebbetzin, the perfect lady, dispensing advice over tea and running me down to all her friends over bridge. And not to know a soul!"

Rachel felt a wall of tears crumble in her chest and she wept loudly, all at once, like an unhappy child.

"You're crazy even to consider it," she sobbed. "It would turn into hell for both of us, and for Aaron too. There's no escape from here, no place to go to get away from those people for a day. How far away is the nearest place? A thousand miles? What is it? St. Louis? Chicago? Who wants to go to St. Louis or Chicago for a vacation? However awful Gateshead is, at least New York is right there. . . ."

Rachel no longer saw anything but Seymour's face, outlined against a glass wall, the yellow evening sky behind it. She was unaware of people, unaware even of herself, except as the vehicle of her desperation.

238

"I don't care!" she cried. "I won't go!"

Seymour slapped her. He did it because she shook and cried so and her eyes were blind with anger and tears both. He thought she was no longer in control. He was right. She had let out a long scream, it trailed from her last words into a "Waaaaaaah" like a child's, her blind eyes on his face, yellow with the reflection of the sunset. So he slapped her, and she stopped. A few people walked down the corridor, tip-tap, tip-tap, their heels clicking on the hard floor. They walked around Rachel and Seymour and looked back at them furtively when they were a good distance away. No one stopped or came between them. When Rachel's scream faded into sobs, the heels clicked on and the heads no longer turned. It had not been a scene the spectators would long remember.

Rachel wiped her eyes and swallowed down her sobs and walked away from Seymour and toward the boarding gate. He followed at a distance and maintained the distance until they were on the plane. Rachel sat by the window and looked at night falling quickly across the sky, the band of gold growing smaller along the horizon and the still pale moon hanging a frosty light in the void. Rachel kept her back turned to Seymour and they did not speak to each other. She felt her eyes large and ringed like a mist around the moon; now and then a sob rose up in her throat. She paid attention only to the night outside and in her head the same words of denial raged over and over again.

They arrived in New York late at night and once more it was raining and humid. A fine spray of water swept across the airport lights. Warm air dipped into the space around Rachel. She kept her distance from Seymour and said nothing for a long time. When they came home she went up to kiss Aaron, who moved to wake himself.

"How was Omaha?"

"It's a nice place to visit, but I wouldn't want to live there."

239

8

Summer was everywhere, in humid green profusion. Rachel savored its jungle heat. She walked barefoot and wore no bra. Summer brought her closest to the good memories of being young. (Rachel did not miss her youth, nor wish to recapture it, but she liked playing with her recollections.) Summer wiped away the lines of winter, the thoughts of decay, the weight of pale flesh. The air was filled with children's cries until late in the night. The band that played in the park could be heard at midnight, when the wind came from the south, from the ocean.

Betty Diamant called to ask what they were doing for their summer vacation.

"It's vacation enough just to have it summer. There'll be no bar mitzvahs, no Sisterhood meetings, and no Hadassah."

"What about Aaron? Will he be hanging around, enjoying how he doesn't have to go to Sisterhood?"

"Didn't I tell you that Aaron is going to the Catskills with some friends? They all got jobs in a hotel."

"You never tell me a thing unless I ask. Is he working as a waiter?"

"More like a busboy."

"They'll probably exploit him terribly. I'm surprised you allow it, Rachel. You with your advanced political views!"

"He can always come home if it doesn't work out. I'm not going to make the same mistake you made, never allowing me to work. I had to stay around Buffalo."

240

"You didn't seem to mind."

"I didn't say I minded. I love summer too much not to enjoy it wherever I am. I had a glorious time in many ways—sketching, writing in my diary, swimming. I was alone a lot, and that was nice. But still, I lived from handouts."

"Handouts? My Lord, Rachel, you didn't live on handouts. But you didn't *have* to earn money. I can't see working just for the sake of working. Especially, you should pardon the expression, for a girl. And you take it away from someone who needs it."

"All true, Mother. I was just saying how I might have done it differently. If I had had a greater sense of urgency, of discipline, if I had learned independence, I might have gotten started sooner on a career."

"Career? What kind of career?"

"The choice of the word was unfortunate, but I'm a painter, Mother, remember? Your daughter paints."

"Oh, that."

"Well, you see, it's not taken seriously."

"You were always good at it, dear, but I surely never thought it was your intention to make it your life's *work*. You couldn't earn your keep at it. Not that you *have* to."

"I 'earn my keep,' as you say, being a rebbetzin and a housewife and a mother."

"You sound like a women's libber!"

"A lot of feminist complaints make sense, especially when it comes to economics. We live in a capitalist society . . ."

"Oh, Rachel."

"All I'm saying is that I've earned my keep. But to get back to the point of this discussion—if I'd gone off to work summers during my adolescence, I might have learned to stand on my own two feet. That would have been a big help. I might have concluded that I could make it on my own in the world, and not gotten married in order to continue to be supported."

"I thought you married Seymour because you loved him."

"I did. But a lot of people who marry for love continue to lead independent lives."

241

"Not in your day."

"In *any* day, Mother. It's more common now, but I know women of my generation who remained independent. However, that's neither here nor there. I don't cry over spilled milk; I've got enough trouble, being a *shvartse*."

"What *are* you talking about?"

"It's the punchline of an old Jewish joke. A black man is sitting on the subway, reading a Yiddish newspaper and an old Jew taps him on the shoulder and says, 'Excuse me . . .' "

"Rachel! I didn't call you to hear Jewish jokes."

"I'm sorry. What were we talking about?"

"Summer vacations. I wanted to make you an offer, but now I don't know, you're so edgy."

"Edgy? I'm not edgy."

"Nervous. Yes, you are. Argumentative."

"Me?"

"Yes, dear."

Rachel knew that her mother always invoked the nerves as a means to maintain the upper hand. It was her oldest ploy.

"What's the offer, Mother?" Rachel knew she sounded edgy now. Her mother's prophesies were self-fulfilling.

"Are you sure you're ready to hear it?"

"Yes, Mother."

"Professor Dinsmoor asked if we knew someone who would rent his house on Cape Cod for a month this summer. Your father and I thought that you and Seymour might enjoy the four weeks away—I'll pay for it. It's a simple house. I was there several times; we rented it ourselves the year the Dinsmoors were on sabbatical and went to England. It's near Wellfleet. There's no heat or anything. Two small bedrooms, as I recall. It's a charming place. . . ." Betty Diamant's voice trailed off in sudden embarrassment over her gift. "What do you say?"

"It's a wonderful idea. Thanks a lot! I'll talk to Seymour—I'm sure he'll be delighted, too."

"Now I want you to know, Rachel, that this is for *you,* primarily. You've been working hard, and you

242

had the operation—you're supposed to have some rest. I don't mind telling you that I know Seymour takes very little of the burden off your shoulders. Your women's lib ought to start closer to home."

"I don't want to discuss that," said Rachel, in what she thought was an ominous tone. But her mother disregarded both the tone and the words.

"I like Seymour, you know that; but his mother spoiled him from the day he was born, and you're reaping the harvest. I want you to take those four weeks on the Cape, no matter what Seymour says. Do you understand?"

"Yes, Mother." There were times when Rachel welcomed her mother's hardheadedness.

Seymour was, in fact, pleased. Rachel reported about half the conversation to him. She kept, as she always did, her mother's criticism to herself. It caused her some small grief, now and then, to be caught listening to her mother's judgments, particularly when she knew them to have some justification. But it would not do to be in league with her mother against her husband. It was a part of Rachel's nature to bear these hurts alone. She thought it disloyal even to talk to Sally about them, though sometimes she wanted, desperately, to have that kind of confidante.

The Fourth of July dawned bright and hot. It was a perfect day for the Fourth. A parade had been scheduled to go the length of Gateshead's Main Street and end at the bandshell in Harbor Park, where a concert of patriotic music was to take place. The reviewing stand for town dignitaries had been set up near the church on Deacon's Hill. The state senator had promised to be there and the state assemblyman said he might come. All of the local clergy had been invited, and all but Truscott Boothby and Seymour Sonnshein had turned up. *Those* two, true to their ideals, refused, citing their stand in support of the separation of church and state. It was, as usual, a stand not shared by the rest of Gateshead's spiritual leaders.

Aaron had left for the Catskills the week before and had written one cryptic postcard: "I miss you. Thanks for all your past kindnesses. It's going to be

243

lots of fun (and work!). Your loving son, Aaron." His mother decided he was homesick and sent him a long and cheerful letter.

Rachel went early to the parade; she loved parades. Seymour did not go at all. He fixed himself a cool drink and settled down in the lawn chair under the willow tree and began reading the books he had brought home from the library the day before. The Grogs were away on their annual vacation.

The parade was a good one. It had all the ingredients to make the heart beat faster and to let the spirit soar. A contingent of Marines and the high school band led the march; they were followed by a platoon of soldiers, and a group of drum majorettes from the Catholic Youth Organization. The Veterans of Foreign Wars and Jewish War Veterans marched, as well as Cub Scouts, Girl Scouts and a brigade of volunteer firemen. Police on motorcycles and a Holy Name Society bagpipe band were on hand. Boy Scouts and military cadets, the Ladies' Auxiliary of the American Legion, and the Christopher Columbus Chapter of the Public Works Department union were all represented. The Steuben Society sent a band, as did the Sons of Poland.

No one was missing but Seymour Sonnshein, who sat under his tree, and Truscott Boothby, who was missing only from the reviewing stand. He stood beside his wife's wheelchair on the steps of the bank.

"Rachel, Rachel," he said, "where have you been?"

Abigail wore dark glasses and did not return Rachel's greetings.

"We went out to the boondocks for an interview."

"How was it?"

"The interview went well, but I hated the place."

"Don't leave us, Rachel. Seymour is needed in Gateshead."

"By whom?"

"By yours truly. And by his congregation. They are lucky that he represents them to the town."

"If only *they* realized that."

"I tell them, I tell them every chance I get. I always

244

sing Seymour's praises . . . and I tell them," he added, almost in a whisper, "what a wonderful wife he's got. It isn't often these days one sees a well-regulated, happy marriage."

"I trust your faith isn't misplaced."

"You're not happily married then?" Truscott Boothby seemed to have been eagerly awaiting such news.

"Oh, I am, I am," said Rachel, wondering why she had made a statement that was sure to mislead Truscott. "It's just that you made it sound so . . . well, so *perfect*."

"Nothing perfect about *this* marriage," said Abigail. "Right, my love?" She turned to Rachel. "Never trust a clergyman," she said. "They're full of lust, all of them. They'll bed you in no time flat. How's your rabbi, dear?"

Rachel smiled at her. "Fine, thank you."

"You heard about Sydelle Prawn's illness?" asked Truscott Boothby.

"Yes," said Rachel.

"Have you been to see her?"

"Lord, no. I always dream about being a good neighbor, but I'm such a coward when it comes to illness and unhappiness. Maybe I'll go this afternoon. Bake some brownies and pay a call."

The last of the bands had come down the hill and the children trailed behind it, stepping high as children will. There was a big crowd down in the park and Rachel sat at the very edge of the dock, swinging her legs above the water. The band played Sousa marches. It was all as it should be in a small town in America on the Fourth of July.

Seymour was asleep beneath the willow tree, a book in his lap, his mouth slightly open. Rachel kissed him on the forehead and he started up, confused, even a little frightened.

"Oh, Rachel, it's you."

"Happy Fourth of July."

"Do you want to watch the fireworks tonight?"

"Of course I do. What a silly question."

245

"The Goulds invited us over. They live on that high hill above the harbor and say the view is beautiful."

"Not beautiful enough to make me want to go to her house."

"I said we'd probably come."

"Well, say we won't."

"What have you got against them?"

"Not against *them,* against *her.* Charlie isn't my type either, but he doesn't matter."

"You're being irrational."

"No, I'm being jealous."

"You needn't be."

"She's younger, prettier, and richer than I am. And she takes up a big space in your heart, it seems."

"She's not half the woman you are, Rachel."

"Cold comfort that is."

"It's not an easy time. I don't complain to you."

"Truscott Boothby said our marriage was ideal."

"Isn't it? I need you to love me, Rachel."

"Me and who else?"

"I used to think nobody else, but you're a painter now."

"Go ahead and blame me for your infidelities."

"You'd better come with me tonight."

"Don't let's talk about it now. I'm making brownies."

Rachel had no energy for the argument, no appetite for contending with Seymour. She did have her mind on her painting. Argument was Seymour's way of drawing her to him, invading the private place of her work. She went quickly into the house, fixed a gin and tonic for herself, and brought together the ingredients for the brownies.

The brownies came out smelling deliciously of hot chocolate. They were moist inside and crisp on top. Rachel ate one hot and arranged the rest on a plate. Then she took some back for Seymour—mostly the corner ones. She covered the plate and the brownies with Saran Wrap and finished her second drink. She felt finely tuned, only slightly tipsy; just enough to make the trip next door to see Miss Prawn seem a little less difficult. Rachel put sandals on her bare feet

246

and went out the front door. "I'll be at the Prawns'," she shouted to Seymour, and didn't wait for his answer.

Rachel rang the doorbell before she had collected her thoughts and was startled to see how fat Clarabelle had gotten.

"I've come to pay a sick call," she said, quickly and too lightly. She tried not to stare at Clarabelle's fat arms. "How is Sydelle?" asked Rachel, and lowered her voice from its too cheerful treble.

"Poorly," said Clarabelle. "I sometimes think she's failing so rapidly she won't see the end of summer. She doesn't notice how the yard looks. She has no pleasure in anything. I'm glad you came—we see so few people now."

She led the way to the darkened living room. Two French doors opened into a sunporch filled with plants, but the doors were closed against the day's heat and the shades were drawn over the rest of the windows.

"Rachel Sonnshein is here," said Clarabelle Prawn, at the moment Rachel saw Sydelle sitting deep in an armchair, her eyes shut. She opened her eyes and raised her head to look at Rachel; her eyes were still bright.

"Someone's come to see me, and it's the good rabbi's wife. I'm not even one of your flock."

"I don't visit the flock."

"You should, my dear. That's what ministers' and rabbis' wives are for."

"I've always wished I were good at the things rabbis' wives are supposed to be good at. But I haven't the talent."

"Talent's not what you need, Rachel. You merely need the will and the time. I doubt that you really want to be good at being a rabbi's wife, anyway. You may want to be good at painting. I'm not criticizing, you understand. I think you *should* want to be good at painting. God knows I understand women not wanting to be household drudges."

"You sound lively enough. How are you feeling?"

"On the whole, I feel rotten," said Sydelle. "I live from day to day. The garden's gone to weeds, my sis-

247

ter stuffs herself while I grow thinner. But I'm not in pain, that's a blessing. I'm weak, and always tired; I miss my visits to the library. I miss talking about things other than domestic details. It would be nice if you came to see me now and then. Death isn't catching and, as yet, I'm not a sight to avoid. It would relieve my boredom. You know, I sometimes wish for the days of the anti-war movement; everyone who shared our commitment was a friend. We saw each other all the time. You do remember?"

Rachel nodded. She had (with some surprise) met Sydelle on the picket lines. It was before she knew her well enough to have seen that aspect of her. Sydelle stood with the peaceniks on their silent vigil in front of the Civil War monument week after week. She paid no attention to the taunts and jeers of the people who drove by; she stood erect and proud in her London Fog raincoat, and held one of the banners Rachel had made.

"There was such camaraderie," Sydelle went on. "We met once a month to plan for vigils and demonstrations."

It was an awfully long time ago, thought Rachel.

"What's happened to them all?" Sydelle asked.

"I've lost touch myself," said Rachel. "That's the curse of suburbia. We only inhabit the same place such a very short time."

Sydelle's head drooped. Her eyes closed. There was a long moment's silence in the room. The clock ticked with sudden ferocity and the teakettle whistled shrilly from the kitchen. The full weight of summer pressed against the panes of the windows. The white tulle curtains rippled, as though stirred by a passing flutter of wings. The damask drapes moved ever so slightly. Perhaps it was the cat.

"You needn't stop talking," said Sydelle. "I'm listening."

Rachel was not certain whether to believe her. She sensed that Sydelle closed her eyes and dropped out of the present as though rehearsing for death's eternal darkness. She had already moved away from the conventions of daily life, had withdrawn into this room (she slept downstairs now, in what used to be her study), and lived only with her thoughts and with the sounds, the patter, of Clarabelle's reports on the weather and on stories of human interest gathered from *Newsday*.

Clarabelle came back into the room now, carrying the teapot and the plate full of brownies. She placed a large napkin on Sydelle's lap and gave her tea in a mug. (She and Rachel drank from china cups.)

"You must try Rachel's brownies, just one," she said.

Sydelle moved slowly, as though she had to will it.

Rachel, sitting in the Vuillard room, suddenly felt the rush of her own strength, her youth come to rescue her. Her bare brown feet in their sandals looked ready to leap and to run. Outside, out in the hot green summer world, dust settled on the flagstone sidewalks and other struggles raged.

The two sisters spoke sometimes as though animated by a single ventriloquist. They had, in the past, moved with one rhythm as well, and Clarabelle still seemed to sit—heavy and placid as she was—waiting for Sydelle to come forward, to get up and arrange the flowers or stroke the cat. The cat lay still and round upon a small piece of colorful cloth that had been put on the rocking chair for her.

The telephone rang. Rachel looked at her watch. Clarabelle seemed to think Sydelle would answer, and got up slowly, after the moment's hesitation.

"It's for you, Rachel," she said. "Your master's voice."

Seymour sounded testy. "What are you doing there?"

"Visiting." She was embarrassed that he had called, though she didn't want to show it. She was quiet.

"You've been there a long time. When are you coming home?"

"I don't know," said Rachel, as though he had asked a difficult and serious question.

"Well, make it soon then. I've been alone all day."

Rachel hung up. Sydelle had nodded off again.

"He wants you home?" asked Clarabelle.

249

"He called to ask me something."

"Men are like that, my dear. That's why we never married."

"I'll come again," said Rachel.

"Don't wait too long," said Sydelle, without opening her eyes.

"Thank you for the brownies," said Clarabelle.

Rachel saw that she had eaten almost half of them. They walked to the front door together. Rachel said a hasty good-bye and jumped down the front steps. Once again she exulted in her own strength, the vigor of her body.

"You shouldn't have called," Rachel told Seymour. "You really had no business interrupting my *one* visit. It pointed up the fact that you didn't go. You're a neighbor too, and a clergyman. You could visit a dying old lady."

"Did she tell you that? You know she doesn't care for me. I needn't prove to her how good and kind I am. I have enough with my own sick and wounded."

"Did you tell the Goulds we're not coming?"

"No, I didn't. I thought you might change your mind."

"I just don't feel like seeing them. They're not friends of mine."

"Natalie is very fond of you."

"I'm tired of hearing that. It's her business to like me, anyway. It's in *her* interest to get on the good side of me. I don't have to toady to her."

"Do you mind if I go alone?"

"Not in the least. It will give me an evening off to do some work."

"There'll be other people there. It won't look right if I come alone on the Fourth of July."

"You want my stamp of approval on the whole thing. I'm not inclined to give it, though."

They sat in the living room. Rachel suddenly noticed that it had grown threadbare, and the dust had accumulated again. The couch needed to be re-upholstered. The lining of the drapes was torn. The screen in front of the fireplace was rusting. But they were

250

moving in September. She would worry about it then.

Rachel climbed up to the attic and left Seymour alone with the TV. It was too hot in the attic to do anything, even with the window fan turned on. The place was bearable in summer only after the sun went down. Rachel went into the bedroom, lay down on the bed, and looked at her bare brown arms and felt to see if her belly was still flat. To see if she hadn't become a fat cow. She felt virtuous about her visit to Sydelle Prawn. Rachel fell asleep, her head on her arms, lying the wrong way on the bed, her bare dirty feet on the pillow.

Seymour woke her at seven o'clock. He was gentle about it. He sat next to her on the bed and touched her face with his hand very softly.

"Rachel."

He was so gentle and so delicate that she knew— even in her sleep—that he wanted something from her. What was it?

"Are you coming with me?" he whispered.

"Goddamn it," said Rachel, with spittle in the corner of her mouth. "Goddamn it."

Seymour put his hands under Rachel's shirt and touched the nipples of her breasts. They puckered at his fingertips. Ever so slowly he unwound her skirt, moved the flat of his hand down across her belly and felt for her clitoris. He lay down on top of her. His hands met over her pubic hair and rubbed her sweetly. His penis lay against her back, down where the cheeks of her ass spread out. Seymour rocked slowly while his hands moved in their different rhythm. His head was next to hers, turned so his tongue could lick the soft pink of her ear. Rachel was caught up in his rhythm, and quickly came, just as Seymour—pressed against her, flat on top of her—shuddered as well and sighed into her deep breaths. She felt the warm wet semen spread over her back.

The Goulds lived high above the water in a converted carriage house. It had been written about and

251

photographed in splendid color for *Newsday*. Natalie and Charlie had posed beside the free-standing fireplace. The Barcelona chairs were shown neatly lined up next to the glass-topped dining room table. Bowls of flowers were everywhere. The only things in bad taste at the Goulds' were the paintings. They were large, colorful abstractions of the sort seen most frequently in corporate offices.

Rachel had taken a bath and put on a pair of white Levis and a colorful Guatemalan shirt. She had been silent in the car with Seymour, but he did not seem to notice. His own good humor was all too obvious.

The air was soft and filled with fireflies. The leafy trees were like dark fans spread out against the yellow sky of dusk. The pale horizon undulated with the bluffs. A thin band of mist rose from the flattened sea.

Rachel and Seymour arrived just before dark, and Charlie Gould served them gin and tonic. Japanese lanterns were strung along the periphery of the patio, lighting the way to the long and winding driveway. It was a touch that moved Rachel. She thought of a tender past and white summer suits—photos in her mother's album, and memories of F. Scott Fitzgerald's books. Natalie Gould was lying in a hammock. Rachel thought she looked fragile. She was casually dressed; she had made an attempt at bohemian carelessness. Rachel's eye searched for discordant details of costuming; she was not about to forgive Natalie Gould a single fault. The patchwork jeans were most certainly from Bendel's, and her loose Greek shirt had been designed in Paris. Her thong sandals were delicately wrought. Her feet were delicate too. Rachel thought them too small and narrow. She detested Natalie's feet. There was a beautiful silver choker around Natalie's neck.

"Hello, Natalie. That's a beautiful necklace," said Rachel.

"Oh, thank you. I'm glad Seymour convinced you to come." She was pointedly silent for a moment.

Seymour could not see Rachel's eyes in the dusk, but knew the look storming up in them. "Rachel pretends not to like parties," he said.

"I'm just shy," said Rachel.

252

"A very private person," said Natalie, softly. "I wish I had your self-esteem."

"I was born with it," Rachel muttered, "but I never show it in public."

Charlie Gould sat on the low brick wall of the patio and swung his leg. He wore no socks. He did not usually talk very much, but tonight he seemed particularly out of sorts. Rachel felt bound to him, yet could think of no way to approach him. She was a stranger. The landscape in which he moved was utterly foreign to her. She imagined Wall Street. It was like footage from an old newsreel to her. A run on the banks. People in dark clothes, moving jerkily. "How's business?" wouldn't do at all. Neither would a question about the Mets. He had been a football player. He didn't look as though he cared a fig about baseball. Rachel did not think she would like him and, looking at his swinging loafer, didn't think he would like her.

"I hear you went out to Omaha," Charlie Gould said to Seymour Sonnshein. "How was it?"

"All right. Interesting."

He seemed unwilling to give Charlie Gould an opening. But Charlie Gould took it—that was his nature.

"You thinking of taking that job?"

"It hasn't been offered yet."

"You might be happier in a nice-size city like that. I have a feeling you don't dig suburbia."

"I don't 'dig' anything. I'd stay here until the end of my days if I didn't have to be subjected to contract negotiations every couple of years. Voted upon by people who are not my peers. It's a hell of a way to make a living."

"You want lifetime security?"

"University professors get tenure."

"Nobody in the world ought to have tenure. We don't have tenure in the business world. You produce or you fail. It's as simple as that."

"How do you judge a rabbi's performance?"

"Management studies show it can be done."

"Do you really believe that people vote for or against a rabbi on the basis of his competence?"

"Probably not. But that doesn't mean they couldn't.

253

You can figure out most things with a ruler. If congregations learned that, emotions could take a back seat."

"But they never *do*," said Seymour.

"Rabbis play on people's emotions. It's what they're paid for, after all. They shouldn't complain when the tables are turned. I never met a rabbi yet who didn't bitch all the way to the bank. Yours is a parasitic profession, my friend."

Rachel was filled with loathing now. She could feel her heart pounding. "You're full of crap."

Charlie ignored her. Seymour seemed to think it had all been said in fun. He laughed.

"Rachel gets very excited," he said, adding, "with some justification, of course. I'd love it if the nature of my job were different, were like it used to be. And I wouldn't mind being measured, as you said, with a ruler. Filling out time sheets, passing civil service exams—it would be a snap after what I go through now."

Seymour leaned back in a captain's chair, and his dark hair caught the soft light of the Japanese lanterns. Natalie's eyes were on him. Rachel imagined her stretching a hand out to him, in her languid, rich way. Charlie Gould smiled. The light from the living room, billowing out in the gathering darkness past the sliding glass doors, just reached his face and went no further. The long slash of his open shirt exposed the dark flesh of his chest.

"In this world, Rachel," he said, and his swinging leg beat time to his words, "the race goes to the swift, as you must know. To the guy who can sell himself or sell his product, who can show the biggest profit. Profit's the thing. If a painter can sell his work and make a lot of money, I take my hat off to him. I applaud him. He's a genius. I don't care if the product stinks. I just hope, for his sake, that the lousy product doesn't catch up with him. But I think in the art world it doesn't, not until after he's dead and buried and his kids have spent his money on dope."

"The American Dream," said Rachel. "Making it by selling shit."

"Pretty words will get you nowhere," said Seymour.

254

Rachel could not read him through the fumes of her fury.

"The trouble with all you radical utopians," said Charlie Gould, "is that you don't know what life's really like."

"We never met a payroll," said Rachel.

"You took the words right out of my mouth."

"I was being sarcastic."

"It's all the same to me," said Charlie Gould. "It's my money buys your pictures."

"Shall we talk about something else?" said Natalie Gould.

"Anything you say," answered her husband.

The fireworks had begun. Rachel looked out over the black water and saw the shower of stars, the puffs of light, the brilliant dance of a thousand sparks arching into the summer night. She tried to put her mind to rest, to close it off against the anger so that she might see the fireworks pure. The crackling bursts of frozen blooms rose into the night sky and dropped and dropped and fell to nothing. But the words still rankled. An edge of hostility obtruded into her sight.

Some other guests had arrived. Rachel finished her drink and went to get another. Charlie poured it for her and chatted with his friends all the while. Rachel knew none of them. They were not members of Shaare Tefilah, nor did they live in Gateshead. They came from more exotic places. Natalie and Seymour talked quietly in a corner of the patio, shadowed by night. Rachel felt like an intruder. She held her drink high and walked between them. Their voices dropped off like fading firecrackers.

"Hi, dear," said Seymour and touched her hair, moving it back from her forehead in a gentle gesture. She did not have the guts to resist. Or perhaps she wanted to maintain the bond in front of her rival.

Guests drifted out to the patio to watch the fireworks. The women wore long skirts and talked about the lovely view and the enchanting house and the perfection of everything. The men wore blazers and open-necked shirts and talked about the decline in the price of gold and the cost of tennis racquets.

255

Rachel had heard it all before. She took her drink and walked away from the patio, across the sweeping lawn, down to the edge of the small bluff that ended on the beach. She heard Seymour call out "Rachel!" but he did not call very loudly, nor did he repeat his call, so she continued on and found a rock on which to sit and watch the fireworks arch up and out above the water. Sitting there (not very far from the house but far enough to be out of sight, far enough to hear only murmurs, not words, far enough to see without being seen), she allowed the sweep of her anger to fan out and include Seymour, permitted herself the wish that he be gone, that she might be free. She sat in the darkness and gave herself up to the fireworks, having dared to think what she had never thought before. It was a liberating thought at that moment, and coincided with the end of the fireworks. Three or four bursts in colors red, white, and blue broke all at once high in the sky. There was an after-sound like a sigh, a collective "Ooohhhhh" that filled the night.

Rachel walked back into the circle of light, the glow of the lanterns, looking for Seymour. She still always looked for Seymour. He was in the same chair.

"You're back," he said, sounding both pleased and wry.

"I hadn't meant to spend the evening like this."

"I never knew you to spurn a good meal," he said, and they went together to fill their plates with an assortment of delectable things. There were fat pink shrimps and crisp white cauliflower, tiny pancakes and salmon mousse and cucumber salad, and tomatoes stuffed with crabmeat. They ate alone in a corner of the patio and watched the moths dancing in the haunted summer night.

It was one o'clock when they got home and fell asleep in their beds without talking about what was going on in the black privacy of their heads.

The following day, Rachel called Sally and asked if she would like to go to the city.

"I can't. My parents are here. How about next week?"

"We're leaving for the Cape. But let's have lunch

256

before I go. We can take sandwiches down to the beach."

Rachel went into the city alone. She took the train and held *The New York Times* up in front of her face so that the possibility of encounters was lessened. The train reached Penn Station on time and Rachel fled up the stairs and out of Gateshead's way. She felt truly free as soon as she was on the subway. There was no need to hide; she was among strangers. She took the local to 79th Street and went crosstown on the bus. The Metropolitan Museum was full of summer visitors. Rachel headed for those galleries which were relatively empty. Mannerists and primitives were not much in demand, and neither were Greek vases and Etruscan bronzes. Rachel didn't care all that much for Greek vases and Etruscan bronzes herself, but she always came through that part of the museum and looked at several pieces to discipline herself. She was like one of those people who learn a new word from the dictionary each day. She walked past the Euphronios *krater* (lit dramatically in the dark still room), past the Chinese vases, past the stand where they rented out taped lectures, and into the room at the top of the stairs. Most times it was presided over by Raphael's *Madonna and Child Enthroned with Saints,* but lately a *Deposition* with a greenish Christ had taken its place. Rachel did not usually linger among the works of the High Renaissance.

"Hello, Rachel!"

The two women spoke in unison, startling Rachel, who had believed herself safe. They were congregants from Gateshead—Sisterhood members on a guided tour. (Rachel remembered their names several hours later, on the train going home.)

"What are *you* doing here?"

"We're on a special tour. You can join us if you want to learn something. Our lecturer is terrific."

"No, thank you. I already know something."

"What do you make of all this *goyishe* art?"

"It was made for *goyim; they* like it."

"Doesn't it make you nervous? Doesn't it make you a little sick?"

257

"I'm not easily upset, even by the most gruesome martyrdoms. The painters who painted them often took great care to imagine the wounds and paint them properly. St. Sebastian is a great favorite."

"Who?"

"St. Sebastian. He was shot full of arrows."

"They did worse to the Jews."

Rachel didn't want to be reminded. She felt anxious and nervous, surrounded by Christian saints, accused by Jewish women. No great painted image existed for the deaths of six million Jews. Photos of stacked corpses. The eyes of the women were on her, full of accusation. A rebbetzin should take Jewish martyrs more seriously than a *goyishe* saint with a tin plate on his head, stuck full of arrows like a dart board.

"I must be on my way," said Rachel, going quickly to the room with the Giovanni diPaolo and the Sassetta.

"Hello, Rachel."

This time the voice calling her name was familiar and loved. Rachel turned around and saw Ben. She had seen him too recently to expect him to be the Ben of yesteryear, but she was shocked, just the same, by his pallor and by the dark hollows around his eyes.

"Ben!" she said and touched his arm—she had never been able to keep her hands off him. She kissed him and he kissed her back in his offhand way, as though he didn't really mean it.

"We still seem to meet in the same places," he said.

"I meant to call you."

"Why didn't you?"

"I don't know. . . . I'm working. I find it hard to do anything that changes the delicate balance of my life. I'm stuck in Gateshead and when I come to the city my day is taken up by doing things I can cross off my list. . . ." She pulled a tattered piece of paper from the pocket of her denim skirt. "And then, too, I didn't want to seem aggressive."

"Rachel-Rachel, I think about you now and then. Not all the time, mind you, but now and then."

He wore a blue oxford shirt and a denim chore jacket, washed out until it had a grayish-yellow cast

258

to it. He wore chino pants with paint splattered on them and old blue boating sneakers. He was as tall as Seymour, but thin as a rail. His thinness made Rachel want to touch him; she had never forgotten what it felt like against her flesh.

"You always liked the Sassetta," she said, "even before I did."

"What do you mean 'even'? I taught you all you know."

"You say that all the time. You must not believe it."

They stood next to each other and the years slipped away. They did not look at one another but only felt the other's presence. Ben put his hand on Rachel's arm, awkwardly, as he had always done it.

"Let's look at some pictures together, and then take a Fifth Avenue bus to the end of the line and have a drink and see what happens."

"All right," said Rachel, casually, although the waves of old-new desires had begun lapping at the seat of her pants.

They looked together at the Vermeers and at Poussin. Controlled surfaces, perfect clarity. Out of the way of nature's passions and its suns.

"It's taken me a long long time to 'see' Poussin," said Rachel.

"You were always a slow learner. You had to fight your way through all that art history they taught you at Barnard and learn to see the way a painter sees."

"You always liked giving out little digs like that. But I would like to remind you of the fable of the tortoise and the hare."

"I bet your husband, what's-his-name, likes to provoke you, too."

"What makes you say that?"

"So it's true?"

"I suppose."

"My insight has been kept intact through the long harrowing years. What *is* his name?"

"Seymour, as you well know."

"Exactly right for a rabbi."

"Exactly right for me."

"I would deduce your Seymour sees rather less with

259

his eyes and more with his mind. And has a soft heart, mushy with need for love."

"You needn't criticize him."

"I don't see you bringing him along to look at the pictures you love to look at."

"I do it best alone."

"Or with me."

"Or with you."

"Remember, I'm jealous. He carried you off. Took you away from me."

"He was there first, remember? You took me from him."

"For a brief while, I did. Took you on a short fling to the nether world. Introduced you to wicked Greenwich Village, to free love and Mary Jane. But you reverted to type. Buffalo will out."

"Do you think we would have been happy?"

"*You* might have been, Rachel-Rachel, because you *are* happy. I would have been sad, as ever."

The seventeenth century grew absurd around them. Curled flowing wigs, satin and lace. Marble garlands. They hurried on to the eighteenth.

"I love the eighteenth century," said Rachel, "but not in painting so much."

"You love your idea of the eighteenth century. It's part of the college education you received."

"It's also the birth of Romanticism. Think of all the people born in the eighteenth century. Turner and Beethoven and Goya. Kasper David Friedrich . . ."

"You didn't used to know who he was."

"I'm a slow learner, remember?"

They looked at each other and away again, back at the paintings.

"For painting, what century would you pick?" Ben asked.

"The fourteenth, I guess. The century in which we met—so to speak. You taught me to see it with modern eyes. You made the connection for me."

"It was the only connection I made?"

"Don't say that."

"I didn't *say* it, it was a question."

260

"You made a lot of connections. It was the one with your dealer I objected to most."

"You just drifted out of my hands, back to what's-his-name . . ."

"You went to Europe . . ."

"We talk about the same thing every time we meet."

"We've got nothing new to share, as yet."

"I *should* have taken you to Europe with me."

"You would have left me alone to talk in cafes."

"You could have come with me."

"I'd have wanted to keep busy with other things —painting, going to the Louvre."

"I went to the Louvre."

"I have a drawing you did. It hangs in my studio. God, were you good!"

"I know the one—done after the *Battle of San Romano,* one of the great paintings of all time. I was fascinated by those plumed heads, the lances setting up the rhythm, the unfurled banners. You kept my drawing all these years?"

"I loved it. I loved the artist."

"Paolo Uccello?"

"Him too."

They had reached the nineteenth century in France. Ben and Rachel looked at the Cézannes for a long time.

"He chained himself to that mountain, didn't he?" said Rachel, after a while.

"He was like one of those saints who go into the wilderness to tame their rebellious romantic spirits."

Rachel and Ben walked down the grand staircase. They took a Number 1 Fifth Avenue bus and got off at the corner of Houston and Broadway.

"It wasn't called SoHo when we were young," said Rachel. "Do you still see anybody from those days?"

"Most of them are gone. Moved away to California or Paris. O.D.'d. A very few became famous. The ones I still talk to escaped from Pilgrim State to Westbeth. The ones cancer didn't get, or desperation or electric shock. Artists with baby carriages. Spiritual parents to the generation of the sixties."

261

"What's your wife like?" asked Rachel.

They were walking in the hot afternoon sun. The asphalt was soft and black bubbles rose on it. The streets smelled of live garbage. Cheese and salami and fresh fish sent up their own good odors above the waste, and the buildings didn't reach too high. Bleecker Street, west of Sixth Avenue, was still Italian. The sidewalks were crowded. Ben kissed Rachel on the forehead and a shopkeeper hooted. He kissed her full on the lips and a couple of boys laughed raucously and yet in admiration. Out here on the street everyone was actor and critic.

Ben took Rachel into a bar where he was known. The bartender greeted him. A couple of men were watching the ball game. It was nice in there. Not only cool but dark enough to make watching the ball game easy.

"What's happening?" asked Rachel, but the men didn't believe she cared.

"You still like baseball?" said Ben, and they sat down at one of the tables.

"I still like baseball, better than ever. You didn't answer me about your wife."

"What's there to say? I'm faithless enough being here with you. She's a good woman."

He got up and fetched two beers.

"She's got to be good to put up with me. I still talk about what I'm going to do and I'm forty-five and never going to do it. She just quietly goes about her business, never talks about what she's going to do. She's a social worker, a supervisor in the welfare department. I'm a bum. *You* couldn't have stayed 'nice' married to me. What makes Annie good is that she doesn't expect anything great of me. You would have kept saying 'you have so much talent, don't waste it,' and you would have become sour with the years, still hoping, still expecting."

Rachel saw the truth in that clearly enough.

"She doesn't come up with ideas like wanting to be an artist," he said. "She does everything well. She cooks, she sews, she's taken up weaving but she doesn't

262

make it into something spiritual. She isn't full of all the middle-class bull about one thing being more worthy than another. She saw me when I was down, way down, and she picked me up."

"O.k., o.k.," said Rachel, "I understand."

There was a flurry of action in the baseball game; the opposition had scored another run. The men watching complained loudly. "Take the fuckin' pitcher out already."

"I'm not putting you down, Rachel, for being middle class. It isn't that. It's only that we gambled, each of us in our own way, and I lost. And sometimes you think you lost, too, but you didn't. You only think you did."

Ben's hands lay on the table. They were long and very thin. They had never been terribly clean and they had paint around the cuticles, as always. Rachel put her hands over his.

"I want to go to bed with you," she said. "Very much. The way I used to when there were always all those people around and I never got to be alone with you."

Ben slid his hands back over hers.

"I used to drink with Mason and his friends. You were so jealous of that girl. The wild one. What was her name?"

Rachel had not thought of her in years. "She was beautiful. The kind of beautiful girl who drove me crazy because I wanted to look like that and didn't and wanted to be like that and wasn't. An oval face. Long blond hair and nothing to tie her down, no one to call her back. She was free free free. I don't remember her name either."

"Do you really want to sleep with me?"

"Yes. I have never slept with anyone else since I married Seymour. I am scared of strangers. But I know you. I am not even being unfaithful. I loved you once. Maybe I'll always love you. You are the painter in my life. We see through eyes that are alike."

"Where are we going to go?"

"A hotel room."

263

"The fastidious suburban lady coming into the city to fuck the disreputable bohemian in a roach-infested bed."

"Don't make fun of me. I'm not all that sure of myself this very moment."

"Neither am I."

They finished their beers and walked back out into the sunshine. Summer in the city. The men were still watching the ball game. Rachel didn't say anything to them.

They found a hotel. Rachel saw the lobby and its furnishings very clearly, but they made no impression on her—body and soul rested with Ben. He was fumbling awkwardly at the front desk.

"You have five dollars?" he said. "I need five dollars more."

Rachel took the bill out of her wallet and gave it to him. The clerk stared at her leather pocketbook. It was the only expensive thing about her. For the rest she might have been any whore with dirty feet. The kind that gave tourists who came to the Village the feeling that they were screwing arty girls.

The room was small. Rachel looked at herself in the mirror that stood on the dresser, leaning against the wall. Once upon a time it had hung from a nail; a hole bursting with plaster in the papered wall attested to that. The room was surprisingly clean, though sparsely furnished. There was a smell of cleansing powder in the air.

Ben stood by the window for a long time.

"Are you sorry you came?" Rachel asked him, no longer certain herself that it had been a good idea. The unfamiliar room, the green chenille bedspread, the dirty window—all these seemed to take up the space between them.

"I'm not sorry I came," said Ben, still looking out of the window, "but I don't know how to begin making love to you. There are lots of things we haven't told each other. Things left over from the olden days and unresolved. Now they're overlaid with sediment and I don't know where to begin. What was it we

264

loved about each other? And what did we hate? Are *you* sorry you came?"

"I thought it would be simpler."

Rachel sat on the bed. She left her sandals on the floor and drew her feet up, put her arms around her knees. It was a conscious gesture reverting to her youth. They were both aware of the room's gray presence, its faded wallpaper and stained armchair. Rooms like it had once figured in Rachel's fantasies. They came out of those self-same Depression novels and plays she had used, when she was very young, to insulate her from a world she felt would crush her if she did not keep it at a distance. But she knew, suddenly now, that these rooms were more constricting yet, that if she *had* to return to them each night and hear the mice scurrying in the walls and the water dripping in the tub, she would exhaust her imagination merely in trying to see that it did not become a tomb instead of a prison.

Ben took off his jacket and the blue oxford shirt and stood near the window now in his T-shirt and his chino pants. His skin was very pale. Rachel remembered that he did not often go out into the sun, or take off his clothes except in the dark. He was ashamed of his thinness and always cold. Ben drew the shade over the window and the room became dim. In its dusky light desire revived. Rachel felt her cunt clucking for Ben, and saw his pants puffed out over his penis. When he took them off she saw it more clearly still, cradled in his shorts, and the throbbing of her cunt made her legs grow weak. She pulled off her denim skirt and her flowered blouse and undid her bra. In the dimness, the white strips her bathing suit had left on her body looked whiter yet and the brown of her shoulders and thighs seemed the color of rust. She pulled the chenille spread from the bed and turned down the sheets. They were clean but old and soft from washing. She still had her underpants on. Ben lay down beside her and the tip of his penis touched her leg through the slit in his shorts. It went through her boldly, that touch, until her whole body was filled

265

to bursting with desire. They pulled each other's underwear off and now touched flesh to flesh. They closed their eyes so that they could not see but only feel each other. They put their lips and their fingers over each other's skin, tasting and stroking blindly and deliciously, delicately and agonizingly. They wanted to pitch the throbbing desire to the highest point before letting it go. When it seemed that there was no place left, no place at all in the dark of their touching and burrowing, when their panting had almost reached a cry, they found each other, blindly too, and at the very instant Ben thrust his prick into Rachel they came. Their backs arched in a leap that made them yelp with pleasure and melded sweating bodies into a single figure.

Rachel and Ben dropped apart slowly, like petals from a flower. The room had gained something through the spending of their desire. It was a familiar room all at once. Their clothes were scattered over it. A beam of sunlight shone round the sides of the window shade.

"What time is it?" asked Rachel.

"I haven't got a watch."

Rachel lifted her limp arm from his chest and looked at her wristwatch. It was five minutes after three.

"When do you have to be home?"

"I told Seymour it might be late. After the rush hour anyway. I said I might do something time-consuming, like taking a trip around Manhattan."

Ben leaned over to take a pack of cigarettes from his pants pocket.

"You shouldn't smoke; you'll die before your time."

"Who tells you I want to live?"

"Don't you?"

"Not always."

Rachel kissed him. He had covered himself up with the sheet and Rachel sat next to him with her legs crossed. Little bubbles of his semen still burst from between them. They had sat like this in the olden days and planned what to do with each other in the years ahead.

266

"Sometimes I think how nice it might have been, going to Greece with you," said Ben, "or Mexico, or Italy. I used to make it up, how it would be. But then I lost the memory of you. It's clearer again now, but it will be all about this afternoon from now on. The other things are impossible to dream about now. Sometimes I look up at the ceiling when I wake up alone and think that everything in the world has congealed into a square of pavement. That's my self-portrait."

"Don't be so melancholy."

"Don't act like you're Joan Fontaine in *The Constant Nymph*. I don't mind the romance, but the sentimentality kills me."

Rachel had forgotten his bitter turn of mind. The way he could turn some fledgling thought of hers to dust. To turds. She dressed and went to open the window shade.

"Seymour will smell the semen on you."

"I'll take a bath when I get home. I might even go for a swim. It stays light late now."

Ben buttoned his buttons and they left. Quietly, the way they had come, without trying to remember the way the lobby looked, setting the key down gently on the counter.

Rachel went to a movie—she never after could remember what it was—and took the 7:35 home, carrying her secret fit to burst. Nobody on the train guessed it. They didn't even seem interested. She saw no one she knew. She walked as though she owned everything in sight, but still no one guessed she had just slept with an old lover in a flea-bag hotel and been unfaithful to her husband for the first time in almost twenty years of marriage. Seymour was out when she got home and Rachel thought nothing about it. She was too full of what she had done. She took a bath and put her clothes into the washing machine and was in the backyard, having a drink, when Seymour got back.

"Where have you been?" she asked.

"At the library."

And if Rachel knew that he was not telling the truth she gave no hint of it. They did not talk much

267

the rest of the evening. Seymour did not ask what she had done in the city. He was trying to keep his own life under control.

Truscott Boothby called early the next morning. "I just saw your good husband," he said. "I know he's not home. He was going up to the hospital to visit the sick. Will you meet me in town next week, Rachel?"

Filled as she was with Ben's sweet kisses and gentle caresses, Rachel could not think of Truscott Boothby in bed next to her, all muscle and booming shoulders and blue eyes like steel.

"I don't think I can," she said. "Honestly, Truscott, I can't." She gave him no reason but he understood that she would not love him.

"You seemed to respond to me. I thought surely you meant it. You'd meet me for lunch. We could go to a museum."

"No, no," she said. "A lot of things have come up. I don't dare. I can't handle it."

"If anyone can, you can."

"No, Truscott, believe me!"

He hung up angrily. Rachel knew he felt betrayed. He had declared himself, on the strength of her encouragement, which she had just withdrawn. He would undoubtedly feel even worse had she told him that it was another man who came between them.

A week and a half later Rachel and Seymour drove up to the Cape in their convertible. Rachel's fortieth birthday would fall in the middle of their stay. She claimed not to put much stock in birthdays (even fortieth ones) because it embarrassed her to think she might be discovered among those women who counted the years and feared old age. Still, she never failed to mark the date on the kitchen calendar, and had seen to it that Aaron circled it in his pocket diary.

Rachel and Seymour put the top of the convertible down and listened to the radio and ate in tacky diners. Now and then Seymour put his hand on Rachel's bare thigh (she wore shorts cut down from an old pair of jeans—they permitted a few pubic hairs to curl out

268

below the frayed leg). They said very little, exhausted as they were by the turbulence within them.

Rachel remembered summers of her childhood and long trips east to the sea. They were characterized, at a certain point along the way, by whiffs of sea air wafting in through the windows of the hot car and the sight of the soil turning to sand beneath the short, wind-stunted trees. The color of the land changed as soon as you got close to the sea. And suddenly, with a splendor that was not dimmed by time or habit, the horizon would grow sharp and flat, would become a metallic gray line 'twixt water and sky. It was the ocean, and on it the sun would dance or whitecaps sparkle, or perhaps a line of breakers far out would curl toward the shore.

Rachel never had enough of it. And the houses to which she had come, through the years, were always utterly plain and stark like the sea itself. They were never really strange; she "knew" them within hours and never woke up in them choked by the sense of being lost. They returned, like old friends, subtly altered but recognizable, in her dreams forever after.

Driving in the open car, heading toward the sea, Rachel ordered all the spaces in her mind.

She thought, too, about the hotel room. It had already become a memorable space. She would evoke it in her dreams to come, slightly altered, slightly changed, but recognizable, even without Ben to occupy it. She would set imaginary figures in it. It was no wonder then, that she had always liked paintings in which the rooms (landscape) dominated the figures. That was the reason why, finally, the art of Michelangelo with its great roiling figures, and even that of Rembrandt, however deeply moving, however gloriously painted, did not occupy first place in her pantheon.

The radio and the wind in their noise kept Rachel isolated from Seymour, even as they touched. It was part of their closeness that they did not need to talk.

They found the house without trouble. A note in the mailbox (it was not for the mail, which came to a post office box) told them where to find the key to the

269

house. It unlocked the kitchen door, which was the one most generally used—the front door was creaky and swollen in its frame.

The high dune grass grew everywhere. It swept up to the foundation of the white, two-story frame house like the sea, and when the wind turned it into flickering waves, the illusion was complete. A sandy driveway led straight to a weathered garage. There was nothing else for a long, long space—and then the pale beach and the blue mirror of the ocean. Though the house looked fragile, there in that emptiness, it was not. It had been built in 1911 (the date was incised in a cornerstone) and had weathered even the 1938 hurricane. It was brilliantly white, bleached like a bone in the sun. No splash of color came near it, no flowers grew in its vicinity, no shrubs of any kind, and even the red brick chimney had weathered into a subtle orange-brown. Looking toward the ocean on a weekend you could see the bright round spots of beach umbrellas, towels and beach chairs, and they were the only flowers in the landscape. Even within the house the colors were subdued. It was as though the sun in all its strength had gone right through the walls which the wind couldn't breach. The blue cushions had lost their deep dark saturated hues and the pink tablecloth had turned nearly white. The furniture (what little there was of it) was white wicker or white painted wood. The floors had been painted too—gray or yellow or aquamarine—and then splattered with dots of bright enamels: *whoosh!* Rachel could feel it done, with a paintbrush soaked in color and the arm swung wide. Scatter rugs were made of cotton, washed out pale over the years. Rachel loved the house at once, and began (the very next morning) to draw its rooms, one by one.

The vacation—like most things for which the hopes held are too high—proved less than perfect, though when she thought about it later, Rachel remembered its beauties and forgot its raw and painful spots. That was her way.

Wellfleet was the nearest town. All sorts of interesting people were said to be in the vicinity—writers, painters,

270

and intellectuals—but Rachel and Seymour did not know a soul. They went to the post office and to the general store; they went swimming every sunny day and lay on their beach towels and smiled at the solitary walkers, but no one (not even those who smiled back) spoke to them. It was not intentional, of course; it simply meant that the others had a full life and many friends, while Seymour and Rachel were castaways in the Dinsmoors' white clapboard house. It might not have rankled so much if they had not been aware of the splendid social life all around them. There were picnics in the evenings, with large bonfires, softball games on Sunday mornings on the school field, and large parties where the artists danced late into the night. Had they been marooned among the rich and socially prominent, they would not have yearned so for their company, they would have worn proudly the yellow badge of their pariahdom. (Rachel would have thought about the Revolution.) But it was painful to be so alone among those to whose station you aspired, to be an outcast among an elite you admired.

Rachel and Seymour were together constantly—and constantly alone. It might have been their honeymoon, except for the twenty years of burrs and barnacles that had accumulated on their marriage and made them tend to look backward to find fault, rather than forward to make plans. All those years as rabbi and rebbetzin had not prepared them for the life of solitude. Rachel rather liked it, but it oppressed Seymour and his unease made her anxious. She was too bright and cheerful with him and cooked too much, using forbidden foods. She bought clams and lobsters and shrimp. She broiled sirloin steaks and made pot roasts with bottom round, browned in bacon fat. All of it made her feel guilty (why could she not rid herself of that stupid guilt?), but her meals tasted awfully good. They had bacon and eggs every morning and got fat. Rachel had to lie down on her back across the bed in order to zip up her jeans. The swimming and running they did to slim their waists only made them hungrier for the rich *treif*. Rachel liked to cook, it was a change from her drawing and painting and fed her sense of being a wom-

271

an who could do a thousand things and do them well. It made her feel strong and self-sufficient. The gloomier Seymour grew, the more Rachel cooked, and the better her meals got. She atavistically played out the role of the Jewish mother. "Eat, eat," she seemed to say, "you can't be unhappy if you eat." And Seymour ate to see if it would make him happy, while Rachel ate because it tasted so good. One day, when she had made a bouillabaisse, serving it with fresh, home-baked French bread and was sitting there, grinning over it as she ate with undisguised pleasure, Seymour said to her, "I never thought I would see the day that you would become a full-fledged fat Yiddishe Mamma . . ."

". . . who serves bouillabaisse?"

"My emphasis was on the 'fat.' "

"You're very sweet today."

"I can't stand to see you eat like that. You stuff your mouth with lobster and mussels and corn and the butter drips down your chin. It's disgusting."

"I have to enjoy it while I can."

"I doubt you'll die tomorrow."

"I doubt it too, but I'll have to go back to Gateshead all too soon."

"And that's like death to you?"

"No. Not like death. I'm not that dramatic."

"So you say. But you do participate in your own small dramas. This place is perfect for them. It bores me. It fills me with anxiety. I should have brought something to read, a project, some work. I thought I'd come here and do *nothing*. I hoped *we'd* do nothing, both of us together. I should have known that you would withdraw and leave me stranded. You spend the morning by yourself, drawing and painting. At the beach you dream and read *Anna Karenina*. You have shut me out."

"I set myself these tasks . . ."

"It's summer and we're on vacation."

"When I finish *Anna Karenina* I'm going to start on *The Decline and Fall of the Roman Empire;* you can have that until I get to it."

"I've read it. And you don't understand. I want to

272

do nothing morally uplifting. I'm not determined to improve myself, the way you are. You believe in your own perfectibility. I don't. Neither in yours nor in mine. I like talking, having social encounters. I suppose it has to do with my being a rabbi—I'm always up to my throat in conversations. They're not always pleasant, but they fill the air, make me think on my feet. I'm a talker. It's silent here—unbearably so. All you hear is the wind and the surf, and in the village the chatter is all around me—I feel as though I don't exist."

They sat across from one another, at the bleached wooden kitchen table. The bouillabaisse bubbled in a large enamel pot on top of the gas stove. Its odor mingled with that of the bread, which had suffused the house all day. Rachel had no idea of the date, nor the day of the week. It rained outside. The kitchen lamp hung low over the table, the corners of the kitchen were dark, but Rachel and Seymour were caught in a pool of yellow light. The rain fell softly on the roof, fog was sweeping in from the sea. Distances and directions were wiped out, the isolation of the house seemed complete. Although there was a radio in the house, and summer books (the kind found at church fairs and in second-hand stores), everything was connected to someone else, to strangers.

"I even miss the TV," said Seymour. "It brings me news of a world I've grown dependent upon. I'll have to start work on my holiday sermons soon. I'll have to plan the year. It all seems very unreal here. Especially in the rain and the fog, with no one to talk to. I don't mean that you're no one, Rachel, but you're shut off, solitary. You're just the same as the house, it's no wonder you like it. You sit there, your inner rooms are clear and clean, and you look out to sea. Sometimes I think you might be having visions, or become withdrawn to the point where I can't call you back. Listen to that foghorn!"

They were silent while the bleating horn faded out and came mournfully back. The white fog was at the door now, the window screens glistened with droplets of water. It had stopped raining, there was no longer

273

the rustle of falling water, nor the gurgle of the gutters carrying it down into the sand. And then the telephone rang. It seemed like a shocking and frightening intrusion. The fog and the silence of the windless night had severed all connections with the rest of mankind.

Seymour answered the phone. As always, he did not hurry, nor catch his breath in fear. Rachel thought "Something is wrong with Aaron" and listened to hear the kind of sound Seymour's voice made. He said, "Hello, Cy," in a cheerful voice, and Rachel knew it was the congregation's business. Then Seymour's voice dropped to low and sad and he said, "Oh, I'm so sorry to hear that." She got up from the table to wash the dishes and turned the stove off, dipping a last piece of bread into the fish broth. Seymour came back from the hall where the old black telephone stood, on a rickety table, with the names of strangers on a card next to it. The plumber's name led all the rest.

"That was Cy Glatt. Michelle Shulman Halprin's father died. He wanted to tell me so I could call them. They want me to do the funeral, but didn't call me because I'm on vacation, which is considerate. But I think I ought to go back. I'll need all the friends I can get. It doesn't guarantee they'll be my friends, but it might leave them with a grateful enough feeling to influence their vote. I think they're on the fence. Don't you think it's wise for me to go?"

"Will you be back for my birthday?"

"I thought you didn't care about birthdays."

"I don't."

"If I can make it I will, but you know how it is with funerals. If it doesn't work out we'll celebrate later—I promise you a fancy dinner in New York."

Rachel rather liked the idea of being alone for a little while. She wanted the time to move through the house, through her life, without distractions.

"I'll be able to take care of some other business while I'm home," said Seymour. "I can check our mail. I should have heard from Omaha by now."

274

Rachel had almost forgotten about Omaha. She realized how little she wondered about what went on in Seymour's mind. Did he think about Gateshead? Did he dream about Natalie? As far as Rachel was concerned, it was "out of sight, out of mind" both for Gateshead and Natalie Gould. And as long as Seymour was on the Cape with her (no matter how glum, she thought), he was out of Natalie's way. If only he didn't begin to pine for her. Pining was bad, it made the object pined about seem better than she was. Rachel knew Seymour would go to see Natalie in Gateshead. He was laying his plans now. She watched him get busy with telephone calls. He seemed pleased.

Rachel put the bouillabaisse into a bowl and let it cool on the table before storing it away in the refrigerator. The kitchen was clean and neat now. There were only useful tools in it. She wore a pair of jeans and a T-shirt with no bra. Her hair was longer than usual and had reddened in the sun. Seymour was as dark as an Indian and his curly hair lay softly on the nape of his neck. Thoughts darted through Rachel's head, without stopping at any one impression, while Seymour went about, purposefully now, finally in charge of something, finally engaged. Rachel looked over the kitchen before turning off the light. It presented a lovely scene. She stopped her wheeling thoughts and looked at it closely. All other considerations trailed off; she no longer heard Seymour at all. The red lobster claws, the bunch of daisies in its thick blue bell jar, the checked cloth (no, the checked cloth would have to go), the bread, the plain bowl. (The checked tablecloth was definitely too cute.) It needed a lemon. An eggplant. Maybe the earthenware pot. Rachel arranged everything on the bare table.

"What are you doing?" asked Seymour, from the doorway.

"Rearranging the still life."

Seymour sighed.

Rachel brought down her black sketchbook from the spare bedroom in which she worked, and her box of forty-eight magic markers, and spent the next two

275

hours drawing the still life on the kitchen table. She prowled around her still life and drew it from different angles. It was midnight before she stopped and put the food way.

Walking upstairs after the kitchen was cleared, she heard Seymour's voice, like squirrels on the roof, intense, furtive, just above a whisper. She stopped where she was, in the middle of the stairs; her bare feet had made no noise, she was not heard. He was on the telephone in their bedroom. Rachel crept the rest of the way up the stairs. The light was dim, coming out from under the door; the foghorn still wailed in the distance, she heard it again now; she had not heard it while she worked, had not remembered hearing it. Rachel stood at the top of the stairs, only a yard or two away from the bedroom door, and listened.

"I'll see you this weekend after the funeral. I'll have to miss Rachel's birthday . . . no, she says she doesn't mind. She's working, as always . . . no, she doesn't know. I long to see you. I miss you."

Rachel felt the words crushing her heart. She had never heard Seymour say them to anyone else. He had said them to her, they were hers alone, they did not belong to anyone else.

"I do love you, you silly girl."

Rachel's crushed heart pounded. She did not want to hear any more, at the same time she wanted to know it all, to hear the very worst, to bruise her heart ever more (as though building up a case on the basis of which she could act, even if action eluded her at that moment). As she stayed in her place, listening, her strength seemed to ebb (her vaunted strength!). For one moment she put her hands over her ears, but the silence left her open only to her pounding heart and she freed them again. As long as she was there, unknown, unobserved, she must hear the end of it. She hadn't chosen to eavesdrop. It wasn't as though she had opened a letter not addressed to her, or lifted a receiver knowing that Seymour was on the line. She had happened upon the conversation innocently, on her way to bed. She had stumbled across his betrayal without wanting to. She had forced thoughts of Natalie

276

out of her mind, tried to forget Gateshead, tried not to worm her way into Seymour's mind.

And now, as she leaned against the bannister and heard Seymour tell Natalie Gould that he loved her, she could no longer shut her ears or close her mind. She had to confront her crushed heart and Seymour's duplicity. For it was not his infidelity that pained her (had she not slept with Ben scarcely a month ago, in a dingy hotel room in Greenwich Village?) but his duplicity. He had told Natalie Gould that he loved her. How could he love Natalie Gould as he loved her, Rachel Sonnshein, his wife? Rachel did not doubt his love for her, she had never doubted it, but she could not imagine sharing it with anyone, least of all with Natalie Gould. (Could she share it with a friend, with Sally perhaps? She believed that she could. She had not tested it, but it seemed a reasonable belief. At that moment, anyway.) He had been able, all this time, all these months, to deceive her, to build up new layers of love, new feelings of tenderness for someone else. It meant that he had constructed a new and different life for himself out of her reach, her sight, her knowledge and her own love. No, perhaps not out of reach of her own love, for he must think that she would forgive him. He believed himself to be pure in heart; he did not think those new layers of his love spoiled the old. He counted on her to cut through the layers and find the shining perfect kernel and recognize it—because she loved him.

Rachel knew all that, even at the instant of her discovery, there in the dark hallway. But it did not help her, did not assuage the pounding of her crushed heart, did not drive out the jealousy storming through her mind. Rachel had believed that her strength guarded and protected her against jealousy. It did not. She was sick with its taste now, nausea bloomed from out of her bloodied heart. Seymour was still; did he hearken to Natalie's voice or was he listening for hers?

"I'd better hang up now," he said (he was hearkening to Natalie's voice). "I'll see you tomorrow. I can't wait. You are lovely in my mind, just like you were..."

277

Rachel ran quickly down the stairs, silently on her bare feet. She could stand to hear no more. She could also not be caught at her eavesdropping. Eavesdroppers deserved what they got. She was lying on the living room couch, holding *Anna Karenina* on her stomach, when Seymour came downstairs to look for her. Only the small table lamp was on, its sixty-watt bulb casting barely enough light upon the pages of the book; but, then, she couldn't see to read the words anyhow.

"You'll go blind, reading in the dark."

Seymour was more cheerful than he had been all night. He thought his secret was safe. He bent down to kiss Rachel on the top of her head. She moved away.

"What's the matter with you?"

Truly he thought she knew nothing. Rachel had not formulated a plan of action. She acted instinctively. Seymour had said "I love you" to a stranger. He had given away a word that belonged to her.

"You're mighty cheerful," Rachel said.

"I love you," answered Seymour.

"Don't say that."

"But it's true."

Rachel knew that she could not admit that she had heard him say the same words to Natalie Gould. Perhaps he even knew it, but counted on her unwillingness to admit it to keep her from bringing it up. "Rachel, Rachel," he said with a sigh, and it reminded Rachel of Ben and she had to balance the hotel room against what she had heard. But she had not told Ben that she loved him, and he was no stranger; he was already a part of her past; he had returned one day and she had received him.

It was not the same thing and yet, perhaps, it was. Rachel found that she could say nothing, nothing at all. It was a dark night and they were alone. Seymour held tight to his innocence, his purity of heart. Rachel was not certain of the purity of her heart, and she wanted peace. Blessed peace.

"Seymour, Seymour," she said, but her heart lay crushed within her still, and the anger would not go away, it fluttered on wings of nausea. There was a

278

thick and evil taste in her mouth. She longed to read *Anna Karenina*. Tolstoy would comfort her with the greatness of his understanding. It was as though she had a painting by Vermeer to contemplate—there was no dross, there was only the balance of perfection. A comprehension that transcended the moment's evil taste. It could transcend the crushed heart and only death would snatch it from sight, and death came to everyone. But in the meantime you had to live and learn. To fill the spaces.

"When are you going?" Rachel asked. "I hope you're not taking the car."

"How else will I get home?"

"There's a bus."

"And in Gateshead?"

"In Gateshead there are taxis."

"I have to attend a funeral, Rachel."

"And I'll be here all alone. Suppose I need to get groceries, go to a doctor. Suppose there's an accident?" Her anger was climbing on top of her, like a clawing cat. It fastened on the car. "You can't leave me here without a car. All alone without a car!"

"I have a funeral . . ."

"You're going to fuck around."

"Stop talking nonsense. You heard Cy Glatt's call."

"You're going to fuck around and take the car too!"

"I can no more be without a car in Gateshead, going about my business this week, than I can the rest of the year. I don't want to have to ask anyone else for a favor. You can manage here. I'll buy you groceries before I leave tomorrow."

"Why can't you at least buy a second car?"

"Not now, Rachel, not until I find out what's going to happen with me and my job."

"And when we live in that development? Far away from everything? The only thing nearby is the *shul*, and I can't buy bread there, or milk."

"We haven't moved there yet."

"But we're going to."

"I'll deal with it when the time comes. I don't want to discuss it now."

"I don't want to discuss it now either, but I'm al-

279

ready going to be stuck, the first time of hundreds, while you go fucking off to Gateshead."

"It's only two days, Rachel. Three days at the most. I thought you liked hanging around this house, doing your precious work. You never wanted to go anywhere with me while you had the chance. We've been stuck here for two weeks and you've practically become a recluse, but now you want to go traipsing off just because I need the car to go back to Gateshead and work my ass off to conduct a funeral—right smack in the middle of my summer vacation."

"The funeral is a welcome excuse for you."

"You want to call Michelle Shulman Halprin and ask her?"

"I don't mean that there's no funeral, only that you're going back for more than a funeral. You only accepted the funeral because you want to fuck Natalie Gould."

"You seem to be obsessed with that idea. Is it the only thing your little mind can think up to throw at me?"

"Isn't it enough?"

"It's more than enough. You're so hysterical you've blown it into a monstrous accusation and I won't even try to defend myself. I'll be back in a couple of days. I can't say 'No' now, it would be worse than if I had said it in the first place. Do you want me not to go?"

"I didn't ask you not to go. I just thought you might leave me the car. But never mind."

Rachel was weary. She was always the first to tire in an argument. Seymour had a great deal more stamina than she did; his resources in battle were immense. He knew now that she had given in. He suspected she had given in on more than the car.

"I'll shop for you in the morning before I leave." He started to touch her again, but wisely refrained.

Rachel sat, bent over the closed book (her finger marked the page where she had pretended to be reading), and did not look after Seymour as he bounded upstairs. She sat for a while, stunned and worn. She tried to cry but couldn't. It was like trying to throw up when you were merely vaguely nauseous. You put

280

your finger in your throat and retched and retched until your throat was sore and never got relief. Rachel went looking for the vodka, feeling dramatic and Russian as she drank it neat, but it only gave her a headache. She went upstairs at three in the morning, when she was certain Seymour was asleep. The fog outside was like a shroud and the distant rumble of the surf like a funeral march.

When Rachel awoke the next morning, Seymour was gone. There were three large bags of groceries on the kitchen table (containing delicacies such as smoked oysters and gooseliver paté as well as staples enough to hold an army for a week) and a note that promised love forever, complete, eternal. The sun had burnt the fog away. It was a beautiful day.

Rachel was happy to be alone. The burdened evening had disappeared with the fog. She was on her own, a tower of strength, alive and talented: an artist. Taking her breakfast outside, Rachel drank coffee and felt the gentle wind in her hair and the warm sun on her shoulders. She wore no more than a thin robe and her body (fat as it had grown) felt supple and useful. She could expect no more, useful was enough. Maybe everything would turn out all right.

Rachel spent the morning working on a second series of drawings of the still life. Everything was changed by the light of the sun. In the afternoon she took *Anna Karenina* and went down to the beach. The surf was light and easy, but Rachel walked down to the public beach so she would not have to swim alone. She was a good swimmer, but respected the sea too much to take chances with it. She sat at the outermost edge of the crowd, far enough away so as not to be distracted by radios or conversations.

The next day was Rachel's birthday. A hotel postcard arrived from Aaron. He had written "HAPPY B'DAY from your one and only son" beneath the advertising material.

The telephone in the sun-lit house rang frequently.

Saul and Betty Diamant called and announced that they had sent a check.

"It hasn't gotten here yet," said Rachel.

281

"You sound depressed," said Betty Diamant.

"Who, me?" asked Rachel, pumping cheer into her voice. "Why would I be depressed? I'm just beginning my life, looking forward to the next forty years."

"I'm glad to hear it."

"I wouldn't want to be twenty again."

"I hope you're getting your rest."

"Yes, mother." Rachel did not tell her that Seymour was in Gateshead.

Michael and David Diamant called, from their respective offices.

"How's it feel to be grown up?" said David.

"Any gray hairs yet?" asked Michael.

Even Milton and Sadie Sonnshein called.

"Where's my son?" asked Grandpa Milt. Rachel told him that Seymour had been called to Gateshead for a funeral.

"He must be very worried about his job," said Milton Sonnshein.

"I wouldn't let *my* husband get away with that," said Sadie Sonnshein.

"How are you feeling?" answered Rachel.

Seymour was the last to call.

"Happy Birthday!" he said. "I love you."

"That and a token will get you a ride on the subway."

"That's not how the line goes."

"But you get the point."

"Why are you angry?"

"I'm not angry."

"Has your mother been making trouble again?"

"It was *your* mother who said she wouldn't have allowed *her* husband to be away on her birthday."

"She's full of bullshit. My mother has only her suffering to hold over my father's head."

"What's been happening in Gateshead?"

"Nothing much. The funeral went o.k. You ought to write a condolence note. The place here is dreary and dank—you didn't leave it in very good shape."

"Any more complaints? And how's your love life?"

"Pretty rotten. Rachel?"

"Yes?"

282

"Do you love me?"

"Of course I love you."

"I need your love. I miss you. I love you very much."

"Only me?"

"Only truly you."

"Are you alone?"

"Of course I'm alone."

"What about Natalie Gould?"

"She doesn't matter. Are *you* alone?"

"Utterly alone."

"Well, stay that way. I'll see you soon."

"When?"

"Monday, probably."

"O.k. Good-night."

"Good-night, Rachel."

The house seemed very silent after Seymour had hung up and Rachel had put the receiver back. She went from room to room and looked out of every window. There were only distant stationary lights visible. Nothing stirred; there was no sound. Rachel checked the doors again and closed the downstairs windows, even those she had left open when Seymour was there. It was the deep of the night and even the sliver of moon had set.

Rachel undressed and took a bath in the old-fashioned tub. She heard the water heater go on. The house sighed and creaked and settled around her. Rachel looked at her body. The two white strips of flesh where her two-piece bathing suit covered her glowed against her deep tan the way white flowers do against the earth. The pink scar went up her stomach like a zipper and stopped just where the tan began. The hair that fell down the nape of her neck was wet. Rachel let her legs float and lie still. Her breasts broke through the flat plane of the water. She let her arms float too, and rested there until the water grew cool. She wrapped herself in one of the large beach towels and climbed into bed. When she was dry she sprinkled powder under her arms and on her crotch and put on one of Seymour's large white T-shirts. She went downstairs once more and checked the doors and turned the lights off except the one in the hall and the small

283

lamp in the living room. White powder footprints traced her steps through the house. Back in bed she pulled the quilt up around her neck—it was a cool night—and turned off the light. The glow from the downstairs hall shone softly out from under her door. A dog barked somewhere. The room became slowly visible. Gradations of black appeared. Rachel made out the dresser and its white coverlet, the rocking chair, and the shapes of the pictures on the wall. The door was outlined in faint light and the window—shaded by curtains—was made up of two black rectangles on black.

Rachel thought about Seymour. She suddenly remembered that there were things she wanted to tell him, things she'd forgotten or crushed in her anger. Seymour was alone in Gateshead, in a house gone sour on a close summer night. She turned the bedlight on. Its sudden brilliance blinded her. She dialed the Gateshead number. It rang for a long long time, but no one answered. She thought she might have gotten the wrong number and dialed again. The same ring curled in her ear. She didn't hang up until it had rung more than ten times. Still nobody answered.

Rachel woke up very early the next morning. It was a cool and overcast day. The ocean was an unfriendly gray color and hinted at autumn. Rachel made breakfast. She felt a need to forget the evening, a need to work, but she could not. She was thinking about her invisibility, dreaming of fame. Dreams of fame were bad for working, the worst thing there was. Rachel cleaned out the refrigerator and polished the top of the stove. She made the beds and folded the laundry which had lain clean in the basket for days. Between each of these chores she would sit for a while in the spare room that she used as a studio, but nothing she touched engaged her. Sometimes she stared out over the dunes to watch for small changes in the light, to see how the sea gulls swooped and soared. She tried to see if the sun would break through the overcast, but the sky was a dull long gray, like the sheets on Ben's bed. There was nothing to whet her appetite for work. Her

284

mind—like the gulls swooping in the sky—returned again and again to the same place. She heard the empty ringing of the phone in her ear and felt abandoned. She did not feel that her work had merit, at least not merit enough. The house was a cell that day and Rachel had need to escape. She could not bear the sight of anything around her. The objects seemed ratty and strange and common.

The telephone rang. For a moment Rachel thought it was the telephone in her head, the one in Gateshead. When she realized it was the one in the next room her angry heart jumped with the thought that it was Seymour. But the words she had mustered earlier flew out of her head. Rachel answered the telephone. It was Aaron.

"Hi, Mom." His voice was strained by too much cheer and some trepidation.

"What's wrong?"

"Why should anything be wrong?" Aaron asked, but clearly his voice contradicted his words. It broke a little. "I quit my job, I'm in Boston now. I took the bus last night. I had to leave. It was no good."

"Are you coming here?"

"That's why I'm in Boston. There's a bus leaving for Wellfleet that gets there at twelve thirty-five. Can you meet me?"

"I haven't got the car. Dad took it back to Gateshead for a funeral. But don't worry, I'll get there. We can take a cab back."

"Twelve thirty-five, Mom."

"Are you o.k.?" asked Rachel, hearing the money slithering away in the coin box in Boston. "You could have called collect."

"Sure I'm o.k. We'll talk about it when I get there."

"You're not sick?"

"I'm not sick. Good-bye, Mom."

The operator's voice came breaking in upon Aaron's last words. It was probably a recording; it went through its spiel without pausing for the good-byes. Rachel hung up.

That was the end of that day's attempt at work. As it turned out, it was pretty much the end of work for

285

the rest of the vacation. No wonder artists make rotten parents, thought Rachel, surveying her worktable. They always reserve the last bit of strength for themselves, come what may. Rachel put her things in order and closed the door to her studio. She had the melancholy sense that she was leaving it forever.

The telephone rang again. This time it was Seymour.

"Aaron's coming," said Rachel. "He just called. Where were you last night?"

"Why is he leaving his job?"

"He didn't tell me. Just said he was arriving at twelve thirty-five."

"Is he all right?"

"He said he was. Where were you last night?"

"Home. I called you, remember."

"I tried to get you back later. You were gone."

"Impossible. You probably got a wrong number."

"I tried twice."

"So you dialed wrong twice. What's with Aaron? Should I worry?"

"I'll find out when he gets here. I think you're lying."

"Are you sure he didn't say anything to you that you're hiding?"

"Are *you* sure you're not hiding something from *me*?"

"He's not in any kind of trouble, is he?"

"I told you he said nothing but 'I'll be there at twelve thirty-five.' And I don't have a car, of course."

"Nothing about being sick?"

"No. Where were you at two-thirty this morning?"

"In bed. Asleep."

"With Natalie Gould."

"You're crazy!"

"I may be crazy but that doesn't change the facts. I called at two-thirty this morning and you weren't home."

"I didn't answer."

"You always answer."

"Where could I possibly go at that hour of the night?"

"You tell me."

286

"Natalie's got a husband. You don't think he'd let her out at that hour of the night."

"He was probably away on a business trip. Or you went to a singles bar."

"I wouldn't do that."

"Then a doubles bar."

"It's not my style."

"What *is* your style? Fucking in the back of the car? Going to a hotel in the city? A motel in Westbury? For all I know the whole congregation knows what you do, where you go. All except me. I'm the only one in the dark. A laughingstock."

"I'd never do that to you."

"You would too! You've never been able to resist those silly women who make goo-goo eyes at you. You let that cheerleader flatter you silly when you were eighteen."

"I was seventeen."

"It hurt then and it hurts now."

"I think you're being hysterical. My relationship with Natalie Gould is no threat to you whatever. I love you."

"You say that and expect it to wipe all your sins away."

"But I do love you."

"You say that to her too. I heard you."

Rachel's voice had risen to a tremulous cry. She hadn't meant to say that, but having spit it out she repeated it.

"I heard you," she screamed.

There was a long silence.

"Rachel, listen to me," said Seymour, trying to sound offended. Rachel heard him change the tone in his voice. "I'm really more concerned about Aaron right now than about you and your shrewish behavior. Call me as soon as he gets there, will you? Tell me he's all right."

"Oh, fuck you," said Rachel, and hung up on him. In a few minutes the phone rang again.

"Don't hang up on me," said Seymour.

"I can't argue with you, you're slippery like an eel."

"I am what I've always been. You know me, you've

287

always known me. I love you, Rachel, as I've loved you since we were kids."

"Go fuck yourself."

"Don't be angry, Rachel, please."

"Good-bye!"

"Call me about Aaron."

"Good-bye."

Rachel hung up again and decided not to answer, should it ring once more. It didn't.

Rachel made Aaron's bed and aired out the room. She put the suitcases she had stored there out in the hall, fluffed the curtains, set a bunch of dried flowers from the living room on his dresser, put clean towels on his chair. Then she went downstairs and baked a chocolate cake. Its fragrance seeped through the house.

Shortly before noon she set out for town. The sun shone blindly through the clouds. It had a hot sting. The back of Rachel's neck was damp, her feet sweated in the old blue sneakers she had worn to walk more easily. Rachel knew no shortcuts; she had passed this way only by car. Small bubbles pocked the asphalt of Route 6. She thought about hitchhiking and tried putting her thumb out when a car went by. She felt foolish when it didn't stop. She tried again, and this time she felt disappointed. By the third car her disappointment had turned to chagrin. When the fourth and fifth cars went by she felt unwanted and tried no more. She got to the bus stop by twelve-thirty. There was a bench under a large elm tree and she sat down and watched the world go by. She felt that her walk had increased her virtuousness, and it had also given her a new perspective of the town. Pedestrians saw the landscape differently and this one (being old and settled) was made for walking. Summer tourists strolled around, holding maps and looking pale or sunburnt. There were a lot of bare legs to be seen. Naked flesh. Beach flesh. Rachel watched them and did not see the bus arrive or notice that it was twenty minutes late.

"There you are, Mom," said Aaron, who was carrying a suitcase in each hand and a rucksack on his back. His hair under the Mets cap was long and he seemed

288

very tall. He was thin but did not look sick. He looked quite strong, in fact.

"You look healthy enough," said Rachel, and had to stand on her toes to kiss him on the cheek.

"I lugged a lot of heavy trays." His voice seemed deeper than before.

"Have you had lunch?"

"I had a big breakfast. I met a guy on the bus to Boston whose father runs a cafeteria and he fed us for free."

"I baked you a chocolate cake."

"Thanks."

"What happened?"

"What do you mean?"

"What happened that you came home?"

"Let's relax a little first, Mom. Take me home, show me around, let me hang up my hat."

They walked to the luncheonette where the town's cabby spent his free time, drinking coffee. He drove Rachel and Aaron back to the house.

"Is that it?" Aaron asked, as they turned down the long driveway. "Wow! A real beach house! I'm glad I came."

Rachel showed Aaron his room and he threw his suitcases down and kicked off his shoes. In a minute the room was a mess. They went downstairs and sat together at the kitchen table. Aaron ate a piece of the cake. It was still warm. He drank a glass of milk. Rachel ate a peanut butter and jelly sandwich. The sun had not quite made it through the clouds but the kitchen was milky white with light. The wild daisies in the bell jar drooped a little. Aaron looked all around him, studied the place.

"You cook better than the chef at the hotel."

"Your father is going to call. He'll be back Monday."

"Can I go to the beach?"

"You can't swim by yourself, that's a rule around here. There's undertow."

"I just want to go down and get my feet wet. Please, Mom?"

"No swimming," said Rachel.

While he got into his bathing suit, she cleaned up the

table and felt matronly. A towel was wrapped around her waist. Would she need a whole new set of fantasies when she got old? Maybe she could become the fat lady who ran a diner and leaned on the counter reading the *Daily News* when things got slow. Aaron sprinted out of the house across the dunes, and down to the water's edge. Rachel took off the towel.

She followed Aaron at a discreet distance and sat off to the side, not quite invisible, but not right smack in the open either. Aaron frolicked in the waves. He ran into the white water and tumbled down in the boiling froth. He ran along the edge of the sea, along the curving lines where the water licked as the tide came in. He collected shells and threw stones. Rachel thought about the luncheonette. She could hang her pictures on the walls. Wouldn't it be nice to be the fat lady in the diner and not worry about Art? She would be known for her good chocolate cake and be a comfort to lonely travelers.

Aaron came wandering back, wiping himself dry with the pink towel. He had known his mother was there.

"You've been watching me all along. It's beautiful. Maybe next year I can get a job at a seaside hotel."

They walked along the narrow path through the dunes. The white house looked delicate, its lines were spidery.

"What happened?" asked Rachel, thinking the question would catch Aaron by surprise. But he was prepared. He had become watchful, he was gliding out from under his mother's grip. He ran ahead. He was getting away from her.

Back in the kitchen he said, "Time for a drink."

"I'm supposed to say that," said Rachel.

"I'll take a beer."

"You didn't answer my question."

"It was a personal thing."

"Love?"

"Yes," said Aaron, quietly.

The light in the kitchen had turned golden in the late afternoon. Rachel threw the daisies out.

"Tell me about it when you feel like it."

290

She had reached the perimeter, she was content to wait for his words to open the space for her, let her in. She felt she ought to know. The telephone rang. It was Seymour.

"I told you to call, why didn't you?"

"I thought you said you'd call me."

"Did Aaron get there?"

"Yes."

"How is he?"

"O.k."

"What happened?"

"He's fine. A little misunderstanding, that's all."

"Let me talk to him."

Rachel gave the phone to Aaron. She felt as though she stood on a high promontory, looking down at her husband and her son from a great distance. She saw them separately, running through a maze, destined not to meet. It was a shocking image. Aaron was talking to Seymour in a cool, friendly voice. He was noncommittal, he had made no plans as to how he would proceed. The story locked inside of him would be a different story when it was told to Seymour. Rachel knew that. Did parents struggle, always, for the stories their children told? (Even if they were lies?) A sharp tinge of anxiety struck Rachel just below her breastbone. It was almost like pain. How much strength it took to cope, day by day, conquering your own fears and those of the people who clung to you. Rachel got the vodka out and made a large martini. She threw three small green olives into the glass and sat on the porch swing. She would not listen to Aaron's part of the conversation. Thank God, Seymour's was locked into the receiver. Aaron came out to join her on the swing. They rocked. Rachel's anxiety gave way slowly under the influence of the strong drink.

"This is just like a Mickey Rooney-Judy Garland movie," said Aaron, "except for the view."

"Those movies always ended happily," said Rachel.

"I guess it isn't, then. The porch swing fooled me. It's the first porch swing I've ever known."

"What did Dad say?"

The martini had just about dissolved the sharp sliver

291

of her anxiety and left a stain like spent tears in its wake.

"The usual. He wanted to know how I was. He acts as though I were very fragile."

"Are you?"

"I never used to think so. I'm not so sure now."

They sat and watched the darkness gather. The sky paled, the landscapes were silhouetted in black against it, the clouds turned purple. Slowly, the sky blackened until the stars became visible. Rachel heard Aaron's soft breathing. He had fallen asleep. He held the empty beer can loosely in his hand, between his lean hard legs. Rachel took it away gently and went into the house to prepare dinner. She heated the left-over bouillabaisse and made a large salad and boiled fresh ears of corn. The French bread was growing stale, so she spread it with butter and garlic and browned it in the oven.

Aaron stood sleep-dumb in the doorway. Rachel was startled.

"Did you forget about me? I smelled the food and it woke me. I'm starved."

They sat down together and ate and began to talk about how they had spent their summer. They skirted the large issues and concentrated on the small ones. They grew used to one another, slowly, in the course of the evening. Rachel told about Miss Prawn and about the Fourth of July. Aaron told about the cooks and waiters and chambermaids, about small crises in the kitchen, pillow fights in the dormitory. They talked about the baseball season and washed the dishes together.

"Is there a TV?" asked Aaron.

"No. And if there were one you could probably get only one or two stations."

"They're called channels on TV, Mom."

"Maybe we should go to bed?" said Rachel. "You probably haven't been getting your sleep."

They went upstairs. Rachel noticed that Aaron's jeans hung loose on his hips. "Thin," she said, patting his ass.

"Good-night, Mom."

292

They both slept well and got up early on Sunday morning. They walked into the village and bought the Sunday *Times* and got a ride back from a young man in a green pick-up truck. It was a beautiful day and Rachel packed sandwiches and beer into the cooler, as well as fresh peaches and tomatoes. They went down to the beach and had a picnic, all by themselves. The ocean was gentle, the waves curled over in small breakers. Rachel and Aaron swam past the breakers and floated on their backs to look at the cloudless sky.

After they had eaten, Rachel stretched out on her towel, cradled by the hot sun of August and the constant hiss of the surf. She slept a little while. Aaron sat beside her, on the pink towel. He was reading *Ulysses,* which he had taken to the Catskills as a gesture of intellectual snobbery and been stuck with. He got to like it.

Rachel awoke slowly. The sound of the surf had changed. It was louder now; the tide had turned and the waves risen. She stretched out her arms and inadvertently touched Aaron.

"You know you snore?"

Rachel yawned. She caught the whiff of beer and mustard stealing through her suntan lotion. She sniffed. It was odd, but Aaron had no smell. He seemed bone clean and scrubbed, without an odor of his own. Rachel playfully ran her finger down the bumps of his backbone and rested the palm of her hand on the flat triangle just above where his bathing suit began.

"You've lost weight."

He bent down and kissed her squarely on the mouth. Rachel was taken aback by the strength of his kiss. She tasted salt water and the faint breath of garlic and beer—but his body remained odorless.

"Race you to the water!" she cried, jumping to her feet.

Of course he beat her into the surf. The waves were now about five feet high and breaking smoothly. Aaron and Rachel rode them when they could and dove beneath them when they couldn't. They clenched their hands behind their backs and held their bodies like smooth fish to ride the length of the wave in its froth all

293

the way to shore. When they did it right it felt like going ninety and they yelped cowboy yells and thundered along, high on the speed of it. They spent a long time in the water. Afterwards they dried themselves and rested. When it seemed to be nearing supper-time they went home. They had no watch with them, but the sun had started to cast long shadows and its strength was diminished. A cool touch of autumn's grave rose from the sand. Aaron prepared a fire on the rusty grill and they had a Campari with soda and cooked hot dogs until they were black. The smoke rose straight into the August evening air. There was no wind, the weather was perfectly still. The sun set without a cloud to mar the sweep of the sky. Gold and orange faded to lavender. The water was flat and a darker violet. The dunes were razor-backed, the grass sharp as quills. Bonfires flickered far away and the lights appeared slowly, like the stars, in the houses to the west. It was the sort of evening that—in the best of times—celebrates the end of summer.

It grew cold that night. Fall hovered in the breath that Rachel sent into the air as she went out to dump the brown bags of kitchen garbage. She lit a fire in the living room hearth and drank a cold beer with Aaron. They stayed close to each other, without quite touching.

"Do you think a person ever gets over an unhappy love affair?" Aaron asked.

"If he's in reasonably good mental health." Rachel decided she would not say very much at all.

"Do you mind if I light a joint?"

"Go right ahead."

Memories of Ben bubbled up in her mind. She sat with her legs crossed on the couch. Aaron went upstairs and brought a little metal box down from his room. It had once held English lemon drops. On its cover was a picture of several yellow lemons. Aaron took a carefully rolled joint out of the box and lit it.

"Would you like some?"

"I belong to the drinking generation."

"You never tried it?"

"Long ago I did. But it always made me sleepy. I

294

used to try and turn on, and while the rest of the people forgot time and place and floated among a host of ornate impressions, I watched the clock and cut out in time to get back to Barnard before the curfew. We had to be in by one-thirty and I always made it. I used to go home alone from the Village because it seemed silly to ask Ben—that was my boyfriend—to leave the party just to take me home. I never cared for those ceremonies. I was independent in some ways. I used to go through the crowd of couples at the dormitory gate and realize they felt sorry for me (the ones who saw me from their clinches) because it looked like I didn't have a date. I kept my smug little secrets to myself. I'm sorry, Aaron. I didn't mean to go off so long on my own track."

"That's all right, I'd rather listen than talk, but I can't listen too well, either. Sometimes I think I'm going to die from the hurt. I want so much to be near her. Just to sit and watch her, even if she doesn't look at me. But when I was there and did that and she pretended I didn't exist it was worse. She wouldn't have me any longer, she made me feel as though I had a disease. That's why I came home. I ran away. I hoped she might ask for me back. I know she won't but hoping is better than being told the truth."

"Who was she?"

"She was a guest at the hotel. I guess she was a little screwy. She must have been, to bother with me."

"Why should she have to be screwy to bother with you? You're a good kid. A girl ought to be proud . . ."

"She was married, Mom. She was twelve years older than me."

"Twenty-eight?"

"Yes. She didn't get along with her husband, she said. She was up there without him. She would come down to the pool and just sit there, with a book in her hand—the same one every day, a book by Hesse—just looking out at the water. As though it was an ocean or a lake, not a dumb chlorinated swimming pool. She was pretty. I guess now I'd say she was a Jewish-American Princess, but I didn't see that at first. She seemed lonely and full of discontent and I was right there,

295

ready to comfort her. She told me I was mature for my age, and I was pleased."

"Of course you were pleased," said Rachel.

"I've always been a bit on the outside at school. I didn't always like what I saw, not until this spring, when Frannie came along. Being in love with her made things come easier. It brought me into all the things high school is for kids."

"High school never changes," said Rachel.

"But Frannie was just a kid. Suzannah was a woman. She led me to believe that she had *suffered*."

"That is always the way."

"She told me to come to her room after work. She had some grass. I went a couple of nights later, when I wasn't exhausted, and we had a couple of joints. She got undressed and said, 'Don't mind me,' and I sat there and looked at her and got stoned. We made love. It was weird. She said I was sweet; I think she thought I was a virgin. She told me about how awful her husband was, how he always put her down. She made her life sound like something out of the 'Hundred Neediest Cases.' I told her about myself. I told her things I shouldn't have told her, I felt awful about it later."

"You have to be careful whom you trust with your secret life."

"I know that now."

Rachel sat quietly, sipping her beer. It was growing warm in her hand. She hated Suzannah in her heart.

"Before I knew it, I didn't see it coming at all, I was in love with her. Maybe it happened as soon as we made love. I thought I was bringing her something special. I don't think she felt that way."

"Women are supposed to and men are not supposed to. You had it turned around. I think it happens a lot nowadays."

"I started hanging around with her in my free time. The other kids thought I was crazy. I stopped going into town with them and when we played softball after dinner she would come and watch until she got bored and then I'd be wild to go after her and lose all interest in the game. The manager sort of warned me. He said guests screw boys all the time, but don't make it so

296

obvious. He didn't want my work to suffer. I think that was what he was afraid of. She liked me hanging around, listening to her, being her pet, until one day she suddenly turned on me with, 'Stop hanging around me like a puppy dog, I didn't mean for you to become sappy like that.' I make her sound cruel . . ."

"She was!"

"It seems that way now, when I'm telling it, but I *was* sappy. I tried to be nicer—she said I didn't understand her—but of course I was miserable and I *was* becoming a pest. I thought if only I can show her that she needs me—but she already had someone else, she had her eyes on a guy who had just come up there, a divorced guy with a kid. He was awful. Tanned, with hair on his chest and aviator glasses. I saw him and thought how can she like *him?* She told me I was a bore. She avoided me. It drove me crazy. I finally busted in on her early one evening and said, 'Just let me sit with you. I won't do anything, we'll just talk. I'll just *be* here for you.' She called the desk and said one of the help was bothering her and they sent up a security guard. I guess he didn't believe her. Didn't think she needed protection from me. He just walked me back to the dorm and brought me a cup of coffee and said, 'Be careful with them Jew broads.' I don't know what he thought I was. I know he thought *she* was a whore. There I am, with a broken heart, and I have to listen to a cracker security guard's advice! I almost cried. He meant well, but I didn't want to hear him put her down. She was unhappy, I know she was. . . ."

"That's no reason to make *you* miserable. You're a sweet kid, you don't deserve an unhappy woman."

"I thought the love I brought her was a gift, without strings, I only wanted to keep on giving it, but then she made it seem as though I had brought her shit."

"Part of knowing how to love is to be aware of the needs of the lover. You'll learn. Try to put her out of your mind."

"But it still hurts. It hurts a lot. I left the hotel because I couldn't stand being around her any longer. I was so miserable and each day she reminded me of my misery. It was as though she had not only hurt me

297

but humiliated me as well. It was the way it is in dreams, you know what I mean? When you dream that your dog's been run over or your mother is dead and the whole world is laughing? She tried to make light of my feelings. 'You're a kid,' she said, 'you'll get over it. Think of me, in analysis three years and I'm unhappier than ever.' "

Rachel had followed it all in her mind, had seen it reeling off like a movie, but the woman's face was a blank.

"That's what happened," said Aaron, "that's the story."

He had gained enough control over it to have told it. The two days home had done that much. If he cried, he cried at night when he was alone. He sighed. He had shared his story with his mother. It seemed to help a little. Rachel took his head in her hands and kissed him. She knew that she was telling him, "I've won you back, you're mine, you'll always be mine," but she did it anyway. Knowing what a dreadful thing it was to do, what an old mother trick it was, she still crowed in triumph. But her heart ached for him too, she felt the burden of his misery upon it and thought (only fleetingly) that it was hard to be a mother.

"It *will* go away," said Rachel, rocking him as she had when he was a baby and his head rested, like now, on her shoulder. "You *will* get over it, you will," she said. Was she making a promise that she had no power to fulfill? She tousled his hair roughly and pushed him gently away; she had that much sense left and that much self-protectiveness too. "You're a good kid," she said. "You'll love somebody again one day soon. Somebody who's worth the love you have to give."

The next day was Monday and in the middle of the afternoon a purple Pontiac drove up to the house, honking and bouncing up the length of the dusty driveway. It was Seymour.

"Look what I bought for your birthday!" he shouted.

Rachel and Aaron gathered around and admired the purple Pontiac.

298

"It's almost new. I got it through Cy Glatt's brother-in-law. The convertible will be our second car. We'll need two cars when we move."

Seymour greeted Aaron with great delicacy. They shook hands. Seymour looked him over carefully, as though to find the place where he had been patched together. They went walking on the beach. Aaron told him another version of his story. It too was the truth. The weather was gorgeous and Seymour stayed the rest of the week. They went riding in the purple Pontiac and picnicked and swam. Seymour and Aaron talked about stories from *The New York Times* which Seymour bought every day. Rachel and Seymour bickered. In the small house there was no place to talk alone. Words not spoken got twisted into mutant shapes. Seymour said he was tired of all the seafood Rachel cooked. She said that he didn't help her enough.

On Sunday Seymour said he was going back to Gateshead. He said he had work to do, the holidays were coming around, he had to look after things. Rachel was relieved, though she tried not to show it. She didn't even care about Natalie Gould at that moment. She had stopped imagining her in Seymour's arms. It was easy to do when she needed to be alone.

"I'll leave you the car," said Seymour. "I can take the bus back. Then you two can drive home Friday with all the stuff."

Rachel drove him down to the bus stop. A few of the maples were beginning to turn. Red and yellow leaves fluttered at their crowns, as though singed by the cold nights and the clear air. Seymour kissed Rachel. It was a little peck of a kiss, given from a great distance.

"I'm sorry," he said, referring to God knew what. "It really was a nice vacation. But I'm nervous, edgy, uncomfortable. I can't lie around any longer."

Rachel kept every one of her thoughts to herself. She watched the bus go down the road, winding in and out of the traffic. Once again she felt guilty relief.

That night Rachel and Aaron went to a movie and ate dinner out. The car gave them new freedom. When they came out of the movie theater it was warm and the wind stirred the elm trees with a summer breeze. They

299

walked over to the park and watched the men of the slow-pitch league play under the lights. Kids and dogs tumbled in and out of the dugout. Fall was still some weeks away. The crickets chirped, the smell of hay drifted up from the field by the pond, and the moon was full and round, big as the sun.

The weather turned wet toward the end of the week and there was talk of a hurricane. Rachel and Aaron cleaned the house and secured it against the storm. They left a note of thanks stuck to the refrigerator with masking tape. They packed the car and drove back to Gateshead.

It was the weekend of Labor Day.

9

On the ride back to Long Island, Rachel mourned the disappearing seascape. Aaron kept the radio on full blast and his thoughts to himself. They made good time. Rachel drove aggressively—she was proud of her verve behind the wheel of a car. Humming along the highways, fifteen miles in excess of the speed limit, she kept alive the dream of running away. The window was open, her tanned left elbow rested on the door: Rachel felt sustained by the *idea* of her freedom. The month at the Cape had seduced her into thinking that she would, during the coming year, insist on her right to live her own life. It was the amateur's belief that you could be all things to all people (the family, the congregation), and still be an artist.

"Are you happy to be going home?" asked Aaron.

"I'm happy to be alive," said Rachel. "That way I still have a chance."

"At what?"

"Realizing my fantasies."

"And what are they?"

"Making the hit that wins the World Series. Pitching a perfect game. . . ."

"You mean getting into the record books? You could drop a third strike."

"Not me, Aaron. Not me."

They arrived in Gateshead in the late afternoon. The day was hot and oppressive. Thunderstorms swept along the coast; lightning rent the black clouds over the Sound. The Plymouth convertible stood in the drive-

301

way of their house. There was no room for the purple Pontiac, and Rachel had to leave it at the curb. The first thing she saw as she got out of the car was the high grass. Seymour had apparently made no effort to see that it was cut. The trumpet vine was growing wild; weeds choked the bright phlox growing beside the porch. Rachel wondered if the inside of the house would reveal an even greater neglect. She remembered the impersonal chaos of Seymour's room at the Seminary: dust under the bed and papers piled on every chair; books stacked on the shelves, not in a row but in precarious piles; clothes scattered on top of the papers and heaped on the bed. She would come up, in those days, and make order and they would lock the door (most often the dusk of winter evenings wiped clean the face of the ugly room) and make love on the narrow cot.

Seymour was watching the news on television. The living room seemed reasonably clean. Rachel looked into the kitchen; the floor there was full of crumbs but the rest of the kitchen was neat. There were no dishes in the sink and no coffee stains on the table.

"You didn't leave a mess—inside," said Rachel, and kissed Seymour on top of his head. "I appreciate it."

She went to help Aaron carry the luggage, the boxes and driftwood, the shells and stacks of drawings into the hall.

"You *do* know we have to move in two weeks?" said Seymour.

"Why isn't the grass cut?" Rachel answered.

"I thought *you* had made the arrangements. Didn't you ask the Schwartz kid?"

"Since you were here and I wasn't, you could have reminded him when you saw it wasn't done."

"Do I have to be responsible for all this domestic shit? Don't I have enough to put up with from the congregation? You're worse than they are."

Rachel had not been home five minutes and already they were testy with one another. With the High Holy Days approaching, Seymour's temper was not likely to improve. Rachel wished she were back in the white clapboard house on the Cape, alone and unencumbered.

302

Outside, the wind rose. The sky had darkened and the thunder had drawn nearer. Large drops of rain slapped the window. The television set sputtered with static.

Rachel brought her luggage upstairs. The bedroom was orderly, though not very clean. Rachel felt an odd sense of oppression. The storm moved closer, the branches of trees whipped the roof of the house. What was it that so disturbed her? She had never liked storms and was afraid of lightning, but it was not the black skies (after the brilliant summer sun she had memorized at the Cape) that oppressed her and gave such a sinister air to all her rooms. And then—suddenly—the insight broke like a clap of thunder: Rachel knew what had happened, knew all at once what it was. She sat down on her bed and was filled with angry trembling. Another woman had been in this house, it was the touch of *her* presence that Rachel detected in the unstudied neatness everywhere. The enormity of her discovery brought a terrible pain in the wake of her trembling; Rachel suddenly saw the evidence of betrayal and plunder everywhere. It was as clear as if it were the odor of cheap perfume or the sign of a telltale object left upon a table. None of these things could be found anywhere, though Rachel looked (oh how she looked!) for them. There were no torn stockings in the waste basket, nor empty shells of Tampax. There were no bobby pins (old-fashioned sign), not even a hair or two in the bathroom sink, not a single piece of forgotten clothing which Rachel could lift with a crooked finger and present as evidence. The signs were much more subtle than that. Rachel discovered the spectral feminine presence in order, not in disorder. The sheets were tucked most strangely, the towels folded and hung by a hand not her own— Rachel saw that hand at work in the arrangement of the medicine cabinet, she saw it on her kitchen shelves. Once she had found it out, she saw it everywhere. She kept the knowledge to herself for the time being, adding to it, bit by bit, for hours on end. She was filled to bursting with rage, but could not let it go, the cause of it was so new she had to test it for accuracy, she had to let the evidence on which it was built

303

accumulate. (Rachel valued her control.) She waited for the moment it would burst—pricked by the needle-point of some other, minor, provocation.

Outside, the storm broke with great ferocity. Rain lashed the windows, trees bent almost to breaking, the waters of the bay ran up on the sandy shore. For a scant quarter of an hour the skies above Gateshead were in turmoil and then the storm moved on. The evening sun appeared in a pink sky, the thunder grew distant.

Aaron had noticed nothing. Seymour was, it appeared, content to have them home again. Rachel husbanded her anger. In bed, that evening, Seymour said, "I feel lost when you're not here with me, you mustn't leave me by myself, Rachel. You belong at my side."

His prick was hard and stood straight up; he was covered only by a sheet.

"What a pretty sentiment," said Rachel. "You deserve an award for play-acting."

"What is that supposed to mean?"

"You know full well."

"I know nothing at all except that you've come home from a vacation that you claim was ideal—a dream without responsibility or care—and instead of being loving you're full of hostility, full of rage. What is it you want from me?"

"Nothing but the truth."

"The truth is that I love you. Come to bed with me."

"You think all you have to do is offer me your love and I'll forgive everything."

"Isn't that what it's all about?"

"I don't ask *you* to forgive my bad behavior all the time. I try not to behave badly."

"You're a saint."

"I don't bring men into your house. I don't fuck other people in your bed . . ."

"What are you talking about?"

"You mean to tell me Natalie Gould *wasn't* here?"

"Did you come all the way back from Cape Cod to throw accusations in my face? Did you come home just to give me a hard time?"

"I came home to love and to cherish you and what

304

do I find? I find that you've had Natalie Gould here." Rachel raised her voice to the roof, the anger came screeching to the surface. "You brought that bitch into my house, don't ever tell me you didn't. I know, I can tell. You think I'm a damn stupid fool but I know *you* don't keep the beds made and the sink clean. *You* never folded the laundry in your life, you don't put the dishes away, you barely even run the dishwasher. . . ."

"You're concocting some paranoid fantasy, Rachel. I swear it, Rachel, you're crazy."

"It's not a paranoid fantasy and I'm not crazy. You're not going to pull the Russian shit on me—get me committed as nuts because you don't like what I have to say."

"You haven't the slightest feeling for me in my loneliness and my misery, and you dare accuse me like a screaming fishwife, raving and ranting about Natalie Gould?"

"Who was it then, who was it you brought here?"

"No one's been here but me. I did get someone to straighten the place . . ."

"Who? Who?"

"I don't know her name, Roosevelt got her for me. I wanted the house to be nice for you. I wanted to welcome you back to a clean place and what do I get? Shit is what I get."

Seymour had tuned his self-righteousness up into a fine anger. He meant to blunt Rachel's fury. He did this all the time and was most successful at it. Rachel shrank from him, the logic of her silent raging broke to pieces. Had she been wrong? The trouble was that she always thought that she was wrong, was the first to think it. In the end, Seymour always successfully beat back her attacks. She got no satisfaction and licked her wounds; her moral superiority was little comfort, but she reasoned that she needed her peace.

"You're a shit and a bastard," said Rachel.

"I told you to leave me if you don't love me. . . ."

"I never thought to leave you."

"That isn't true either. You always hold that thought in abeyance. It's your trump. It's what you keep back, deep in your heart, the thing that makes a final sham-

305

bles of your saintliness. You hold on to your moral superiority, but it's a lie—you will leave me, you *can* leave me. I don't have that choice. I'll love you always."

Rachel was silent.

"I heard from Omaha," said Seymour. "They took someone else."

"You didn't tell me."

"You never gave me a chance. You were too busy with your raving ranting accusations."

"It's probably just as well, you would have hated it there too."

"Do me a favor, Rachel?"

"What?"

"Leave off your criticism until after the contract negotiations. Just don't bother me until then."

"And you—will you continue to deceive me?"

"I'm not deceiving you. I told you how I feel. I love you best of all. Nobody comes near to you in my heart. I will never leave you. But I need the affection of other women. You think that's terrible, I know. Just remember how you feel about your work. Compare it to that. It's as desperate a kind of need as mine, it can never be filled, you'll never be satisfied. *I* can't fill it. It isn't only that you're not content to be *merely* a wife and a mother. If that were the case I'd tell you to fuck off. You're driven. You want more than that. You want to be a *real* artist. You get impossible, rotten, when you're not working. It claims more and more of you. Why should my need for affection—my need for love—be any more terrible? When I tell you it's no threat to you, why can't you believe me?"

"I believe you. I may even understand you, but what my head assents to my heart may reject. I can't help that. And the need I have for work has to do with all sorts of other things, things that you cannot take personally, as I take your women personally. It has to do with immortality, with being visible, a person in my own right. It has to do with a need that is really inexplicable, mysterious like the process of life itself."

"You ought to know not to take my women personally either. And have you ever thought that per-

306

haps it has to do with my own small need for 'immortality' too? To be loved is to become a part, however small, of another's life, to become entwined in their memories. It takes you out of the tiny circle of your own domesticity, makes you an actor on a larger stage. That's immortality, in a very small way."

"Only if the woman is George Sand or Alma Mahler."

"How like you, Rachel—to think big!"

"If fame and fortune ever smile on me, I'll take you away from all this. We'll move to New York, leave Gateshead forever. We'll abandon it to the Republicans and the amateurs and you can find yourself a really grand woman."

"I thought you never thought of fame and fortune?"

"Did you really think that?"

"I thought there was some lack of competitiveness. You can afford to be pure, you don't have to live by your work. I'm not putting you down. You offered me a really grand woman, after all, but not tomorrow."

"You don't put me down but you're saying that I'm not wholly professional, that it's *your* financial support that makes it possible for me to work. You're just putting me in my place, I see."

"That's how it is, isn't it?"

"Yes," said Rachel, "that's how it is."

"You're still angry with me?"

"Yes, I am."

"Why? Because I said your dream is only a dream?"

"No. Because you kept a woman in my house."

"I kept no one."

"You did."

There was nothing left to say. Rachel and Seymour both lay on the edge of exhaustion. They took refuge in sleep. No words of affection passed between them that night; they were drained of all speech. At best, the hoard of bitterness had been let go. They had, for now, talked themselves out.

It took no time at all for the old routine of Gateshead to close over Rachel's head. Bar mitzvahs (unscheduled in July and August) followed one another

307

in rapid succession, even before the Jewish holidays. Invitations to them accumulated on the kitchen bulletin board. Rosh Hashanah was just around the corner; the move to Astro Lane only two weeks away. Rachel saw no hope for herself before the middle of October. She would simply have to say to hell with painting until then. Though it was still summer (the flowers bloomed in the rich heat, the trees were a deep green under the cerulean sky), for Rachel autumn had begun. The windows of clothing stores were full of wool and corduroy suits in plaids and dark colors. Long-sleeved heavy sweaters were draped all around. It made Rachel glum. The development on Astro Lane made her even glummer. She had gone to look at it again; the house was empty and seemed unbearably tacky. The congregation was having the outside painted yellow (the front only, the sides and rear were made of white asbestos shingles which never needed paint) and had sent the janitor to cut the grass.

The new synagogue was being readied for the High Holy Days. It wasn't quite *finished,* but it would be ready. A thousand men, women and children could come to pray on Rosh Hashanah and Yom Kippur, at fifty dollars a family. Tickets were being sold; they went like hot cakes. Religious sentiment made its yearly appearance among the Jews of suburbia. A temporary office had been set up in the lobby, a billboard out front announced the Grand Opening for the Holy Days: Come Worship With Us. Floodlights lit the sign at night. Seymour's name was in tiny letters at the bottom; the cantor's name was smaller yet. Cy Glatt's name was the same size as Seymour's, but its letters were fatter.

The moving men came bright and early on the fifteenth. The day was clear and hot, there was not a cloud in the sky. Rachel and Seymour carried the small things in the two cars—clothes on their hangers, dishes, boxes of odds and ends. Rachel planned to leave the contents of her studio until last, but she asked the movers to carry away the old mirror. It had been in the attic when they moved into the house, but Rachel

308

decided she deserved it, for all the affection she had bestowed on the house.

On Astro Lane, the neighbors' children gathered to watch the movers. Rachel bought bubble gum on one of her trips through town and offered it to them. Most of the kids took it, a few even returned for seconds, but one little girl told Rachel, "Ever since that lady on Moonshot Place gave out poison at Halloween, my mother doesn't let me take candy from *anyone*. You aren't mean like that?" she added.

"I'm real mean," said Rachel, with a smile, "but I don't poison little girls."

"Do you poison *big* girls?"

"Not usually, though sometimes I'd like to."

She thought of Natalie Gould in her large house beside the bay. Maybe she wouldn't have the guts to come this far into the kingdom of the lower middle class.

Rachel knew it was a waste of time to feel bitter about the house. In order to come to terms with it she had devised a fantasy in which she owned a house from which she might never be evicted. It was a house on the beach, a house very like the Dinsmoors', and she saw it like that, but not quite, in her mind. She knew that even the most primitive house would be expensive—exactly *how* expensive, she couldn't guess. In an excess of optimism she opened a savings account with a deposit of fifty dollars. She had not told Seymour and was scheming to find ways to add regularly to the little cache. It was, as the feminists rightly said, awful to be so utterly dependent. Rachel vowed to find a way to earn some money. Maybe Sally could get her an adult-ed class, or she could conduct art tours, like Hildegarde Kaye.

Once she had laid the plans (however fragile) for a safe haven, Rachel could think of the house on Astro Lane as no more than a temporary abode. The basement, which she had several times inspected, was large enough to be made into her studio, even though it smelled of dampness and mildew. Fluorescent tubes would give it the necessary light, whitewashing the floors and walls would increase the brightness. She

309

would worry about Seymour's contract when the time came. It did no good to eat your heart out. She decided that, come what may, she wouldn't eat her heart out. She could always run away.

The movers were done by nightfall and Seymour took Rachel and Aaron out for pizza. They sat in the last booth in the small restaurant and ordered the special. A bottle of wine sat in front of them, wrapped in a brown paper bag. They drank it out of paper cups supplied by the establishment and were tired and content enough to feel that life wasn't really so bad. A couple came in with their three children, all five of them waddling tubs of lard.

"Don't look!" Seymour cautioned, but it was too late.

Murray Buchholz called to them across the room. "Hi, Rabbi!" he said. "Whatcha eating?"

Seymour did not answer.

"What's the rabbi eating?" asked the oldest boy.

"Eating *chazzer,*" roared Murray Buchholz.

"I think you should find another line of work," said Rachel to Seymour.

The first night in the new house was confusing. Rachel woke up several times and didn't know where she was. (They slept without sheets, wrapped in their quilts, amid a welter of boxes and cartons.) Seymour had trouble falling asleep, and Aaron read until two in the morning. Rachel woke up innumerable times and had to figure out the shape and layout of the room each time and then (before she dared get up) decide where the bathroom was located. At five o'clock in the morning she awoke for the last time and found Seymour missing. He had gone downstairs to make breakfast in the small kitchen. Their large white table just barely fit between the window and the open archway that led to the dining area. They ate silently. The window faced directly upon the monstrous silhouette of the synagogue. Against the paling sky of early dawn it looked more than ever like a factory. "I wish it was a factory," said Seymour.

At ten o'clock Rachel returned to the old house to move her studio. There was a small crowd on the side-

310

walk in front of the Prawns'. Betty Grog was there, in her housedress, and the neighbors from across the street. The mailman, too, had stopped on his rounds. Rachel heard the wail of the ambulance as she pulled into her driveway. It whined up the street and stopped at the Prawns'.

"What happened?" Rachel asked the mailman, though she could well enough guess.

"One of the sisters died, the one's been sick. The writer."

Rachel shook her head and clucked her tongue. She suddenly hoped she wouldn't meet Clarabelle.

"You all moved out?" the mailman asked.

"Just about."

Betty Grog had seen her and turned away.

"It'll be hard on Miss Prawn," said the mailman. "They might put her in a home."

Rachel packed all her equipment in the car—the easel and pads and tubes of paint and rolls of canvas and stretchers, brushes and jars and cans and boxes of paper scraps. The little table she used to mix her paints, the masking tape and charcoal and magic markers and pens and inks and pencils. And all the paintings, finished and unfinished, which were stacked against the wall. It was necessary to make another trip. By the time she came back, the sidewalk was empty again, the Prawns' house slumbered in the midday sun.

Rachel unloaded her things one by one and carried them into the basement of her new house, which was half filled with boxes of stuff for which the new house was too small. There was a lot of work ahead of her.

"When will you do it?" Seymour asked.

"Not before the holidays, that's for sure!" said Rachel. "Sydelle Prawn died."

"I'm sorry to hear that."

"No you're not," said Rachel. She was angry about the house. She was angry about a lot of things.

The week before Rosh Hashanah, the tail end of a hurricane swept across Long Island, uprooting trees and turning summer into autumn overnight. It rained

311

for ten hours and the basement was filled with two inches of water. It poured in under the basement door and trickled through the casement windows. Rachel went down and tried to shovel the water into the washtub. It was no use. She put everything on blocks of cement and on rickety chairs and an old table. The water rose, still. She shoveled it with a snow shovel, like a maniac, like the sorcerer's apprentice, wearing a pair of rubber boots.

"This is unusual," said Seymour. "We won't have another hurricane for ten years maybe. Don't worry. Just keep everything on blocks."

"I won't be able to work here," said Rachel. "You can't put me on blocks." Her arms and back were sore from all the shoveling she had done. "I'll have to find a place to work. A room in town."

"How will you pay for it?"

"I'll manage. Don't worry about it. I can paint pets from photographs or people's houses for their Christmas cards. Anything. I'll be a whore. I'll lead art tours."

"Don't do anything rash. Think about it. We have to pay for Aaron's college next year. I may be fired."

"We'll worry about *that* when it happens. Stop holding it over my head. You always ask me to put things off. For twenty years now you've told me, 'Wait until next year.' That worked for the old Brooklyn fans, but even *they* didn't have to wait more than twenty years for another pennant."

"You don't care about me at all. You're unconcerned about my career, my livelihood, you just want to pursue your dream."

"What can I do for your career that I haven't done?"

"The list is endless, but I'll begin by suggesting that you make an effort to reach my supporters. Try being a rebbetzin for the next two months. I mean, really *try*. Invite people to the house, make them feel welcome, make them feel that they have a place in our lives."

"But they don't."

"That's beside the point. It costs you nothing to do some entertaining, reciprocate once in a while. Every-

312

one entertains in this town except you. It's the suburban way of life."

"And a shitty way of life it is. You used to knock it too. What happened? Did Natalie Gould put those ideas in your head?"

"Nobody puts ideas into my head. All I said was that you ought to have some people over once in a while."

"Give me a list and I'll make a party. It's easier than arguing with you. Pick a night and a group and give me money for booze and food and I'll make quiche without bacon and I'll smile. I just don't want to discuss it all night. And I *am* going to find a studio. I'll do anything you want, but I won't argue."

The hurricane had brought fall in its wake. It was cool and clear for days afterward. The grass went to seed and the flowers drooped and got tangled up in stalks and weeds, turning gray as dust. A block party was planned for the weekend. Rachel found a mimeographed invitation in her mailbox. "Beer and hot dogs for everyone. Meet your swinging (haha) neighbors. Have a ball. Join in the once-in-a-lifetime bash."

A volunteer fireman came by to collect money for the party. "Anything you want to give," he said.

Rachel told him she was new in the neighborhood.

"What we have left over we donate to charity—muscular dystrophy."

Rachel gave him two dollars. "We don't drink much beer," she said.

"I suppose you don't care about crippled children either."

Rachel forked over another dollar.

The block party was held on Saturday night at an intersection in the middle of the development. The men worked hard all day to set up tables and connect lights. The women stood in small clumps, children clinging to their legs, and wondered if the weather would hold. They criticized (goodnaturedly, of course) what the men were doing. Rachel watched them for a while from her bedroom window and reported to Seymour what she spied. They had come home from a bar mitzvah, filled with liver knishes, sweets, and raw

313

vodka. It was a warm September afternoon, warm enough for the beach. Aaron was in his room, listening to his new radio.

Seymour slept his usual *Shabbos* afternoon, post-bar mitzvah sleep, with his mouth open, snoring a little, the sheet drawn up to his chin. Rachel had taken her party dress off the minute she got home and put on a pair of shorts. She thought about sitting in the backyard, but there she would have to look down upon the synagogue and listen to the neighborhood machines and children and dogs, as well as the banter of the cheerfully busy fathers. Why was it she liked the life of city streets and couldn't bear the life of a suburban development? She used to watch for hours from the window in Ben's flat and never tire of the view. She was accepted as a watcher. It was what some people were. She put a pillow under her arms the way the old ladies did, so as not to feel the hard sill of the window. On Astro Lane and Moonshot Place there were no watchers, only Peeping Toms.

Manny Lebow, builder of Le Beau Foret developments in several suburban locations, had learned about beauty and grandeur in Las Vegas. He dreamed of incorporating the fantasies of Caesar's Palace and the MGM Grand Hotel if ever he got a chance to build a really classy development. In the meantime he had an unlisted telephone number, taken when the first of the back stoops collapsed. When the first cesspool went he had gone on another gambling junket, and when the wiring proved faulty he had gone into bankruptcy. Before he became a builder (when he was merely the owner of a prosperous lumber yard), he had been president of Shaare Tefilah.

"He went in above his head," the people who knew him said. "Manny was not cut out to be a builder. He didn't know from plumbing or electric, and the unions gave him a hard time. The unions ruined him."

In the meantime, the people who had bought his houses spent thousands fixing them up. But nobody had as yet solved the problem of the water in the basements after a rainstorm.

Rachel's basement had still not dried out. Mildew

314

had begun to appear on leather and wood. Rachel looked for her sketchbook. Its black cover was turning green. She took most of her things up to the spare bedroom, next to the entrance hall, where it was dark and a door led to the garage. "Why don't you use that as a studio?" asked Seymour. Rachel knew why she didn't—it was an awful, depressing little room, without proper light and space. You could fix the one, but not the other. Besides, there was a foul spot on the ceiling, dripping water from the upstairs bathroom.

Rachel took her sketchbook and drove down to the harbor in the convertible. She sat down on a large rock above the water and drew the pier. The sun felt warm and soft, a coolness of early evening rose up from the water, a coolness of autumn, but the sun's heat still triumphed. Rachel was happy to be alone, back in the familiar surroundings. It was pleasant to see the people walking, sitting, fishing. A modern-day afternoon on the *Grande Jatte,* though Rachel understood the need to see it more harshly. There weren't many gardens left. The only one of Rachel's faculties not ever confounded by sentimentality was her sight. She drew a couple of boys playing catch, and the shirt-sleeved man who watched them. When the afternoon grew misty and the water lavender-gray, she put her felt-tipped pens in their box and walked away from the cooling stones and the lapping waves. She went up Main Street where the Saturday afternoon left-over hippies lounged and crew-cutted men shopped for hardware. Rachel went into the Pleiades and had a cup of hot chocolate. There was a handwritten sign up on the mirror behind the counter that said Room for Rent. Rachel saw it right next to her own reflection. A telephone number was penciled in below the underlined words.

"Where's that room?" Rachel asked the waitress who worked her end of the counter.

"It's right upstairs."

"Do you know anything about it?"

"The nut who owns this building put up the sign, that's all I know. You looking for a room?"

"Looking for a studio," said Rachel, in the same

315

clipped tone of voice. She often found herself mimicking the person she was talking to and wondered if they noticed. Probably not. People were too involved in their own words and always raced ahead to answer you.

"You a painter?"

"Yes."

"Go up and see her, don't call. She lives right above here. She'll treat you better if she sees you."

Rachel finished her hot chocolate and went upstairs. The hall was dark and the linoleum patched. A single lightbulb burned in a fixture built for three. Rachel rang the doorbell. She waited a few minutes, rang again and waited some more. The door opened suddenly. The woman who looked up at Rachel had frizzy gray hair. She was smoking a cigarette.

"I came about the room."

"Eighty bucks a month."

"Where is it?" asked Rachel, though it sounded like much too much rent.

"Is it for you? I won't rent to hippies or colored or Puerto Ricans."

"How about Jews?"

"Long as they pay the rent. You Jewish?"

"Yes. May I see the room?"

The woman led her up another flight of stairs and showed her the room. It faced out the back onto a small lot and an empty garage. It was about nine feet square and furnished with a bed, a table, and two chairs. There was a small refrigerator and a two-burner gas stove under the single window.

"The bathroom's down the hall," said the landlady.

"I don't really need a furnished room, and eighty a month is steep."

"Rooms are hard to find."

"I'm looking for a studio."

"You an artist?"

"Yes."

"I'm sorry you wasted my time. I don't think I'd take a chance on you, anyway. Artists are fire hazards."

"Well, thanks for letting me see it."

316

Rachel went back into the dusky street, determined to continue the search she had just begun. It excited her to think about having a room of her own. She liked the idea of having a foothold on Main Street. She noticed that almost half a dozen buildings had For Rent signs in their windows. After the holidays she'd look in earnest. Rachel's excitement caused her to feel a stirring in her bowels. She returned home in the convertible and took a satisfying crap.

Back on Astro Lane and Moonshot Place, preparations for the block party had been concluded. The men and women of Le Beau Foret (most of whose trees had been bulldozed to make room for the development) had gone home to wash and to dress. A barrier of saw horses had been set up by the block's auxiliary policeman to keep the traffic out. Rachel had to move some of them to get back to her house.

"Where have you been?" asked Seymour, who was still half asleep.

"I looked at a room."

"What sort of a room?"

"A studio."

"You're serious about it, aren't you?" he murmured, between the sheets.

"Dead serious."

"Who's dead?" mumbled Seymour.

Rachel went back downstairs. Aaron was watching TV in the living room with the cathedral ceiling. He had drawn the curtains across the picture window so that the temple wasn't visible, glowing in the early night for *mincha-maariv*. Aaron had been rather more inward since the summer, but Rachel did not think he was unhappy. He had come out from under his love affair intact. Slowly he would move out of the constricting circle of Gateshead High. He went to the city on Sundays when the L.I.R.R. and the subways and buses ran for half the price. Frannie did not accompany him; her mother did not allow it. They drifted apart.

Rachel wondered, idly, whether she would notice when it came time for Aaron to extricate himself from the web she had woven. It *was* a web. She kept hear-

317

ing the child, even in the deepened voice. She expected he would always come home, she would always hear the child.

"I think I'll try to get into Columbia," he was saying. "That way I can be in the city all the time."

Rachel heard her own voice too, or thought she did. She assumed he would walk along the same paths she had walked. At such times she did not see him as anything but hers, her own child, not Seymour's, whose characteristics she noticed but dimly. She had never, as many women had, counted on children to bring her ultimate happiness, yet she was not averse to counting on Aaron when self-doubt assailed her. When her work went poorly, when winter evenings could not be dislodged from her soul, she turned to Aaron for confirmation of her self, just as she looked to Seymour to provide the mirror that told her she was a woman.

None of them felt at home in the small, tacky house, but they held on, gritted their teeth, tried to find ways to make it matter less. Seymour's way was the most mysterious. He did not connect to things; he seemed to float in pure thought as well as on impure gossip. His ear was sharp, he heard the whispering of friends and foes. He did not see his surroundings at all. He was blind to dislocation and the ugliness of banality.

The block party started at eight o'clock. The big bonfire was lit and the kegs of cold beer opened. Music blared into the night and spotlights shone down from the branches of the trees like small yellow moons. No one was dancing as yet, but some figures (from Rachel's windows they appeared as shadows) moved in time with the music. The smell of cooking hot dogs filled the air, the flames of the fire flickered against the spotlights and the smoke spiraled upward and out of sight in the darkness.

"Do you want to join them?" asked Rachel.

"Not really," said Seymour.

"It's not nice if we don't show our faces."

"You go."

"I don't want to go alone."

"You can always run away, it's right in front of your house. Just say 'Excuse me' and vanish."

318

"What happened to your old courage? Your aplomb? You didn't act like this when you were friends with Marcie Kubelik and everyone wanted to dance with you at the prom."

"That was before they discovered the murmur in my heart. It was during a time in my life when I thought all the light in the world was mine to give. I was the brightest star."

"They'll think you're not friendly."

"Let them think it. I need my friendliness for more important things. I'll come out to rescue you if you look to be in danger of rape, or if you're having too good a time, or both."

Rachel put on a long skirt. She was still sticky from the afternoon sun and the dust of the streets. She should have bathed, but the block party looked to be sticky too. So she merely combed her hair and put a pair of earrings on and splashed some cologne around the various creased places on her body. "Have fun," said Seymour. Aaron had gone to the movies. Rachel stood for a few minutes in the shadow of the forsythia bush that grew beside her driveway. She watched for a good moment to make her entrance, but all moments were really the same. It was like plunging into cold water. She left her hiding place boldly. No one paid her the slightest bit of attention. She tried to look cool, unconcerned, at ease in society. Rachel felt a little bit miffed that her entrance had caused no stir. She wandered among the groups of friendly neighbors. "Put a smile on your face and a song in your heart," she said to herself, but try as she might she couldn't produce a song in her heart. It kept getting stuck in her throat. She did hum a little melody—the theme from Brahms' *Haydn Variations*. It kept coming back to her all night. Rachel went to get a glass of beer.

"Hello," said a ruddy-faced man. "You're the new people at number 64, aren't you?"

"Yes," said Rachel.

"We live at number 86, the house with the red shutters. Have you met my wife?"

"I haven't met anyone yet."

The man called to a blonde woman who looked at

319

him and turned back to what she was doing. "Excuse me, I'll get her, she must not have heard me," said number 86 and left. He never returned.

"Do I know you?" a short man with pale hair asked her.

"I don't think so, we're new here. We live at number 64."

"You want to dance?" he asked, making dancing gestures the way smoothies in the movies did.

"I'm not very good."

"Suit yourself," he said, offended.

"I was only warning you."

"I'll be back for you later," he answered and sashayed off to grab a woman who squealed loudly before she let him swing her about. She was wearing a short skirt, and her twirling motions exposed her underpants. There were shouts of "Aaahh" from several of the men. Those women who had not been asked to dance looked on in disapproval. The fire flickered gaily, the music was loud, mostly popular tunes from the years of everyone's youth—the forties and the fifties. Rachel swayed with her hips, this way and that, just as she had done at high school dances. Gateshead had slipped away. She was back home in Buffalo, attending her first dance.

Rachel drank a second beer. She knew no one and everyone looked familiar. The haggard couple doing the two-step were her neighbors to the right. She had heard that they had eight children but she had not as yet been able to count them herself. There was a baby who was always screaming; the older children went to parochial school. They were like slum children, wide-eyed and predatory. Seymour ignored them and Aaron tried to amuse them by making weird faces. Rachel (as usual) tried to act friendly, but they giggled furiously at her one-sided conversation.

Their name was McKeever. Edna, the mother, had introduced herself the day the Sonnsheins moved in, and told Rachel that they ate meat but twice a week and once it was hamburger. John McKeever, the husband, kept having to fix the car. He was an insurance adjuster.

320

The McKeevers danced past Rachel and said, "Hello." John was already a little drunk and Edna looked pained. Rachel saw the light in his eyes (it was more than a reflection from the bonfire) and concentrated her attention on Edna.

"How's the baby?" she asked.

"I think I caught his cold," said Edna, and sniffed.

John, sober, always kept his eyes down when he talked to women, like a dog being chastised; drunk, he grew bold and looked straight out at the women of the world. One day, his lust would find a response.

The music stopped, the dancers stood still, their arms hanging down. Rachel searched her mind for something to say to Edna McKeever, but John's bright eyes disturbed her.

"How are you, neighbor?"

Rachel turned around. A heavy-set man with curly hair had spoken.

"I'm Bill Quincy."

Rachel did not usually remember a name for longer than it took to pronounce it, but Bill Quincy's was easy—she saw it each day on the mailbox. He was her neighbor on the left and his mailbox had a large eagle decal on it and bold letters that said *Wm. Quincy, Jr.* Bill Quincy had a pool in his backyard and sod for grass in front of his house. His rhododendron were well-fed and bedded in wood chips. But the pool was the pièce de résistance. There was room for precious little but the pool in his backyard. Rachel saw it daily from her bedroom window. A sturdy stockade fence enclosed it, a purring filtering system cleaned it, and bright red rubber animals bobbed on its blue surface. Oh, how blue that pool was! Rachel could think of nothing but the blue blue pool as she listened to Bill Quincy tell her about the Civic Organization, of which he was president.

"We want to keep streetlights out of here," he was saying. "I'll have to get you and the reverend to sign the petition."

"Why don't you want streetlights?"

"We want to preserve the rural character of the area."

321

Rachel said, "Oh." She had wondered why it was so dark at night when you drove into Le Beau Foret from the main road. "A lot of the houses are lit up with floodlights," she said. "That's not very rural."

"People are afraid of vandalism," said Bill Quincy, "and the ladies fear rape."

"Then you *ought* to have streetlights."

"We have to weigh the preservation of the environment against the paranoia of a few nervous nellies."

The short man with pale hair jigged by again, and this time he grabbed Rachel by the hand, set her glass of beer on the table, and started to fox-trot with her. Rachel felt stiff and awkward.

"Relax," said the man. "You're much too tense."

"I have to think about what I'm doing," said Rachel. "The only dance I can actually do well is the polka."

"You and the Polacks," said the man. "You were right about being a lousy dancer."

The remark offended Rachel. She tried all night to think of the snappy comeback she might have made.

Just as she was beginning to feel that her feet were at last obeying impulse rather than will, the man danced her back to the table where she'd left her beer glass and said, "Thanks for the dance," before whirling another partner into the street.

Rachel sat down on a redwood bench and tried not to think of her bad performance. Life *had* come full circle—back to high school, back to those uncertain times of trying to imitate cheerleaders and prom queens. It had dawned on her but slowly that she was a ridiculous and awkward parody of them. Only when she finally saw herself clearly, in that foolish stance, did she begin to look for her destiny elsewhere. Now, on a mild September night, in a development on Long Island, she had suddenly forgotten the lessons she'd learned long ago. She had tried again. Tears sprang to her eyes as she felt the hot adolescent pain once more. She sat alone and thought about how she had gone back to her room at home in Buffalo, after her social failures (and Seymour pursued by Marcie Kubelik) and restored her self-assurance. She had drawn herself in the full-length mirror: self-portrait

322

upon self-portrait, clothed and naked, in poses that both echoed the art she had learned and delineated the person she wanted to be.

"Do you believe in Jesus?"

The question startled Rachel out of her reveries. A woman with pink-orange hair rising into a fragile mound atop her head had spoken. She was drinking Coke from a bottle and leaning on the arm of a stout man.

"I'm a rabbi's wife," said Rachel.

"I told you," said the stout man, who wore a tie. "Now will you leave her alone?"

"I'll call on you soon," the woman promised Rachel with a wink. The stout man frowned.

Another woman, this one alone, wedged herself in front of the Jesus lady.

"I've heard all about you from Natalie Gould, one of your congregants," she cried. She had flowing, shoulder-length hair and was very intense. "I live by myself down the block. I'm divorced and into films. Maybe we can get together for coffee one morning."

How did she come by Natalie Gould? The name had fallen straight into Rachel's heart, like a hot ember.

"Are you interested in AR?" the woman plunged on.

"In what?" said Rachel, still trying to dislodge the painful name.

"Aesthetic Realism. We meet once a week. It's marvelous for the gifted. Natalie tells me you're into painting."

"Yeah," said Rachel, "I paint. But I don't think I'd be interested in Aesthetic Realism. I'm too busy just trying to find the time to paint."

"I *love* women who assert themselves when it comes to their work. Good for you, Rachel Sonnshein! You believe in the life of the spirit, I can see—not many around here do." In a whisper, she added, "The men all want to fuck me and the women are bored and full of hate. By the way, my name is Katherine Penfield."

She was like a recorded telephone message—she didn't listen, she only spoke.

"Do you like films?" she asked.

323

"I like the movies," said Rachel, realizing that they had already established a kind of relationship. Katherine Penfield was bursting into ecstasy while she, Rachel, made small beeping noises, meant as irony, but not perceived as such.

"Another film freak!" Katherine Penfield shouted. "Welcome to Le Beau Foret!"

"Come dance with me, Katherine," said John McKeever, tilting toward her. He swept her away.

Rachel put her beer down for the last time and left the party. Nobody noticed. Inside the house, she turned the porch light off.

"Did you have a good time?" Seymour asked.

He was watching an old Western on television. The shots drowned out the music outside.

"No."

"I'm glad I stayed home. Did anyone pinch you?"

"No."

The party continued until the small hours of the morning. Rachel could not sleep and watched from her window. She wore her nightgown and her feet grew cold in the middle of the night. The Jesus lady fell asleep with her head on her arms, her hairdo collapsed. Her husband sat in conversation with another man, straddling a bench, their bellies close and nearly touching. Katherine Penfield danced and danced and never touched her partners. Edna McKeever began to clean up. Bill Quincy peed in the bushes.

The fire burned low and, at the end, a carload of kids drove whooping through the barriers and threw firecrackers into the dying flames. Their car roared off, and the men laughed and reached for the cunts of their women. When it had grown dark and black and was close to the hour when visions occur and the soul speaks to the devil, the party ended, the music stopped, the lights went out. Rachel stayed at the window a while longer. The moon had risen. It was still almost full. Less than two weeks to Rosh Hashanah and a new moon. There was a rustling here and there, the yapping of a dog. Rachel saw shadows move and lengthen in the moonlight, flicker darkly from cover to cover among the bushes. A few of the neighbors were still playing, giggles and thrashing sounds came out of the darkness once, twice, and then there was silence and the shadows stole away and finally, at long last, there was only the chirping of insects in the white night. Rachel put her head down on her arms and allowed herself the pleasure of tears, she was not certain why. Seymour pretended not to hear her.

Preparations for the High Holy Days kept Rachel and Seymour occupied for the next several days. At no other time of year were their traditional roles spelled out as clearly. Seymour went about on synagogue business and spent untold hours preparing his sermons, while Rachel stayed home or shopped. Each year she found herself in the same frenzy of trying to put her house and wardrobe in order.

Rachel cleaned the new house thoroughly and put the rest of the curtains up. She polished the silver and washed the windows. She made Aaron try on his good suit and shoes. Neither of them fit, so she took him down to Wittkover's men's store and bought a pair of gray flannel pants and a dark blue blazer, and then sent him down the street to Schnabel's shoe store to buy a new pair of shoes.

"Get loafers, please. I don't want to see you in boots, in sneakers, moccasins or work shoes."

For herself she bought another floppy hat and a calf-length flowered dress. Because her legs were still brown from the summer sun she decided to skip the pantyhose. Her pumps were out of style but comfortable. On the second day of Rosh Hashanah she would wear her good suit and on Yom Kippur one of her long dresses. On Kol Nidre night the good suit with a new blouse and the hat would do.

After standing in line at the bakery to place her order for the round holiday *challehs,* Rachel drove to the fishstore on Jericho Turnpike to buy whitefish and pike and a small piece of carp for the gefilte fish. She stopped at the kosher butcher's to pick up a plump pullet and a brisket for pot roasting.

325

"Didn't see you for a long time," said Hymie, the butcher.

"I went on vacation and ate *treif*."

"I know you're kidding me," said Hymie, smiling at their little joke.

When Rachel got home she put the fish through the food grinder with onions and carrots, and added eggs, salt and pepper, a touch of cold water, a little matzoh meal. She shaped the mixture into balls and threw them into a large pot of boiling water, swimming with more onions and carrots and the bones and heads of the fish. She cooked them until they floated on the top, puffy and white, flecked with specks of carrot. The whole house smelled of fish.

On the last morning, *erev* Rosh Hashanah, Rachel baked an apple pie and a sponge cake and ran out for the honey she had forgotten and a bouquet of flowers. She was so caught up in her preparations that she never once thought about painters and painting. At noon she went to have her hair cut.

"I haven't seen you in ages," Waldo said.

"I look it, don't I?"

Rachel didn't think she looked such a mess; why did she sound like all women who go to hairdressers? She listened in silence while Waldo snipped away and talked about his analyst and his sailboat and the two weeks he had spent in East Hampton. Several faces smiled at her from under the hairdryers, and disembodied voices shouted "Hello" much too loudly on account of the buzzing in their ears. The entire Jewish female population of Gateshead, Long Island, and perhaps even the world, was having its hair done.

She set the table in the afternoon, while she was making the salad and the soup and matzoh balls and skimming the fat from the gravy. By five o'clock she was finished and went to bathe and dress. When she came downstairs and saw the festive table set only for them, she grew sad for a moment, thinking that her efforts ought to provide for more than three people. A *real* rebbetzin would have invited some lonely strangers to share their feast.

Seymour, wearing his black suit, his hair trimmed and washed, his body showered and powdered and deodorized, walked down to the synagogue at five-thirty.

"Are you coming with me?" he asked Aaron, but Aaron was neither dressed nor showered.

"I hadn't planned on it—isn't it enough if I come tomorrow morning?"

"And the next day," said Rachel.

"Suit yourself," said Seymour and left the house by the kitchen door.

"You ought to have made the effort," Rachel told Aaron. "We leave him alone too much with his Jewish chores."

She watched Seymour walk down the empty suburban street, where no one ever walked save the children going back and forth to school. It was not yet dark, the evening breeze stirred the moist vapors of the day, the sky yawned pink above the flaming trees and Seymour's solitary figure looked so—so eternally *Jewish,* walking toward the Jewish factory below, to begin another year. Rachel lit the candles and murmured the holiday blessing.

Aaron showered and shaved and sat with Rachel, prim as a preacher's wife, on the couch in the living room waiting for Seymour to come home. The new building, visible through the picture window, was brightly lit. Streams of yellow light burst from its long narrow windows and shattered on the crusty, still unplanted earth. Aaron drew the curtains, Rachel picked up the day's newspapers and read that Jews all over the world were about to celebrate the arrival of the new year. The obligatory picture of an old man wrapped in his *talith,* holding a ram's horn to his mouth, accompanied the article. The picture had been taken at the Beth David Home for the Aged: "Jews Usher in New Year at Sundown."

At seven-thirty Seymour came home and sat down to dinner with his wife and son. At his place stood a silver beaker which he filled with wine. He recited the *Kiddush* and made the *hamotzi* over the shining

327

round loaves of *challeh* covered with a linen cloth. He cut off a piece and broke it into smaller portions, one for each of them. Rachel felt the loveliness of the moment without distracting afterthoughts. Even sentimentalized, it carried a curious dignity and banished an unruly world.

She served the dinner and they ate, wrapped in peace and contemplation. No one called to disturb them and before going to bed they telephoned Buffalo and wished parents and relatives a good *yom tov*. It grew cold that night and there was a light frost. When Rachel woke up in the morning the air was biting crisp and clear.

"There's a bag of garbage on the front lawn," said Aaron, when he came down to breakfast.

"Probably the dogs again," said Rachel, and went out in her robe and slippers to clean it up. She saw that it had clearly not been dragged there by the neighborhood dogs but thrown from a car in the night. She bent down (her feet wet from the cold damp grass) and collected the rinds and peels and tins and put them into a plastic bag. As she stood there—like an early-morning harridan—a car with four young men in it drove by and honked brassily. She looked up and saw their laughing faces and guffawing mouths. Straightening from her task she made an obscene gesture at them. They screeched to a halt, their laughter choked off, and for a moment it seemed that they might pile out of the car and attack her, but they did no more than shout evil words at her which she tried not to hear. They drove off with a hot-shot roar on their wide tires. Rachel did not tell Seymour what had happened, and continued to curse the dogs.

Seymour and Aaron left the house together, the morning of the first day of Rosh Hashanah, the "birthday of the world," as Seymour said in his sermon. Rachel was alone in the house for a brief while. She always went to *shul* a little later, like most of the women, after preparing everything for the midday dinner. Roosevelt was posted at the door, taking tickets.

"Nice crowd," he said to Rachel. "The rabbi be pleased I'm sure."

328

"It's not him they come for, but to see the new building."

Roosevelt cackled, as was his wont. He was dressed soberly, in a suit as black as Seymour's and a shirt as white. A chauffeur's hat covered his head from ear to ear. Seymour wore his white robe, and the high white *yarmulke* which covered his head from ear to ear. The cantor wore the same.

The new building was as yet bare of decoration and there was something cave-like about its interior. The *bimah* looked stark and empty, like a modern stage; the ark was cavernous—only the mantles of the Torahs and the silver breastplates touched it with color and light. Rachel found a seat near the front of the sanctuary. The pews had not been installed, the floor was filled with an acre of folding chairs from the funeral home. The huge sliding doors were opened so that the sanctuary extended the entire width of the building, through what would soon be known as the "social hall." By the time Seymour was ready to give the sermon all the seats were taken. Children's high voices peeped and their mothers shushed them. Old ladies made comments in quavering voices. Others whispered or talked or waved at distant relations. Seymour waited them all out. When it was quiet enough he began his sermon. On the High Holy Days he spoke longer than on the Sabbath and he let loose with more rousing rhetoric. The stamp of the time, the year, the political event, was always on his words. His illustrations came out of daily life. Sometimes he told a joke. Again and again he reached back to the Bible and his voice thundered out the ancient words, in sonorous Hebrew and in the melodic English forever shaped (even for Jews) by the King James version of the Holy Writ. Outside, the sun shone brilliantly and the sky's blue was endless, though only slivers of it were visible through the clear and narrow windows.

Small bitter thoughts crept into Rachel's mind, hard as she tried to banish them. She wanted to feel love and hope and ecstasy, but the reality of Gateshead kept obtruding. She saw the familiar faces and wondered whether they were friend or foe. While Seymour

329

preached she wondered how many of them would vote against him when the time came. The faces told her nothing, yet she sensed their discontent. The good feelings of their early years in Gateshead were gone—they could nevermore be recaptured. The congregation had changed, Seymour and Rachel remained the same. They were, like Truscott Boothby, constant in their commitment to social causes. But in suburban Gateshead, what had been fashionable in the sixties was no longer fashionable today. The men and women who had welcomed the Sonnsheins to Gateshead ten years before were a tiny minority now, and many had grown weary of congregational politics. The newcomers wanted nothing to do with social justice, they wanted to find personal salvation and self-fulfillment. They talked about "creative potential." They were politically conservative and religiously naive. They wanted their rabbi to incorporate the "wisdom" of Kahlil Gibran and the "philosophy" of *Jonathan Livingston Seagull*. They also wanted a rabbi who would offer himself as a religious scapegoat and set them an example of piety which would show them the way to heaven, and lead them straight into the laps of their *bobbes* and *zaydes* of blessed memory.

The ones (and there were many, alas) whose children had gone astray—married out of the faith, left school, refused to become doctors or docile housewives, became fanatics in pursuit of spirituality—were especially bitter. They blamed Seymour for the ills of a society he himself had roundly condemned. They saw him as the messenger who brought news of the decline of the family, the dissolution of the religious community and the death of God. For this they wanted to be rid of him.

"Surely I don't love these Jews enough," thought Rachel, once again. She was afraid that she no longer even understood them. She longed for a bond, a shared dream. The congregants rustled, stirred in their seats. The rabbi had gone on long enough. When the sermon was over there was much sighing and murmuring and a small exodus from the sanctuary. Rachel's thoughts fastened on mundane things, dinner and the telephone bill and the rattle in the old car.

An hour after the sermon, the morning service ended. It was one-thirty in the afternoon. The congregation filed out, and Rachel noticed again how many strange faces there were. When she and Seymour had first come to Gateshead, the congregation had been relatively small. They fitted comfortably into the old building and Rachel stood beside Seymour and greeted them, almost as friends. They were her Jewish comrades, her confrères, sharers of her Jewish secrets. She had felt pride in her role—yes, pride— and felt that it mattered what they did; they had a place, they were needed, in good times and in bad. Now she felt only bitter ambivalence. Sour faces grew like so many thistles around her. People stopped talking as she walked by. They glanced at her sideways, their jaw muscles tense, as though they had to clamp their mouths shut to keep the nasty words from spilling out. Rachel stood alone in the lobby and watched the Jews of Gateshead greet Seymour with handshakes and manicured smiles and heavily inflected good *yontiffs*—happy new years. Some complimented him on his sermon, many more did not. Rachel felt threatened. The very stones of the building smelled of the tomb.

Rachel did not wait for Seymour. As soon as she had found Aaron she went home, through the parking lot and the stubby field. She stumbled over rocks and blocks of cement and heard the honking of car horns as she skipped among the goldenrod and climbed (new dress and all) over the low wooden fence into her own backyard. (Only it wasn't her own.)

"You'll sit with me tomorrow," she said to Aaron.

"What's the matter?"

"The place is lousy with enemies."

"Don't be paranoid, Mom."

Rachel put her apron on and turned the heat up on the pot roast. She had prepared another good dinner. Seymour came home and was pleased with the way he had preached his sermon.

331

"What's the matter with you, Rachel?" He was relaxed and expansive, like an actor after a good performance.

"It's getting harder and harder to feel sympathetic toward those people. You can't imagine how antagonistic they are," Rachel said.

"Don't bring me bad notices right now, I'm feeling good. My sermon went well."

"It did."

"They're only a small group. A handful of malcontents. I'm a pretty good rabbi as rabbis go, don't you think?"

"You're terrific," said Rachel. "I love you."

They sat down to dinner and blessed the New Year.

The second day of Rosh Hashanah was cool and overcast. The blue of the sky had been wiped off by the pale wash of clouds. The smell of burning leaves (forbidden though it was) graced the air. Rachel and Aaron sat together on folding chairs in the barren sanctuary. Without the sun to brighten it, a look of desolation crossed the room. There weren't as many people at services on the second day of Rosh Hashanah, but to Rachel it seemed as though the enemies had multiplied. She tried to hide behind her dark glasses. The second days of holidays were always depressing, like warmed-over meals. Rachel didn't like to go through the same motions twice. Seymour preached well, but the reduced congregation and the hard seats made her nervous. At the conclusion of services they walked back home together and Rachel put another holiday meal on the table. They ate, while outside, in the development, a bulldozer roared at work and children shrieked at play. The sun had come out from behind the flat white curtain of clouds.

"Let's go away," said Rachel.

"Where to?" Seymour asked.

"Let's drive to the ocean."

"The city is closer."

"How about Coney Island then?"

"You're crazy."

332

"I thought you felt like escaping too?"

"Yes, sure."

"Then let's pretend that we can. Let's not be bound by anything and just go off somewhere as though we were lovers."

"Do you want to come?" Seymour asked Aaron.

"Not if you're pretending to be lovers."

They drove away together. Traffic was relatively light. It was the second day of Rosh Hashanah. Coney Island was somnolent in the pale sun of a September afternoon. Seymour and Rachel walked along the boardwalk. Many of the concessions were closed. Rachel thought the signs beautiful and the faded glory of honky-tonk touching. The ocean was tame and muddled, not like the splendid Atlantic of Cape Cod, all curling waves and wind-blown spray. They walked for a long time.

"If I get fired I'll quit the rabbinate."

"And what will you do?"

"Look for another Jewish job. But we'll leave suburbia. I think you're right about it. It's never going to work."

They both wanted to think it was simple. They walked hand in hand.

"I bet I could get a job," said Rachel.

"Doing what?"

"I'd do anything if it meant we could get out of Gateshead."

They walked barefoot down to the water's edge.

"Let's cast our sins into the water," said Seymour. "It's the time for *tashlich*."

He turned his pockets inside out and Rachel cleaned the lint from her jeans and from the pocket of her denim jacket. Seymour recited the appropriate prayer and they watched the ocean gurgle gently over their odds and ends. They kissed and walked on, arm in arm, not tempted by sex, merely tender. Later they went to a movie and by the time they came out of the theater it was night. The holiday was over, the Jewish stores in Brooklyn were open again. They stopped for a corned beef sandwich.

333

"L'shonah tovah," the waiter said.

The ten days to Yom Kippur passed quickly. Rachel was suspended in the autumnal void. She spent the days keeping order—shopping, going to the cleaner's, washing, ironing, doing several months' sewing. She had put aside all hope of painting until she found a studio. She was in limbo and had to walk gently because of it. The workmen were busy getting the offices and classrooms ready for the start of Hebrew school. The staff was supposed to move in before Sukkoth.

Rachel and Seymour and Aaron ate early *erev* Yom Kippur, before the fast. They walked, all three of them together, through the streets of Le Beau Foret, feeling peculiar in their good clothes among the neighbors who went about their business as usual and paid the wandering Jews no mind on this, the holiest day of the year. Rachel thought they walked on foreign soil. It was not often that she had so strong a sense of it. Most times her alienation had something willed about it, but on this evening, *erev* Yom Kippur, just before Kol Nidre, to be Jewish in a suburban development seemed to her to be particularly perverse.

"If God had meant the Jews to live in suburbia," she said, "He would not have led them out of Egypt."

Not a single seat was empty in the sanctuary of Shaare Tefilah. Many people stood along the walls as Kol Nidre began. Darkness was falling, the cantor's voice rose in the ancient chant, the elders of the congregation stood upon the *bimah,* holding the white-clad Torah scrolls. By the time the third rendition of the Aramaic text had ended and the last note had fallen on the cement-block walls, the Torah-bearers we glad to put their burdens down. Rachel listened, as she did each year, while following the Hebrew words on the pages of the prayerbook, trying to *understand* their meaning. The solemn moment was clothed entirely in history—its stiff and ancient words made clear, each year, how precarious was the life of the Jews. Stone throwers and storm troopers and the armies of the Czar rode the waves of memory. Perhaps

334

Rachel did not love the Jews enough, but she loved them with sufficient fervor to be counted with them tonight. She had no choice perhaps, she thought, but, *given* the choice, she would still be there. In some distant corner of her soul she knew that she must be counted.

The appeal for money started as soon as the last note of the Kol Nidre had faded away. Cy Glatt read a long speech from index cards. It would do nothing to spur the giving, but was a necessary prelude to it. Cy Glatt deserved his day in the sun, his evening before the multitudes. Ushers passed among the crowd to collect the pledge cards once Cy was done with his boring speech. Complicated arrangements had been made so that the cards had neither to be marked with a pen nor torn, activities which were prohibited on this Sabbath of Sabbaths, the holiest day of the year. "Turn down the tabs on your cards," said Cy Glatt through the microphone. "Give as much as you can." The spell of the evening had been broken; the crowd chattered as crowds will. Even Seymour's sermon, entitled "Is This the Fast I Have Chosen?" could not quite still the rustle of commercial transactions. The ushers counted the pledges and Cy Glatt announced the result at the end of the service. More money than ever had been subscribed. The new temple was a success.

The Sonnsheins walked home in the light of a ten-day-old moon that was rising in somewhat lopsided splendor over the remaining trees of Le Beau Foret.

By one o'clock the next afternoon, when the morning service had ended, Rachel was hungry and had a splitting headache. Seymour stretched out for an hour on the living room couch and fell asleep. Rachel dozed in the armchair until wakened by the telephone.

It was a young child who said, "My mother asked me to call and ask you when *yiskor* is."

"I don't answer the phone on Yom Kippur," said Rachel and hung up.

A minute later the mother herself called back.

"Services begin again in an hour," said Rachel.

"But when is *yiskor*?" the woman insisted.

335

"Jews are supposed to pray all day on Yom Kippur," said Rachel.

Seymour murmured in his sleep.

"I had to feed my family," said the pest, "but I want to come back and say *kaddish* for my dead mother."

"Come any time, the rabbi can't be bound by schedules."

The phone cracked down in a loud whack.

"She probably tells the whole town how awful it is that we answer the phone on the holiest day of the year."

"Why didn't you tell her when *yiskor* was?" Aaron asked.

"I'm not sure, and I'm full of resentment today. Let them call Cy Glatt if they want information."

The next call was from *Newsday,* asking if they wanted to subscribe to the paper. "I'll cancel," said Rachel, "if you don't stop bothering me on the holiest day of the year."

Truscott Boothby was the last to call. "Isn't your celebration over with?" he asked. "Did Seymour talk about slavery and about liberation? I wanted to come by to hear him, but your janitor wouldn't admit me."

"You need a ticket," said Rachel.

"That's what the man said. My Lord, you Jews act peculiar sometimes, selling tickets to talk to your God."

The afternoon wore on and Rachel's headache galloped back and forth in her head. At three o'clock Seymour returned to the synagogue and Rachel sat in the backyard briefly and closed her eyes. The McKeever children were putting a sock over the head of the kitten their father had bought them. From behind the stockade fence that protected the Quincys' pool came the sound of WABC and the splash of warm blue water.

Rachel rinsed out her mouth, and walked down to the synagogue through the thistles and rocks at five o'clock for the *neila'h* service. She had made it through another Yom Kippur, another year—almost. On Rosh Hashanah the names are inscribed in the book of life, and on Yom Kippur they are sealed. It

336

says so right in the liturgy. Rachel wondered what the new year would bring—she always wondered that, wondered if she'd be alive the next time around. She promised herself to work hard. She was sad and hungry. Evening had come again. Thank God. Another Yom Kippur done.

"*Sh'ma Yisrael.*"

"*T'kiah G'dolah.*" Blast of the shofar.

Rachel vowed to love the Jews a little more.

10

Between Yom Kippur and Sukkoth Rachel found herself a studio. She went out one day, wearing a demure skirt, stockings, and loafers, and rang the doorbell of every building on Main Street which displayed a For Rent sign. Her mode of dress—a deliberate reversion to the fifties—brought her polite greetings wherever she went. It was simply amazing what a conventional appearance accomplished. Alas, she soon found out that owners of newly furbished buildings were looking for tenants able to pay high rents: dentists, lawyers, insurance brokers or even, if they were very lucky, doctors. Rachel was more in a class with summons-servers, seamstresses and thrift shops. Hers was a marginal profession.

Most of the landlords who interviewed her seemed to be relics of Gateshead's illustrious past. They had once had the cream of the village for tenants. *All* the professional men had maintained offices on Main Street, and upright Christian couples had lived above their hardware stores and flower shops. Those days had passed into history, but witnesses to the passing were few. No one remembered the last good year, or could say exactly how the change came. Even the "newcomers" hadn't come all at once, like a horde of locusts; the developments sprang up piecemeal. One day there was a pleasant field, open to the sky, the next time you drove by there was a "model" on it (festooned with pennants) and six gaping foundations. The newcomers had spawned the hippies who loitered

338

in doorways even after the papers said that the sixties were over and the youth of America had gone back to conventional pursuits. The decent folk all died and were buried far away; the old graveyard on the hill was full.

In the end, Rachel rented a room over an antique shop which belonged to a couple named Camilli. They were elderly people and lived in a large apartment on the second floor. They rented out the third floor, where there were four "offices." The Camillis, like everyone else, had been waiting for the right tenants. A seamstress occupied the one front suite, and one of the rear rooms held the cluttered desk and swivel chair of a bail bondsman. Mrs. Camilli showed Rachel around. She wanted a hundred dollars a month for the front office. She hoped for a tenant who would put gold letters on the large window that faced the street: "Attorney at Law." The rear room—across from the bail bondsman—was next to the toilet and looked out over a weed-covered lot and some old fences and garages and the fire exit of the movie house next door. It had two high windows and a northern exposure and needed a coat of paint. Mrs. Camilli wanted sixty-five dollars for it.

"If I paint it and fix it up and pay my own electric bill, can I have it for fifty?" asked Rachel. She liked the room and sensed that Mrs. Camilli liked her.

"All right, but I need a month's security, and if I find a tenant who'll pay me sixty-five dollars, I may ask you to leave, or to match it. . . . Is your husband Rabbi Sonnshein?"

"Yes, he is."

"You know, *I'm* Jewish. My husband is Italian. Not from the south, you know, but from Bologna. Most people don't understand the distinction. Dominick comes from a distinguished family, but over here they called him a wop. My own family never forgave me for marrying a Gentile. My father sat *shiva* for me. Nowadays Jewish girls marry Gentiles all the time, but in my day hardly ever. We never had children. Sometimes I think it was a punishment. Your husband has been very nice to me. A lot of rabbis wouldn't

339

bother with a Mrs. Camilli, but he came to see me in the hospital. I tell you the truth, when you first walked in to ask about the room I wasn't sure. Painters are not reliable people and these days anyone can say they're a painter. But when you said your name was Sonnshein, I thought, 'That nice rabbi's wife, how can she be a bad person?' "

Rachel returned home happy, filled with stories of her day's adventure.

"I found a place."

"How much does it cost?" asked Seymour.

"Fifty bucks a month."

"I just hope you can pay for it."

"Me too."

Sukkoth arrived in brilliant autumn weather. A large *sukkah* had been constructed by the janitor and decorated by the children of the Hebrew school on the grounds of the new Temple. They had hung apples and gourds from the rafters and tied ears of Indian corn to the latticed walls. Seymour had, as always, built his own *sukkah*. Though not by nature inclined to be good with his hands, he had made it a point of honor to do this one task. Seymour's *sukkah* was frail indeed, a perfect structure to support the Talmudic interpretation that man's life on earth was forever at the mercy of the elements, a marginal gift at best. You saw the stars and the full harvest moon through the pine branches that swayed on the chicken wire stretched across the rafters of Seymour's *sukkah*. It was always on the verge of falling down, but it never did. Rachel always thought that Seymour's childlike *sukkah* was a marvel of faith. When Aaron was small he had played in it. Seymour made *Kiddush* in it the first days and last days and the Sabbath in between. Sometimes they ate in it, as they were meant to. The neighbors peeked over at them, their curiosity tinged with puzzlement. Had they asked about the structure, Seymour would have been glad to enlighten them. But they never did.

Rachel worked hard to refurbish her studio. She painted the floor gray and the walls white, washed the windows and hung fluorescent lights. She scavenged

340

for pieces of furniture, and found an old armchair, a small table, and a low couch without a cushion. The studio soon became home to her. The view from the window was limpid with autumnal melancholy. Rachel did sketches from her high chair beside the window to get back in shape after the long hiatus since summer. She nailed two pieces of homosote against the western wall and tacked her canvas against them. Slowly she worked her way back into the *seder* painting and decided to do a series, with variations, in which she pared down the details, concentrating on sections of the laden table and fragments of figures. She tacked up reproductions of Piero's Arezzo frescoes and Uccello's *Battle of San Romano*. She worked in her studio from early in the morning until Aaron came home from school, and found that she minded Le Beau Foret less, now that she spent most of her time on Main Street.

Rumors in Gateshead were rife that Seymour's "opposition" had decided to run a slate of candidates for the Board of Trustees of Shaare Tefilah, to make certain that Seymour's tenure of office—should he be re-elected—would be marked by an unfriendly majority. Unfortunately, rumors were the only things to reach Seymour's ears, and rumors were difficult to fight. Like the sullen faces of his enemies, they represented clear signs of hostility, yet they could not be used in a campaign to get support for Seymour. His friends in the congregation—led by the indefatigable Natalie Gould—did their best to reach the "uncommitted." In language, action, and aroused passions, the whole affair began to take on the aspect of a political campaign. All that was missing were buttons and shopping bags. Ambivalent as both Seymour and Rachel were about the blessings of Gateshead, they did not relish the idea of being driven from it. Again and again, sympathetic observers would say, "People lose their jobs all the time. There are plenty of pulpits around; Seymour will find something else." "You'll end up with more money." And, "It's all for the best, you'll see, even if he's fired." Rachel's mother had said that. She secretly hoped that Rachel and Seymour might

341

turn up in Rochester, or perhaps Syracuse, if not Buffalo.

"We've been here ten years," Rachel said to her mother. "It's so dirty, the whole business, so undignified. These people are behaving like CREEP."

"Who?"

"Richard Nixon."

"If that's how bad it is, Seymour should have found another profession."

"We were young then, we didn't know."

Seymour was nervous and tense about every sign and signal sent out by members of the congregation, and became almost paralyzed by the currents of love and hate that flowed around him. Even *indifference* seemed to represent a position—how could anyone claim to be unconcerned about his fate?

Truscott Boothby called one day.

"I hear wild stories about you. You are rumored to have seduced young virgins, boys as well as girls. The sauna at the 'Y' is steamy with talk. They say you insulted the oldest living member of the congregation on the Holy Days, and give your money and support to the A-rabs. Lawyer what's-his-name is convinced you are engaged in real estate swindles, and it's said your wife meets disreputable men in the city. If that is so, I should be very angry."

"Don't tell me bad news," said Seymour, "especially if it's bad news I can't do anything about."

"I called about something else, actually. You must help me, Seymour. Jane Winthrop and I have been working our butts off to set up a day-care center down the street from your Temple. The building we want belongs to one of your parishioners who had promised to rent it to us for a reasonable price if we fixed it up. But someone's been after him, claiming there's opposition in the neighborhood, and he's raised the rent 100 percent. We need the space desperately. It's not the most convenient place, but it's the only one large enough. Will you talk to the owner? His name is Sol Wasserman."

"You couldn't have picked a finer fellow," said Seymour. "The man is my sworn enemy. He's in

342

charge of the gang that's trying to get me. Anything I say he'll be against. Maybe I could tell him I don't want the day-care center and he'll become its most enthusiastic supporter."

"Things are that bad?"

"They couldn't be worse."

"All right then. I'll try to get to him some other way. We're having an open meeting next month at my church, to thrash out some of the things that seem to be troubling your good neighbors. Will you come to that and be on my side?"

"I'll gladly do that," said Seymour. "If they're going to crucify me, it might as well be for something worthwhile. I'll go out with a bang instead of a whimper. You can count on me."

Seymour told Rachel about the stories Truscott Boothby heard.

"They are merely distortions of the truth," said Rachel. "It is true that you have seduced Natalie Gould."

"She is not a virgin and I have never had a hankering after boys, large or small. . . ."

"You did tell old Mrs. Javitz that Judge Koppelman is a crook."

"I didn't know he was her son-in-law."

"You're *not* a knee-jerk Zionist, and your father told you last year that he was leaving you sixty acres on Lake Erie."

"What about this disreputable man you've been seen with?"

"I bumped into Ben at the Met one day last spring."

"You didn't tell me."

"I thought I had."

"How many other things didn't you tell me?"

"Not many, and they're all forgettable."

"Regrettable?"

"Forgettable."

Rachel knew that Seymour was only fishing. Trying to find some small indiscretion with which to ward off her next attack on his relationship with Natalie Gould. He did not really suspect her of anything with Ben. If she brazened it out, lied in her teeth, he would accept it. His mind was elsewhere. He was more jealous

343

of the present than of the past, over which he had triumphed. Rachel, growing defiant in her assertions of innocence, suddenly saw her own behavior reflected in Seymour's. He too warded off inquiries with brusque and self-righteous lies. She had simply never believed that she could do it. She had such faith in her own innocence!

Seymour knew that the cantor, the principal, and Roosevelt all held views on the subject of his contract. The secretaries claimed to be neutral, but everyone knew that they were not. Millie Fertig liked Seymour; her sister-in-law couldn't stand him. The two secretaries argued about him all the time.

Millie defended him: "He's awfully intelligent, I don't care *what* you say."

Fay grew vehement: "He's a disgrace to his profession. He eats *treif* and he sympathizes with the Arabs."

"That's not true," said loyal Millie.

"You've seen him yourself."

"About the Arabs, I mean."

"And how about the last Russian Jewry march. Where was he?"

"He said he was done marching, it did no good. He said there were other ways."

"He marched for the niggers long enough."

"I can't stand your nasty talk," said Millie. "It's unseemly. You work for the *shul* you should stay neutral."

"And *you're* neutral?"

"I've never taken a public stand. You go to all those teas and cocktail parties they're running to drum up the opposition."

"You defend him every chance you get."

"I defend him against those libelous statements. That's no more than human decency."

"If only half of them are true it's enough. He should be fired. Ten years is enough. I don't mind speaking my mind. I have a right. It's a free country still."

Their arguments, like most political arguments, led nowhere. Millie came to work every morning with a

344

long face and made soothing remarks to Seymour. On the theory that he should know what was happening she told him all the gossip. She was by nature pessimistic; it never occurred to her that her resigned and hopeless support had a depressing effect on Seymour. Fay was curt and glassy-eyed. She whispered to people when there was no need to whisper. Seymour began to avoid the office whenever he could. Millie took his messages and called him at home to tell him which ones were important. When Fay answered the phone she said, "The rabbi did not come in today. I have no idea where he is."

Millie's litany of bad news had no end. She reported that Mel Stirnweiss was circulating a petition asking that Seymour be required to make a "firm and positive stand" in support of Jewish settlement on the Left Bank, while Shirley Himmelfarb had introduced a motion at the Sisterhood board meeting censuring Seymour for expressing political opinions in the pulpit.

Millie often forgot that Seymour, her confidant, was the object of all these machinations. Once, meeting Rachel in front of the Pleiades luncheonette, she almost wept in anger at the latest bit of gossip. It seemed that Lew Pines, the barber, had told all his customers that Rachel walked barefoot into the sanctuary and that her feet were dirty.

"I wear sandals and my feet are clean."

"The truth doesn't matter to them," said Millie.

In the midst of all this it became known in Gateshead that Seymour favored the establishment of a day-care center two blocks down the street from Shaare Tefilah. At the same time Cy Glatt came out in support of bingo—over Seymour's strong objections.

"You're against bussing little black children to a day-care center so their mothers can work, but you're ready to bus adults to a bingo game every week so you can separate them from their money."

"Exactly!" said Cy Glatt. "The spics who work for me love bingo. I'm doing them a favor. What's the matter, Rabbi? You against the spics having fun? I

345

thought you preached we should all do our own thing, only the spics and the niggers should do even more of it."

"I don't remember preaching that," said Seymour, "but I *have* preached that you shouldn't, as the Bible says, put a stumbling block before the feet of the blind."

"I'm only getting back for the *shul* a little of the exorbitant wages I have to pay them."

"From what I hear you pay the minimum and fire them rather than raise their pay."

"Stick to religion, Rabbi," said Cy Glatt.

Things were not going well at all.

Rachel felt guilty that she was managing to work hard and turning out good paintings while all of this was going on. She had succeeded in putting a wall between herself and the congregation—the studio proved to be her salvation. She worried that she was disloyal to Seymour, washing her hands of the trash that flooded in on him day by day. And yet, her efforts to finish a series of paintings and thereby create a small beginning to an *oeuvre* were, after all, a step toward self-sufficiency; and a self-sufficient rebbetzin stood a better chance of being a helpmeet to her husband in his time of need than a clinging vine. Seymour didn't always agree with this assessment.

"It's not as if you had a *real* job. We can't live on promises and I need your help *now*."

"What do you want me to do?" she asked, resentful at the prospect of an intrusion, and miserable over her resentment.

"If you don't know by *this* time, I can't tell you."

Seymour withdrew into his suffering and Rachel continued in her daily routine. Once a week she went to New York to look at works of art. Most of the time she went alone. She talked to Sally on the telephone and they met, regularly, for lunch. Some evenings, falling into bed at midnight (she did all her household chores at night, in order to have a full day at her studio), Rachel felt so tired that she thought she might simply go to pieces one fine day. She dreamt of not rousing herself in the autumnally cool dawn but

346

staying in bed for months and months. Luckily, she slept soundly and when the alarm *did* ring, the prospect of a day's good work always sent her flying back to her studio. By the time she had finished her second cup of coffee and was possessed by the labors at hand, whatever anxiety she'd felt before had fled from her as if by magic.

Seymour went mechanically through the motions of his job. He visited the hospital daily, counseled the distraught, answered his mail, and met regularly with his supporters. He spent the hours from three to six (when Hebrew school was in session and many of the mothers appeared) at his desk. Since Fay Fertig left at two-thirty, he was able to avoid her almost entirely. He looked in on Sisterhood meetings and even went to the *minyan* now and then.

Rachel made a trip into the city on one of the last warm days of October. She walked and walked, trying to store up the day for the winter. If she could experience it intensely enough she would always remember it. The end of summer was finally at hand, everyone knew it. The old people sat up against the walls of the buildings and closed their eyes and put their faces into the fuzzy sun. Rachel did not carry a handbag, but wore an old jacket with enough pockets to carry all her things, save the black sketchbook. She wore comfortable walking shoes. She felt young and unencumbered. It made her think of Ben again. Being young and unencumbered in Greenwich Village was to want to be with him. Rachel went through the galleries of SoHo, but most of what she saw that day depressed her. It was either stridently bad or almost nonexistent. A piece of string cast on the floor, a fingerprint upon the wall. Rachel did not want to give so much of herself to so small an enterprise. The only things she saw all day that gave her pause were a group of Rauschenbergs at Castelli. Rachel spent a while with them, and their delicacy and gossamer beauty retrieved the day for her and lifted her spirit out of the glumness to which the *schlock* had condemned her.

When she grew hungry, Rachel went into her fa-

347

vorite corner restaurant to have a sandwich on thick brown bread, a bowl of soup, and a glass of cider. She sat alone at a table and in her mind the words formed in slow motion, like a dryer winding down, the drum turning ever more slowly. "I wish—I wish I could live here," was how the first sentence began. "If only I could live here," thought Rachel, while her eyes sought out the faces and angles and the dusky light of the streets—"to live here, to come home to New York." She wondered if she dared say it out loud, let her lips move and tune her throat. After a while, the words fell into the proper rhythm and rattled along while she ate, becoming divorced from thought, just fitting themselves to a small personal melody. She wondered whether the wish was irredeemable. She thought, once again, about running away. Had she gone too far, was she too old to start over? She thought not, but what would happen when she left Seymour and Aaron behind? The idea thrilled and frightened her, at the same time she knew it would lead her into a dark night of troubles. She would have to put up with the contempt of all who loved her—she would surely be a pariah. A lot of women were running away, it was true. What was also true was that many of them found that the husbands they left behind breathed freer than they did.

Running away would mean she had to hack it alone. All alone. Utterly and completely alone. She could no longer simply plan to hitch a ride or jump a freight to the Petrified Forest. That dream belonged to a distant past. She would have to make other plans. She needed her solitude, but she could only manage it as long as someone waited for her in the wings. She had to come dancing off the stage into his waiting arms. That was not merely her heritage from the movies, but an acknowledged source of her strength: she must be loved.

Rachel's mind returned to thoughts of Ben. His name insinuated itself into the sing-song of her wish, to wish to live here, to wish I could, I wish—with Ben, Ben, Ben. . . . How talented he had been! He had known exactly how to give shape to his fantasies.

348

He had learned the lessons so easily—it had taken *her* years and years. She was going to find him again; she had known it all day. She had merely postponed the moment when she would admit it to herself. She would find him in the bar where he hung out. All she needed to do was call home to say there was a late afternoon movie at the Museum of Modern Art she wanted to see. Her heart sang. It was a beautiful day, the last day of summer. She would run away with Ben. They would finally be alone and talk about painting and turn their backs on middle-class life and on suburbia. They'd live for art!

Rachel walked west to the docks. The New Jersey shore was pale gray and pink in the hazy heat of the afternoon. The sun, sliding down through a cloudless sky into the Meadows, filled the city with the soft light that reflects from the waters. Rachel watched the Circle Line boat steaming down the Hudson. She waved. She wished she were on it. She thought some children waved back; the boat was far away. It was so hot that Rachel took off her jacket. She folded it neatly and put it down on a tar-soaked wooden beam and sat on it.

Rachel drew in her black sketchbook until four o'clock, when she went to a phone booth and called home, collect. Aaron answered.

"Accept the call! Accept!" cried Rachel.

He did. She gave him a little spiel about the five-thirty movie at the museum and missing the rush hour. She had looked up the name of the movie. It was an old Marlene Dietrich film.

"What do you want to see *that* for?"

"It's not so much the movie, but I hate to come home with all those sweaty men."

She was putting some truth into the lie.

"The World Series starts next week," said Aaron.

"I know," said Rachel. "So what?"

"I wish we had a color TV."

"I promise you I'll buy one as soon as I become rich and famous."

"What if I can't wait that long?"

"Then you'll have to get out and become rich and

349

famous yourself. In the meantime, just think that a black and white TV is a distinction in Gateshead. You don't want to be one of those awful rich kids, do you?"

"Nobody in Le Beau Foret is *rich*."

"But they all want to be, so they can have color TV in every room. It's the only thing they live for, and it's the way America will conquer the world."

"Don't lecture to me, Mom. I just want to watch the World Series in color."

"Go visit a friend this year and maybe by next year we'll have a color TV. Dad may get re-elected and get a big raise to boot."

"He says 'never.' "

"Never what?"

"He'll never get a color TV."

"He says a lot of negative things when he's upset and he's been upset lately, as you well know."

"Do you really think they'll fire him?"

"Let's not talk about it on the telephone, Aaron. On a collect call, yet. I'll see you later."

Rachel hung up. She felt free and relieved. She walked to the bar, but on the way her excitement became stained with doubt and fear. Not the kind of fear that involves the body becoming hurt or mutilated, or has to do with facing an enemy or a sudden threat. The fear Rachel felt had to do with the unknown, it was the fear of complications and disorder. Was she going to go down the bramble path and lose her way? To have slept with Ben once might be excused for old times' sake, but going to look for him, to proposition him, as it were, was something else again. She wanted so desperately to wipe Gateshead from her mind—it had become a prison. She was condemned to see enemies everywhere. Though she loved Seymour as ever, she felt an awful, guilty twinge of contempt, watching him struggle in the grip of the enemy. Even his friends—even Natalie Gould—were enemies, in some sense. They all belonged in Gateshead. He was their victim. How awful it was to feel scorn for the victim. How much worse to betray him as well.

Rachel sat on one of the high stools at the bar.

Ben was not there. She ordered a gin on the rocks. It seemed less of an uptown drink than a martini, less lady-like than a Bloody Mary and more powerful than a beer.

"You mean a martini?" the bartender asked.

"No, I mean a gin on the rocks. I like gin," she added, as if the man cared.

She was sipping at it, glad for its soothing qualities, when Ben came in. She had almost forgotten that he was the reason she was there. She had begun to think that she was merely having a drink in a bar. She saw him while he was still in the street. Ben stepped into the soft darkness of the room. Rachel was where he saw her immediately. He said nothing, but sat next to her. There was neither surprise nor happiness on his face. He merely looked at her as he might look at the familiar picture of Franklin Roosevelt that hung next to the mirror behind the bar.

"Hello," said Rachel.

Ben nodded his head. (Later, Rachel realized that she had expected a kiss.) He was ashamed of his emotions. Much as he loved his sensitivities, he detested his emotions for fear they might play him dirty.

"Are you waiting for someone?"

"Always the joker," said Rachel. "Same old Ben, never a serious moment. It might crack him up."

"You're so right, Rachel," he said. "Right and serious to the end."

"You always hold my seriousness against me."

"You refuse to see the absurdity of life."

Ben ordered a beer. The bartender returned to the other end of the bar, his arms folded, listening to an elderly man, a regular customer who worked as a security guard. He wore his dark blue jacket with a patch on the shoulder. Rachel sat drawn up on her stool, close to Ben. They spoke in quiet tones. Rachel could not admit to her purpose.

"I knew you'd come here one day," said Ben. "You're always looking for me. I knew that the first time we bumped into each other. You've been looking for me all these years. When we made love it was you coming 'home.' "

351

"I didn't know it was so obvious. But you know I love Seymour. I *do*," she said, loyally. "Only right now there's a lot of shit. I can't stand it any longer. I hate it in Gateshead. I hate being the rebbetzin. I even hate the rabbi sometimes."

"You'll always be in that fix. Because it was me who opened your eyes, but you went and followed Seymour. You'll always be indebted to me, you'll never be able to let go. You're spoiled, Rachel. If you'd stayed with me you'd cry for him."

"That's true."

Rachel's thoughts hadn't moved as swiftly as his. She was pained by his bluntness. Of course she was a more heroic figure in her own sight. But *spoiled*? She put her hand over Ben's long, paint-stained fingers. He very nearly pulled them away. He would have done it, once, long ago. He was less certain about his irritability now.

"I don't think I'm spoiled. I wouldn't have put up with my life all these years if I were spoiled. I always thought that I'd earn my freedom one day. I put in my time, so to speak—why shouldn't I be allowed to become a painter now?"

"It's nothing that's *allowed*. You have to insist on it. With your life, if necessary. With your happiness, surely."

"I understand that. I know I've got to make the choice. That's why I'm here. I need support. I'm asking for your help."

"You think *I* can help you? My God, Rachel, I can hardly help myself."

"I've got to escape from Gateshead. Its provincialism is killing me, I can't bear the desolate landscape. Can you imagine what it's like not having friends with whom you can *talk*?"

"Talk about what?"

"Painting. Serious things. Art."

"You really want to sit around and talk about painting? Rachel-Rachel, you are unrelentingly serious."

"What do *you* sit around and talk about?"

"I have different conversations with different peo-

352

ple, but I try to keep them cool and light. 'What detergents do *you* use to get those greasy stains out?' My wife and I have a pact: we talk about *Beowulf* from ten to twelve on Saturday mornings, about the Crusades on Sunday nights and about Ann Landers all day Tuesday."

"Be serious."

Ben finished his beer and ordered another. "I'm trying hard not to hear what you're getting at. Where were we?"

"Talking about friends."

"Friends are o.k. Especially when the TV's on the blink and the bars are shut. They're the picket line between you and the drop to the river. They mark things down in their notebooks. They keep track. I'd be lost without them."

"You always were. But I keep seeing you all alone, now."

"They left me, one by one. I owed them too much. They saved my life once too often. Oh, Rachel-Rachel, where did the good times go?"

"Hey, Ben," said Rachel (and as she said it saw the moment flashed on a screen, saw herself doing the bit Barbara Stanwyck used to do, or Betty Field or Margaret Sullavan or Jean Arthur, the same way she'd put her hand over his earlier—an act from the movies but true nonetheless), "do you want to try it again?"

"Try what again?"

"Try love again."

"You're making bad rhymes, Rachel. You're a sentimental poet. Rod McKuen. A suburban rhymester ..."

"Rhymestress, if you please."

"... gone berserk in a city bar."

"You of all people ought to appreciate my clichés. You always loved the tacky."

"That was before I lived it. When I had the distance of a sensitive artist ..."

"Do you want to—to run away with me?"

"You're joking!"

Rachel sighed. Of course it was a joke. What else

353

could it be? Whatever had made her think she could count on Ben?

"Yeah, I'm joking," she said.

"You want to bring back our lost youth. It won't work. You think you can rewrite the ending. No, Rachel."

"We make our own endings. I believe that."

"You want to make a movie."

"I want to escape."

"To a shabby room, a cracked mirror and me?"

"There's no place for me in Gateshead."

"Your place is beside your husband the rabbi, what's-his-name."

"My place is in a gallery on Fifty-seventh Street."

The security guard had stopped talking to the bartender. They were studying a small portion of the bar in front of them. Pretending not to listen. When Rachel and Ben stopped talking they began to make rasping noises, as though taking up their conversation. Ben ordered another beer and a second gin on the rocks for Rachel.

"Let's sit at a table. You got money to pay for this?" he asked Rachel and winked at the bartender.

Rachel gave him the five dollars she had saved for a book at Penn Station to read on the train.

The tables were like small islands. There were green-checked tablecloths on them, and in the center of each one, a vase with a plastic rose and a sprig of plastic lilies-of-the-valley.

"The setting is perfect for you," said Ben. "All we need is a black piano player. You came all the way from Gateshead, Long Island to proposition me, you deserve the best. But you're not living a movie, Rachel. It's true, we made love to each other, not long ago. It was our *Brief Encounter* and it was nice. But it didn't mean all that much."

"Didn't it?"

"I don't think so. Even though you came running in from the suburbs today to find me. That's sweet, Rachel, it really is, I'm not putting you down. In fact, I'm touched by your faith in me. But I *can't* help you, you know that, sweet Rachel."

354

"You're leaving? You won't even make love to me again?"

"Not if it entangles me in your escape plans. I haven't the strength. It's one of the reasons I've been faithful to Annie for all these years. I told you all this before. You just forgot, you don't want to remember. And you haven't met Annie, she's not real to you. But my own habits, and that includes my habit of faithfulness, are completely entwined with hers. I bet it's the same with you and your rabbi."

"He's not always faithful."

"That's part of the habit too. If he were always faithful he would have destroyed you long ago with moral righteousness, with jealousy. His guilt keeps him honest. I know how it is. I know his kind of love and your need for it. Just as I understand your wanting to make a dramatic gesture, shock your congregation. You ought to wear a button that says 'Live Art, Not Life.'"

"Art *is* more real. Shit, Ben, that's why I'm here."

"No it isn't, Rachel, and that's why I'm leaving. I've got too many problems to face, day by day, that have nothing to do with art. I can't take any more. I'm a lousy provider, a rotten husband, a terrible father. Rachel: I can't have an affair with you. I would love to have an affair with you. I love you. Maybe not the way I used to. I mean, I'm not able to love you in that young way I had. I'm not able to do a lot of things. I'm a failure—by every standard Americans have devised. It's hard as hell for Annie to live with me, I can't make it any harder for her. I love her too much. She took me on—as I told you—after you went back to your rabbi. I was a mess. Not because we split, I was just a mess, generally. My nose was running, I needed a haircut. There were holes in my head and my soul was scuffed. I lived in a single room, in terror. I couldn't work. I spoke in fewer and fewer words. I painted crazy little pictures with lots of detail— hair and bottle openers and hot water bottles. And then Annie rescued me. She came in one day and the cockroaches went away and the words came back and I got my hair cut. I have to stay with Annie. I owe her

355

whatever good years I've had. I couldn't stay with Annie and start seeing you again. I surely couldn't run away with you. Forgive me, Rachel, for disappointing you."

He leaned over and kissed her. And then he stood up.

"I have to get home," he said, "and you have to get home, too. I'll see you sometime. Give my regards to the rabbi, what's-his-name, if you tell him you saw me. I'm sure I like him better than he likes me. I love you, Rachel."

He walked quickly out the door. The men did not look after him, they looked at Rachel. She sat at the table for a while, trying to convince herself that she hadn't wanted it to end any other way, that it was for the best, that she had nothing to cry about. She almost succeeded. She took the bus crosstown at Christopher Street and walked down First Avenue to Houston and bought a beautiful smoked whitefish and some creamed herring and pickled salmon. By the time she got to Penn Station the rush hour was over, the tickets were cheaper, and she was home a little after eight-thirty.

"How was the movie?" asked Aaron.

"Pretty good, but I'm tired and there's a headache starting up in the back of my head."

Seymour was out. He did not come home until late and wanted no part of the whitefish or the herring or the pickled salmon at such an hour. He didn't ask Rachel about her day, nor did he tell her about his. Sleep released them from their troubling silence.

Rachel did not mourn Ben for long. The more she thought about it, the more determined she became to rely on herself alone to find the way out of Gateshead. The weather grew colder, the days shorter; Rachel went to her studio every day, right after breakfast. She had finished work on the *seder* painting and was doing a series of small variations on it. She was well pleased with her progress, though she wished she could show her work. It was meant to be seen. At the very least, she needed to talk about it—she wanted encouragement. She would have to see about that, after the contract negotiations, after the first of

356

the year. She knew it would be hard (she had no connections whatever), but she was convinced that her work was good enough. She kept at it with single-minded determination. To hell with Ben.

Rachel went regularly to Solti's Bar and Grill, down the street from her studio. Sometimes she met Sally there for lunch, or had a quick bite with Seymour when he was on Main Street and came up to see her. He never told her he was coming, he simply bounded up the stairs and appeared at her door. She wondered what he expected to find.

On summer afternoons Solti's was often crowded with fishermen and visiting yachtsmen, but as the evenings grew longer and autumn cleared the harbor of pleasure craft, the bar became a hangout for local drunks. They were neat drinkers, all of them, working men who didn't work regularly, quiet clerks who couldn't face their empty rooms, and lonely women who were afraid to drink at home and didn't want to admit to being lonely. The place had dark yellow walls and pressed metal ceilings brown with grease. It hadn't been painted in many years. A large smiling rotogravure picture of John F. Kennedy hung high above the bar. There was a color TV in a back corner of the room, next to the kitchen. It was hard to see, except from the bar, and sat dark and still during the lunch hour, when all the tables were filled and Solti's was noisy with the chatter of shopkeepers and the laughter of women fresh from their weekly exercise class. The hamburgers were excellent, the drinks large, and the clam chowder had been praised in *Newsday*. George, the owner and bartender, turned the TV on at three-thirty, when the lunch crowd had left and the solitary drinkers started to appear.

Rachel had taken to stopping at Solti's for a drink before she went home in the afternoon. It was quiet there and she could unwind. She was working every weekday and Sundays as well; only on the Sabbath did she rest. (But since the Sabbath was given over to bar mitzvahs, she didn't perceive it as a day of joy unto the Lord, free from toil and devoid of care.) On Sundays most of the stores on Main Street were closed

357

and the cacophony they brought to Gateshead was stilled. Rachel parked her car right in front of her building and looked down on casual domestic scenes from the window of her studio. On nice days, the men who lived nearby brought kitchen chairs out into the alley and sat sunning themselves alongside their dogs. Children played on the ground (squatting on their haunches to make markings and signs in the dust) or bounced rubber balls against the stone wall of the movie theater. The women crossed their legs, sitting on their back stoops, and rested their hands in their laps while they talked to each other. Young men leaned into the open jaws of their automobiles to tinker with carburetors, distributors and water pumps.

Rachel would sit near the window and watch. If someone looked up and saw her she waved. Sometimes she drew the scene below her. She had taken photographs of it as well, and planned to record the changes in time and season as seen from her tall window. As it grew colder, and the wind started up with a whine from the harbor, the children vanished and the adults moved indoors.

On the Sunday of the second game of the World Series, Rachel planned to go to her studio as usual. A light drizzle fell on Gateshead. In Boston, where the game was being played, the weather was even worse. By rights, the season should have been over; it had grown too cold for baseball, which was meant for the long lazy afternoons of hot summer. It needed the rhythms of summer, its colors and light. For the World Series, a slight nip of autumn in the air was quite enough.

Seymour was at home, asleep. He slept badly these nights, tossing and turning in the grip of his congregational *tzuris,* and dozed off frequently during the days. He would have preferred to hide and sleep in his bed all day and all night, escaping from the increasingly acrimonious voices around him, but neither his conscience nor his supporters would permit it. The latter called him day and night, to egg him on, to plan strategy, to discuss alternatives. His alliances with the proponents of the day-care center had brought him new

358

friends among the rich WASP ladies who performed good deeds, but they weren't members of Shaare Tefilah, and neither were the left-wing Jews who perennially manned the barricades against war and racism but kept a smug distance from "merely" Jewish matters, as they were proud to point out when they bragged that they never set foot inside a synagogue except to pray for peace.

Aaron had gone to a friend's house to watch the World Series. The friend had a color TV set in his own room, a pool table in the basement, and a tennis court beside the swimming pool on two wooded acres in Gateshead West.

"He's a nice kid, regardless," said Aaron, when he saw his mother's nose wrinkle the first time she saw the boy drive up in a Porsche. "Besides, you told me to find someone with a color TV."

"He has an unbearable self-assurance."

"He's not one to be polite to mothers."

"I'd take care of him if he were *my* kid."

"Why are you so angry with him? You barely know him."

"He's a snotty rich kid and will never get his comeuppance."

"He's not very happy, Mom."

"I'm sorry to hear that."

She *was* sorry that her reaction had been instantaneously negative, just because of the damned Porsche. She realized that she was suffering along with Seymour, despite herself.

Rachel got to her studio right after lunch. The building was quiet. Neither the seamstress nor the bail bondsman came in on Sundays. Rachel went straight to work. She had seen what was wrong in the picture on her easel the minute she walked in the door. It sprang directly at her, as though it had been a hole or a smear. She worked steadily for an hour or two (she easily lost track of time when she worked) until she heard the voices raised in argument in the apartment below. Ida Camilli and her husband were having another fight. They fought most often on Sundays, when the shop was closed. Rachel couldn't hear the words—the building was old and its walls thick—but she could hear their angry sound. She could distinguish Ida's high voice and Dominick's low voice. The anger flowed between them like a current. Sometimes the voices came together as one, sometimes they broke apart and one voice became triumphant. Rachel wished she had a radio to drown out the sound of battle. It was disconcerting, like a sharp wind rattling at the windows.

Rachel cleaned her brushes and put on her denim chore coat and went out into the street. The drizzle had stopped but the clouds above were gray and low. They turned dark above the waters of the bay and whitecaps skipped across the water. The boats tossed at their moorings. At Solti's the TV set was tuned to the World Series. There were six customers at the bar and George was wiping glasses with a clean white apron.

"What's the score?" asked Rachel.

"One to one, top of the fourth."

The Red Sox had won the opener 6–0. Rachel ordered a Bloody Mary, which was not a sissy drink at Solti's, and sat down at the bar to watch the game.

Two stools away from her sat a young man Rachel had noticed before. She had wondered about him in a casual way. She had found him handsome and let it go at that, the first time around. The second time she thought that handsome men were generally a bore and why had she, upon seeing him, not dismissed him from her mind? Rachel knew that handsome men, like pretty women, were not likely to make good friends. Their awareness of the world was blocked by the impression they made on others. They were always *noticed,* they could go nowhere as observers; they were always the observed.

The Red Sox went ahead in the sixth inning, 2–1, when Rico Petrocelli singled to score Yastrzemski from second. The young man was watching the game along with everyone else, but was also watching Rachel, not in an obvious way, just looking at her now and then, trying to find the right moment to speak directly to her. But she was too absorbed in the game. He wore a blue checked shirt and a gray cashmere sweater. He decided all at once that he didn't need the right time.

"You for Cincinnati or the Red Sox?" he asked.

"The Red Sox," said Rachel. "It's the first time I've ever rooted for an American League team in the World Series. I'm a National League fan from way back." She was careful to explain herself.

"I like the Red Sox myself. I spent a couple of happy years in Boston. Went to college there, but never finished." He sounded jolly, though Rachel detected a morose tone, like a bass accompaniment, in his voice. "I had to go to work," he said. "Still, I think one day I'm going back. My name is Larry Silver."

In Boston, the game had been halted because of the rain. George turned down the sound.

"What's your name?" asked Larry Silver.

"Rachel Sonnshein."

"You any relation to the rabbi?"

"I'm his wife."

"What are you doing in a bar on a Sunday afternoon?"

"Watching the World Series. Having a drink."

"I've seen you here before."

"I have a studio around the corner."

"You a photographer?" he asked.

"No, I'm a painter. What do you do?"

"I'm a salesman."

"What do you sell?"

"Cars. You interested in cars? I'll gladly sell you one. I can sell anything." He took out one of his cards and gave it to Rachel. "What do you drive?" he asked.

"A 1965 Plymouth convertible," said Rachel, smugly.

"One of those!" said Larry Silver with a low whistle. "You need a new car for sure."

"We have a new purple Pontiac. I love the convertible. It runs like a dream." Rachel rapped her knuckles against the curved wooden counter of the bar.

"I know your kind," said Larry Silver. He was short and slim. Almost dainty. He wore, Rachel noticed, loafers and crew socks. His pants were dark blue flannel.

361

"Why are you here?" asked Rachel.

"I had a fight with my wife."

Rachel looked back at the TV screen. The game had not yet resumed. She felt that the conversation was going to be a strain. Larry Silver's handsome face looked less handsome once you saw it animated by his conversation. His nails were bitten to the quick.

"Everything will probably look better when you've made up with your wife," said Rachel. Once it was out she was startled that she had actually said it. Larry Silver, she thought, must have a powerful beam of some sort built into his brain, to draw such a sappy statement from her. Rachel felt as though her mind had melted down into an Ann Landers column. She was trying to be kind. It was condescending. She blushed.

"If I talk to your husband and tell him my troubles, will he say I should turn to God and follow His laws and commandments?"

"No," said Rachel, defensively. "Seymour is smarter than that."

"Who's Seymour?"

"My husband."

"The rabbi. I see. I never knew rabbis had first names. He won't give me a lot of inspirational talk and send me on my way with a blessing?"

"I doubt it. Of course I never heard him talking to anyone who's come to see him with troubles."

"He doesn't tell you?"

"People's private conversations? Of course not."

"Not even if it's hot stuff?"

"No."

"I don't believe it."

"It's true. He never even tells me who comes to see him."

She drank the last of her Bloody Mary. Drained the glass until the ice was sucked up against her teeth. Larry Silver motioned to George to bring another of the same. He was drinking Chivas on the rocks.

She didn't know whether to thank Larry for the drink. He hadn't paid for it yet. Maybe he didn't plan

362

to. It made her nervous. She was unused to the etiquette of bars.

The game resumed. George turned up the TV sound. It was still wet in Boston. The players could be seen wiping the rainwater off their bats.

"They're starting to play again," said Rachel. Her eyes left Larry Silver's face and went back to the baseball players on the little screen.

"It's not feminine to be such a baseball nut," said Larry Silver. "I bet you know old line-ups."

"Only for the Dodgers," said Rachel. "I have a lousy memory. I like what's happening at the moment and I understand it perfectly, but I can't replay the hand the way bridge players can. Why do you think it isn't feminine to be a baseball fan?"

"Girls can't play. You have to have the feel of playing in your bones before you can understand what's going on."

"I played a lot when I was a kid."

"Don't the men resent you for knowing more than they do?"

"A lot of men I know I can only talk to about baseball. Especially in suburbia. Especially in the congregation."

In the ninth inning it was still 2–1 in favor of the Red Sox. Rachel felt that it wasn't good enough. She had the firm conviction that you could feel victory in your guts. Could tell whether your team could make it or not. She felt uneasy about the Bosox. The groundskeepers kept putting dry sawdust around home plate. Bench led off for Cincinnati with a double, and the Red Sox took out Bill Lee. "Shouldn't do that," Rachel muttered. Drago, the relief pitcher, got two out. "Maybe it was the right decision," said Rachel, but she felt nervous still. It didn't feel safe. It wasn't over yet. Bench was on second. It wouldn't be so bad if he were only on first. This way, with a single, he could score. He did. Concepción hit the ball on a high bounce over second. Doyle could make no play. Bench scored the tying run. Then Concepción stole second. Rachel's heart fell. Had she been at home she

363

might have started busying herself, folding the laun-cry, so that her heart's desires might not foul things up. Also in order to be able to look away if the bad end-ing she feared took place. Here she was stuck. She saw it all. Ken Griffey hit a double. Rachel knew it was over. "Bastards should've kept in Lee," she said. The Red Sox went down in order in the bottom of the ninth.

"Too bad," said Larry Silver. He didn't care.

"Shit," said Rachel.

"You got money on them?" asked George.

"I never bet," said Rachel. "I don't know why I get so involved in these things."

"Women are emotional. You should meet my wife."

When Rachel got home Seymour said, "You don't do anything for me anymore. You've become a strang-er. You even sent Aaron away."

"He wanted to watch the World Series in color."

"And you?"

"Me too."

"I thought you were working."

"I was, but the Camillis were having a fight so I went to Solti's and watched the game. They have color too. The Red Sox lost."

"Fuck the Red Sox. I'm losing my job."

In the end the Cincinnati Reds won in seven games. It was one of the most exciting World Series ever played.

11

Winter had begun to bite; the last of the dead leaves rattled in the streets. It was November. The lawns of Le Beau Foret had been swept clean. Even Rachel had raked leaves on a warm Sunday when Indian summer flared briefly for one last time. Aaron helped and it didn't take them long. The neighbors nodded stiffly at them. They had heard that Seymour was among the supporters of the day-care center to which they were all opposed.

"It's enough we have a church next door," Bill Quincy said.

The storm over the day-care center grew in intensity. No one admitted it was the blacks who were hated and feared. A decade of civil rights struggles had taught even the worst of the bigots not to say "nigger" in public.

"Such facilities lower property values."

"We're not against the little children, but it will attract crime to the area."

The mothers of the Hebrew school formed a committee which appeared at the hearing at St. James the Apostle. They booed Truscott Boothby and hissed at Seymour. They made unexpected friends among the *goyim* and were invited to houses where they had never before set foot.

"We only want the best for our children—we're not racists," they said, again and again.

Newsday sent a reporter to interview the mothers as they left the meeting.

365

"Rabbis and priests have no business meddling in neighborhood affairs," said Fern Glatt, who lived several miles away. "I don't want my daughter raped coming out of Hebrew school."

"By three-year-olds?" asked the reporter.

"Somebody has to pick them up."

"Would you rather their mothers stayed on welfare?" asked the reporter.

"They never had day-care centers when I was a kid, and my mother worked just the same."

After the meeting the mothers went home and talked about the best way to keep the nigger babies from polluting the fresh country air of New Gateshead.

On the Saturday before Thanksgiving Rachel accompanied Seymour to yet another bar mitzvah. The celebrants' name was Applebaum and the reception was being held in the basement playroom of their large old house in Gateshead, not far from Sweetwater Street. To Rachel it felt like a homecoming. The Applebaums were the sort of family who did all things in a spirit of manic enthusiasm. They were former peaceniks and had tramped with Rachel to vigils and demonstrations. On the front lawn of their house stood a piece of junk sculpture. Rachel had never seen sculpture on a suburban lawn before—only birdbaths and dwarfs. The work of art was made from parts of automobiles, and had the names of all the Applebaums incised upon it.

The luncheon had been prepared at home; the family had cooked and baked for weeks. It was a vegetarian repast, redolent of exotic spices. For the bar mitzvah a ping-pong table was set up in the playroom and covered with colored lengths of crepe paper. Matching streamers hung from the ceiling. The room had little furniture, but contained an organ around which the Applebaums gathered to sing folk songs from every land. They had also transcribed Beethoven's Ninth for recorder and organ. The children's paintings covered the walls and macramé hangings dripped down between them. As a memorial to the victims of the Vietnam war a Buddhist altar had been set up in one corner. It was gaily decorated with fruits and vegetables, as though it were a *sukkah*. A poster honoring Cesar

366

Chavez and his cause hung above the fireplace. All in all, it was a memorable place.

Celeste Applebaum, the bar mitzvah's mother, appeared, smiling, at Rachel's side.

"Rachel Sonnshein! How glad I am you could come."

Rachel was holding a plate loaded with vegetarian goodies in one hand and a glass of wine in the other. The Applebaums served no hard liquor. (This and the lack of meat were certain to make Seymour glum. He was elsewhere, engaged in a conversation with a pretty lawyer for the Hospital Workers' Union.)

"The rabbi seems depressed," said Celeste Applebaum.

The Applebaums were faithful if unpredictable supporters, but they exhausted Seymour and alienated much of the rest of the congregation.

"I want you to come and meet my Aunt Eleanor," said Celeste Applebaum. "She's involved in the art world too. I told her about you, but she doesn't believe me."

Aunt Eleanor was a short woman with a mannish haircut who wore a long black skirt and a white blouse. She looked skeptically at Rachel. Celeste Applebaum remained cheerful.

"Aunt Eleanor says the only rabbi's wife she ever heard of who called herself an artist did scenes of the Holy Land in stitchery. I told her I saw nothing wrong in stitchery, but she's partial to hacked-up pieces of felt on the floor."

"Not exactly," said Aunt Eleanor. "You are a painter?" she asked Rachel, who nodded without further committing herself. "I'm director of the Museum at S.U.N.Y./North Shore. My name is Eleanor Hirschfeld."

The forthright manner in which she introduced herself struck Rachel as uncommonly sympathetic. It was rare to hear anyone, let alone a woman, announce the pertinent facts about her person with such clarity. Eleanor Hirschfeld had told Rachel exactly who she was, and would soon find out whether she was dealing with a rebbetzin who did biblical heroes in needlepoint.

367

She sized Rachel up quickly, asking her where she had studied, discovering within minutes what she knew and where her painterly empathies lay. (Eleanor Hirschfeld could talk to anyone, but if it did not involve money—a donation to her museum or the gift of a painting—she did not suffer fools gladly.) They sat down together in the corner of the basement playroom and talked about painting and painters. Eleanor Hirschfeld, with a Ph.D. from the Institute of Fine Arts at N.Y.U., specialized in Baroque painting but cultivated an interest in twentieth-century art as well. Museum work had been a blow to her scholarly aspirations, but she enjoyed the daily contact with living artists and their art.

"Does the rabbi require that you come to all these ghastly functions?"

"We never talk about it. I've just always gone to them."

"I can't *imagine* having to go to one of these every week of my life!"

"It goes with the thrill of being married to a rabbi."

"I can't imagine *that* either."

"I loved it, in the beginning. It was so outlandish. Not every girl on the block could boast of having one. But I must admit it's beginning to pall."

Seymour had finished as many vegetables as he could stomach and was talking in a corner of the basement to Marty Applebaum. Rachel sensed that he was not having a good time. She saw him look at her continually. Out of the corner of her eye Rachel saw Seymour shake hands with Marty Applebaum. Within seconds he stood beside her.

"We must go home," he said, right in the middle of one of Eleanor Hirschfeld's sentences. He was always childishly awkward when he did things he knew were rude. "I have a lot of work to do."

"I thought the Sabbath was a day of rest," said Eleanor Hirschfeld.

"Not for rabbis."

There were things Rachel had not yet dared to take up with the curator. She was enjoying the conversation, a rare one for a bar mitzvah party. Seymour

368

stood still in a stubborn pose. Rachel looked angrily straight at him but he avoided her eyes. He knew full well he never did a thing on *Shabbos* afternoon but sleep off the martinis he drank at bar mitzvahs.

"I'll be ready in a little while."

Rachel smiled at Seymour because Eleanor Hirschfeld was watching, but she tried to look sternly at him through her smile. The curator knew exactly what was going on. Rachel had to decide whether it was better to leave so as not to risk an argument (Seymour was ready for one) or to stay to prove that she would not be intimidated. She chose to stay.

"What is your work like?" Eleanor Hirshfeld asked Rachel.

This was the question Rachel had been waiting for. She tried to answer succinctly, but it seemed as though she couldn't stop.

"We *have* to go," said Seymour.

"You'd better do as the rabbi tells you," said Eleanor Hirschfeld, and Rachel disliked her, at that moment, for her mocking knowledge.

"Would you come to my studio and look at my work sometime?" Rachel asked.

"I'd love to—call me next week and we'll set a date?"

She gave Rachel her card.

Seymour stood poised for flight. He nodded curtly at Eleanor Hirschfeld.

"My wife's a very good painter."

It was his first pleasant remark within earshot of Eleanor Hirschfeld. She smiled a curator's smile, all brightness and teeth, and said, "I'm certain she is." She shook hands with Rachel and said, "We'll see each other soon."

The Sonnsheins drove home in silence. Rachel thought happily about her conversation with the curator. She was buoyed by hope and excitement, though annoyed with Seymour as well. Would he always blunder into the connections she made? She decided to ask Eleanor Hirschfeld to lunch. Could it be true that someone with taste and the power to be helpful to her was actually interested in coming to her studio?

369

Seymour appeared contrite, now that he could no longer do any damage.

"I'm sorry," he said. "I just didn't like her very much."

"She knew, but I don't think she held it against me."

"Do you think she's a lesbian?"

"Good heavens, why would you suspect her of something like that?"

"I'm not criticizing her, or questioning her competence. It was just speculation."

"The thought never crossed *my* mind at all."

"Just imagine it: a woman of a certain age—she must be close to sixty—unmarried, hostile to men."

"Hostile to *you,* perhaps."

"Do me a favor—watch out."

"For what?"

"Complications. She'll take advantage of you."

"How can she? It's me who wants something from her. She's doing *me* a favor."

"That's when you have to be careful. What will she want in return?"

"If some adoring bitch of a woman had spent the afternoon slobbering all over you, we'd still be at the party. Nothing *I* could have said would have dragged you away. Here I was, for the first time in my life, making a contact, and not only did you do your best to embarrass me, but now you're saying there's a worm in the apple."

"I'm saying no such thing. Nobody could be happier over your success than I. Just watch out for her, that's all."

Aaron was sitting in the living room when they got home. He smelled of Seymour's after-shave lotion and wore a clean shirt.

"I've got a date."

He hadn't taken out any girls since his unhappy love affair of the summer.

"We're going to the movies and then to Friendly's for a soda. Just like in *Andy Hardy.*"

"Who's the lucky girl?" asked Rachel.

"Cindy O'Neill. She's black."

370

"She's what?"

"Black. Like in 'spade.' "

There was silence for a moment.

" 'Bougie' black," said Aaron, "like in bourgeois."

"Will she convert?" asked Seymour.

"I haven't asked her to marry me yet. We'll see what happens after the movie."

"Andy Hardy goes to Harlem," said Rachel.

"Garbage on the lawn again," said Seymour.

"When they fire you we won't have to worry about any of that."

Seymour hauled off and smacked her across the face. Once, very fast. Rachel felt the sting but it hadn't hurt. It hadn't even moved her to a reaction. She had been talking like that, skimming across the top, thinking that anything went. Apparently it didn't. Aaron caught his breath. He looked at Rachel, saw that she didn't flinch, didn't cry, and let out his breath again. But he looked for a moment at Seymour with challenge.

"Don't joke about it," said Seymour.

His voice was quiet. It did not take back the slap but slid over it. The three of them turned away from each other, wanting to forget. To be alone. The telephone rang. Seymour was released. He hurried into the bedroom and closed the door. He stayed there a long time, talking softly, so he could not be heard.

"I'm leaving, Mom," said Aaron.

Rachel had not been aware of the honking car horn. "Does she have a car?"

"It's her mother's station wagon," said Aaron. "I'll be glad when I've finished drivers' ed."

"Then I'll have something else to worry about. Don't be late," she said, but it was merely the formula she used to say good-bye.

Seymour came down the steps from the upper landing. "I'm going out."

Rachel didn't ask him where he was going. She spent Saturday night alone in the house, like a cat, prowling, sniffing at things, touching them. Listening to the wind.

Three days later Rachel took her courage in hand and called Eleanor Hirschfeld to invite her to lunch.

371

"There's a nice place around the corner from my studio—we can eat there before I take you up to see my work."

Rachel was nervous and prepared everything carefully. She cleaned the studio and tore up the drawings she thought were bad, put the others in order, set the paintings in neat rows. She took twenty dollars out of the bank so she would not be watching the prices. They might even decide to have two drinks.

Eleanor Hirschfeld wore a tailored suit. Rachel felt awkward and young. She remembered Seymour's admonition. Eleanor Hirschfeld carried her eccentricities coolly. A steady, cold rain beat against the windows in windswept gusts. George had turned the lights on. Eleanor Hirschfeld told Rachel about her education, her travels. She kept away from intimate revelations but made frequent reference to the foibles of her colleagues, the weaknesses of her acquaintances. She put down the mighty and extolled the insignificant, without identifying with either. Rachel found that conversation flowed well—she had been afraid of long silences—and she managed payment of the bill admirably and without undue fumbling. She left a generous tip.

They went out into the November rain and walked quickly up the street to Rachel's studio. Eleanor Hirschfeld loped along on strong, thin old-woman's legs. She looked carefully at Rachel's paintings and drawings and collages. She was unhurried in her perusal and did not feel it necessary to make constant exclamations. She made no quick judgments either, but Rachel noticed that she was obviously relieved not to have been disappointed.

"Your collages are far more abstract than your paintings."

"I use them to work out relationships. I'll see something—a view from the window, let's say—and transform it into an abstract collage and it will tell me something new, capture some intuitive vision."

Eleanor Hirschfeld sat back in Rachel's found armchair and looked straight at her.

"I gambled on my instincts," she said. "They are,

372

as always, sound. You're very good. Why haven't you ever had a show?"

"I suppose I didn't want to take a chance. For a long time I worked like an amateur, and I didn't dare show my work to people who *know* something. I assumed I'd be rejected—the way it is when I take around petitions against war and racism."

"Part of every artist's talent must consist in taking chances. I'm certain you know that. You must also take chances in offering it to the public. To your peers. To potential buyers and sellers. If you don't mind June —a slow month—I will give you a show at our college gallery."

Rachel smiled. She felt the smile spread all over her face, move into her scalp, down to the back of her neck.

"Wow! Thanks a lot."

Her language burst apart into little rainbow showers of exclamations. She reverted to her high school self. She suddenly had no other memories of success to draw upon; it was like being chosen editor of the yearbook, captain of the regional girls' softball team. Eleanor Hirschfeld cut through all that sharply; her crisp voice spoke to the present.

"We'll have to choose the work carefully. The show should revolve about the *seder* paintings, but I think the small seascapes are good too. I don't so much care for the collages. Too much Schwitters in them."

"I'm very grateful," said Rachel. "I don't know how to thank you."

"Don't be grateful, grateful people are a bore and become obsequious, which causes their benefactors to doubt the wisdom of their choice. I know what I'm doing. I don't hand out charity."

Eleanor Hirschfeld shook hands with Rachel.

"We'll talk about it again, and I'll send you a letter of confirmation."

She put her plastic raincoat on over her suit and went back out into the rain. Rachel sat still for a few minutes but her heart was so full of joy it was ready to burst. Her inner voice kept howling "Whooppeee!" and other sounds to that effect. She did a little dance

373

on the clean floor of her studio, holding a painting for a partner. When she was breathless and her heart beat loudly in her ears, she stopped and ran downstairs and across the street to the Pleiades to call Seymour.

"What's the matter?"

"I'm having a show in June," said Rachel, and her voice broke with happiness.

"Mazel tov."

* * *

The night of the congregational meeting drew nigh; the weeks had passed quickly. The air between Rachel and Seymour remained dark and charged with misery. The smallest conflict often broke into a storm of abuse. Aaron lost weight.

Down at the synagogue, the bingo games had begun and a large sign in front of Shaare Tefilah announced them in letters painted red, white, and blue. On the mornings after bingo the Temple was littered with papers and smelled of smoke and old clothes. The money rolled in and the interior decoration was proceeding nicely. A Gay Nineties bar and imitation Tiffany lamps were being installed at the rear of the vestibule.

Seymour's secretaries were tense and argued constantly. The cantor worried about his voice, and Sheldon Greif, the Hebrew school principal, came out strongly against the day-care center. He wanted to place as much distance as possible between himself and the rabbi in case Seymour got fired. He volunteered to give a series of lectures on "The Importance of Being Jewish." Chanukah was approaching and it heralded a difficult time for the Jews of suburbia. *Christmas* was everywhere. It caroled from every shop in town and was worn in bright lights and wreaths throughout the developments. A crèche had been erected across the street from Shaare Tefilah, and Sheldon Greif had to look at it daily from the window of his office. He wanted to institute the celebration of Chanukah in the Gateshead schools while Seymour

374

lobbied to have *all* religious observances banned in public places.

The cantor, clearing his throat constantly, came to see Seymour shortly before the congregational meeting to tell him all the gossip he had heard.

"Spare me the details," said Seymour.

"I just wanted to warn you."

"I'm warned."

"Do you think they'll rehire me?" the cantor asked.

"I haven't the vaguest idea."

"Have you heard anything?"

"Nothing very much. But don't forget, a lot of people aren't talking to me. You're better off asking the principal. He hears everything and talks a lot besides."

Seymour and Rachel stayed home on the night of the congregational meeting. Seymour had asked to talk briefly on his own behalf, but the request was voted down by the Board of Trustees. It seemed a bad omen. Neither Seymour nor Rachel had a taste for dinner that evening. Aaron claimed not to be hungry. A pall hung over the house. At around eight, Sally called.

"I'm bringing over a quiche I made. You may get hungry while you're waiting. If not, I'll stop by after the meeting and we can have it then—either for the celebration or the wake."

"We call it *shiva*," said Rachel.

Sally arrived ten minutes later with the quiche, hot from the oven. It was steaming in the cold November air. Along with the quiche Sally had brought a gallon of white Italian wine.

"Go and drink, I'll be back later. I promise to do my best with the one vote I have. I may even open up my big mouth and say my piece."

Rachel watched her drive out of the driveway and head down to the *shul*. A stream of headlights wavered along the road to the parking lot.

"It's the biggest crowd since Kol Nidre," said Seymour. "That means my enemies are out in full force."

Rachel felt she ought to disagree but she could not. Her own heart was wrapped in apprehension. Too

375

many of the people she saw on Main Street had lately been unable to meet her eye. If they had been giving away bumper stickers, most of them, she was afraid, would say *Better Dead Than Sonnshein* or some such thing.

Rachel felt profoundly discouraged. More than likely, the people streaming to the synagogue had come to do Seymour in. They were angry and frustrated. Life had not delivered all the good things they had hoped for. They were not particularly happy in Gateshead; the suburbs had not brought them peace of mind. Money ran through their fingers like sand. All they could do to show their frustration and anger was to vote down school budgets and can the rabbi. Many of them were resentful thinking that Seymour and Rachel moved through the community at their own pace, calmly, absorbed in each other, independent. Rachel didn't seem to mind not having a fur coat, or being unable to spend a winter holiday in the Bahamas. Seymour was an employee, dependent on them for his livelihood, but he didn't show it. He didn't flatter them, and he let his wife run down Main Street with paint on her jeans. They weren't eager to join their congregants at their pleasures; they didn't seem to need marriage encounters. As a result, it was suspected that they led weird and exotic secret lives, but no one had ever caught them at it.

"They'll surely fire him," thought Rachel. "He doesn't share their concerns—he never did. The message he tried to bring them fell on deaf ears: Learning and study, a life of the spirit, social justice—it means nothing to them. He's failed."

"You may squeak by with a few votes," Rachel told Seymour, but her voice carried no conviction. "Maybe the opposition will go too far. That sometimes happens, you know. A reaction sets in."

"Stop talking," said Seymour. "I can't stand listening to your prattle."

Rachel fixed herself a Bloody Mary. Seymour took a Scotch. They stood beside each other, looking out at the Temple building.

"It's not the way it was when we came here," he

376

said. "The congregation, the town, everything's changed. I don't think *we* have changed. I don't think I've stopped being a good rabbi. I'd hoped to build a special kind of community but it didn't work."

Rachel put her arm around his shoulder but he stayed coiled and tense and she took it down.

"I suppose it needs a small congregation to realize *my* kind of Jewish community, but a small congregation is no longer viable. Or so they tell me. A small congregation can't pay its mortgage, can't hire a cantor, teachers, a principal. It's the litany you hear all over. So you opt for a big one and what happens? It never has enough money to pay for all those things either. It needs yet a bigger building, more staff. And you end up with bingo and a catering establishment."

The Temple was brightly lit. The parking lot, crowded with cars, was still and dark. A northwesterly wind had started up, blowing across the bleak space between their house and the synagogue. Rachel noticed that there was a draft around the windows; it stirred the curtains. The telephone rang, startling both Rachel and Seymour.

"I'll get it," he said.

"Could it be someone with the vote?" asked Rachel.

It was not quite nine o'clock. The caller was Betty Diamant.

"I'll let you talk to Rachel," said Seymour.

Rachel didn't very much feel like talking to her mother.

"I hear they're voting on Seymour's contract tonight. You didn't tell me."

"How did you find out?"

"Mothers find out everything. You remember Ellie Ignatow? She's got a cousin in Gateshead. Not in your congregation, but she has her ear to the ground, she hears all the news."

Rachel mumbled sounds.

"Speak up," said Betty Diamant. "What's the matter with you? Can't you talk? Is Seymour nearby?"

"Yes. No, I can't."

"He should never have become a rabbi. All those

377

years he spent in school he could have gone into teaching, become a professor. He'd have tenure by now. Neither of you would have to go through all this."

"How's Daddy?"

"Fine."

"And everybody else?"

"Fine too. Except your mother-in-law, who's still complaining and looks like death warmed over. Don't tell Seymour."

"I have to keep the phone free. I'll call you tomorrow."

Rachel hung up.

"What did she want?" asked Seymour.

"She called to wish you good luck."

"It'll be all over Buffalo tomorrow."

"It already is."

Seymour turned on the television set and switched it from channel to channel. He could find nothing he wanted to watch but left the box turned on to an old movie, without the sound. The black-and-white shimmering screen gave out an illusion of activity, of something happening. Rachel picked up a copy of *The New Yorker* and leafed through it. She couldn't read.

The telephone rang again. Rachel shivered. It was ten-thirty. All the cars were still silently parked in the lot. Seymour reached the kitchen phone at the second ring. His answers—as far as Rachel could make them out—were monosyllabic. "Yes," "No," and grunts. He hung up on a resigned "O.k."

"What happened?"

"Cy Glatt wanted to know if I was willing to reverse my stand and come out against the day-care center. He asked me to 'compromise.' They're going to take the vote shortly."

"Those bastards! Oh, Seymour—why don't you just quit. Resign! Go somewhere else."

"It's no different anywhere else. Jews put the same bastards in charge of every congregation in the world."

"Some rabbis seem able to handle it. How in God's name do they do it?"

"Show me *one* who hasn't gone through this. You've heard them bitch at their get-togethers. But they're like

378

everyone else, they forget about the bad times once they're over. They block out the memory of these evenings from one contract to the next. And besides, every rabbi thinks he'll do better next time. Next time he'll know how to handle it, or next time the congregation will be nicer. And really, what else can he do? What's he fitted for but to be a rabbi? He can't turn around and become a shoemaker. He can't even count on his wife to support him. Back in the *shtetl* he could sit in the *Beth Midrash* and study Torah, while his wife ran the store or sold fish in the marketplace."

"I'd love to be able to support you," said Rachel. Her voice was a whisper. "If only I could! Maybe one day. Then you can quit for good."

"It's kind of sad, you know, the whole thing. And it isn't entirely the fault of the Jews. It's America—the American Way of Life: Bigger is better. Conglomerate! The *successful* rabbis are the ones who run a large congregation as if they had trained to be captains of industry. Entrepreneurs! They don't tell you that at the Seminary. They *know* it, but they won't tell you. They teach you a lot of Talmud and the names of all the kings of Israel, and send you out into the Jewish community with a Master of Hebrew Literature and a pat on the back."

"Do you want to stay here even if the vote goes your way?"

"I no longer give a damn. I don't know what I want, except that I want the waiting to end."

At a quarter to twelve the telephone rang. It didn't seem to startle Seymour. Even before he answered, Rachel knew it was the *real* call. Seymour knew it too. Lights were springing up all over the parking lot, the sound of motors being revved could be heard in the clear winter air.

"Yes," said Seymour.

There was a tiny silence.

"What was the vote?"

Rachel's heart sank. (Later she remembered that it had seemed to do that, literally. Had collapsed in her chest where it had beaten loudly, and fallen to her stomach, where it sat, like a silent stone.)

"Thanks for calling," said Seymour. And hung up. "I lost."

There were no tears in his eyes but his voice quivered slightly, like the voice of a young boy. Rachel went to embrace him, but he would not allow himself to be embraced.

"One hundred ninety-two against me, one hundred sixty-five for me."

"That's a lot of votes."

"Don't rub it in."

"I meant altogether. They had a big turnout."

Nothing she could say was right, thought Rachel. Words were useless. Not even affection seemed to help. A whopping rejection like that cuts deeply into the heart. Seymour stood in the center of the living room, looking toward the windows. The parking lot was fully alive now. You could feel its presence even with the curtains drawn. A few shrill voices rose above the coughing, gunning motors. Rachel thought she heard joy and exultation ring through them. She wanted to run out the kitchen door, across the grass and the stubble and the hard winter ground and wreak vengeance. Beat in the headlights of the cars, smash the fenders, break every window in the place, frighten the bastards out of their wits. The fantasies raced through her head like a brush fire, crackling, leaping, burning with anger and hatred.

Sally came into the house without ringing the doorbell. She walked up the flight of stairs into the living room. Rachel knew she had hoped to come running, clapping and shouting in joy. She was alone and very quiet.

"I'm sorry," she said, "truly sorry, Seymour."

She sounded as if she had come to pay a condolence call.

"It was terrible!" she said, and all at once she was crying.

Aaron had come out of his room and was standing on the second floor landing, big-eyed and silent. The four of them stood locked in place, like actors in a drama. The thought crossed Rachel's mind that the

380

sound of the cherry trees being felled in the orchard ought to come from offstage—but it was honking horns she heard, and car tires squealing on the frozen earth.

"What awful people," said Sally, swallowing her tears. "What miserable shits."

The telephone finally released them. Loosed them from their poses. Seymour went to answer it. His voice on the phone was low. Rachel assumed it was Natalie Gould at the other end.

Sally had wiped the tears from her face and taken off her coat. Aaron had slipped down the stairs on his stockinged feet.

"I hope I never have to listen to such crap again," said Sally. "I'm sending in my resignation in the morning."

"Natalie and Charlie want to stop by for a minute," Seymour called out.

"Hell no!" cried Rachel. "I'm in no mood for the Goulds. Tell them we don't need any sympathy. Tell them we don't want their crumbs, tell them . . ."

"O.k., o.k., calm down," said Seymour.

". . . no more Lady Bountiful descending into the slums with alms and sweet words for the needy. . . ."

"Shut up!" said Seymour.

"Tell them I'll bomb the place tomorrow. I'll bust every pane of glass and pop every light bulb."

"You're acting crazy," said Seymour, when he came back into the room, but he spoke without rancor, gently, as he might if she were mad indeed. Relief was beginning to dawn upon his pale, drawn face.

"You've been fired," said Rachel. "I don't have to put up with the Natalie Goulds of this world anymore."

"She's not so bad," said Seymour. "She's been a real friend."

Sally had gone to fetch the quiche and the wine from the kitchen.

Rachel suddenly felt very hungry.

"I'm starved."

"Me too," said Seymour.

"Will I be able to go to college?" asked Aaron.

"Of course, stupid," said Rachel.

381

The telephone rang again. It was Millie Fertig this time. Seymour had to comfort her. His voice was resigned.

"It's not the end of the world," he told his secretary "You'll like the new rabbi, too."

"Where will we get the money from?" Aaron asked.

"Dad will get a settlement, I'm sure, and there'll be another job. Don't worry. You'll finish high school here, we don't have to leave before summer. Please don't worry, baby."

"Do I have to go to school tomorrow?"

"Of course."

"All the kids will know."

"Only the Jewish kids—maybe. And what do you care? Make up one of your movie scenarios for them, and remember: most people don't care about your troubles. If it were a *scandal* it would be another thing. Trouble is just embarrassing, that's all."

"I'll tell them we're *glad*. I'll tell them we always wanted to leave."

No sooner had Seymour hung up than the phone rang again.

"I'm waiting for the first obscene phone call," Rachel told Sally. "Boy, will I give them an earful!"

"You're really angry," said Sally.

"It's just finally coming out."

Seymour sounded weary on the telephone but he was very polite.

"That was Jody Goldstein," he said when he returned. "They're new members, a nice couple. They're resigning, too."

The quiche was very good.

"It has bacon in it," said Seymour.

"Do you mind?" asked Sally.

"I only commented on it. I'm free to eat all the bacon I want, now that I've been fired. Tell us what happened."

"Can you stand to hear it?"

"I'm drinking lots of wine."

"The people who spoke *for* you were very good, some of them gave moving speeches. But they just

382

couldn't prevail against all the venom, and the self-righteous accusations. . . ."

"But what did they *say*?"

"They said nothing of substance. They simply spewed out complaints. The stuff they brought up was absolutely ludicrous, it had almost nothing to do with the *real* question which, I thought, was whether or not you were a competent rabbi who fulfilled his obligations to the congregation."

Rachel sighed.

"They complained you didn't come to the *minyan*. One lady got up and said she was shocked to tears when you drove up to her house on *Shabbos*. She said you could have left the car around the corner."

"What about the day-care center?"

"That was the only *issue* that was raised. I couldn't have believed—if I hadn't seen it with my own eyes —that a bunch of reasonably well-educated middle-class people could rise to such passion over a day-care center!"

"Little black toddlers playing within sight of their virgin daughters . . ." said Rachel.

"They raved on and on about how Seymour had made the *goyim* in this neighborhood anti-Semitic and how he believes in brotherhood but only with *shvartses,* not with his own flesh and blood: the Jews of Russia. They said you praised Arafat and criticized Kissinger."

"Who defended him?"

"Oh, you know, the nicer sort of people. The ones who don't have axes to grind, the good-hearted ones, the 'liberals.' But the trouble with them is that they don't understand what motivates the others, they aren't themselves *driven*. They're no match for the fanatics. They gave their little speeches, saying that they thought Seymour had been a good rabbi, a force for peace and friendship in the community. They praised him for speaking out on important issues, said the Jews of Gateshead ought to be proud to be represented by such a man. None of that has the force of hostility, of course, and it's no match against crude

383

gossip. The barber said something about Seymour and a Hebrew school teacher coming out of a motel on Jericho Turnpike—but the chairman ruled him out of order on that one."

"How about the officers?" Seymour asked. "Cy Glatt?"

"The officers said they had decided to endorse you, but it came out as a half-assed recommendation. Cy Glatt said that, as president, he ought to remain neutral. He said he'd had his differences with you over the years, especially about bingo, which has proven to be such a financial success. He said that you came back from your summer vacation for Michelle Shulman Halprin's mother's funeral. He *tried* to be fair. But Wasserman, the bastard, he blasted you. Said you were the best thing ever to happen to the niggers of Gateshead and suggested they elect you rabbi of the A.M.E. Church. Then you could stuff your face with some of their *chazzer* chitlings."

"Did they mention me?" asked Rachel.

"Lord, yes," said Sally. "They dragged you in by your bare feet. Told how you came into the sanctuary without shoes on. They said you didn't know how to dress, and that you weren't interested in the Sisterhood or Hadassah. That you didn't relate to the women of the congregation. That you hang out in bars."

"She does, indeed," said Seymour.

"We had such hopes," said Sally, with resignation. "When Seymour first came to Gateshead, a lot of us thought the Temple would become a place we could be proud of. A place where learning was stressed, where we could come for Jewish culture, for the best of the Jewish tradition. We thought our kids might learn more than a bunch of prayers by rote for their bar mitzvahs. We didn't think they'd want to turn it into a bingo parlor."

They were exhausted. Seymour yawned. Aaron had fallen asleep with his head thrown back against the cushion of the armchair. Rachel cleared the dishes from the table. Sally kissed her and went home. It was all over.

384

12

Rachel awoke on the morning after the congregational meeting and had no idea where she was. On the edge of waking, she remembered that something terrible had happened but didn't know exactly what it was. She opened her eyes, saw the room and remembered. Seymour had been fired. That was it. There was nothing else, or was there? Desertion? Death? Cancer? No. Only that Seymour had been fired. It suddenly seemed to announce itself from all the corners of the room. Clothes were strewn everywhere, last Sunday's papers still lay about, the dressers were piled high with letters and books and the contents of Seymour's pockets and her handbags. She closed her eyes again but could not go back to sleep. Her anxiety was too strong, she could not escape it; it was like a terrible pain. She wondered if she were dying.

"Not now," she thought, "not now. I'm going to have a show in June. I want to live."

She drew the warm covers about her. Seymour was still asleep. He muttered words in a strange tongue, tossed and turned, became entangled in his sheets as though struggling against a shroud. Rachel looked at the clock. It was close to ten. Aaron must have left long ago. The phone had been still; they were abandoned by the world. Rachel noticed the water stains beneath the windows where a driving rain had entered. She saw the ineradicable spots on the wallpaper, ink stains on the floor. The place was a slum. Thank God they were leaving.

Rachel bolted out of bed and found her slippers and warm robe. It was cold in the house, the curtains hung like rags in front of the windows. When she passed Aaron's door, Rachel looked in and saw that he was still asleep.

"Aaron? You have to get up. It's almost ten o'clock. You're late for school."

"I'm not going," he answered, and Rachel realized that he was not as deeply asleep as he made out.

"O.k., then," she said, and went down to make breakfast.

Seymour came into the kitchen looking ghastly.

"What shall we do today?" asked Rachel, trying hard to be cheerful.

"How is this day different from any other?"

"I thought I'd stay home with you, if you wanted me to."

"Don't trouble yourself. I've got a lot to do. First I'm going to see a lawyer. Then I think I'll go into the city."

"Would you like me to come along?"

"No. I want to be alone. I'm going to do what you always do—escape from Gateshead."

Aaron stayed in bed and read *Paradise Lost*.

"Do I have to answer the telephone, Mom?" he asked, as Rachel prepared to go out.

"Just let it ring today. Why don't you come down and we'll have lunch together at Solti's?"

"I may just do that," said Aaron.

Rachel's studio was chilly. She tried to work and to avoid thinking about the congregation, but her thoughts kept turning to the outcome of last night's meeting. Her anxiety left her when she took a Valium, but her chagrin hardened into anger. She thought about revenge. She devised plots, warfare, plans of attack. She imagined herself picketing in front of the synagogue. She thought of hurling a bottle of Manischevitz through the Temple window, but ended up seeing herself led away by police, looking wild and crazy. It would be in the news: "Rabbi's Wife Desecrates Temple That Fired Him." Perhaps she could

386

paint a slogan on the ugly blank wall? Defile the kitchen with pig's blood? Such fantasies left her exhausted and cleansed of her anger. She began to think that the worst was over.

Aaron came by for lunch. Rachel did not return to her studio that afternoon, but took him to the Big Mall and bought him a down-filled parka. It was the time of year when the streetlights go on at four o'clock. Seymour came home very late.

The next day, Rachel went to the best *treif* butcher in Gateshead and bought a sirloin steak. She came home early and broiled it with lots of onions. She made french fries. For dessert she baked a chocolate soufflé and served it with mounds of whipped cream.

"Call Golda Garfinkle," said Seymour. "She's already called you three times."

"Do you think she voted for or against you?" It was impossible for her to think of any congregant except on those terms.

"Probably against me," said Seymour, who had wondered the same thing.

Rachel called Golda.

"I'm sorry about the vote," said Golda. "I voted for Seymour. Morris didn't, but I did. He made a lot of enemies, your husband did, but I'm not one of them. I disagree with him a lot of the time, but I think he's honest. We need more honest people. Morris has a small mind. He likes to run people down; he talks too much."

Rachel said nothing. Golda's clear, purposeful voice excited her. It was as if Golda had all at once penetrated the wall of silliness which had grown up around her and imprisoned her.

"This is probably the last time I'll ever call you with this kind of a request, but I think it's important you honor it. I want you to be on a panel at the December Sisterhood meeting. You owe me one, remember? And it would be nice if you didn't leave us on a note of bitterness."

"I'm not bitter," said Rachel, "just mad. What's the panel about?"

387

"We're planning a literary discussion, 'The Writer Looks at the Jew.' Mainly, we'll deal with Philip Roth. The other two women I've asked to be on the panel take a rather jaundiced view of his work. You can be his defender. Didn't you once tell me he's your favorite writer?"

"He's not my *favorite* writer, but I think he's terrific at describing the Jewish scene as *we* know it."

"And mean as hell."

"All satirists have a mean streak. And 'Eli the Fanatic' is still one of the best, one of the truest, stories about suburbia I've ever read."

"I'm sure you'll have a lot to say, Rachel. I look forward to it. It's a funny thing, but I'll miss you when you're gone—even if you sometimes disappointed me and didn't show up at meetings and kept yourself aloof. I know you don't care for me very much but I've always been rather fond of you. People like me just don't make the slightest impression on you. They didn't at Barnard, they don't here. I'm not saying I blame you, but still, it's been painful to me that you didn't see me."

Golda hung up rather abruptly, afraid and ashamed of what she had finally had the courage to say. Rachel was mortified. Through all of Golda's brittle conversations, this vein of longing had run and she had not realized it.

The Sisterhood meeting was on the first Tuesday in December. Rachel had decided to make Philip Roth's stories the battleground on which she would meet suburbia. She would let him speak for her, use his words as her weapon. She was delighted with the assignment and studied his texts with the care she had, twenty years before, expended on her college papers. Copying passages out of *Goodbye, Columbus,* she decided to make her swan song to Gateshead a raucous one.

The night of the Sisterhood meeting was bitter cold and clear. Rachel wore one of her more outlandish outfits—a long tunic of brilliantly colored cloth over a pair of buckskin pants. She had found that her fantasies of violence and revenge were turning into fan-

388

tasies of fame and renown. What better way to thumb her nose at Gateshead, she thought, than to return in glory? It would be the sweetest victory. It had been the dream of many artists (indeed many revolutionaries) to parade through the streets of persnickety hometowns and petit-bourgeois neighborhoods in just such a victory. Sometimes, in the grip of these dreams, Rachel thought it appalling to want to become a great painter for such petty reasons. But she knew full well that the roots of ambition are hidden and deep, and that the compulsion to work long years in pursuit of some inner vision must be fueled by stubborn fires.

Rachel approached the Temple with trepidation. On the threshold of her bravely imagined confrontation, she felt doubt and fear. The building seemed to her a fortress, her means to conquer it slender. She imagined another response to her, years hence: "She may be a famous painter now, but she was a lousy rebbetzin then."

There was quite a crowd at the synagogue for this Sisterhood meeting. Because it was almost Chanukah, the ladies had set up a book fair in the lobby. Everyone was buying gifts. Rachel was suddenly moved by the abiding Jewish love for books, so obvious even here in this cement block factory of a suburban synagogue. Truscott Boothby, for all his right thinking, his courage, and his social conscience, would never think to institute anything resembling a literary discussion group at St. James the Apostle. The closest his parishioners ever came to a public confrontation with literature was when the Citizens' Committee for Decency Under God raided the shelves of local libraries for books they thought awakened prurient interests.

Touched to the quick and feeling chastised, Rachel decided to squelch her hostility and to enter the lists smiling. She sat through the brief meeting, trying to read her notes.

Golda Garfinkle introduced the panel. There was Rachel, "who needs no introduction," Doris Weingarten, "a member of the Reform Congregation, who was born in Hungary and came to the U.S.A. in 1947. She is the mother of three children and a writer. Her

389

work has been published in *Reader's Digest, Parade,* and *Parents' Magazine.*" And last, but not least, Sondra Spiess, "whom we are pleased to welcome. She is a recent arrival to New Gateshead and already teaches an adult education course at the high school entitled, 'The Female in Literature: Victim, Genius, and Priestess.' Ms. Spiess is divorced and the mother of a little girl."

"The *proud* mother of a little girl," amended Sondra Spiess, "who hopes she'll never fall into the clutches of the likes of Philip Roth."

There was an appreciative chuckle from those who heard her.

Rachel studied the two women while Golda read their biographies. Sondra Spiess looked like what might once have been called a *zaftig* girl—smart but probably a little nutty. She seemed to be about thirty. If she had been Rachel's age she might have been a strident leftist; now she was a shrill feminist.

Doris Weingarten was chic and slender. Rachel calculated that she was in her early fifties. If she had come to America from Hungary in 1947 she must be a survivor of the Holocaust. "Oh, Lord," thought Rachel. It was almost impossible to go up against survivors in a discussion—it didn't matter what the subject was. Rachel peeked at Doris Weingarten's arm to see if there were numbers, but Doris Weingarten wore a long-sleeved cardigan over her frilly dress. Rachel gathered her notes in a neat pile and hoped she wouldn't have to go first.

"Our own rebbetzin will start the panel off," said Golda Garfinkle.

Once Rachel began to speak she lost her uncertainties; she was in complete control. She barely looked at her notes. The sentences came together clearly and logically as she spoke them. She did not begin by defending Philip Roth; she pretended that he needed no defense. He was a writer who fit into the American tradition—she made that plain—a Jewish writer who had (like most of his generation) read Kafka and understood something about his haunted Jewishness. The audience was attentive.

390

Rachel concentrated on "Eli the Fanatic," which seemed to her a peerless example of Jewish pain and insecurity in suburbia. Rachel told her listeners that there was a little bit of the *kike* (gasps from the audience here) in every American Jew—and that each was ashamed of that as well as proud and afraid.

"We are ashamed of the bearded *chassid* in his odd clothes, for he reminds us of our past. We are proud because he reminds us how far back our heritage goes, but the pride is tinged with fear. We know that his brothers—*our* brothers—died because of that heritage. We're ambivalent. We tell ourselves, out here in the land of the *goyim,* that we may be Jews but we're Americans first. We want to push the stigma of our Jewishness out of sight."

It was going well. The audience was still, having survived its horror at her use of the work *kike.* Rachel made certain to say "we" whenever she meant "you." It was something she had learned from Seymour. He did it in his sermons all the time, even when he obviously didn't mean it.

"Philip Roth's ear is absolutely perfect," said Rachel.

She warmed to her subject; she was feeling good.

"If we're truly honest with ourselves, we must recognize the sound of our own voices. It doesn't make any difference whether we came from Brooklyn or Buffalo or Beaver Falls. A hundred tomes of sociological studies will not tell us what a single simple story does."

Golda Garfinkle indicated that Rachel's time was up.

"Let me just add this one thought—Roth has discovered his connection, and by extension, ours, to the terrifying modern world of Kafka. Kafka is our *chassid.* A central European, a German-speaking Jew from Prague, an artist, a genius, he looks at the world and he sees the concentration camps. Though he died of TB at the age of forty-one in 1924, he had seen the horror, he knew, he knew...."

Golda Garfinkle, looking at her watch, stood up. Rachel sat down out of breath and deaf with the pounding of her heart. There was a rain spatter of applause.

391

"Thank you, Rachel," said Golda Garfinkle, and nodded to Sondra Spiess to proceed.

"In her entire and lengthy presentation Ms. Sonnshein did not once mention women. How can you talk about Philip Roth and not mention women? We have become so brainwashed that we are able to deny the evidence before our eyes. We block out the whole of our history. We allow Philip Roth to kick us when we're down—which is where he wants us, you better believe it—and come up talking about Kafka! What about Mrs. Kafka?"

"There was no Mrs. Kafka," murmured Rachel, "only his mother. That was part of the problem."

"Does Ms. Sonnshein not for a minute, not for a tiny minute, feel the agony of Brenda Patimkin? If it seemed so real to her why didn't she cry for that poor, exploited girl? Brenda Patimkin is the callously portrayed victim—the paradigmatic victim—of the Jewish male's narcissism."

There was some loud applause from the back of the room.

"The Jewish Princess is a figment of the self-hating Jewish narcissist's imagination. Mothers and daughters are blamed for the male's impotence. The *shikse* becomes a sex object. No one escapes. No one who shares our bodies and our vulnerability."

Rachel's heart beat slower now. She was recovering from the excitement of her performance. She did not listen very closely to Sondra Spiess. She knew what was coming. If she was apprehensive about anything it was Doris Weingarten, who looked annoyed now and was busily writing a response to Rachel into her typewritten notes.

"We laugh at the jokes and the banter," Sondra Spiess was saying, "and through it all we forget the suffering of Roth's women. We think it's all a big joke—in truth, it is a great tragedy. When I agreed to come here tonight I had hoped we might talk about Jewish women as authors. I find you talking about Roth and Kafka instead. When will you learn who the truly oppressed really are?"

The audience grew a little restless. They didn't really

care about Philip Roth's misogyny. What they cared about—desperately—was his contempt for the Jewish middle class. They called it "anti-Semitism." They knew that this word was powerful enough to foil his accusations of complacent materialism and vulgarity.

Sondra Spiess got very little applause when she sat down.

Doris Weingarten rose and looked around. She put all her notes away. She spoke fluently in accented English, and it had the effect of bringing her words like gifts from a remote authority. She, a foreigner, was so privileged to be here, grateful for the opportunity to share her views with the good ladies of Shaare Tefilah. Doris Weingarten spoke for a vanished Europe. Did anyone there, including Rachel, know its story better than she did? She talked about the camps, but in an offhand way, like a storyteller who knows exactly what effect she wishes to achieve at every point in her tale. The audience was captivated. Doris Weingarten said that she was often reminded of prewar Europe these days in America. Then, quite without warning, she began her attack.

"This writer you talk about, this Philip Roth, we know all about his kind in Europe. He is the Jew who oils the propaganda wheels which turn against us. He is the tool of the anti-Semites. . . ."

She paused to take a sip of water.

"Americans are naïve—you are a trusting people. Believe me, do not trust such men who wash your linen in the marketplace. There was a writer in Europe, in Vienna, whose name was Joseph Roth—perhaps he was related—who wrote such books, such trash, full of nasty Jewish characters. They burned his books. Of course, the Nazis burned *all* Jewish books, but first they learned from him that what they preached was true, the Jews thought so themselves!"

Doris Weingarten sat down to prolonged applause.

Rachel's heart beat furiously. She wanted to respond, but Golda Garfinkle asked for questions from the floor. The first hand raised belonged to Fay Fertig.

"I think Mrs. Weingarten is a brave woman and deserves our gratitude. My question is 'What can *we*

393

do against these sick writers? I want to know how we decent people can be heard?' "

"A good question," said Doris Weingarten. "Thank you. I have a suggestion for you and it is quite simple. Do not buy the books. That is all. If nobody buys the books, soon they won't be printed."

"It seems to me," said Rachel, before Golda had a chance to call on the next questioner, "it seems to me that it says somewhere that the truth shall set you free, though that may be a *goyishe* quote. In any case, I think that Roth portrays us very accurately, alas, and we ought to be more concerned with understanding ourselves than in silencing him."

"If you had seen the death camps," said Doris Weingarten, stopping Rachel in her tracks, "you would not talk like that, Rebbetzin. Jewish writers in the present time *must* keep in mind the Holocaust. It is as Elie Wiesel says."

"Not *all* Jewish writers can do that," said Rachel, "especially if they are Americans. Artists must work out of their own vision and memory . . ."

"Art is not therapy, my dear."

"I said work out *of*, not work out . . ."

"Women *must* work out their problems in their art," said Sondra Spiess. "I agree with you there completely. But it is men who have access to publishers, men who are editors, who make the choices. Women have to fight this, they have a responsibility to the movement."

"But that's politicizing art!" cried Rachel. "One of you suggests we censor writers, the other one says women must follow a party line. That's outrageous."

Golda Garfinkle, trying to maintain civility, recognized a woman whose hand had been waving throughout this exchange of views. She stood up and cleared her throat.

"Excuse me, I want to ask the rebbetzin something. Rebbetzin, what I want to know is why does a Jewish writer have to use so much filth? *Portnoy's Complaint* is terrible. Can't Philip Roth say what he wants to say without the dirty words?"

394

"To tell you the truth, I didn't so much care for some of the writing in *Portnoy's Complaint* either," Rachel answered. "It got boring. But I think it's very funny, just the same. I laughed at it the way I laugh at Jewish jokes—with pleasure, recognition, and a certain amount of masochism. We're a minority in a hostile world, we can't change that, but we can laugh. Jews have always done that."

Rachel spoke slowly. She wanted the woman to understand her but she was also making the answer up as she went along. It had not been in her notes.

"As for the obscenity—what you call filth—I really think there's a lot more obscenity going on in this country today than the few dirty words that are in this book. Do you really think," she said, her voice rising, "that it is obscene to say 'fuck,' but not obscene to let children be chewed up by rats and people get poisoned by industrial wastes? Wasn't it obscene to napalm innocent mothers and babies?"

The word "fuck" certainly had its effect. Having said it Rachel had meant to go on, but she was drowned out by the rising babble of exclamations and whispered comments. She lost track of her thoughts. Doris Weingarten looked disdainfully at Rachel. Sondra Spiess said "Whew" in disbelief. Golda Garfinkle sat like a statue.

"You sound like a fishmonger," said Doris Weingarten. "What a way for a rebbetzin to talk! Shame on you!"

"All I said was 'fuck,'" said Rachel, "to indicate that there are worse things in the world . . ."

"We've gotten away from Philip Roth," Golda Garfinkle, having come back to life, interrupted sternly. "Interesting as this discussion may be, it is not the point of our literary investigation. I suggest we have a brief and final word from our panelists now, and continue our discussion over coffee and cake. Sondra, would you begin?"

Sondra Spiess was not pleased with the way the discussion had proceeded.

"More attention should be paid to sexual stereotypes

395

in American fiction—Philip Roth's books are one long ode to male supremacy."

She sat down abruptly. Her friends in the back of the room applauded.

Rachel decided to return to that part of her paper which she had been forced to leave out earlier.

"I want to close with the plea that Roth be judged as an artist. The question we ask should be: Is he a good writer or a bad one? If he is good we can begin to discuss his vision—regardless of our feelings; if he is bad he'll be forgotten soon enough."

"Who decides?" came a cry from the audience.

"Let his peers decide," said Rachel, "and history."

"And what about *us?*"

"The more we know, the more we learn and read, the better we can judge. All I'm asking for is *informed* judgment."

Doris Weingarten rose to sum up.

"You had a poet—I forget his name. He was an anti-Semite, but, so they said, a great poet. He made broadcasts in the war, he said to kill the Jews . . ."

"Ezra Pound," said Rachel.

"I see you know his name," said Doris Weingarten. "You had a college education. You spent the happy years of your youth at school. You did not learn about life in the death camps. You learned at the university."

Rachel blushed, as she was meant to, and looked away.

"Yes," said Doris Weingarten, "it was different for me. I spent my youth at Theresienstadt. You have heard of Theresienstadt, Rebbetzin? Do not tell me to judge your poets by their pretty rhymes. Those pretty rhymes sent my family to their deaths."

"Pound's case is extreme," mumbled Rachel. "I don't defend Pound."

"Philip Roth's self-hatred is also extreme."

Doris Weingarten spoke directly to Rachel and then she turned back to her audience.

"I leave it to you to decide. You are Jews, all of you. You have a Jewish conscience. You know, I think, that the life of a single Jew is worth more than

396

all the great books and beautiful paintings created by man. Jews must pay attention to the persecution of *Jews.* Forget about the others. Why should we care about them?"

Rachel leaned forward, her face burning now, her heart shouting.

"I tell you why we should care," she said, not in a loud voice but in a voice choked with passion. "We should care because our tradition tells us to care. The most moving, most touching, most glorious thing about the Jews has always been that we *cared* so desperately. We showed concern for victims of persecution everywhere, we wanted to do away with exploitation and injustice, and we never asked the question whether it was worth the death of *one* innocent to save the world. We knew it was a foolish question. We knew you had to fight for right and justice for everyone before you could truly have it for yourself. If there's one single reason to keep the Jews alive, it's for the compassion we feel for suffering."

Rachel was quite beside herself. A decade's worth of anger poured out of the small tear that had opened in her heart.

"Jews are supposed to remember what it was like to be slaves in Egypt. It says so, right there in the Bible. And I believe it, I really do. If *we* don't bear witness to these eternal words, who will? *We*'re supposed to be 'a light unto the nations'—if *we* don't 'proclaim liberty throughout the land,' what would be the point of our remaining Jews? We might just as well all go and convert. It was Emma Lazarus, a *Jewish woman,* who wrote the poem engraved on the Statue of Liberty. I say we're here to remind America what those words *mean.* We're not here to be like everyone else, we're not here to worry about *appearances,* about what the *goy* next door thinks. The Holocaust was a terrible thing . . ."

Rachel summoned the courage to look straight at Doris Weingarten as she said this.

". . . it has traumatized every Jew alive today. It has become the reason we want to insulate ourselves

397

against the world. We surround ourselves with luxuries, we say we no longer care about others, and all because we can't forget the Holocaust. But it is my contention that we must remember the Holocaust just as we remember our slavery in Egypt: *not* for the sake of revenge, but for the sake of compassion—what the Jews call *rachmones*. I hope and pray that we will never forget our role as 'compassionate ones'—that even though Hitler brought death to six million, he didn't bring death too, to *our* hearts and *our* spirit. . . ."

Rachel stopped. She felt relief, she felt an unnatural high, she had cleared all the rage from her soul.

The audience was silent. A flutter of sighs danced through the air. There was scattered, embarrassed applause. Golda Garfinkle rose slowly to her feet. She looked slightly shaken.

"Thank you," she said. "Thank you, Rachel . . . thank you, everyone, for a very stimulating evening."

Coffee and cake were served. Golda Garfinkle came over to Rachel, who was gathering her papers together.

"You were wonderful, so full of passion!"

She looked genuinely moved.

Sally came forward just then, beaming.

"Your friend was great," Golda said. "Too bad that most of her speech probably went over everyone's head."

"*I've* always known about Rachel's gifts," said Sally.

At that moment an excited personage appeared. It was Katherine Penfield.

"I had to come to hear you—my dear, you were magnificent! But you should be ashamed of yourself." She giggled a little. "I know you waited a long time . . ." she paused, dramatically, "but you finally did it!"

"What's that?" asked Rachel.

"You got up in front of the entire Sisterhood and you said *fuck* to them."

Rachel, tired and talked out, felt herself collapse inside, growing relaxed and soft and oblivious. It was her fate, she thought, to be misunderstood in Gateshead, even by those who wished her well.

398

The December days were growing shorter and it rained for almost a week, driving daylight into ever longer nights. The cold rain beat on the roofs and whipped against the windows.

Seymour had begun to return to life, as it were. Freed from the need to lobby on his own behalf, he worked diligently to make his last six months at Shaare Tefilah exemplary. Some of his detractors even had second thoughts about him. Seymour had become quite friendly since they had "liberated" him. Fay Fertig said he was a new man. "He's well rid of the lot of you," said Millie. Seymour spent one day a week in the city, exploring opportunities for a different kind of job. He hoped that something might turn up at one of the many Jewish agencies and philanthropies.

Aaron was filling out his college applications. He wanted to go to Columbia, but had decided—on the advice of his advisor—to try a few other colleges as well.

Rachel, too, felt liberated now, as though she had already said "good-bye" to Gateshead forever. She worked steadily and felt strong and virtuous for it. Her self-assurance was still fragile—no matter how brave and sure she felt, a minor defeat could shatter it. She took care not to pin too much hope on the show. It would not cause miracles to happen. It was but a tiny beginning. She told herself over and over again what a tiny beginning it really was, and went to her studio punctiliously every day.

Late one morning, a few days before the winter solstice, the sun finally came out and bathed Gateshead in pale light. Scraps of blue were visible behind the snow-laden clouds. Rachel left her studio, filled with thoughts of the new year. She drove around Gateshead for a while and then headed east, toward the Sunken Meadow State Park. Bundled in her pea jacket, her boots up to the knees of her paint-stained jeans, she walked along the beach. She was deep in fantasies, dreaming of openings, interviews, her picture in the paper, when, quite suddenly, she saw the empty space beside the famous self of her dreams. Where was Seymour? Rachel realized, then, that one of the forces driving her ambition was the desire to take him away with her. Seymour, her husband, her lover, had to fill the space beside her. It was to *him* she wanted to bring the gift of her fame. She loved him. It had been months since they had been alone together, had talked, had peeled off the dead layers of daily routine. Rachel drove toward home. She must see Seymour, she had so much to tell him.

There was a strange car in the driveway. "Shit!" thought Rachel, "he's got a visitor." She pulled up in front of the house and saw that the car was not unfamiliar after all. It was Natalie Gould's Mercedes.

Rachel ran across the lawn. The front door, which she had left unlocked that morning, was securely fastened. Her eyes watered as if from a sudden biting wind. Her first impulse was to turn around and drive away with a roar. She would return later, full of self-righteous accusations and livid with sharply honed fury. Her second impulse, fast upon the heels of the first, was to brazen it out. To see, once and for all, the awful truth. To look on the mocking face of adultery.

Rachel had her key with her but she banged loudly, frantically, on the door and rang the bell madly. She heard Seymour's voice from far away.

"Who's there?"

Rachel unlocked the door and burst into her house. "It's me."

Her voice, which she had thought was strong, was hoarse and feeble. She saw Natalie's coat on the chair in the downstairs hall. Seymour's voice was still far away.

"Rachel?" he cried. "Rachel?"

She went up the five steps into the living room. Natalie's pocketbook lay beside the couch, her shoes were next to it. A good and expensive pair of shoes.

"I'll be down in a second," Seymour called out to her. "Stay there!"

His voice was unnatural, high with nervousness, and taut.

"Don't bother!" Rachel cried.

400

She knew for certain, at last, that he was in the bedroom with Natalie Gould.

"I'm leaving!" she shouted.

"Wait! Wait! Don't go! I want to talk to you."

Rachel ran back out the front door and into her car. She wasn't thinking. She wasn't even feeling very much but a buzzing in her head and freezing heat waves roiling up in her. She acted mechanically—started the car, put it in gear, drove on squealing wheels around the corner. Her only impulse was to escape, to drive away, out of the development, out of the well-known streets. Away. Anywhere at all. Just away. Rachel drove blindly for hours. Only her instincts saved her from accidents. She did not want to destroy herself; if anything (she thought, as thought came flooding back into her head), she wanted to destroy others. She drove out of Gateshead, toward the city, toward New York. At Glen Cove Road the traffic was stalled and she turned around and headed east. There was no point in running if you had to stand still. She drove on the Expressway, thinking to head for Montauk and the sea. But by the time she got to Holbrook she was running out of gas. She had no credit cards with her. Rachel bought two dollars worth of gas and drove back toward Gateshead, her head filled with fantasies of revenge. Lush visions of mayhem. She thought about beating Natalie Gould senseless with a baseball bat. She thought of slashing the tires of her fucking Nazi car. Strangely, she could not summon her vengeful feelings against Seymour. The thought of seeing him bruised and bloodied filled her with pity. She recognized that she was ill-equipped to inflict real physical damage when she tried to imagine Seymour beaten to a bloody pulp.

Rachel called Seymour from a telephone booth on Jericho Turnpike. He sounded contrite; he was ready to hear her abuse. He was quite still. Rachel screamed at him over the telephone, her invective distorted by sobbing, her curses ruined by repetition.

"You're wrong," he said.

"Wrong about what?" screamed Rachel.

401

"I love you."

"Fuck you fuck you fuck you!" she cried.

She had not known how close she was to tears until she began her harangue. She sniffled and sobbed and shrieked into the mouthpiece, while the wind blew through the cracks in the booth.

"Why did you do it?" cried Rachel. "You didn't have to push it in my face. You wanted to get caught. Did you want me to catch you? You probably did. Or else you took me so for granted that you didn't care if I found out."

"You have it all wrong—we weren't in bed."

"Oh, fuck off," wailed Rachel. "There's no way you can lie your way out of it."

"Where are you?"

"In a phone booth."

"In what town?"

"Only a dime away. I wouldn't waste more than ten cents to call you."

"Come home. I'll take you out to dinner."

"I don't want to see you again."

"Ever again?"

"If I had money with me, or credit cards, or even my checkbook, I'd be long gone. You wouldn't see me again."

"Don't leave without saying good-bye."

"You're a son of a bitch."

"Don't you love me anymore?"

"Would I be so angry if I didn't?"

"Rachel—I love you. Believe me. Don't be mad."

"I like being mad. I want to kick her ass. Smash in her teeth. Pull out her hair. Gouge out her eyes."

"Really?"

"Next time I will. I promise you. Don't try it again."

"I won't. There won't be a next time."

"I don't believe you. You've lied before. You keep on lying. But I'm telling you: next time I'll blacken her eyes and tear up her cunt."

"Rachel!"

"Deposit five cents for the next five minutes, please."

"Are you coming home? Rachel?"

402

eading. "I didn't tell Aaron what happened. Why ou left. I did say you were angry with me."

"He probably knows."

"If he wants to know. I don't think he does. He nderstands about your being angry with me. He's an-ry with me himself half the time. But he won't forgive ou if you leave us."

The light in the room was unflattering. Seymour ad dark circles under his eyes. His hair was in windy isarray. Seymour looked needy. A character out of Rachel's storehouse of Depression plays.

He leaned down to kiss her, his lips wet with de-ire, but she saw him—in her mind's eye—with Nata-ie. Making the same gestures, loving Natalie with words and movements that had belonged to her alone.

"Fuck off," said Rachel. She pushed him away with all her strength. "You bastard."

Tears were in her throat. She stood with clenched fists to ward him off.

"I love you, Rachel."

She sobbed aloud. She cried and cried and had to open her fists, her body had grown soft, she couldn't cry and fight at the same time. Seymour embraced her. His hard prick knocked at her crotch. Rachel cried in pain and rage and pleasure. Natalie Gould disappeared from her mind's stage. Seymour rammed hard against her several times. She could not bear it; she felt her own desire burst open like a ripe fruit. His body moved in on her and she cried out again and bit him on the shoulder. Her anger gave way before her desire. The shock of Seymour's repeated thrusts turned her yearning cunt into a voracious mouth. She pulled off her jeans. Seymour had opened his fly; his naked penis looked dusky and swollen. Rachel, eager and strong, pushed Seymour down upon the old couch and he fell willingly. She held him like a triumphant wrestler. She sat on him, sat straight down on his protruding prick, her knees squeezing his hips. She felt him go right up into her, she rode him, the lips of her cunt opened and closed, opened and closed, and Seymour bucked, arched up to go right through her. She was there, all there, and they came.

404

She knew for certain, at last, that he was in the bedroom with Natalie Gould.

"I'm leaving!" she shouted.

"Wait! Wait! Don't go! I want to talk to you."

Rachel ran back out the front door and into her car. She wasn't thinking. She wasn't even feeling very much but a buzzing in her head and freezing heat waves roiling up in her. She acted mechanically—started the car, put it in gear, drove on squealing wheels around the corner. Her only impulse was to escape, to drive away, out of the development, out of the well-known streets. Away. Anywhere at all. Just away. Rachel drove blindly for hours. Only her instincts saved her from accidents. She did not want to destroy herself; if anything (she thought, as thought came flooding back into her head), she wanted to de-stroy others. She drove out of Gateshead, toward the city, toward New York. At Glen Cove Road the traf-fic was stalled and she turned around and headed east. There was no point in running if you had to stand still. She drove on the Expressway, thinking to head for Montauk and the sea. But by the time she got to Holbrook she was running out of gas. She had no cred-it cards with her. Rachel bought two dollars worth of gas and drove back toward Gateshead, her head filled with fantasies of revenge. Lush visions of mayhem. She thought about beating Natalie Gould senseless with a baseball bat. She thought of slashing the tires of her fucking Nazi car. Strangely, she could not summon her vengeful feelings against Seymour. The thought of seeing him bruised and bloodied filled her with pity. She recognized that she was ill-equipped to inflict real physical damage when she tried to imagine Seymour beaten to a bloody pulp.

Rachel called Seymour from a telephone booth on Jericho Turnpike. He sounded contrite; he was ready to hear her abuse. He was quite still. Rachel screamed at him over the telephone, her invective distorted by sobbing, her curses ruined by repetition.

"You're wrong," he said.

"Wrong about what?" screamed Rachel.

401

"I love you."

"Fuck you fuck you fuck you!" she cried.

She had not known how close she was to tears until she began her harangue. She sniffled and sobbed and shrieked into the mouthpiece, while the wind blew through the cracks in the booth.

"Why did you do it?" cried Rachel. "You didn't have to push it in my face. You wanted to get caught. Did you want me to catch you? You probably did. Or else you took me so for granted that you didn't care if I found out."

"You have it all wrong—we weren't in bed."

"Oh, fuck off," wailed Rachel. "There's no way you can lie your way out of it."

"Where are you?"

"In a phone booth."

"In what town?"

"Only a dime away. I wouldn't waste more than ten cents to call you."

"Come home. I'll take you out to dinner."

"I don't want to see you again."

"Ever again?"

"If I had money with me, or credit cards, or even my checkbook, I'd be long gone. You wouldn't see me again."

"Don't leave without saying good-bye."

"You're a son of a bitch."

"Don't you love me anymore?"

"Would I be so angry if I didn't?"

"Rachel—I love you. Believe me. Don't be mad."

"I like being mad. I want to kick her ass. Smash in her teeth. Pull out her hair. Gouge out her eyes."

"Really?"

"Next time I will. I promise you. Don't try it again."

"I won't. There won't be a next time."

"I don't believe you. You've lied before. You keep on lying. But I'm telling you: next time I'll blacken her eyes and tear up her cunt."

"Rachel!"

"Deposit five cents for the next five minutes, please."

"Are you coming home? Rachel?"

"Good-bye," said Rachel and hung up.

She drove to her studio. The sun was goi[ng] in a narrow bank of black clouds, but the eve[ning] shone brightly in the yellow-blue sky. It was t[he] evening time when every form was etched in [a] clarity against the light of the setting sun. [She] watched the sky fade and turn to night from [she] watched the A&P sign burn pure red beside the sun. When the moment had passed she went [up] to her studio. She switched on the lights and fe[lt sud]denly giddy with relief: her pictures still were [there]. They leaned against the wall and they took on a[nd] and beautiful reality.

"I am a painter!" said Rachel.

She pulled the pictures out and looked at the[m] a long time.

Rachel forgot about Seymour and Natalie. Sh[e] returned to her own world, the only world that [mat]tered. Here, the control was all hers, there wa[s no] way another hand could ruin it. Rachel poured her-self a vodka and decided to stay right there, with her pictures. The pictures were good. If only the memory of the afternoon's humiliation would die! What good was her sharp vision if her muddy thoughts kept in-truding on it? Rachel tried not to think, but it [was] impossible. And what about Aaron? Poor, inno[cent] Aaron, she thought, and realized that she was thin[king] sentimentally and didn't even mean it. Aaron was [nei]ther poor nor particularly innocent. He could d[o] right on his own.

She set to work on a collage. Rachel lost herse[lf in] her work and barely heard the familiar footstep[s on] the stairs. Seymour burst into the room.

"I knew you'd be here. Do you know what time i[t is?]"

"Nine o'clock?" she guessed.

"It's almost eleven. Aren't you coming home?"

"I hadn't thought about it," said Rachel.

In truth she had not. She had been thinking [of] the bits and pieces of colored paper on the table [before] her, trying to decide if she wanted flatness or th[e] sky-blue illusion of depth.

"We need you home," said Seymour. He w[as]

Afterwards, they rested under the bright lights with their eyes closed.

"What are you going to do?" Seymour asked.

"I'm staying here. I want to be by myself. Don't think you can make everything all right with your cock."

"I did make everything all right with my cock," he said, smugly.

"No, you didn't. You came back to me, you did that, and I took you in."

"Are you coming home?"

"I'll see. I'll think about it. Maybe I'll go away for a little. Take a vacation—alone. I'm a free woman now."

"What do you mean by that?"

"I mean that what happened this afternoon gave me my freedom. I'm no longer beholden to you. I could have killed you this afternoon."

"You wouldn't have done that."

"I had every right to. I could have murdered you both. I can still leave you, and maybe I will. The thing is that I've stopped hiding my head in the sand, stopped being willfully blind and ignorant. You've had your princely way for years now, while I've been your handmaiden, guilt-ridden for every minute I've taken for myself. No more. I saw it all very clearly today and, like they say, the truth shall set you free. We're equals now."

"You won't leave me?"

"I don't think so. But you have to go now. Go home, leave me here by myself."

Seymour did go. Rachel worked very late, alone in her studio. Surrounded by her work she felt the good hope late night brought her. When she could finally keep her eyes open no longer, she wrapped herself in her coat and the bright Indian bedspread and fell asleep on the couch. She thought briefly about her prospects and decided that she could survive, even alone.

Rachel woke up confused. She saw the room bit by bit and knew where she was. She also remembered Natalie Gould. She looked at her watch. It was seven-

405

thirty. The hope had vanished in the clear morning air. When she thought of the future, she heard empty hearts knocking, saw blank days stretching toward old age.

Rachel went downstairs to have a cup of coffee at the Pleiades. The coffee tasted awful. She was overcome by a terrible sadness, sharp as morning sickness. She knew that her place would never be there alone on Main Street, surrounded by movie fantasies and odd disheveled characters. It was time to go home.

Seymour and Aaron were having breakfast. They were not surprised to see her.

"Hi, Mom!" said Aaron.

"Hello, Rachel," said Seymour.

The place was a mess. Still and all, it contained most of what she had lived these past twenty years. The faces were not only familiar but beloved. Rachel took off her coat and began to make order in her house. She allowed the love of her family to surround her. She did not explain herself—it was, for the moment, enough to be home.

That night was the first night of Chanukah. It wasn't a big deal, it never was, but the brightly colored candles burned with a soft and gentle flame in the silver menorah. Rachel made potato *latkes*. They purchased presents at the last minute. Aaron had gotten a new book on baseball for his mother and a shetland sweater for his father. Seymour gave Rachel a silver necklace and Rachel gave Seymour a beautiful book on Matisse. They purchased a hi-fi set for Aaron and all that night played Mozart and the Beatles.

Snow was in the air. In three days it would be Christmas. The year had reached bottom; there was no place to go but up toward spring. The congregation had started to interview new rabbis. Between Christmas and New Year's five of them appeared in Gateshead. They were of different dispositions and backgrounds; none of them resembled Seymour in the least.

"Let's go to the city," said Seymour, after the fifth rabbi had been by to inspect the house.

406

They packed a suitcase and went to New York. Aaron said he would stay home and open the door to the rabbis. He said that if he got into Columbia he'd be in New York every day next year.

Seymour and Rachel saw six movies and ate in three French restaurants and went to a concert at Carnegie Hall. They watched the end of the year on a TV set in their hotel room. They drank champagne and decided to move to the city, come June. Seymour had been promised a job with a Jewish cultural foundation; Rachel would have her show. They couldn't guarantee the future, but they decided that they must stay together. Who else could understand the language they spoke— private and hermetic, developed and refined over these many years? They loved each other.

The announcer on the television screen shouted that the ball was about to descend from the top of the Allied Chemical building. He began to count. Rachel switched off the sound. Flakes of thick white wet snow streaked across the screen and fell outside their window. They had returned to the city, the city of their dreams.

"Happy New Year, Rachel."

"L'shonah tovah, Seymour."

ABOUT THE AUTHOR

SILVIA TENNENBAUM has been a rabbi's wife for twenty-six years. She was born in Frankfurt am/ Main, Germany, in 1928 and came to the United States with her mother and stepfather, the conductor William Steinberg, in 1938. She graduated from Barnard in 1950 and married Rabbi Lloyd Tennenbaum in 1951. He has had congregations in Lynchburg, Virginia; Huntington, New York; and Cold Spring Harbor, New York. The couple has three sons. Silvia Tennenbaum's work has appeared in *Midstream, Stories for the Sixties, American Review* and *Newsday*.

RELAX!
SIT DOWN
and Catch Up On Your Reading!